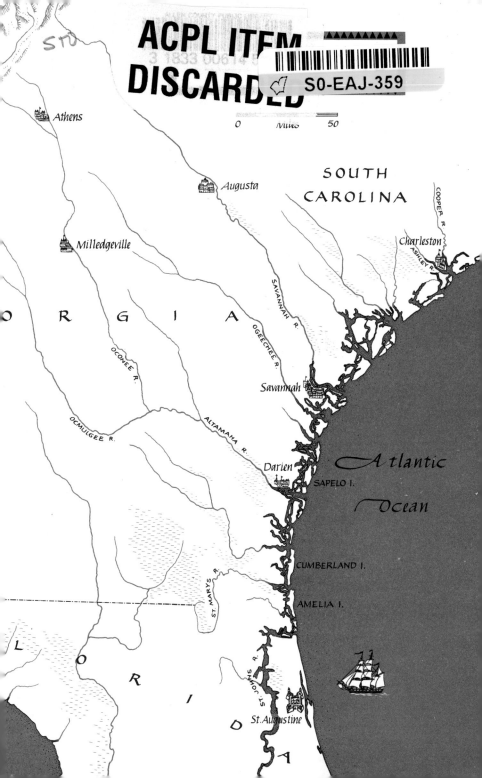

0   Miles   50

Athens

SOUTH
CAROLINA

Augusta

COOPER R.

Milledgeville

Charleston

ASHLEY R.

G E O R G I A

SAVANNAH R.

OGEECHEE R.

OCONEE R.

Savannah

OCMULGEE R.

ALTAMAHA R.

A tlantic

Darien

SAPELO I.

Ocean

CUMBERLAND I.

ST. MARYS R.

AMELIA I.

F L O R I D A

ST. JOHNS R.

St. Augustine

This novel about America in the early 1800s is brimming with romantic adventure, swirling action, and fascinating characters.

It centers on the turbulent events that led up to the acquisition of Florida by the United States. We follow the career of a young lieutenant from Connecticut — Jonathan Ames — who renounces his commission in the U. S. Army to join the flamboyant general Gregor MacGregor in his plans to liberate Florida from the Spaniards by force of arms.

Ames is actually acting on instructions of his government — his secret mission: to report on affairs in Florida directly to William Crawford, Secretary of War, and through him to President Madison himself.

Through Ames's eyes, a vivid panorama of life in the new nation unfolds — from the political intrigues in Wash-

Satan's Back Yard

ington, to the bustle of high society in
Charleston, S.C., to the frontier violence of Florida under the Spaniards.

Based on extensive historical research, this novel offers a highly read-
able tale of romance, politics, and
military adventure — set in one of the
most colorful and crucial periods of
American history.

Also by *Sam J. Slate*

AS LONG AS THE RIVERS RUN

Satan's Back Yard

SAM J. SLATE

Doubleday & Company, Inc.
Garden City, New York
1974

Library of Congress Cataloging in Publication Data

Slate, Sam J
    Satan's back yard.

    1. Florida—History—Cession to the United States,
1819—Fiction.   I. Title.
PZ4.S61978Sat [PS3569.L26]   813'.5'4
ISBN 0-385-00501-6
Library of Congress Catalog Card Number 73-17771

For *Sallie*
with love

1801195

PREFACE

This is a novel, not history, about the last years of Spanish rule in Florida and how it became our twenty-seventh state. However, with events, treaties, dates, battles, I have tried to adhere to the rigid patterns of history. The actions and characterizations of historical figures like Jefferson, Jackson, Madison, Monroe and Crawford are based on careful research. The fictional characters are a product of the writer's imagination. Any resemblance to persons living then is purely coincidental.

I deeply appreciate the courtesies extended me by Mrs. Lilla B. Hawes of the Georgia Historical Society in Savannah; Mrs. Minnie Pringle Haigh of the Charleston (S.C.) Library Society and Mrs. Kimball Oliver of the Sherman, Connecticut, Library.

I am indebted to John Talmadge and especially to the late Lee Barker for their useful suggestions and professional criticism after reading the manuscript.

SATAN'S
BACK YARD

§ CHAPTER 1 §

"Mawnin', Johnny. What's all the fuss about?"

Lieutenant Jonathan Ames, a recent graduate of the United States Military Academy at West Point and military aide to the Secretary of War, William H. Crawford, scowled at being called Johnny.

"Sir," he said, "President Madison wants to see you. He requests that you come to the Octagon House at your earliest convenience."

The huge Georgian smiled. "All right, Johnny. But first some coffee. Know what's on Jemmy's mind?"

Ames winced. Crawford's casual reference to the President of the United States seemed most improper, yet he knew Madison and the former United States senator from Georgia were firm friends. Madison had persuaded him to resign from the Senate and serve as United States Minister to France during Napoleon's final turbulent years. Crawford served his country well. When he returned to Washington in 1816, Madison appointed him Secretary of War.

"Sir, I don't know. A messenger just said the President wanted to see you immediately."

"Oh well, we'll soon find out. But first let's have some coffee."

Ames spoke to an orderly and watched the secretary go to his

(1)

desk and calmly inspect the morning post. He was a gigantic man, all of six feet three, with a large long head, compressed lips and shrewd but kindly eyes deep set in his handsome face. The young officer, in the few months he had served Crawford, had quickly discovered why he was considered the most popular man in the Senate. Beneath his gracious affability and fund of amusing stories was an astute and studious man with clear judgment.

A Negro servant entered the room with a silver tray. "Your coffee, sir. Cream or sugar?"

"Just black, thank you. Put it on my desk."

"Yes, sir."

"Coffee, Johnny?"

Lieutenant Ames mumbled "Thanks" and drank his coffee in silence.

The jovial Crawford eyed his aide with perceptive gray eyes. Immaculately groomed in his blue uniform and highly polished black boots, the slim young officer from Connecticut wore his thick black hair clubbed. Soft dark eyes glowed from beneath arched brows; he had high cheekbones and a stern mouth. Reared in the strong Puritan faith, sin to Ames was a dark and evil thing. His code was one of strict obedience, self-discipline and control. He will make a fine officer in our new army, decided Crawford, and God knows we need them. Almost lost the war with England through the stupidity and bungling of our field commanders, especially in upper New York State and around Detroit.

Crawford finished his coffee and told Ames he would return shortly. As he walked swiftly down Pennsylvania Avenue he saw the tall leafless poplars gaunt against the gray December sky. Pigs, goats and cows grazed on the commons and dogs, big and small, scampered and barked in the muddy streets.

Washington City was still marked by the ravages of the British invasion two years ago. The President's house, or palace, as it was called, was a gutted ruin. While it was being repaired, President Madison lived in Colonel Tayloe's home, known as the Octagon House. It was a most unusual octagonal structure, with glass panels in many of its walls, glistening mahogany woodwork and a graceful staircase rising to the third floor.

The Capitol, on a low hill overlooking a sheep pasture, was badly burned. Repair work had started but it was progressing slowly. After living in Paris he realized that Washington was a squalid village. There were a few elegant houses, but mostly cottages and unpainted shacks adjacent to tumbled barns and sheds.

On arrival at the Octagon House, Crawford was immediately ushered into the President's office. "Mawnin', Mr. President," he said as an aide took his hat and coat and left the two men alone.

"Good morning," replied the President. "I appreciate your promptness." He smiled at the Georgian, who was a foot taller than Madison. A small, precise, neat man, he was dressed in black knee britches, silk stockings and silver-buckled shoes.

Crawford remembered that the Yankee writer, Washington Irving, had called Madison a "withered little applejohn." He chuckled at the apt description, thinking how wrong it is to judge a man by his appearance. Crawford knew the President was a man of courage, foresight and integrity, whose thinking and actions shaped the course of American history.

"Bill," asked the President, "ever heard of a General Gregor MacGregor?"

Crawford thought for a moment. "No, Mr. President."

"He is, or was, one of Simon Bolivar's generals." He picked up a scroll of heavy linen paper. "In this letter to me General Bolivar says, 'MacGregor, a former British officer, fought well and bravely with the forces of liberation in Venezuela.' He requests that I grant his trusted and beloved General Mac-Gregor an audience."

Crawford looked puzzled and Madison explained. "I met Bolivar when he was in the United States about ten years ago. He'd been studying in Paris and was on his way back to Venezuela. He visited General Washington at Mount Vernon. Mr. Jefferson had him for dinner and I saw him several times. You know, Bill, he idolized Washington. Always wore a miniature

(3)

of the general, which he said was a present from Lafayette."

The President tilted back his chair and reflected. "I certainly misjudged him. Thought he was just another young European fop. He was a small man with a trim mustache, black side-burns and always wore a sky-blue coat and long white panta-loons. He talked glibly of freeing South America from Spain and establishing a United States there."

"I'd say he's done pretty well," said Crawford.

"Indeed he has," replied Madison.

"Does General Bolivar indicate the purpose of MacGregor's visit?" asked Crawford.

"No. I received Bolivar's letter this morning with an en-closed note from MacGregor." He picked up a small piece of paper. "He's staying at Tennison's Hotel under the name of Colonel Robert Gregory of London and would welcome an opportunity to explain his mission, which he assures me will meet with my approbation and enhance the glory of the United States of America."

"Ah," laughed Crawford, "when a general talks of glory he means fighting. Another scheme to free Florida from Spain. Anyhow, that's my guess."

"I expect so, Bill. But we need Florida. One day we'll get it. Would have years ago if Congress had supported me." The President frowned, puckered his lips, got up and slowly paced the large room.

Crawford knew he was thinking of the East Florida Rebel-lion led by Governor Matthews of Georgia. His patriot army had occupied Amelia Island, besieged St. Augustine, but had needed help from the United States Navy to storm the city. Congress had refused Madison's request for aid, fearing war with Spain. James Monroe, the Secretary of State, had abruptly revoked Governor Matthews' authority. The Americans re-treated to Georgia with heavy casualties. Matthews, indignant, left for Washington vowing to "blow up the State Department and shoot Monroe." The old Revolutionary War hero died of pneumonia en route.

Still determined to take Florida, Madison named Governor David Mitchell of Georgia to command another expedition.

Once again the Americans occupied north Florida and moved on St. Augustine, expecting help from Washington. Congress, in June of 1812, declared war on England and refused to support the occupation. The patriots, under the leadership of John MacIntosh, attempted to set up a government. The Spanish governor, Sebastin Kindelan, met with the Indians and offered a thousand dollars for MacIntosh's scalp and ten dollars for the hair of each patriot. The Americans evacuated and left behind a ravaged and ruined land.

Madison, still angry, went back to his desk.

"As you know, I've been trying to buy Florida from Spain. Mr. Jefferson always said the United States must have all the land east of the Mississippi River and I agree. George Irwin, our minister in Madrid, reports no progress. The Spanish minister here, that slippery fellow Don Diego de Onís, wants to barter Florida for settling the Louisiana boundary at the Mississippi River. We insist on the Colorado River in the south, the Columbia River to the north, which will extend our boundaries to the Pacific. These discussions have been going on for over a year. Just talk, talk, talk and nothing ever happens." The President smacked his desk with his open hand. "Those damned Spaniards. Why couldn't the English, the French or even the Dutch have discovered Florida? That old fool Juan Ponce de León and his wild dream of a fountain of youth. Bah, Florida has been nothing but a fountain of blood the past three hundred years."

"Georgians living along the border certainly agree with you. They call Florida 'Satan's Back Yard.'"

With a quizzical half smile Madison asked why.

"Florida is a hornet's nest of pirates, bandits, thieves, Creek Indians and runaway slaves from Georgia and the Carolinas. It's poorly policed by a couple of Spanish regiments. There is no law, no order, just violence and constant raids into south Georgia."

"Satan's Back Yard, fountain of blood—it's all the same," said the President.

"I agree." Crawford smiled. "Still I don't think it's fair to put all the blame on old Ponce de León."

"Why not? If he hadn't believed in a fountain of youth the Spanish would probably have stayed in Peru and Mexico. That's where the gold was."

"Maybe, but Ponce de León didn't go to Florida seeking a fountain of youth. He probably never even heard of it."

"But the history books . . . ?"

"Mr. President, you know how damned inaccurate historians can be."

Madison chuckled, remembering the report that he had withheld supplies to Andrew Jackson at the battle of New Orleans. "God knows, you are right." He waited for Crawford's explanation.

"Ponce de León came to the New World with Columbus on his second voyage," said Crawford. "He helped conquer Cuba, Puerto Rico and other Caribbean islands. As a reward he was named governor of Puerto Rico and served in that post for fifteen years. He was happily married and enjoyed life. Suddenly he was removed from office because influential Admiral Diego Columbus wanted the place for one of his own men.

"Now in his fifties, Ponce de León must recoup his fortunes. He returned to Spain and talked with Charles V, the Holy Roman Emperor who also wore the Spanish crown. Charles granted him the title of *adelantade* and jurisdiction over newly discovered lands, especially the island of Bimini.

"Blown off his course by a tropical storm, he landed on the southern tip of Florida shortly after Easter of 1513. He thought it an island and named it La Florida because it was discovered at the time of the flowery festival. On a second voyage three years later Ponce de León was killed by an Indian arrow.

"There is nothing in the records of his voyage, the patents from King Charles or contemporary reports about the fabled fountain of youth. Years later a Spanish historian, Herrera, wrote a biography of Ponce de León and dreamed up this legend of a spring that rejuvenates. In no way does it fit that ruthless man who wanted only gold and slaves."

(6)

"Interesting, most interesting," said Madison. "You talk like a history professor, Bill."

"I was, once."

"You? I didn't know."

"Yes, I taught school in Augusta for several years."

The President laughed. "Now, Professor, advise me. Should we see General MacGregor?"

"Suppose," Crawford said thoughtfully, "I see him first, find out what he wants. This fits into my duties as Secretary of War."

"Fine. Go ahead."

"If," continued Crawford, "he has a plan to swiftly invade Florida, establish a stable government and apply for admission to the Union, it might work. The few Spanish at St. Augustine, Pensacola and Fort San Carlos would offer little resistance."

"Perhaps. But we must not get involved in an adventure that might mean war with Spain."

"I understand. When I was in Paris everyone seemed to agree that King Ferdinand is a vain, stupid man. Spain, ravaged by both the British and the French, is weak, divided and bankrupt. She is in no condition to fight."

"Neither are we. God knows how we'll pay for the last war. Congress has refused to pass new taxes. See this MacGregor but insist that he remain incognito. I don't want Madrid to know we are talking with one of Bolivar's generals. Find out his plans and what he wants."

"If he plans to invade Florida I can tell you exactly what he wants."

"Yes?"

"A king of France said, an army always wants three things —money, money and more money."

"No money, men or supplies. But talk with MacGregor, evaluate the man and get back to me."

"Yes, sir. I think I'll arrange to have dinner with MacGregor in a small Georgetown inn. A South American general dripping medals and decorations might cause talk if he came to the office."

"Good idea. Express my regrets and say I'm at Montpelier for a Christmas vacation."

"Certainly, sir."

"And, Bill, would you mind reporting to Montpelier if your meeting with MacGregor is important?"

"It will be a pleasure. This is Tuesday. Suppose I plan to ride down on Friday?"

"Take the new steamboat down the Potomac. It's faster and much more comfortable. I'll have a carriage meet you at Ocquina Creek, or would you rather have a saddle horse?"

"A horse, please. My big carcass just doesn't fit a carriage."

"Certainly," laughed Madison. "Dolley will be delighted. And I think Mr. Jefferson will be with us on Sunday. He promised to ride over from Monticello if his lumbago improved."

"It will be a great pleasure to see Mr. Jefferson again. I'll come even if I have to exaggerate on MacGregor's importance."

Madison said, "You don't need an excuse to visit Montpelier. You are always welcome."

"Thank you, Mr. President. Now I'd better get back to my office." Crawford stretched his long frame and slowly got to his feet. "With your permission I'd like to have my aide at this dinner."

"Your aide? Who is he?"

"A young lieutenant, Jonathan Ames, a recent graduate of West Point and a very fine young man."

"Is he trustworthy?"

"Yes, sir."

"Then it's your decision, but I want this meeting with MacGregor a secret. Idle gossip in Washington about our meeting one of Bolivar's generals won't help matters in Madrid. Discuss it with no one. I repeat, no one. Understand?"

"Yes, Mr. President," answered Crawford in a surprised voice.

Madison gave him a perceptive look and explained. "I'll tell Monroe when I meet him later this morning. God knows, he faces much more important problems. Naming his Cabinet, paying our war debts and wondering about the Russians in

California. Besides, he's had another one of his bilious attacks and there's no need to burden him further. Anyhow"—and he gave a wry smile—"I'm still President and I will be until March the fourth. That's nearly three months away. I wish it were tomorrow. Can't wait to get back to my Virginia farm." He tinkled a small silver bell and a servant appeared with Crawford's coat and hat.

Walking to the door with Crawford, the President added, "If MacGregor has a reasonable plan I'll arrange a meeting with Monroe. If he's just another adventurer, why worry him?"

The Secretary of War nodded his agreement and walked slowly back to his office. His thoughts turned to James Monroe, the recently elected fifth President of the United States. Crawford had considerable respect for this tall Virginian but no real affection. He was honest enough to admit part of his feeling was envy. He had wanted to be President and believed he could have been elected if he had aggressively campaigned for his party's nomination.

He recalled vividly a dinner some nine months ago with Senator Abner Lacock of Pennsylvania. The Virginia-born senator and strong supporter of Monroe told Crawford a bitter caucus fight might split the party and ensure the election of a Federalist. "Monroe," Lacock had said, "was the last of the Revolutionary 'worthies' who could have a claim to the presidency, whereas Crawford was young enough to serve after Monroe had gone to his grave."

Lacock was persuasive and Crawford knew that both Jefferson and Madison favored Monroe. He wondered now if he had been wise in saying that "his feelings would not permit him to oppose Monroe," and that Lacock was free to quote him. Lacock did to John Binns, editor of the Philadelphia *Democratic Press,* who published the story and praised Crawford's magnanimity in an editorial.

He took a neutral stance and, while refusing to announce his candidacy, he did not withdraw his name from consideration. He said he would bow to the will of the party. His popularity in the halls of Congress almost overcame Monroe's two years of active campaigning. Monroe was named the

Republican candidate by a narrow margin—65 votes to Crawford's 54.

The divided Federalist party nominated Rufus King of New York, who was easily defeated in the electoral balloting. Crawford felt he deserved Monroe's gratitude for stepping aside in favor of his senior colleague. He believed, as next in line for the presidency, that he should be appointed Secretary of State. He had never liked being Secretary of War. He refused the office at the outbreak of the 1812 war and accepted it only on his return from France at Madison's insistence. Many of Monroe's friends had told Crawford he would get the Secretary of State job; however, he had not heard from Monroe and was concerned.

Arriving at his office, he called in Ames, summarized his conversation with the President and emphasized the need for secrecy.

"Johnny," he concluded, "go to Tennison's Hotel, see this MacGregor, or Colonel Gregory, and ask him to dine with me at his earliest convenience. Then reserve a private room where the food is good but we are unlikely to be seen."

"What about Wylie's Tavern?"

"Excellent. Now off with you, but out of uniform before you go to the hotel."

"Yes, sir," replied Ames and departed.

Late that afternoon Lieutenant Ames returned and told Crawford he had seen MacGregor and arranged supper the following evening.

"Splendid, Johnny," boomed Crawford, "and what's your opinion of the general?"

"I could not help but like the general. He's affable, amusing and speaks fluently of his experiences in both the British Army and with Bolivar in South America. He's quite handsome." Ames grinned. "His wife said his grandfather, who was the Laird of Inverardine, was known as 'MacGregor the Beautiful,' and that her husband is his exact image."

"So his wife is with him?"

"Yes, sir. She's a very lovely and attractive lady. She was a Señorita Josefa Lovera before her marriage."

(10)

"Yes?"

"The general told me with great pride how he won the Señorita in Caracas even though she was engaged to a Spanish officer. She goes into battle with him, very handy with pistols."

Crawford snorted in derision. "I ain't surprised. Bolivar is reported to have an English mistress who fights at his side. Generals are a strange breed. World would be a far better place without 'em. Anything else?"

"Oh yes, sir. You see the general's wife did most of the talking."

"Predictable . . . go ahead."

"Mrs. MacGregor . . ."

"Señora MacGregor, Johnny."

Flushing, the lieutenant continued, "Sorry, sir. The señora described in some detail how the general won the Order of the Liberatadores by defeating a much larger Spanish army. It's an order, she explained, that General Bolivar granted to very few officers. Then, sir, she showed me an article in the Glasgow *Chronicle*. I copied some of it and with your permission will read it to you."

Crawford nodded and Ames unfolded his notes. It read:

> "The General was a representative of a reputable and ancient family, was a Captain in our Army in Spain, became a Colonel in the Spanish Army, had a Spanish order of knighthood conferred on him and was allowed by the Prince Regent to assume the title in this country. In Spain he fought to free the country from the French invaders, but when he saw a despicable tyranny reward the friends of liberty with dungeons and death he went to South America and gladly joined the party there who are endeavoring to emancipate themselves from the oppression of the Mother Country. His intimacy with one of our Royal Dukes, distinguished for his liberality and Whiggish principles, is said to add to his influence with Bolivar's compatriots."

Ames paused and turned a page. "It concludes this way—

'Sir Gregor is not only a gentleman by birth, education and manners, but also a man of considerable literary attainments.'"

"My goodness," drawled Crawford, "I'm impressed. Do we address him as General MacGregor or Sir Gregor?"

"He never uses the title, Mr. Crawford. Claims it wouldn't be proper in a republic."

"I'm surprised he'd consent to dine."

"Well, sir, he was annoyed at not seeing the President and more so when I explained the meeting with you was confidential."

"What did he expect—a parade, a twenty-one-gun salute and a state dinner? After all he's in Washington City as a Colonel Gregory, not one of Bolivar's generals."

"I said, sir, that you were acting under orders from President Madison, the meeting must be kept secret and he should not come in uniform."

"You mean that he was in uniform?" asked Crawford in amazement.

"I suppose so, sir. He wore a tight-fitting sky-blue coat, white trousers tucked in highly polished boots and a blazing medallion, which I assumed was the Order of the Liberatadores."

"My God," ejaculated Crawford.

"And, Mr. Secretary, he objected to dining with you in civilian clothes."

"But," said Crawford, "he's accepted. How did you persuade him?"

"I just told him those were my orders and that you would be disappointed not to see him. I saluted and left. He followed me to the door, said he, too, was under orders and under the circumstances he would accept. We shook hands, bowed and I made the necessary arrangements at the tavern."

The corners of Crawford's wide mouth crinkled, then he guffawed. "Good work, Johnny. As you seem quite capable of handling this popinjay, I'd suggest you join us at supper."

"Me, sir?"

"Yes, you, sir," laughed Crawford. "After all, Johnny, I know nothing of tactics, invasions and such military matters—that's your profession, that's what you studied at West Point. You listen to this man and advise me."

"Yes, sir."

When Crawford and Ames arrived at Wylie's Tavern they were warmly greeted by the innkeeper and escorted to a pine-paneled room on the second floor. A fire crackled in the grate. It felt good on this blustery December evening.

"This is a great honor, Senator Crawford," said Wylie.

Eyes flashing angrily, Crawford turned to Ames. "Sir, I assure you—"

Wylie interrupted. "No, Senator, the young gentleman was extremely discreet." He chuckled. "I thought it was a rendezvous with a lady. But, sir, I've seen you often in the Senate and on the streets of Washington. You are the tallest man in Congress and I wish you had been elected President."

Crawford winked at Ames, his good humor restored. "That's very generous of you. We are entertaining a distinguished foreign guest, a Colonel Gregory. Please send him to us on arrival and see that we are not disturbed."

"Yes, sir. It's a great honor to have you in my tavern. Anything special you'd like for supper?"

"Your best. I have a lusty appetite this evening."

"Then I'd suggest baked oysters, a canvasback duck and a roast of mutton with all the trimmings."

"Excellent, Wylie . . . excellent. And a bottle of your best claret, please."

"Certainly, sir." Wylie bustled down the stairs and returned immediately to announce Colonel Gregory.

A handsome man in blue broadcloth and a white stock entered the room. He had deep blue eyes, a beautifully shaped face framed by curly brown hair, lightly powdered. Ames was relieved to see he wore no medals. The visitor scrutinized the two men and bowed.

"Good evening, sir," said Ames. "May I present Mr. William Crawford, the Secretary of War."

"This is indeed a great honor, General MacGregor," said Crawford as he stepped forward.

MacGregor shook hands and said grimly, "Colonel Gregory if you please, sir."

"Sir"—Crawford smiled—"we are alone and I prefer to use the proper title for such a distinguished guest. The President sends you his warmest greetings and his regrets that he is not in Washington City at this time."

"No?" queried MacGregor. "Then may I ask where?"

"The President is resting at his Virginia home, Montpelier."

"Then perhaps I could see him there?"

"If it seems advisable after our evening's discussion it will be my pleasure to make all the arrangements. But first, General, a noggin of cheer—rum, brandy, whiskey or perhaps madeira?"

"Madeira would be welcome."

The next hour was a lesson in diplomacy that Ames would never forget. Gracious, tactful and shrewd, Crawford asked numerous questions about Bolivar and the South American countries. He had a wonderful feeling for words, a self-deprecatory sense of humor and his comments were both acute and flattering. MacGregor responded, reluctantly at first, but soon was eagerly explaining events in South America.

"Even now," he said, "Bolivar is returning to Venezuela with a strong army and will liberate the lower Orinoco River valley. He'll establish a republican form of government, similar to yours, and will surely be elected President. He's in constant communication with other patriots, especially José San Martin in Buenos Aires and Bernardo O'Higgins in Chile. They, like Bolivar, though South American born, are European educated, trained and believe their countries must be free. Peru, Spain's richest province, smolders in dissent as do Chile, Ecuador and Mexico. Brazil, too, seeks its freedom from Portugal and soon all these countries together will form a United Provinces of South America."

As they slowly ate their superb dinner and enjoyed the ruby claret, MacGregor discussed Bolivar. "Though untrained as a soldier his triumphs were those of audacity, swiftness and surprise. He has a native genius for strategy and is worshiped by his men. He knows hundreds of them by name and never forgets a face. He shares their discomforts, their food and often sleeps on the ground.

"His obsession is a free and united South America. Spain is corrupt, venal and its South American armies are poorly equipped and led by court favorites. Soon all the countries will be liberated and Spain's only toe hold in the New World will be Florida." He slowly sipped his wine and waited for Crawford's reaction.

"My apologies, General. I've asked so many questions and been so fascinated with your stories about Bolivar that I've given you no opportunity to explain why you are in our country."

"Gad, sir," exploded MacGregor, "I'm sure you know why I seek an audience with your President. Your eyes betrayed you when I mentioned Florida."

"Did they now? Maybe I should wear a pair of old Ben Franklin spectacles. So it's Florida, eh? And you have a plan for her liberation?"

"Yes, Mr. Crawford, but only with the approval and possible help of your government."

"Approval, perhaps—help, no. But we'd be most interested in your idea."

The general frowned and gulped his glass of wine. "I understand you are from Georgia, Mr. Secretary?"

"That's right."

"Then you know Amelia Island?"

"Yes. It's just south of Cumberland Island at the mouth of the St. Marys River. General Oglethorpe, when he built a fort there in 1735, thought the island so beautiful that he named it Amelia after Princess Amelia, the sister of King George II."

"Deuced interesting. Princess Amelia, always known as the lovely princess—so that's how it got its name. And it's a most bewitching isle with drooping willows shading the scarlet hibiscus. Have you been there recently?"

"No, it's been ten years or more."

"Well, I was there last month, as a merchant from Nassau, interested in buying a bit of, shall we say, smuggled goods."

Crawford laughed. "You mean pirates' loot? That damned

little village of Fernandina even has the gall to advertise its stolen merchandise in Charleston and Baltimore newspapers."

"One trader told me the chattels in those flimsy shacks were worth over a million dollars. Anyhow, Mr. Crawford, I had ample opportunity to scout the island and its defenses. Fort San Carlos is in shambles and undermanned. A few hundred determined men could easily storm the fort, then march on St. Augustine. The British and American planters would rally to our cause and boot out the wretched dons. We'd form a government similar to Georgia's and apply for admission to the Union. God's blood, sir, it's that simple."

Crawford started to speak but MacGregor held up his hand. "Sir, I read your thoughts. You must avoid trouble with Spain. But, Mr. Crawford, the United States is not responsible for operations conducted beyond its jurisdiction."

"True enough, General—and speaking as a Georgian I would welcome Florida into the Union. Under Spain it has caused us enough trouble over the years. And I'm sure you are right about Fort San Carlos. But where, sir, will you get your men?"

"I'd recruit them in Charleston and Savannah."

"Maybe, but to recruit men you need money."

"True, Mr. Secretary, but I assume the United States . . ."

"No," replied Crawford. "We'll not finance your expedition. President Madison was explicit on this point. The best you could hope for would be our unofficial blessing."

"I understand, Mr. Secretary, and while I'm disappointed I have other possible sources of funds."

"Such as?"

"I fancy that merchants in Baltimore and Savannah might underwrite such an expedition."

"So they'd get a cut of the spoils—a percentage on all goods sold, eh?"

"Exactly, and an agreement to buy Florida land, say at a dollar an acre."

"Greedy fellows! That ought to swing the deal, but can you expect any help from Bolivar?"

"Perhaps. Depending on the success of his expedition into

Venezuela. He approves my plan, endorses it, otherwise he would not have written President Madison."

Crawford reflected for a moment, realizing the truth in this statement. . . . This general just might have the audacity and verve to take Florida. He needed time to get the latest intelligence from Georgia. Time to talk this over with the President. Nothing to gain by being hasty.

"General, I'd like to make this suggestion. It's now December, no time to mount any expedition. Why don't you consult Bolivar, speak to your merchants and I'll report to President Madison, then we'll meet again in, say, February?"

MacGregor frowned and drank more wine. "I agree, sir, but one final question. . . . Do you approve of my venture?"

"I personally approve of any plan to liberate Florida, but I do not speak for my government. The most you can expect will be hands-off policy. . . . And one final warning, sir—under no circumstances are you to tell anyone of this meeting."

"I understand, Mr. Secretary. You have my word on that."

General MacGregor got to his feet. "I'll see you in two months. Good night, sirs."

§ CHAPTER 2 §

Lieutenant Jonathan Ames paced the Potomac River dock waiting impatiently for the Secretary of War. He had been ordered to accompany him to Montpelier and be prepared to summarize and evaluate MacGregor's plans to liberate Florida. Ames was excited over meeting the President of the United States and grateful to Crawford for the opportunity.

The young lieutenant recalled his dismay on receiving orders to report to the office of the Secretary of War in Washington City. To be an aide to a cabinet member seemed to him a complete waste of his years at West Point. And to serve a Southerner, a disciple of Thomas Jefferson, was demeaning. In Litchfield he had been taught that Jefferson was a libertine, an atheist whose Democratic beliefs would destroy the Republic.

He briskly rubbed his cold hands, wished for a cup of steaming coffee and thought of his boyhood days in Connecticut. His mother had died of smallpox when he was ten. His father, a brilliant but erratic lawyer, deeply despondent, sought consolation in Old Medford rum. A drunken night ride on a frisky mare and he was found the next morning with a broken neck. . . . Jonathan shuddered in the cold December wind as he remembered those confused days. His father was deeply in debt, so the small house, furniture, linen and plate were sold to satisfy creditors.

The town selectmen decided Jonathan was a pauper and must become a bound servant. This was common practice by thrifty New Englanders who sold their slaves south for a tidy profit and eagerly bid for paupers such as Jonathan. They worked for keep without pay. When a boy was twenty-one he received his freedom and the gift of a horse. A girl at eighteen got bedding and a quilt.

Jonathan never forgot his shame and humiliation when he stood in the crowded Litchfield courtroom and heard the bearded first selectman extoll his virtues. Several families wanted his services, for Jonathan was of neat appearance, strong and wiry. He could also read, write and was good at figures. Fortunately the selectman bound Jonathan to Ed Chase, a farmer who Jonathan's father had once represented.

Chase, a dour man, told Ames he was to be considered a member of the family, not a servant. "Your pa saved my farm in a title dispute," explained Chase, "and I'll always be grateful. You'll work for your keep, for I'm poor, but I'll share and see that you are educated."

Chase kept his word. Young Ames rose at sunup to milk the cows and feed the pigs and chickens, then went to school, and, in the afternoons, plowed, weeded and hayed while his classmates played on the village common. When he was seventeen Judge Tapping Reeve, head of the Litchfield Law School, got him an appointment to the new United States Military Academy at West Point. He would have preferred Yale, his father's college. His musings were interrupted by the appearance of Crawford.

"Sorry I'm late, Johnny," he said, "but I overslept. Come on, let's get aboard."

Crawford was warmly greeted by the captain. As they steamed down the Potomac the big man moved easily among the crew and the passengers. He shook hands with everyone, knew many by name and apparently had an endless supply of stories. He obviously liked people and they responded. It was easy to understand his popularity in the capital. As they passed Mount Vernon, about an hour out of Washington City, Crawford saw Ames standing alone gazing at the home of the first President of the United States.

"He was a great man, Johnny," said Crawford. "And I'll always be grateful to him."

"Did you know General Washington?"

"No," answered Crawford. "I saw him only once, when he visited Georgia in 1791. I was a young schoolteacher in Augusta and went to Savannah to hear him speak. You know, Johnny, I was always ashamed of being so big. Then I saw General Washington and how he towered above most men. He must be nine feet tall, I said to myself." Crawford's big laugh boomed. "And suddenly I was proud of my height, of being tall like Washington. Never bothered me again."

It was difficult for Ames to imagine this poised, confident man worrying about his size. He blurted, "Was General Washington as big as you are?"

"Well, not exactly, Johnny. I'm six feet three inches, maybe an inch or so taller than General Washington, but that doesn't matter. General Washington will always be to me the tallest American and one of the greatest. He and Tom Jefferson."

"Mr. Jefferson?" repeated Jonathan. "As great as General Washington?"

"Yes, Mr. Jefferson," said Crawford. "Maybe you'll meet him at Montpelier. I hope he'll be there. I'd like you to know him and decide for yourself if the Federalist lies about him are true."

"As an officer I have the greatest respect for a former President of the United States," stiffly replied Ames.

Crawford gave his aide a warm smile. "And as a born and bred Yankee from Connecticut I suppose you consider him a special agent of the devil?"

Ames flushed and his temper flared. "Sir, I had great admiration for both Judge Reeve and Mr. Timothy Dwight, president of Yale. I've heard them speak at Fourth of July celebrations. They did not approve of Mr. Jefferson."

"No, Johnny, they didn't," replied Crawford. "I've read their speeches. Timothy Dwight screamed that we 'have a country governed by blockheads and knaves.' He predicted that under Mr. Jefferson we'd have anarchy as in France and blood would run in the streets. Your friend Judge Reeve ranted that Mr. Jefferson espoused principles of 'infidelity and despised all laws both sacred and divine.' He termed Mr. Jefferson 'coward, shyster, a betrayer of American rights and dignity.' Incidentally, he was indicted by a federal grand jury for libel."

As he continued, his voice became angry. "And did you know, young man, that at a Federalist banquet in Middletown, Connecticut, this toast was proposed—'To the President of the United States, may he receive from his fellow citizens the reward of his merit, a halter.'"

Ames was astonished. He felt Crawford exaggerated, but he did not have the facts to argue. "Are you sure, Mr. Crawford?"

"Yes, Johnny, I'm sure. The Federalists were scurrilous, false and malicious in their attacks on Mr. Jefferson." In a surprised voice he asked, "Didn't you study history at West Point?"

"Yes, sir, but mostly Greek, Roman and European history. The campaigns of Alexander the Great and Caesar."

"And nothing about America," scornfully added Crawford.

"Oh, we studied the French and Indian wars, the Revolution and General Washington's years as President."

Crawford snorted in disgust. "You graduated in 1815 and you know nothing about Mr. Jefferson except those canards and lies of the Federalists . . . nothing of the great things he did for our country in his eight years as President."

"Well, I know he founded the academy," stammered Ames.

"And he'd be ashamed of its curriculum. It's time those West Point officers realized it's the nineteenth century." Crawford removed his hat, ran his fingers through his thinning hair and spoke softly, persuasively. "Johnny, your Federalist friends were so contemptuous of democracy, so drunk on their vituperation, they refused to admit Mr. Jefferson's accomplishments. But the people knew, and that's why the Federalists have been so soundly thrashed in every presidential election."

Ames gave him a perplexed glance, remembering how surprised and bitter Litchfield had been over the defeat of Charles Pinckney and Rufus King.

Crawford continued, "I served in the Senate the last two years of Mr. Jefferson's administration. I know. Unjust taxes were repealed and millions of dollars paid on our national debt. The public service was purged of parasites and pensioners and its efficiency increased. Rigid economics were enforced in all departments of government. The press was free. No longer were Americans tossed into jail for criticizing those in power. Mr. Jefferson maintained peace with France and England despite incidents. Tripoli, Algiers and Tunis were chastened. We no longer paid tribute to pirates. The national domain was doubled by the Louisiana Purchase without fighting or increasing the taxes. The nation's credit in London and Amsterdam was excellent. Our country was confident, prosperous and peaceful."

Crawford paused and smiled. He wrapped a long arm around Ames's shoulders. "Forgive the lecture, Johnny, but as an American officer you should realize Mr. Jefferson's contributions to our country and be grateful." Chuckling, he added, "Anyhow, as you said, he founded West Point. Otherwise you probably wouldn't be here now."

Ames's frown vanished and he laughed with Crawford, who said, "Come along. We should be landing at Ocquina Creek in a few minutes."

A Negro groom from Montpelier met them with saddle horses. He gathered their small baggage, strapped it to a mule and said it was about forty miles to "Massa Madison's house." He had gotten rooms for them at a "tolerable inn" for the night and they would be at Montpelier late tomorrow.

It was a long cold ride and Ames was relieved when Crawford pointed to the spire of the Orange County courthouse and said they would soon be there. He explained that the President owned over five thousand acres and was one of Virginia's most successful farmers. He grew wheat as a money crop, not tobacco. He raised cattle, practiced crop rotation and had experimented with many new fruits and vegetables. Madison inherited the farm from his father, and with the assistance of William Thornton, the architect of the Capitol, had enlarged and improved the original house. "It's most elegant and compares favorably with Monticello."

As they jogged up the gravel drive Ames saw a handsome two-storied house with a graceful four-columned portico flanked by low, rambling wings. They paused as the groom opened the gate, and Crawford pointed out a large tin cup that was used to measure the exact amount of rainfall. The two weary men watered their horses at a well dug by Madison's grandfather when he developed the land nearly a century ago. They drank the cool water from a gourd and Ames admired Montpelier's beautiful setting. Oak, cedars of Lebanon and boxwood guarded a well-kept lawn, which swept down toward the Rapidan River. Some twenty miles away were the low ridges of the Blue Ridge Mountains. Behind the mansion a grove of oak, walnut and pine trees shielded farm buildings, the smokehouse and the slave quarters. To the right was a formal garden laid out in a horseshoe pattern resembling the seats in the House of Representatives.

They walked their horses up the drive where President Madison, standing on the low steps, waited to greet them. He was dressed in black britches with top boots, rather like those worn by Connecticut farmers, thought Ames. His gray, bright eyes twinkled in his kindly face. Despite the simple costume he bore himself with dignity and assurance. Ames decided that he liked the President.

In a precise voice Madison said, "Welcome to Montpelier," and shook hands.

"Lieutenant Ames, it's a pleasure. Mr. Crawford thinks highly of you. I'll be most interested in your impressions of General MacGregor."

Embarrassed, Ames replied, "Thank you, Mr. President."

To Crawford the President said, "Anything you need, Bill?"

"I'm saddle sore. Perhaps a hot bath and a tot of rum, Mr. President."

In his gentle voice Madison said, "Let's dispense with formalities, Bill."

"All right, Jemmy," replied Crawford, pleased.

"No visitors here, not even any of Dolley's kin. Just Mr. Jefferson. He's a bit tired after that long carriage ride. He's resting and will join us at supper."

Madison led them into a vestibule with a huge semicircular window divided into thirteen parts, to symbolize the original union of states. Down the hall was a large drawing room. "It's called the clock room," explained Madison, "because of a huge old English clock, which regulates our life here." Its walls were covered with paintings, several by Gilbert Stuart, and busts of Washington, Franklin, Jefferson and Lafayette. An enormous persian rug and sofas in crimson damask lent color as the pale December sun came through the tall french windows. A marble mantelpiece—"Sent from France by Mr. Jefferson," said the President—gave the room a studied elegance.

Adjoining was the dining room, where oil portraits of Napoleon, in crimson robes, and Confucius, and a water color of Jefferson, looked down on a large mahogany table and two sideboards covered with family silver. "Upstairs," explained Madison, "is my library. It doesn't compare with the one at Monticello, but I'm proud of it. We'll talk there after supper. Nothing formal, only Dolley and Mr. Jefferson will be here.

"Now, gentlemen, you must be tired." He clapped his hands and a tall, dignified Negro appeared. "Paul, show them to their rooms in the south wing."

"Yes, Mr. Madison."

"And tend to their needs."

"Certainly, sir." He bowed and, turning, said, "Gentlemen, please follow me. Your traps are in your rooms."

Ames was impressed and said as much. Crawford explained that the Negro was Paul Jennings, who had been Madison's valet and faithful friend for the past twenty-five years. Ames did not understand how a slave could be a friend, but asked no questions. He was excited and awed. He had met the President of the United States and found him a warm friendly man. Soon he would dine with the fabulous Dolley Madison and the legendary Thomas Jefferson. It was like a fairy tale. Bewildered but pleased, he slowly dressed for supper. He declined Jennings' offer of help, wondering why a man needed assistance. He had never heard of a valet in Litchfield, Connecticut.

Promptly at seven Crawford and Ames walked into the clock room. An apple-wood fire crackled and candles flickered in silver sconces. Standing beside the President, now in knee britches and silk stockings, was a tall raw-boned man, his faded red hair tinged with gray, dressed in black broadcloth with a white stock. Ames knew this was Thomas Jefferson. He noticed his silver-buckled shoes and suppressed a grin, for in Litchfield it was said that Jefferson wore only laced shoes, which were considered the trademark of Sabbath breakers, tipplers and libertines.

Crawford stepped forward, bowed and shook hands with Jefferson. "May I present my aide, Lieutenant Jonathan Ames, a recent graduate of the Military Academy?"

Smiling sedately, Jefferson said, "Lieutenant Ames, perhaps you will join me in my morning walk tomorrow. I'm deeply interested in the academy and its progress."

"It will be my pleasure, Mr. Jefferson."

To Crawford he said, "Senator, or should I say Mr. Secretary?"

"I prefer Bill, but Senator if you like. Many times I wish that I were still in the Chamber, but the President was most persuasive."

"We needed you in France," said Madison, "and needless to say you served your country well."

"Did you enjoy Paris?" asked Mr. Jefferson.

"Yes indeed. It's a lovely, fascinating city. And I liked the French people. But Napoleon . . ." He glanced at his portrait and scowled.

"I share your feeling," said Jefferson. "He was certainly the Attila of our times, a ruthless killer of millions. Perhaps he was a lion in the field, but in civil life he was a cold-blooded, calculating, unprincipled usurper without a virtue. He knew nothing of civil government, commerce or of political economy. I set him down as a great scoundrel." He sipped his madeira

(25)

and his eyes twinkled. "Senator, I'm told Napoleon once said you were the only man he ever felt inclined to look up to."

The Georgian laughed. "He had no choice, Mr. Jefferson. He's such a puny fellow." He thought for a moment. "I've heard that story too and maybe it's true, I don't know. Certainly Napoleon never said anything pleasant to me. He ranted and snarled that we were base ingrates and should rejoin his fight against England."

"Let's just hope he won't escape from St. Helena like he did Elba," commented Madison.

"He won't," said Crawford. "Besides, he's a sick, tired old man. Must be fifty or so."

"Forty-seven," said Jefferson. "He was born in 1769. Any truth that he was ill at Waterloo?"

"I expect so. In Paris several French officers said he had an acute attack of piles the morning of the battle. He just sat in his easy chair, refused to see anyone or give orders."

"It's possible," mused Jefferson, "that he might have defeated Wellington if he'd struck at dawn. Certainly he wasn't the aggressive general of his previous battles."

A soft voice broke into the conversation. "Good evening, gentlemen."

"Dolley, my dear," said Madison. "May I present Lieutenant Ames, and of course you know Mr. Crawford."

Her friendly, wide-set blue eyes welcomed her guests. She was as tall as her husband, with her black hair piled high. Her ample figure was sheathed in a mulberry hued satin dress with a white silk kerchief at her neck. Ames had once seen her wearing a turban topped with an ostrich plume. He felt slightly disappointed at her simple attire.

Mrs. Madison asked Crawford about his family, teased him about the ladies in Paris and, turning, to Ames said, "It's a delightful change to have a young face in this old house. So many of Jemmy's friends are so wrinkled and gloomy. Lieutenant, your arm please. You must tell me all about yourself at supper."

She led her guests into the dining room, where a lavish Virginia meal was served. Rice soup, round of beef, turkey, smoked ham, macaroni pie, vegetables and, finally, ice cream. Under her skillful guidance the conversation flowed easily. Mrs. Madison seemed anxious to hear of Ames's life in Litchfield.

He described the salt-box houses gay with color—Indian red, gray, green or bright yellow—and the dark peak of Mount Tom brooding over the whipping post on the square where offenders to the "publique weal" were stripped and flogged . . . the "hell fire and damnation sermons" during which young people nibbled orange peels and stuck each other with pins to keep awake . . . the long winters of sleigh riding, with tinkling bells and bearskin rugs . . . rubbing handfuls of snow against a frozen ear or nose.

Dolley grimaced in distaste and said she did not like cold and snow. In his low voice, which Ames could just hear, Mr. Jefferson asked sardonically, "Did you know my great admirer Judge Tapping Reeve?"

Confused, Ames stammered, "Yes, Mr. Jefferson, he was a friend of my father's and helped me get into West Point."

"Probably the most sensible act of his life," drawled Crawford. "My dander rises when I think of his scandalous remarks about you, Mr. Jefferson, and our party."

"Now, Senator"—Jefferson smiled—"every man has a right to his opinions and to freely express them." He paused reflectively. "He was undoubtedly influenced by his brother-in-law, Aaron Burr."

"Burr!" said Crawford. "What a charming unprincipled rascal."

Jefferson chuckled. "Lieutenant Ames, we'd value your opinion of Judge Reeve."

Ames collected his thoughts and spoke slowly. "I remember him best as a pleasant, absent-minded professor. I've often seen him ambling along, his long gray hair flapping in the breeze and holding the bridle of his horse and smelling a flower or watching a bird. Meantime his horse was grazing in someone's garden."

Dolley giggled and the three men grinned. Crawford said, "Johnny, did you ever have a talk with Judge Reeve?"

"No, sir, but I often listened. I worked at Catlin's Tavern in winter—sweeping and washing the mugs. The judge and Mr. Timothy Dwight would sit for hours over coffee discussing religion and politics."

His audience waited expectantly and Ames continued, "They often discussed the nature of sin. They damned the grossness and immorality of the theater, considered Shakespeare's plays the language of vice and said a man who visited a strange woman would never look on the face of God."

Suddenly noticing Mrs. Madison, he mumbled an apology.

Dolley laughed. "Lieutenant, I'm well aware of the peccadilloes of men." She folded her napkin and took snuff from a small silver locket. This shocked Ames almost as much as starting supper without asking the blessing.

"Lieutenant," she asked, "has this evil old man"—she inclined her head toward Crawford—"corrupted you?"

"Now, Dolley," interposed Crawford, "that's not fair. I've taught him a few things about wine, cards and how to bet on horses and even persuaded him to take dancing lessons. A little worldly knowledge will make him a better officer."

"And the ladies?" asked Dolley. "Does your instruction cover our sex?"

"I wouldn't be so presumptuous," answered Crawford. "Besides, Lieutenant Ames is a bit shy with girls."

"Don't you have a sweetheart, Lieutenant?" Noticing his blush, she continued, "A handsome young man in uniform . . . who could resist you? When we retire and move back to Montpelier you must pay us a visit. I'll introduce you to some of our Virginia belles."

Ames said he would be delighted. Madison wagged his finger. "Let's be serious, Dolley. . . . You've told us about sin, Lieutenant, but what did Judge Reeve have to say about politics?"

"Sir, as you know, he was an ardent Federalist. He considered democracy licentious and hated the Union because it gave too much power to the people. He believed the states had a right to secede from the Union."

"That damned Hartford convention," said Madison. Noticing Ames's surprise, he explained. "During the dark days of 1814 many New England Federalists encouraged by commercial interests talked of withdrawing from the Union. The Massachusetts Legislature called a convention at Hartford in December to give voice to New England's opinions. Saner council prevailed and the secession plan failed. The convention did suggest several amendments to the Constitution that would limit the power of Congress to make war, to admit new states or restrict commerce. They also asked for a law preventing successive Presidents coming from the same state. Two in a row from Virginia was gall to those proud Yankees." He smiled and went on, "Anyhow, the end of the war made the Federalists glad to forget the whole thing." Madison got up. "Enough of this idle talk. Let's get to the purpose of Mr. Crawford's visit. Dolley, will you excuse us?"

"Certainly, Jemmy." She wished the men a pleasant good night and left. Madison suggested they retire to his upstairs library. He offered his guests brandy and cigars. Crawford lit a long, tapering Havana, puffed contentedly and said, "Lieutenant Ames and I had dinner with General MacGregor. At my suggestion Johnny saw the general several times and showed him the sights of Washington City. With your permission Ames will report on our meeting and evaluate the general's plan to liberate Florida."

Madison nodded. Mr. Jefferson said, "Lieutenant, suppose you first give us your impression of the general."

Speaking thoughtfully, Ames said, "Sir, he is a battle-tested officer who speaks freely of his experiences in the British Army and with Bolivar. He's a handsome man, brown curly hair, blue eyes and likes gaudy uniforms, pomp and ceremony."

"Then you liked this general?"

"Yes, Mr. Jefferson."

"Senator?"

"I didn't," replied Crawford. "But then I have no use for any generals. That's why the President stuck me in the War Department." The men chuckled and Crawford continued, "He's a real strutting peacock, but he's shrewd. If he can get money from those Yankee merchants for this venture, he's anything but a fool."

"But," asked Jefferson, "can he organize and lead an army or is he just another bird of brilliant plumage, Lieutenant Ames?"

"The general spoke at length about his fights against the Royalists and how he won the battles of Onoto, Alacran and especially his great victory at Juncal. I'd say, Mr. Jefferson, that he was a sound planner and understood strategy. I think he has a practical plan to liberate Florida."

"Bill, what about it?" asked the President.

"I agree with the lieutenant. I think MacGregor can capture Amelia Island and East Florida, but can he establish and organize a government? Will he get us into a row with Spain?"

"Very pertinent questions," said Jefferson. "But first let's consider the general's . . . er . . . shall we say, grand strategy."

"Go ahead, Johnny," said Crawford.

The young officer unfolded several sheets of paper. "May I read from my notes?"

"Excellent idea," said the President, who liked written reports that he could study and examine at his leisure.

"General MacGregor has a five-point plan to liberate Florida," said Ames.

"Point one—recruit an army of five hundred men in Charleston and Savannah.

"Point two—capture Fort San Carlos on Amelia Island and set up a provisional government in the town of Fernandina.

"Point three—issue a proclamation to the Americans and British now living in Florida to join his patriot army and participate in the government, which will be modeled after one of our states. He'd leave it to their discretion when to apply for admission to the United States.

"Four—aided by Florida militia he would storm St. Augustine, the capital of Spanish Florida. Pensacola, on the Gulf Coast, would be the only Spanish outpost left in Florida. MacGregor claims that the Spanish would evacuate it once St. Augustine is captured.

"Five—MacGregor would use Fernandina as a depot to collect supplies for the armies fighting for South American independence. The general says he would return to General Bolivar's staff as soon as his mission is accomplished."

Ames carefully folded his paper and waited. The three men were silent for what seemed to him an interminable time. Finally President Madison reacted. "Very neat and tidy. I suggest we examine his points one by one. Bill, can he recruit five hundred men in Charleston and Savannah?"

"Yes. Lots of soldiers and sailors from the last war are out of work, restless and unhappy. Also there are a number of Napoleon's officers in exile, eager and willing to fight. He'll have no trouble if he can pay them."

"Exactly. Has he got the money?"

"I think so. I told him bluntly—no money, soldiers or arms from the United States. He was disappointed but said he could raise the money in Baltimore and New York."

"What's their interest?"

"Profit. It's as simple as that. Fernandina is a free port. Privateers bring in their loot and sell it to merchants along the east coast. Levy a fifteen per cent tax on sales and it will bring in one hell of a lot of money. Also, if the invasion is successful land values will jump. His backers would have options to buy large acreage at a discount."

"What about the slave trade?" asked Jefferson. "I know Negroes are landed in Florida and sneaked over the Georgia line at night."

Ames spoke up. "General MacGregor says he doesn't believe in slavery and would obey our laws forbidding their importation. He would even like to offer citizenship to the many escaped slaves hiding in Florida."

"He'd have trouble there," observed Jefferson. "It just isn't that easy. But I approve in principle."

"Gentlemen, gentlemen," said the President. "Let's stick to the issue. Can MacGregor take Fort San Carlos, Bill?"

"Yes, sir. A report from reliable sources in Savannah say the fort is old, in bad condition and manned by less than one hundred Spanish dragoons. Their morale is poor. Low pay, often months overdue, and about the only recreation in Fernandina is drinking rum. A determined attack should succeed."

The President looked at Ames, who nodded. "What about the Americans and the few British in Florida? Will they welcome such an invasion?" asked Madison.

"I think so," said Crawford. "As you so aptly put it, Jemmy, Florida is nothing but a fountain of blood these days. Settlers are tired of being robbed by bandits, pirates and the Indians. If MacGregor can restore law and order they will welcome him."

"How many settlers are there in Florida?" asked Madison.

"Two or three thousand, I'd guess," answered Crawford.

"Probably more," asserted Jefferson. "When I was President I encouraged Americans to settle in Florida. I thought if enough Americans went there we might acquire Florida without a war with Spain. Unfortunately, Spain quickly blocked American emigration. First they said all Americans in Florida had to become Catholics. Then about a year later they forbade land grants to Americans."

"Then we agree there are enough Americans in Florida to make MacGregor's point three feasible?" The President looked at his guests but there was no dissent. "Now about St. Augustine?"

"That's a tough nut to crack," said Crawford. "Castillo de San Marcos is a well-built fort with twelve-foot tabby walls, deep fresh-water wells and, with enough food, could stand a long siege. The governor is an Irishman named José Coppinger. He'll fight and MacGregor will need all his skill to take St. Augustine." He glanced at the President and added, "As you well know."

"I certainly do," responded Madison. "If Congress had permitted me to support one of several invasions of Florida by Georgia militia it would be part of the United States today."

"I've often wondered," mused Crawford, "why you didn't order the Navy to support Governor Matthews when he had St. Augustine besieged."

The President frowned. "Why, Bill, it would have violated the Constitution. No President should order our armed forces into action without congressional approval."

"I certainly agree," added Mr. Jefferson. "Only a dictator like Napoleon would take such action." He poured a glass of madeira from a square decanter, sipped and continued. "If Napoleon had kept his word we wouldn't have this problem today."

"How is that, Mr. Jefferson?" asked Crawford.

"When I sent Monroe to Paris in 1802 his instructions were to try and buy New Orleans and Florida. There was certainly no thought of getting all of Louisiana. To our surprise Napoleon offered to sell all the land that Spain, under duress, had transferred to France. He desperately needed money to fight England and didn't dare levy additional taxes on the French people. As you know we got the Louisiana Territory and Napoleon promised to bring pressure on Spain to sell us Florida.

"When rumors of the sale got around, the Spanish were indignant and rightly so. Napoleon had given them his written pledge never to cede Louisiana to any country except Spain. He ignored their protests but at the same time reneged on his promise to force Spain to sell us Florida." He paused, drank more wine and added, "We must have Florida, which is a natural territory of the United States. We can't have a foreign power on our southern doorstep and should carefully consider any opportunity to get it."

"Then you think we should give General MacGregor our unofficial blessing?" asked the President.

"Yes," replied Jefferson, "though we should have someone we trust with MacGregor, someone who can report his actions to the President. For all we know he might be a British agent."

"A British agent?" exclaimed Crawford.

"Yes, Senator, England owned Florida for twenty years and reluctantly gave it up in 1783 for a clear title to the Rock of Gibraltar. The British, through Forbes & Company, dominate

Florida trade today. We've heard rumors that Britain might buy Florida from Spain."

"That's true," said Madison. "A recent letter from our minister in Madrid reports that Spain has several times offered to sell Florida to Britain. It has never been a profitable colony and besides Spain has her hands full with the Revolutionaries in South America."

"It's been my experience," said Jefferson, "that the British never give up. With Florida they might well renew their claims to New Orleans and the mouth of the Mississippi. This MacGregor may be all he claims, an idealistic crusader interested only in freeing the New World from Spain. I insist though that the President must have accurate intelligence."

"I agree with Mr. Jefferson. We must not be involved in another disastrous Florida venture," said Madison.

"It seems to me," interjected Crawford, "that St. Augustine is the crux of the matter. If MacGregor moves swiftly and captures St. Augustine this venture should succeed. A long siege might bring civil war in Florida and perhaps intervention by England as Mr. Jefferson suggests."

"Then we invoke the Congressional act of 1811. You remember, Bill. You voted for it," said Madison.

"Of course. This act passed in secret," he explained to Ames, "gives the United States the right to occupy Florida if it is seized by a foreign power."

"Bill, I assume you and Lieutenant Ames agree with Mr. Jefferson that we should indicate to General MacGregor, if he's successful, that we are prepared to treat with his provisional government."

Both men said "Yes" and Madison continued, "But who will be our observer with MacGregor's forces?"

"Why not Lieutenant Ames?" said Crawford.

"But he's an officer in the United States Army," objected Madison.

"Let him resign and volunteer. I know General MacGregor likes Johnny and would be delighted to have a trained officer on his staff. When this is over Johnny can rejoin the Army and you can upgrade him to a captain or even a major."

"Ever the old fox." Madison smiled. "Bargaining for your friends."

Noticing Ames's expression of consternation, Jefferson said, "This is a most serious step for the lieutenant. I think we should be guided by his wishes."

"Certainly, Mr. Jefferson," agreed Crawford. "How do you feel about it, Johnny?"

"I was trained to be a soldier, not a spy."

"I understand, Lieutenant," said the President, "and I assure you none of us will think the less of you if you decline. However, I might add you are not really a spy, for we hope MacGregor will succeed. You would be expected to help the general in every way. You'd be more like a correspondent but reporting to your President rather than a newspaper."

"But, Mr. President, I'd be deceiving General MacGregor, my commanding officer." **1801195**

"But in the best interests of your country."

Ames jumped from his chair and walked to the large french window. He was confused. Puritan background urged rejection. However, he liked and respected both the President and Mr. Jefferson. He could not believe they would ask him to do anything dishonorable. He also realized the importance of Florida and the expedition sounded thrilling. He would be glad to leave Washington City though he would miss Mr. Crawford. He turned back to the three men and said, "I'll do as you ask."

"Want to think about it overnight?" asked Madison.

"No, Mr. President, I'm ready."

"Good lad," said the President while Jefferson and Crawford smiled their approbation.

§ CHAPTER 3 §

The last week in February, Crawford and Ames held their second secret meeting with General MacGregor at Wylie's Tavern. The Secretary of War told MacGregor of their meeting with President Madison and Mr. Jefferson and said, "Unofficially you have the best wishes of the United States but we cannot be involved."

"Gad, sir!" exploded MacGregor, "I'm disappointed—I had hoped—"

Crawford interrupted. "General, you know why the United States cannot assist you." In his persuasive voice Crawford continued, "You have our blessing, sir, when we could easily have halted your expedition."

MacGregor blinked his eyes. "It would have been simple," said Crawford, "to slap you aboard the first ship to Caracas. Come, General, we have agreed to treat with your provisional government if you are successful. What of your backers? Have you got the money?"

"They are ready, Mr. Crawford, but wanted some assurance from the President."

"You have not told them of our meetings?"

"God's blood—I gave you my word," he said angrily.

"No offense, General. You can assure them that the United States will not interfere. That should satisfy."

"I hope so. What about the new President? He takes office next month."

"President Monroe has been briefed and approves. You probably know that he was Madison's Secretary of State. They see eye to eye on foreign policy."

"Deucedly awkward," grunted MacGregor. "I suppose it's better than nothing."

"Much better," agreed Crawford. "And I might add that you owe Mr. Ames a debt of gratitude. He vigorously supported you in his presentation at Montpelier."

"You think my strategy is sound?" asked MacGregor.

"Yes, sir, I do."

MacGregor beamed. "Dashed if I'm not grateful." Crawford plucked a taper and lit a cigar. Puffing deliberately, he said, "Confidentially, Lieutenant Ames is bored in Washington City. Too much paper work and not enough action." He paused and waited for MacGregor's reaction.

"Indeed, young man, you have my sympathy. Soldiers are trained to fight, not to push pens, eh?"

Ames nodded and Crawford continued, "While I'd hate to lose Lieutenant Ames, I believe he might consider joining you."

"I'm blessed if I understand," said MacGregor. "Would you be acting as a military observer for your government?"

"No," answered Crawford firmly. "My government is not officially aware of your existence. He'd have to resign from the Army and seek a new career with you."

The general wrinkled his brow. "A most serious step for a young man."

"Sir," said Ames, "you resigned from the British Army to fight with General Bolivar."

Smothering a grin, Crawford said, "Lieutenant Ames is a graduate of West Point, a trained officer, and I'm sure would be a most valuable addition to your staff."

"Yes, he would," admitted MacGregor.

"Besides," continued Crawford, "a former American officer would reassure your backers and be helpful in recruiting."

MacGregor turned to Ames. "Lieutenant, would you like to take part in this venture?"

Ames hesitated for a moment. "Yes, General, I would be honored."

"Then I'll commission you a captain."

"General MacGregor," said Crawford. "A captain ain't worth a picayune in frontier country. Every militia squad has droves of captains. He should be at least a colonel." He winked slyly at Ames.

"A colonel, eh? I served for years in the British Army and only got to be a captain. Well, this is a new world, Mr. Crawford, and a colonel it shall be." He chuckled and asked Ames, "When can you report for duty?"

"Sir, I must officially resign from the Army. Mr. Crawford, what do you think?"

"A couple of weeks. Say right after President Monroe's inauguration, which is March the fourth."

"Splendid. Suppose, Colonel Ames, you meet me in Charleston in the middle of March. Get in touch with a Mr. George Blair, who is a member of the syndicate. Start recruiting and look for two ships. Former privateers would be effective. They should be well gunned and each capable of holding at least two hundred men."

He got up, went to his overcoat and returned with an elaborate scroll. "I, too, Colonel Ames, was recently commissioned. Mr. Crawford, I know I can trust your discretion."

"Certainly, General."

MacGregor read:

"Deputies of Free America, north to their compatriot Gregor MacGregor, General of the brigade in the services of the United Provinces of New Grenada and Venezuela, greetings;

"You are to take possession of East and West Florida so their inhabitants there shall have the blessings of free institutions and security of their natural rights.

"You will arm vessels and grant rank to naval and

military officers and establish a free government by the will of the people.

"It is signed by the deputies of Venezuela, New Grenada and Rio de la Plata." He paused. "And my first act is to appoint you a colonel in the forces of liberation."

"Thank you, sir," said Ames. Crawford tendered his congratulations. Ames saluted his new commanding officer and promised to be in Charleston by the twentieth of March. He and Crawford then wished MacGregor "Good night" and departed.

The next morning the secretary called Ames into his office. "Johnny, are you sure you want to enlist with MacGregor?"

"Yes, Mr. Crawford, I'm sure."

"You aren't being hoodwinked by this glib general?"

There was a long pause. "No, sir."

Crawford puffed his morning cigar and recalled the strange fire in MacGregor's handsome face when he talked of battles fought and won, his laughing blue eyes and petulant mouth. He understood why the young officer was impressed. He analyzed his own attitude. He wanted the general to succeed, yet he wondered if this bombastic man could recruit and lead a liberating army. This he doubted. Most of all he did not want Ames to suffer. He was fond of his young aide and now felt a sense of guilt in recommending him to MacGregor. "You know, Johnny, your Litchfield friends will disapprove."

"I suppose so."

"And your fellow officers will scorn you as a renegade."

Ames frowned as he realized the truth of this remark. "And if the expedition fails," continued Crawford, "it will be difficult for you back in the Army, even with a presidential reappointment."

"Impossible, I expect."

"Well, Johnny, maybe I spoke hastily at Montpelier. You must not be unduly influenced by the President, Mr. Jefferson or me. It's your future and we'll understand if you decide not to go."

"Mr. Crawford, I've had time to carefully cogitate." He grinned and explained, "That was one of my father's favorite words. I know it's a gamble, but it will be exciting and I'm tired of Washington City. I do appreciate Florida's importance to the United States. If MacGregor succeeds I'll be proud I was there."

"It'll be a great service to your country. I met with the President and Mr. Monroe a couple of days ago. Mr. Monroe knows about your mission and sends you his appreciation. And the President wishes you God speed and said to remind you there will always be a warm welcome for you at Montpelier. It seems that Dolley took a fancy to you."

"She's a very kind and gracious lady."

"Well spoken, sir, and now back to business. I again emphasize the importance of secrecy. You are to write to me only. Make your letters gossipy and friendly so if one is intercepted it will sound personal. I'll report anything of importance to the President."

"Shall I send letters to this office?"

"No," replied Crawford. "Use my home address. Besides, I won't be Secretary of War in the new administration." Noticing Ames's puzzled expression, he explained. "I'll still be in the Cabinet as Secretary of the Treasury."

"The Treasury Department!" exclaimed Ames. "I thought you'd be Secretary of State."

"So did I, Johnny, but politicians have convenient memories. Mr. Monroe claimed he couldn't appoint me to the State Department without offending Henry Clay, who also wanted the post. He said he'd had many complaints about southern influence in foreign affairs. You'll recall he was Madison's Secretary of State and Madison served Mr. Jefferson in the same capacity."

"I see," said Johnny.

"Well, I don't," said Crawford. "This came in today's post." He tossed Ames a clipping from the *Savannah Gazette and Columbian Museum*.

It was a letter signed by Dr. Jabez Hammond, a member of Congress. Ames slowly read:

"When Congress first assembled, as between Crawford and Monroe, I have not a particle of doubt that a majority of the Republican members were for the former. But caucuses were put off from time to time and finally when held Crawford got fifty-four votes to sixty-five for Monroe. There is no room for doubt that the election of Mr. Monroe was chiefly due to Mr. Crawford's voluntary postponement of his claims."

Ames wanted to say something comforting. The right words didn't come. Finally he blurted, "It's a damned shame!"

"The ingratitude of man, eh, Johnny? Anyhow Monroe has appointed John Quincy Adams Secretary of State. He offered Clay the War Department. He refused, saying being Speaker of the House was more important. He's right. If I were still in the Senate I'd not accept a cabinet post."

"Why don't you resign and run for the Senate?"

"I was tempted, but both Madison and Jefferson insisted I serve in the Cabinet. They said if I left it would weaken the party and encourage the Federalists. Also they promised to support me for President in 1824." He tilted his chair and reflected. "Eight years is a long time. It might be sooner, for Monroe is sixty and not in good health." He suddenly jumped to his feet and paced the room. "Goddamnit, I shouldn't talk like that—forget my words please, Johnny."

"Yes, Mr. Crawford," replied Ames, thinking he would never understand politics or politicians.

Resuming his chair, the secretary gave Ames a letter. "This is a note to my good friend Edward Simms. He will arrange to express your letters to me. You'll find him sociable, knowledgeable and he'll smooth your path in Charleston."

"Is Mr. Simms aware of my mission?"

"Of course not, Johnny. Only three Presidents and your humble servant know. Your secret is in good hands. I told Simms you were a personable young man, seeking excitement and adventure. Simms will certainly approve of liberating Florida and be glad to help. When are you leaving for Charleston?"

"On March fifth. The Potomac is jammed with ships but none are sailing until the day after the inauguration. I've booked passage on a sloop and the captain says we'll make it in eight or nine days."

"Maybe, if the weather is favorable. Anyhow, I'm delighted, Colonel Jonathan Ames, that you'll get to see James Monroe inaugurated as the fifth President of the United States."

"So am I, Mr. Crawford, but, sir, don't call me 'Colonel.' It sounds downright ridiculous."

"You'll soon earn the rank. Now, Johnny, I've got to make arrangements for President Monroe's honor guard. Good day."

March 4, 1817, James Monroe's inaugural day, was warm and sunny. By noon thousands of people had gathered in the capital. The crowd, strolling through the dusty and rutted streets, was the largest Ames had ever seen. They slowly assembled before the temporary structure where Congress sat until the burned-out Capitol could be restored. In front of the frame building a platform, upon which the President would take the oath of office, had hastily been built.

As Ames climbed Capitol Hill he grinned at the absurd reason for this uncomfortable ceremony. Last night, Crawford, roaring with laughter, told him the House had flatly refused to let the Senate introduce their elegant, new, red velvet armchairs into their chamber where the ceremony usually took place.

"They squabbled like schoolboys over a bag of cookies," said Crawford, "and couldn't agree. Finally they compromised on an outdoor ceremony. I'm told Speaker Clay was responsible, got his dander up because he wasn't made Secretary of State. Also, none of the diplomatic corps will be present. Someone forgot to send 'em an official invitation." He wiped the tears from his eyes and added, "Diplomats never dress up with braid and medals and go places without an engraved invitation. It will certainly be a spectacle."

Ames agreed that it was. He watched the President-elect, along with Vice President Daniel Tompkins, arrive on horseback. Monroe sat erect, tautly holding his reins as he joked with his escort. He was greeted with military honors by the Marine Corps and several army regiments. Accompanied by

Madison and the justices of the Supreme Court, Monroe and Tompkins were sworn in.

The President moved to the platform and delivered his inaugural address. He was not a good speaker and read poorly. His voice was almost inaudible and his message did not inspire. He discussed the need for new roads and canals, fostering manufacturing and a stronger defense establishment. He was applauded when he stated that "a country that failed to jealously guard its rights scarcely can be said to hold a place among independent nations. National honor is a national property of the highest value." There was no mention of Florida or the struggle for independence of the South American nations.

Disappointed and vaguely disconsolate, Ames walked slowly back to his boarding house. Somehow this tall gray-haired man with his deeply lined face did not measure up to his ideal of a President. He would have preferred the strapping, confident Crawford. Perhaps I'll watch William Harris Crawford become the sixth President of my country, he thought. This revived his spirits as he methodically packed for his trip to Charleston.

The coastwise schooner, the *Silver Cloud*, all sails set, and riding a flood tide, swung into Charleston's inner harbor. She was nine days out of Washington City and, except for rough seas off Cape Hatteras, it had been a pleasant voyage. Nevertheless, Jonathan Ames was glad to go ashore.

Around him swirled the sights, sounds and smells of the harbor as he waited for his luggage. It was very hot for March, more like a July day in Connecticut. He sniffed the heavy perfume of oleanders mixed with the stench of the mud flats. Sea gulls soared, darted and snatched bits of food from the water. Three great, ugly black birds, which he recognized as buzzards, fought over a dead cat.

Graceful mulatto girls, baskets of fresh fruit or vegetables on their turbaned heads, moved swiftly among the sweating Negro dock workers. Chanting, they unloaded sacks of coffee, sugar and flour. Huge stems of green bananas, wicker baskets of coconuts, oranges and pineapples were piled high under a shed. Ames, wiping his forehead with a linen handkerchief, thought, it's like a foreign country.

Mr. Crawford had recommended the Planters' Hotel. He hailed a carriage and was driven to a handsome building with ornate grilled balconies. When he registered the Negro clerk bade him welcome, saying Mr. Simms had made all arrangements. "He say he come by in the cool of the evening to see if you comfortable and he honored if you sup with him."

Ames replied that he would be delighted. After a hot bath, fresh linen and a light meal he strolled the city's narrow streets. Charleston, it seemed to him, was a town of high-walled gardens, imposing gates and doorways and delicate iron-work porches. Purple wisteria draped over brick walls, roses on bushes and trellises, and camellias and azaleas, were brilliant against somber green leaves. Palmettos, live oaks and tall magnolias shaded the soft-toned yellow and blue plaster houses. The headiness of gardenias, orange blossoms, and sweet olives pleased him. The colorful flowers, the deep shade and the brilliant sun somehow made him think of Litchfield. What a contrast! It was still winter in Connecticut, the trees leafless and the only indication of spring the budding willows in the valleys.

As he walked along he was aware that people bowed or softly said "Afternoon." At first he thought it was a mistake. Soon he realized that both friends and strangers were greeted. It was a courteous town.

Continuing, he saw a small crowd standing on the steps of a public building. It was a slave auction. Fascinated, he pushed forward. Four Negroes stood impassively. There was a man about thirty, a handsome mulatto woman and a young girl. They were obviously a family. The fourth was a huge black man, well over six feet, his muscles bulging under his faded but clean cotton clothes. He slowly flexed his enormous hands and eyed the crowd. Ames felt an instant compassion for him. He'd never forgotten that day in Litchfield when he had been declared a pauper. He shuddered at the idea of being in servitude for life. He admired the Negro's composure—almost studied indifference.

A stout, red-faced auctioneer clapped his hands three times and shouted, "Oh yeah! Oh yeah! These here niggers fer sale." He spat tobacco juice and went on, "This ain't no ordinary sale of no-'count niggers, whar a man buying a nigger mout or mout not git what he was lookin' fer. It's a rare opportunity whar a buyer is sho that fer every dollar he pays he's gittin' his full dollar's worth of real genuine niggers, healthy, well raised, respectful, obedient and willing."

Ames was disgusted. He started to leave but the auctioneer's hearty voice grabbed his attention.

"These here niggers being sold to settle the estate of the late Colonel Stovall—God rest his soul. I'se been instructed by the executor to sell this first lot as a family. We hopes you all will offer a good bid for these trained servants." He pointed toward the family group and continued, "The man's a fine butler, coachman and yardman, the woman's a good cook and the young 'un be ripe in a few years." He leered and the crowd gave a burst of coarse laughter. "Anyhow, gentlemen, these niggers all trained in Colonel Stovall's yard. They's been examined and all enjoy good health."

A slovenly, tobacco-chewing man came forward and allowed as how he'd like to look over "them niggers." Ames heard a well-dressed gentleman drawl to his companion, "That's old Jonas Henderson, the damned nigger splitter."

The odd term piqued Ames's curiosity. "Your pardon, gentlemen, I'm a stranger in Charleston. Would you mind explaining that expression, 'nigger splitter'?"

His obvious Yankee accent caught their attention. The speaker turned and saw a slim young man in a gray suit, white stock and well-polished boots. The man bowed. "Delighted to oblige, sir. He's a nigger trader—buys up families cheap with the understanding they will be kept together, then he splits the family, sells 'em individually at high profits."

Ames expressed his horror at such brutal treatment. "I agree, sir," said the Charlestonian, "but he won't get this family. I promised my wife I'd buy them. We need a cook and my coachman is rheumatic."

He kept his word and bid in the family for $2,200, much to Henderson's displeasure.

The auctioneer then told the remaining slave to stand up. "Are you buying him, too?" asked Ames.

"No, though he's a fine field hand. Hate to see one of Stovall's niggers sold down the river to the cane brakes."

"Cane brakes?" questioned Ames.

"Sugar cane in Louisiana and Mississippi. A big strong man like that will probably last two or three years before fever gets him. A shame, but the quarters on my Edisto place are overflowing. Just can't use another field hand."

The auctioneer, impatient to get on with the sale, said, "Here's a strapping big nigger, good hand and carpenter, too. He's twenty-six, healthy and answers to name of Wash."

Henderson swaggered forward and ordered the slave to open his mouth. He carefully examined Wash's teeth, then his eyes, ears and feet. He gave a grunt of satisfaction. Suddenly he grabbed the Negro's cotton shirt and ripped it off, exposing his broad back. "No whip marks, eh? You must be a good nigger." Wash did not answer.

Henderson slowly circled and without warning crashed his fist into the Negro's groin. He bent double in pain but did not utter a sound. He pulled himself erect, towering over the squat trader. For a moment Ames thought the giant black man would hit him. He hoped he would. He felt a bond of sympathy for the Negro and a loathing for the trader. He flexed his fist and edged toward Henderson. He wanted to smash his ugly face.

"No hernia," observed Henderson. "You be surprised how many of these big bucks is ruptured." He spoke to the auctioneer. "I'll start 'er with five hundred dollars."

For a few minutes the bidding was brisk and quickly rose to $725. There was a lull in the auction and Henderson smiled exultantly.

Ames was angry and felt humiliated at being a spectator. The brutal blow to the stomach revolted him. The Negro shrugged dejectedly and his eyes were sad. Compassion overrode reason and Ames said, "I bid seven hundred and thirty dollars." This is ridiculous, thought Ames to himself, and the crowd seemed to agree. They laughed and someone remarked, "A thrifty Yankee with only a five-dollar raise."

Henderson glared and in his cold unemotional voice said, "Seven hundred and fifty dollars."

Annoyed at himself and hating the swarthy trader, Ames bid, "Seven hundred and fifty-five dollars." Again the spectators tittered and Henderson sneeringly replied, "Eight hundred dollars."

Ames thought, I've disgraced myself. For a fleeting instant he was tempted to walk away, but he glanced at Wash, who smiled hopefully.

He said firmly, "Eight hundred and five."

The determination in his voice brought a scowl to Henderson's face. His profit was diminishing. A slave would bring $900 to $1,000 in the cane fields. Still he'd have to transport him and perhaps wait months for his money. This young man with his nasal tone puzzled Henderson. Most Yankees at slave auctions showed scorn or disgust but never bought.

The auctioneer spoke. "You gonna bid, Jonas?"

"I reckon so, though I just can't figger out why he wants this here nigger." He turned toward Ames and said, "Thought all you Yankees had no stomach fer slavery."

Ames flushed but did not answer. He wondered if he had gone slightly mad. How would he explain to Mr. Crawford? The Secretary of War had given him $2,000 from the department special emergency fund. Would buying a slave qualify? The answer was self-evident, but he'd save this man from the cane brakes. He knew he was swayed by his own experience as a bound servant.

"Jonas," asked the auctioneer, "what you bid?"

"I'll go as high as eight hundred fifty."

"Eight hundred fifty-five," bid Ames.

"He's yourn, you damned meddling Yankee," snarled Henderson and turned on his heel.

Furious with himself, Henderson and the entire proceeding, Ames spun the trader around saying, "Don't speak to me like that."

The slave buyer deliberately spat tobacco juice on Ames's boots. This, on top of his agonized frustrations of the past half hour, sent Ames's temper soaring. He feinted with his right and swung a straight left to the jaw. Henderson toppled. Stunned, he slowly got to his feet. "I'll rip yer gizzard, you Yankee bastard." He whipped a long knife from beneath his coat.

A heavy walking stick cracked Henderson's wrist. The knife clattered on the stone steps. "You miserable wretch! Drawing a knife on a gentleman. Be out of town by sundown and don't ever show your face in Charleston again."

Henderson started to retrieve his knife, decided against it and abruptly departed.

Turning to his benefactor, Ames said, "Sir, I am Jonathan Ames and I'm deeply beholden to you."

"I am Richard Dickey, Mr. Ames, and glad to be of service. That damned scoundrel! He should be horsewhipped." He scrutinized Ames with amusement and in his courtly drawl added, "I'm glad you bought Wash, but, sir, I was surprised when you entered the bidding."

"So was I," ruefully admitted Ames, "for I don't believe in slavery."

"So, despite your beliefs, you now own a slave."

Ames's worried look vanished. "Not for long, Mr. Dickey." He then beckoned to Wash, who came to his side, grinning and exposing gleaming white teeth. "I thanks you, massa. Sho hates to work in 'em cane bottoms. Massa, where we go now?"

"Don't call me 'massa.' I'm not your master." And to the perplexed Negro he said slowly, "I won't own any man. You are free—free to go where you please and do what you please."

Startled, Wash tapped his broad chest. "Me, sah?"

"Yes." And Ames smiled.

To be saved from the fever swamps and suddenly made a free man was beyond Wash's comprehension. Puzzled, he asked, "Me free?"

"That's right, Wash. You are a free man."

Laughing and sobbing, Wash said, "Praise God. I'm free—

I'm free. Oh sweet Jesus, I'm free. Me, free." His big face beamed and he sang softly:

> "I'm just God's own chile,
>   Free as the river wind running wild,
> Oh sweet Jesus, hear me sing,
> Free as the fuzz on an angel's wing."

He halted his song of joy and asked plaintively, "Who'll give a free nigger a job, where'll I go, what'll I do? Oh Jesus, how can a man be free wid no work to do?"

Touched by his lament, Dickey said, "Wash, you know my house on King Street?"

"Yes, sah."

"Go there. Tell them I sent you. Mr. Ames and I will see you in the morning."

"Yes, sah." He walked slowly and dejectedly away.

"It just ain't that simple, Mr. Ames," said Dickey. "Lots of us in the South would free our slaves if it were. There are papers to sign, a bond to post. You must guarantee Wash support or a job. He can't be a charge on the sovereign state of South Carolina. Mr. Ames, where are you staying?"

"At the Planters' Hotel."

"I'll call on you in the morning. Do you know anyone in Charleston who can vouch for you?"

"Not really, though I do have a letter of introduction to Mr. Edward Simms. He has invited me for supper tonight."

Dickey was impressed. "Excellent. I'll explain your predicament to Mr. Simms, who is a friend of mine. Don't worry. We'll help you straighten things out. Good night, sir."

Ames said, "Good night," and walked slowly back to the Planters' Hotel a very confused young man.

He noticed a handsome carriage at the hotel entrance. An elderly Negro, standing beside the two matching black horses, said, "Excuse me, sah, is you Colonel Ames?"

Still unaccustomed to being addressed as "Colonel," Ames stuttered, "Why, yes. Yes, I am."

"Mr. Simms done sent his carriage. Will you kindly get in, sah."

After a short drive they pulled up before a fine Georgian house. A plump man in a white linen suit ambled down the crushed-oyster-shell walk.

"Colonel Ames, I bid you welcome to Charleston. I apologize for not appearing personally at the hotel. You see," he explained with a hint of mockery, "I was detained talking with your friend Mr. Dickey."

Ames reddened, shook hands and said contritely, "I guess I made a fool of myself this afternoon."

"Well, it was the last thing I would have reckoned on." Simms smiled. "But come and let's sit on the piazza, be comfortable and we'll talk." Ames followed his host to a long side porch that caught the evening breeze from the harbor. A butler appeared with two frosted silver mugs.

. "Ah," said Simms, "this should dulcify your Puritan conscience."

Ames accepted the cold goblet and asked, "What is it, sir?"

"A mint julep. Balm for the soul, a reprieve from worry." Jonathan sipped the mellow Bourbon tanged with mint, wrinkled his nose and said, "Mmmmm . . . delicious!" and took two big swallows.

"Whoa, young fellow. Juleps are as deceptive as young ladies. They'll kinda rear up on you if you hurry 'em." He drank slowly, wiped his lips with a linen napkin and sighed contentedly. "I had a long letter about you from my old friend and schoolmate, Bill Crawford."

"Schoolmate?"

"Yes. We attended old Moses Waddell's Academy up in the sand hills. It was a school of high thinking, hard work and plain living." He glanced at his palatial home and continued, "We lived in log cabins, lit by pine torches or flickering tapers. Had three meals daily of cornbread and bacon and studied from sunup till nine at night. A horn roused us for daily prayer and we daily memorized five hundred lines of Virgil or Homer. I expect a graduate of the academy was as rigid and fatalistic in his thinking as New England Puritans." He paused and raised his julep. "I'm sorry my boy but Bourbon makes me talkative and the old enjoy ruminating about school-days."

This was a mysterious world to Ames. He had often wondered about Crawford's young days in the South. "Please go on, sir," he urged.

"Well, Bill went back to Augusta, taught school for a while and then read law. I returned to Charleston, became a lawyer, but we met occasionally on the green-bag circuit."

"What?"

Simms sipped his julep and continued, "Lawyers carried their books in green bags as they traveled on horseback with a circuit judge. We called ourselves gentlemen of the green bags. I must admit though we weren't always gentlemen. Couldn't be and survive. County courthouses packed with mean, hard men who didn't like lawyers, especially if we won. Your mentor Bill Crawford was bigger and just as tough as any of 'em. Saved my skin a couple of times. Take no sass from any of 'em. I remember the time Peter Van Allen insulted him in a tavern—something about the Yazzo fraud. Bill called him out and killed him."

It was difficult for Ames to believe his jovial friend had fought a duel. "The Yazzo fraud? What was that?"

"Bunch of land speculators bribed the Georgia Legislature and got 'em to sell millions of acres of land near the Yazzo River in west Georgia. It was an outright swindle and Bill led the fight against it. That's how he got elected to the legislature and started his political career."

"With a duel?" exclaimed Ames, thinking of Aaron Burr, who had ended his career with one.

"You don't hold with dueling?"

"No, sir."

"Most times I don't, but sometimes a man gets cornered." His voice took on a sardonic tone. "Just as you don't hold with slavery but now you own a slave."

Ames was perturbed and his hand trembled as he drank his julep. The older man was sympathetic. "I understand why you bought Wash. Bill told me 'bout your being bound. Sounds like slavery in another form."

"It can be," agreed Ames. "But I was fortunate. I think both systems are wrong."

"Maybe," said Simms, "but you are my guest and I refuse to argue. Something to be said for both sides. The question is, what you gonna do with your nigger?"

"I just don't know, sir."

"Well, take my advice and keep him."

"But I've given him his freedom."

"I don't mean as a slave—as your servant. He's a good nigger and you'll find him mighty handy. He can cook, wash your clothes, clean your guns, forage for food and drink. Certainly a colonel in this army of liberation deserves a body servant."

"I guess he would be useful," admitted Ames. "But what will I pay him and how?"

"Give him his keep and any spare money you have. It's more than he'd make in Charleston. No jobs here for free niggers. Besides, all the officers will have servants. I'll go down to the courthouse with you in the morning and we'll fill out the necessary papers. Bring Wash here. He can stay in my quarters until you sail."

"Yes, sir, and thank you very very much."

"Now that's fixed, let's eat supper. You can tell me about General MacGregor, his plans and whether I can be helpful."

While they ate a light supper of baked shad, which Simms explained were running in the Edisto, fresh asparagus and hominy, Ames discussed General MacGregor. "He expects to capture Amelia Island, set up a republic and then attack St. Augustine. Once these Spanish forts have been taken he'll seek admission to the Union."

Simms carefully boned a piece of shad. "You've got confidence in this General MacGregor?"

"Yes, Mr. Simms. He's a former British officer and has won many battles for General Bolivar in South America."

Simms nodded, finished his fish and suggested coffee in the library. Ames was impressed with the large collection of books and was very interested in the wall maps, which showed the

Georgia islands and the location of Amelia Island at the mouth of St. Marys River.

"It's cooler in this room," said Simms. "Never open the windows until dark. Bit warm for March, isn't it?"

Laughing, Ames said, "Warm? It's downright hot. In Litchfield there won't be weather like this until July."

Pouring madeira from a crystal decanter, Simms said, "Always been sorry I didn't go to the Litchfield Law School. A young friend of mine went there after getting out of Yale. John C. Calhoun. He speaks highly of the school."

"I remember Mr. Calhoun. Very tall man with lots of bushy black hair. He gave me a nickel once to help him plant an elm tree."

"An elm tree? What for?"

"It was a student tradition. They believed it brought them luck. Anyhow, you should see our elm shaded green on a summer day. It's lovely and peaceful."

"I'd like to. Now, Colonel Ames, I approve of your Florida venture. How can I help?"

"Do you know a George Blair?"

"Yes. Shrewd Scotsman. Drives a hard bargain but honest. Why?"

"He's MacGregor's agent here and I would like to meet him."

"We'll see him after finishing our business at the courthouse. What else?"

"Well, General MacGregor needs two ships, well gunned and each big enough to transport two hundred men."

"No problem. There are half a dozen former privateers anchored in the harbor."

"The general wants to enlist three or four hundred men here and in Savannah."

"Can he pay them?"

"Yes, sir."

"It should be easy then. Lots of young men out of work in these parts. And the town is swarming with French exiles. They are hungry, restless and I'm sure would sign on for hard cash." He sipped his madeira and thought for a moment. "I've talked several times with one of them, Captain Charles Laurent.

Seems like a gentleman and claims he fought with old Boney in Egypt and all over Europe. Might be useful to have a talk with him."

"I'd like that, though I'll let General MacGregor select his own officers."

"Sensible," commented Simms. "When is he coming to town?"

"I'd think the end of this month. Mr. Blair should know."

"I expect so. Now what about those letters to Bill? He wants them sent express?"

"Yes, sir. I promised Mr. Crawford to keep him informed on the progress of the campaign."

"There's a Captain Stratford who owns a little brig called the *John W. Callahan, Jr.*" He smiled and said, "Don't ask me why because I don't know. Anyhow, Captain Stratford trades in Fernandina. Give him the letters and I'll get them to Washington as quickly as possible." He frowned and asked, "Are these to be official reports?"

"No, sir. I resigned from the Army and our government is not supporting General MacGregor. But, Mr. Crawford said information on Florida would be useful in Washington. He is my friend, sir, and—"

"Mine, too," interrupted Simms. "And I'll forward your letters. Damned if I understand why President Monroe doesn't help MacGregor. We could take Florida in a few weeks. But then I don't like Monroe. I wish Bill were President."

"Many people feel that way, sir," observed Ames.

"He should never have allowed Jefferson and Madison to persuade him to step aside. He could have won this election, and eight years is a long time. Many things can happen."

"Mr. Crawford is very loyal to his party and his friends," remarked Ames.

"Too much so, and already he's getting the short end of the stick. Why didn't Monroe appoint him Secretary of State?"

"I don't know."

"That's what he expected, isn't it?"

"Yes, Mr. Simms. He was very disappointed."

"I'd never trust Monroe. Did you ever know Aaron Burr?"

"No, sir. I've seen him once or twice when he visited Litchfield. I was just a boy but I remember the excitement when he killed Alexander Hamilton."

"Most unfortunate, though I could never understand why Burr was criticized and scorned for shooting Hamilton. It was a duel between gentlemen. Burr won. It should have ended there. Instead he was hounded out of the country." He frowned and drank more madeira. "I hold no brief for Burr and his dreams of empire in the Southwest. I only met him once when he visited his son-in-law, Joe Alston, in Charleston and that was years ago." He saw that Ames did not understand and explained. "My good friend Joseph Alston was a brilliant young man and one of the youngest governors of South Carolina. He married Burr's daughter, Theodosia. She was a beautiful and charming lady. They had one son who died of yellow fever. Theodosia sailed on the schooner *Patriot* for New York to see her father, who had just returned from his exile in Europe. The *Patriot* sank in a December storm. Everyone was lost. Joe, in bad health and dejected at the loss of his family, died last year at thirty-seven. Great loss to South Carolina and the nation."

He paused, grinning, then he added, "Madeira on top of juleps sure loosens my tongue. Sorry if I sound like an old bore, but there's a point to my story. Last year Aaron Burr wrote Alston a long letter urging him to support Andrew Jackson for President. The week Monroe was elected Alston showed it to me. If I'd seen it sooner I'd have sent it to Bill Crawford. Mebbe it would have changed his mind. Anyhow, Burr may have been a rascal, but both Alston and I agreed that he was an astute judge of men."

Simms rose from his chair, went to his desk and opened a doeskin pouch. "Alston gave me a copy of Burr's letter. I'll read you part of it." He flipped to the third page of an obviously lengthy missive and read:

> "Naturally dull and stupid—extremely illiterate, indecisive to a degree that would be incredible to one that did not know him. Pusillanimous and of course hypocritical: has no opinion on any subject and will

(55)

always be under the government of the worst men. Pretends, as I am told, to some knowledge of military matters but never commanded a platoon nor was fit to command one. He served in the Revolutionary War, that is he acted a short time as aide de camp to Lord Stirling, who was regularly drunk. Monroe's whole duty was to fill his lordship's tankard and hear, with indications of admiration, his lordship's long stories about himself. Such is Monroe's military experience. As a lawyer Monroe was far below mediocrity. He never rose to the honor of trying a case of the value of a hundred pounds. . . ."

The contempt in Simms's voice disturbed Ames. He had considerable respect for Burr's intelligence. His host returned the pouch to his desk and said bitterly, "Perhaps, Colonel Ames, you were right in resigning from the Army. Could you honorably serve such a man as your commander in chief?"

Ames decided any comment would be superfluous. He thanked Simms for a most pleasant evening and walked thoughtfully back to the Planters' Hotel.

§ CHAPTER 4 §

It was a busy day for the young man from Connecticut. With Mr. Simms's assistance he posted a bond for Wash's support and signed his freedom papers. He had a long conversation with Mr. Blair in his tiny office back of the custom house. He liked the wrinkled, sharp-eyed Scotsman and his blunt manner of speech. Blair said that ships were available "at bargain prices" and with hard money men could be recruited, but he agreed they should wait for General Mac-Gregor's arrival in Charleston. "He's booked passage on the schooner *Gray Goose* and should be here in April. There's much trading between Charleston and Fernandina. No point in giving the Spaniards advance notice. Once we start enlisting or buying ships they'll hear about it. It might give 'em an opportunity to bring in reinforcements from St. Augustine or even one or two nigger regiments from Havana."

This was sound advice and Ames accepted it. Simms nodded his approval. "Might I suggest," said Blair, "that you keep your role here a secret. Be just a visitor from up North, not Colonel Ames." Simms agreed that made good sense, and that he would introduce Ames as the son of an old friend. "But you'll have to move to my house. Can't have you in a hotel. I'll call you Jonathan, if you don't mind?"

Ames didn't mind at all. He felt sheepish each time he was called Colonel Ames and was glad to drop the title.

He made arrangements with Blair to inspect the schooners for sale and promised an estimate of military supplies needed. Blair said to call on him for anything.

"Might as well enjoy yourself the next few weeks. With Mr. Simms as your guide you'll find Charleston mighty gay."

Once he moved into the Simms house on Church Street he realized the truth of Blair's prediction. He had never imagined such luxury. Trained, smiling servants anticipated his every wish. One day he counted them: a coachman, two grooms, a footman, a butler, a valet, a cook with an apprentice and a boy to wash dishes and bring in wood, several maids who were always dusting, polishing, waxing.

Though he was offered breakfast in bed he preferred to join his host on the side porch. Accustomed to the austere West Point fare, he found himself wondering each day what new delight he would be offered. Berries or oranges, cantaloupes or mush melons, broiled fresh fish, creamed shrimp, thin slivers of steak or liver and fresh eggs cooked to "yer druthers" said the butler, assorted hot breads—biscuits, corn muffins, popovers, waffles or tiny thin pancakes—and always hominy. Ames had always considered hominy a porridge, like oatmeal, to be eaten with cream and sugar. He now found the slow-boiled hominy, "spreckled is best," explained Simms, with a huge pat of butter, delicious. The two men talked of many things at breakfast and got to know and like each other.

Simms's wife and two children had died six years ago in a yellow fever epidemic. This explained his sad eyes and why he looked so much older than his schoolmate William Crawford. Running his thin fingers through his long white hair, Simms would talk animatedly about the British occupation of Charleston.

"When the Revolutionary war was won the British stole the bells from St. Michael's Church. A Charleston gentleman found 'em in London, bought 'em and shipped 'em home. Great crowd met the ship and cheered and sang as they were hung in the tall steeple. When the bells rang out again some people cried, others prayed. Charleston was Charleston again."

Ames understood, for it was impossible to imagine the city

without the bells of St. Michael's. Striking the hours and chiming on the quarter hour, the mellow tones regulated and almost seemed to control life in Charleston. It was beautiful in the first flush of spring. The warm moist air, heavy with crepe myrtle and magnolias, the blue mist over the marshes, the occasional trilling of a mocking bird or wood thrush. Great water oaks, gray-bearded with Spanish moss, gave a deep cool shade from the midday sun, which baked the white sandy back yards. He would miss it.

His most vexing problem was Wash, who now lived in Mr. Simms's quarters. The former slave did not seem to understand that he was free. He kept trying to serve Ames but was frustrated at every turn. He was not allowed in the house for he was a field hand. Simms's trained servants scornfully ignored him. He moped around the back yard and whittled with a pocket knife, his only possession. He was perplexed and unhappy and so was Ames.

He had never had a servant, did not want one, and now that he found himself with one, did not know what to do with him. He regretted his impulsive act at the auction. He wished he could give Wash to someone who understood him—needed him.

Simms laughed at his suggestion. "He's a free nigger. You just can't give him away." Sympathizing, he explained. "There's no work for free niggers in Charleston. A few have trades—painters, carpenters, harness-makers and the like—but I know a dozen or more on the verge of starvation. Wash is grateful and he'll be loyal and helpful. Get to know him, find out what he likes to do . . . talk with him."

"I have trouble understanding him, Mr. Simms."

Simms chuckled. "He doesn't find you easy, young man."

One morning Ames encountered Wash under the huge palmetto tree that shaded the icehouse. He decided to be blunt and reach an understanding.

"Wash, do you want to work for me?"

"Yas, massa."

"Damnit, don't call me 'master.' You are a freeman."

"Yes, Mr. Ames," he replied with the glint of a smile.

"Wash, what's your full name?"

"George Washington Lewis."

"That's a very fine name."

"Yas, sah. My mammy, when she christened me, said George Washington free this country from mean folks over the ocean."

"He was a great man and you can be proud of your name."

"Yas, sah."

"Wash," slowly explained Ames, "if you work for me it won't be easy and you might get hurt."

"How come? I seen snow once and it ain't kilt no one. I kinda liked it."

"Snow?" asked Ames. "What nonsense is this?"

"Folks say you come from up North where they have snow and ice most of the year. If we go there I ain't afraid of snow but I don't like ice."

Suppressing his laughter, he said, "We aren't going to Connecticut but to . . ." He paused and instinctively knew he could trust Wash. It was a decision he never regretted. "Wash, I know you can keep a secret."

"I'se close-mouthed, sah. Won't talk."

"Good." He then briefly explained the Florida expedition and why it was dangerous. "Still want to come along?"

"Yas, sah. Spaniards cruel mens."

"All right. I don't want any body servant. I can dress myself. You can help me with the cooking, cleaning guns and scrounging for food. There'll be plenty to do."

"Yas, sah. I do what you say but I want to fight, too. I'se a good shot. Used to hunt with Colonel Stovall and he taught me. I'se mean man with knife and pistol if I get het up."

That could certainly be true, thought Ames as he looked at the huge man. "That's fine then. We'll need all the fighting men we can get."

"Yas, sah."

"So it's a bargain?"

"Yas, Mr. Ames."

"Shall we seal it with a handshake, like we always do up home?" He offered his hand.

Wash's black face was immobile but his eyes registered

surprise, bewilderment and even fear. He shook his head and rubbed his right hand on his pant's leg.

Waiting, Ames finally snapped, "I thought we'd reached an agreement. What's wrong?"

"Nothin', sah." He hesitantly moved his hand forward, gripped Ames's and wrung it firmly. He moved his lips nervously, whirled and walked quickly away. Suddenly Ames knew this was the first time Wash had been treated as an equal by a white man. He was glad he had observed the old New England custom.

Ames first met Charles Laurent in one of the small coffee-houses near the waterfront. It was crowded with French exiles who bragged of their glory days with the Emperor and stretched one cup of coffee into a morning's conversation. They were pathetic in their faded splendor and their poverty. They talked of the pomp of war, the excitement of combat and the thrill of riding through the streets of captured cities.

Laurent said little and eyed his friends with a cynical, detached amusement. The young American was intrigued. The French officer had very black hair, a nose of notable shape, a narrow chin and broad forehead. Burly black eyebrows arched over black eyes as if in perpetual surprise.

After securing a secrecy pledge, Ames outlined MacGregor's plans and asked if he would like to enlist.

He gave a little barking laugh. "First olives and grapes, then rescuing the Emperor and now fighting the Spanish under a British officer. This New World of yours is a strange place."

Puzzled, Ames asked him to explain.

"When the King decreed exile for all of Napoleon's officers I joined an expedition to America. We landed in Philadelphia and got land grants in the Alabama Territory. Our leaders planned a settlement on the Tombigbee River. . . ." He paused and smiled. "Odd name that, eh? Anyhow they decided to plant grapes, olives and mulberry trees for silk. This wasn't for me, so I went to Washington City hoping to get in the American Army." He shrugged and continued:

"A friend suggested I come to Charleston and see Captain

Dominick Yon, who was one of Lafitte's officers at the battle of New Orleans. I did and Captain Yon said my services would be of great value.

"Nicholos Girod, the mayor of New Orleans, and the Lafitte brothers were great admirers of Napoleon. They got the support of a few Frenchmen in New Orleans and Charleston and are now building a ship called the *Seraphine*. Captain Yon plans to rescue Napoleon from St. Helena."

It's incredible, thought Ames. He gave Laurent a cold look.

"I understand," said the perceptive Frenchman, "but nevertheless it's true. But it won't work."

"You mean Captain Yon is giving up?"

"I didn't say that. The *Seraphine* is almost finished. We can walk down to the docks and see it if you'd like."

"I would," said Ames.

"Captain Yon's problem is Napoleon. He's a fat, sick old man, probably dying. He couldn't return to France. They wouldn't have him. Where would he go, what would he do? Would you give him asylum in America?" He paused and answered himself. "Of course not. I saw a recent letter smuggled out of St. Helena. A staff officer there said bluntly that the Emperor wanted no part of their scheme. Meantime, I'm down to my last sou. This MacGregor got any hard money?"

"Yes, he has."

"Then I'll accept a commission."

"Only the general can swear in officers, but I'll certainly recommend you."

"I'd be most grateful. When will the general arrive in Charleston?"

"I'm not sure. Perhaps in the next two or three weeks." He saw the Frenchman's expression and sneaked two bills into his jacket pocket. "A slight advance. You can repay me when it's convenient."

"I do thank you," said Laurent and shook hands with Ames.

Each morning Simms went to his law office on Broad Street, leaving Ames to his own devices. He quickly got in the habit of spending time in the library. It was an elegant, mahogany-paneled room, with rich cherry-red chairs and tables gleaming with a high polish. Hundreds of books jammed ceiling-high shelves on two walls. Opposite a broad low window was a massive desk with inkstand and freshly sharpened quills. It was a comfortable room and the smell of the leather-bound volumes pleased him. There was Gibbon's *Decline and Fall of the Roman Empire,* David Hume's histories of England and Scotland, Jefferson's *Notes on the State of Virginia, Pilgrim's Progress* and *Paradise Lost* and *Tom Jones, Robinson Crusoe, Vanity Fair* and bound copies of *The Spectator* and *The Tatler.* Ames always started his morning with the Charleston *Courier.* He had never been a regular newspaper reader. In Washington City he had found them dull, malicious, often printing little more than rumors and gossip. The four-page *Courier,* in contrast, was fascinating and gave an excellent picture of the city.

The ship-news column stirred his imagination. Today the *Brig Urania* was sailing for Hamburg; the *Thomas Naylor* for Liverpool; the fine copper-bottomed sloop the *Maquit* for Bordeaux and the clipper, the *Huntress,* docked after 111 days from Hong Kong. He dreamed of these distant ports and someday hoped he would see them.

The St. Cecilia Society was giving a concert tonight at the Carolina Coffeehouse and the theater offered *Hamlet.* He had enjoyed *The Provoked Husband* and *Lock and Key,* despite all the Litchfield sermons he had heard on the grossness and immorality of the theater. Mr. Simms had tickets for *Hamlet* and he was eager to see his first play by Shakespeare.

Edmondston's store advertised the arrival of 150 bags of coffee, thirty boxes of brown sugar, 5,000 Cuban cigars, Antigua rum, shrub and Cherry Bounce and two pipes of fresh orange juice. This puzzled him. He had been told a pipe was 123 gallons. He wondered what Charlestonians would do with so much orange juice.

He chuckled at the medical advertising. There were Dr. Dyott's infallible worm-destroying lozenges, Lee's infallible ague and fever drops and a Grand Restorative and Nervous Cordial and Dr. Robertson's Stomach Elixir of Health.

Richard Pearce offered a choice selection of "fresh shoes." Rebecca Bright's freshly boiled green turtle soup was on sale at State Street. Nathan Batchelor's Ice Selling Establishment promised to build for $10 a little icehouse like a piece of furniture which "may stand in any part of the house." Here gentlemen could keep wine, fruit and butter in perfect condition.

He turned a page and noted under news from South America that General Bolivar had defeated the Royalists and the independence of Caracas was secured.

This would please General MacGregor and perhaps speed up the expedition. He was restless, yet he had never been so content. He liked Charleston and found the countryside a vivid brooding land that enchanted him.

Promptly at two each afternoon he would join Simms for dinner. It was the big meal of the day. Soup, a roast and duck or chicken, fish, fresh vegetables and always rice and hot bread. A fruit pie or ice cream and cake and then thick black coffee. Replete, the two men would go to their rooms for an afternoon nap. Simms would go back to his law practice for a couple of hours and return at seven for mint juleps and a light repast. He often had guests for supper. They accepted Ames once they realized his aloofness was shyness and showered him with invitations to fish, sail, attend the Jockey Club races or cockfights or "just come to see us, anytime."

One evening over coffee Simms said he had accepted an invitation for them to dine with his good friend Joel Poinsett. "You'll find him a most interesting man."

Ames sipped his coffee and waited. He knew from experience that Simms liked to talk about his friends.

"Joel's a Huguenot. His family came to Charleston from France in 1700," rambled his host. "He's a few years younger than me but we often hunt and fish together. That is when he's in Charleston.

"He went to school in Connecticut. I believe it was run by your friend Timothy Dwight. You might ask him.

"Then he went to England, studied at St. Paul's and then

studied medicine at Edinburgh. Got interested in languages. He speaks excellent French, Spanish, Portuguese and a couple of Arabic dialects. He wanted to be a soldier but his pa insisted he come home and study law. Didn't like law or Charleston, mostly I expect on account of an unhappy love affair. His sweetheart up and married his close friend and Joel traveled for the next seven years in Europe and Asia.

"When war seemed likely between us and England he hurried home and tried to join the Army. Instead, President Madison, in 1810, appointed him special agent to the Rio de la Plata and Chile. Got mixed up with the patriots in Buenos Aires and in Chile who were seeking independence from Spain. The dons made it too hot for him. He escaped to the Madeira Islands and got back to Charleston a couple of years ago.

"I might add, he's the town's most eligible bachelor . . . the despair of every Charleston mother. I expect he's still in love with Margy.

"President Monroe recently wanted to send him back to South America but he refused. Didn't especially trust Monroe or John Quincy Adams either. Got himself elected to the South Carolina Legislature. Devotes himself to improving transportation, building roads and dredging rivers. He'll go to Congress as sure as I'm sitting here."

He tinkled a small silver bell and ordered more coffee. "There I go, gabbing again. And I don't even have the excuse of too much wine. Sorry, my boy."

He ignored Simms's apology and peppered him with questions. Did Poinsett know Simon Bolivar? General MacGregor? Had they discussed the Florida venture? What was the status of the patriots in South America?

Laughing, Simms raised both hands. "Save those questions for Joel when you meet him tomorrow."

Sunday was a warm day of brilliant sunshine. St. Michael's chimed two o'clock and Simms suggested they walk to Poinsett's house. As they strolled along Charleston's shady streets Jonathan felt a rising sense of excitement. He was pleased to be invited to one of Poinsett's famous Sunday dinners. His adventurous life stirred Ames's imagination. He hoped for an opportunity to question his host, though Simms had warned there would be at least a dozen guests.

They turned in at a gravel walk to a spacious brick house recessed from the street. The small, carefully tended gardens were a profusion of white roses under a canopy of pink crepe myrtle. Four graceful, white Ionic columns guarded the veranda and supported an overhead balcony. They climbed a double flight of steps to an elevated first floor. A carved mahogany door opened and a white-jacketed Negro said, "Afternoon, gentlemen. Yo' hats, please. Mr. Joel in de drawing room."

Simms said, "Thank you. I know the way." He led Ames down a long, carpeted hall. Must be over fifty feet long and almost half as wide, calculated Ames. He saw a curved stairway to the second floor, an extensive library adjacent to the huge sunlit drawing room, which was pleasantly filled with laughing, talking people. Simms bowed to several ladies and saluted one elderly gentleman.

A trim man with black hair curling over a broad forehead stepped forward and warmly greeted Simms. He was immaculate in dark gray broadcloth and his speech was crisp and incisive.

"Mr. Jonathan Ames, it's an honor to have you in my home, sir. My old friend Edward speaks of you often and how much pleasure your visit has given him."

"Mr. Simms has been most kind, sir, and I'm very pleased to be here today."

His kind blue eyes scrutinized his guest. "You are from Litchfield I believe? A lovely town. I went to the Greenfield Hill Academy in Connecticut when Timothy Dwight was headmaster. Did you know him?"

"Casually, sir. He often came to Litchfield to see Judge Reeve."

"I'm told he's done splendid things for Yale. I must write him." Poinsett smiled. "I never really liked Dwight. It seemed to me we spent half our time learning to sing hymns, many of them written by him."

"I can't imagine you singing hymns," said Simms.

"Oh I can with the best of them. I'm sure you know some of Dwight's hymns."

"All of them!" laughed Ames.

"Some evening our young Connecticut friend and I will give you instruction in hymn singing, Edward—good for your soul and your wind, too. But come, Mr. Ames, I have a room full of people anxious to meet you."

An experienced host, Poinsett guided Ames around the large room and introduced his dinner guests. His affable manner and his complimentary and amusing remarks eased Ames's shyness. He had been in Charleston long enough to recognize names like Middleton, Legare, Pringle, Cummings, Gordon and Pettigru. This was the town's inner circle, which dominated its social and business life. Ames bowed, exchanged amenities and sipped a glass of Flip, which was a mixture of whiskey, eggs and cream. "It's an old English recipe brought to Charleston over a hundred years ago by the lord proprietors of the colony," explained Poinsett.

A rosewood mantel clock struck three and dinner was announced. Ames was hungry, although he detested the bountiful midafternoon dinners.

Joel Poinsett shepherded his guests into a formal dining room, saying, "Please, good friends, find your place cards."

Ames was seated on Poinsett's right between Miss Thalia Cummings and a most impressive dowager—Mrs. Gordon. When introduced to Miss Cummings he was startled by her striking looks and unusual given name. He mentioned this to his host, who chuckled. "Her father was a Greek scholar—she has a brother named Aristotle. Thalia, I believe, means blooming, luxuriant. Appropriate, eh?"

Ames agreed. Thalia had lustrous red hair, piled in a high coronet. Twinkling green eyes set in a camellia complexion smiled amusingly at Ames. For a moment he thought he saw the glimmer of a wink. This couldn't be, but he welcomed being next to this fascinating girl.

He glanced down the long, snowy white table, glistening with silver, pale yellow Spode china and Waterford crystal. He fingered a silver goblet and tried to think of an amusing remark for Miss Cummings. Instead, Mrs. Gordon tapped his arm with her white-gloved finger and asked if he had ever been to Newport.

He shook his head and Mrs. Gordon invited him to "come and see us next summer. We have a house there," she explained. "It's cool and refreshing compared to our hot summers. We've been going there for years. Many friends from South Carolina do and there are a few acceptable people from Boston. But Newport isn't what it used to be. Too many common, vulgar people from New York. I've warned Mr. Gordon I would not tolerate such tacky people. If it continues I shall insist we sell our house and go to the White Sulphur Springs in Virginia. It's quite a fashionable spa and I'm sure we would find only ladies and gentlemen there."

Her wordy torrent almost put Ames in a hypnotic trance. In desperation he turned to Thalia, who was aware of his plight, but she just smiled and renewed her conversation with Mr. Poinsett.

The first course was she-crab soup, a local delicacy that Ames liked very much. He watched Mrs. Gordon remove her white gloves and select a spoon.

"Don't you think I have beautiful hands?" Before he could reply she went on, "People tell me I have the most beautiful hands they've ever seen." Between spoons of soup, she confided, "You know, Mr. Ames, all my family adore me."

This time he made no attempt to answer, and confined his attention to the soup and listened. Everyone she knew seemed to be rich, socially prominent, lovely and awash in blue blood. Ames squirmed and managed to catch Poinsett's eye and his host came to his rescue.

Mr. Poinsett, turning to Ames, said, "I believe you were in Washington City when President Monroe was inaugurated. Would you tell us about it?"

Ames described the huge crowds, the impressive swearing-in of Monroe and Tompkins and brought a laugh to the table when he told how the House refused to let the senators bring their new chairs into their chamber.

"Was Tompkins drunk?" asked Legare.

Startled, Ames said, "I don't think so. He sat his horse well."

"There's a story going round that the Vice President has a drinking problem," said Simms.

"I hadn't heard it, sir."

"He was an aggressive governor of New York during the war," said Simms. "I got to know old Dan fairly well when we consulted a few times on harbor defense. Congress, stingy as usual, didn't give him enough money to pay his troops. He borrowed on his own signature and by 1815 his accounts were in a mess. The New York delegation insisted he be given the vice presidency. They believed it would straighten him out."

"Let's hope it does," observed Poinsett. "The parsimony of Congress has ruined many a loyal American. They still owe me expense money for my years in South America."

"And you'll never get it." Legare grinned.

"Probably not," admitted Poinsett.

The conversation became general. It mostly concerned life and people in Charleston. Ames was baffled when Mrs. Middleton spoke of her doubly removed half-second cousins. Mrs. Legare thought the "empire gown" in poor taste for the St. Cecilia Ball but said that she was pleased with the new books in the Charleston Library Society. She recommended Lord Byron's poems but feared Miss Austin's novel *Emma* was not as good as *Pride and Prejudice*.

Poinsett complimented the ladies for their support of the Library Society and said, "Someday there'll be colleges like Harvard and William and Mary, but just for women." He was sternly rebuked by Mrs. Cummings, who said that a lady's chief concern should be "good manners and breeding." "Every lady," she advised, "should write a fine hand, enjoy reading, be able to play a piano or guitar, to manage her servants and household and, of course, dance gracefully."

The diplomatic Poinsett changed the subject and asked Mrs. Cummings if she approved of the new dance, the waltz.

"I most certainly do not, Mr. Poinsett."

(69)

"Not even if the four-inch rule is rigidly observed?"

"No lady," she sternly said, "would permit any gentleman other than her husband to hold her in his arms."

Poinsett smiled and tinkled a small silver bell. The efficient servants removed the soup plates and served a succession of hot dishes, two of which aroused Ames's curiosity. The first was served in a silver casserole and had a flaky crust.

"That's a cooter pie," said his host. "It's really nothing but a terrapin stew laced with cream and sherry. It's quite good. Try it."

It certainly was, decided Ames, and asked about an apple-sized red vegetable that was baked with a topping of fresh herbs.

"That, Mr. Ames, is a tomato, or love apple as it is commonly called. They have been eaten in Spain and South America for years. Stewed down with onions, spices and wine, they make a superb sauce for any hot or cold meat. Good, too, in salads." He took a bite. "See, it isn't poisonous."

Cutting a small portion, Ames tasted. It was delicious. Its tart flavor was a perfect foil for the roast duck and mutton.

Thalia Cummings chided him for refusing rice. "You will never be a true Charlestonian unless you enjoy rice at least twice a day. We are like the Chinese, you know. We worship our ancestors and dote on rice."

"I like rice. I just can't get accustomed to these enormous midafternoon dinners."

"They are a bit barbaric, but we love tradition. I'm sure dinners like this will be served in Charleston a hundred years from now. To enjoy our town you must accept it. You can't change it, Mr. Ames."

"Do you accept it, Miss Cummings?"

"Most of it, though at times it gets a bit tedious." She grinned mischievously. "Do you like to dance?"

Surprised, he answered, "Why yes, though I'm not very good."

She raised her eyebrows. "I thought you Yankee Puritans disapproved of dancing, card playing and the theater."

"Most of them do."

"But not you?"

"No, Miss Cummings. When I was in Washington City, Mr. Crawford—"

She interrupted. "Who is Mr. Crawford?"

"He is the Secretary of War—or was. He's a big, jovial Georgian who enjoys living. He took me to my first play and insisted I take dancing lessons. Incidentally, he's a great friend of Mr. Simms's."

"So Mr. Simms's good friend corrupted you?"

"Hardly that."

"Did you learn to waltz?"

"Why no. I learned the minuet and the gavotte."

"The gavotte is so uncouth. All you do is bounce around. I'd rather ride horseback if I want exercise. But the waltz is so graceful. Why it's sheer heaven."

His looked stirred her to unrestrained laughter. "Don't look so shocked, Mr. Ames. There's a lot of the Puritan left, isn't there?"

He wondered if this girl was just teasing or would she disobey her mother. "Perhaps," he admitted, "but how did you learn to waltz?"

"From Monsieur Laval, my dancing teacher. He says it's the rage in Paris and it will be in Charleston, too, despite all those silly old ladies. It's really divine and the lilting music makes me feel as if I were floating on a cloud. Would you like to learn, Mr. Ames?"

"You mean take lessons from Monsieur Laval? Well, I hardly have time . . ."

"No, Mr. Ames, from me."

His mouth popped open.

"Come Wednesday at four and you'll get your first lesson."

Before he could answer she resumed her conversation with Poinsett and ignored him the rest of the meal. It soon ended with rum ice cream, coffee and glass finger bowls, which Ames knew were fashionable since Mr. Jefferson brought them back from Paris.

As the guests said good-bye, Poinsett whispered, "If you can forego an afternoon nap perhaps we can have a talk."

Ames said nothing would please him more. Poinsett suggested he go in the library and wait.

Ames relaxed in a leather chair, closed his eyes and thought of Thalia Cummings. She had favored him on leaving with an innocent smile and a deep curtsy. Her exquisite insolence enchanted him. He wondered if he should accept her invitation. He decided he had better consult Mr. Simms.

The creak of a door interrupted his musing. Mr. Poinsett entered, smiled and said, "Napping already, Mr. Ames?"

"Oh no, sir. Just thinking of that wonderful repast." He jumped to his feet. Poinsett waved him back and sat on a brocaded sofa. He offered Ames a cigar and the two men lit their Havanas and puffed in silent contentment.

Blowing smoke toward the ceiling, Poinsett said, "Mr. Simms has told me of your mission. Incidentally, your visit has meant a great deal to Edward. He's been a lonely man since the death of his family. He thinks very highly of you."

"I'm glad, sir: Mr. Simms has been kindness personified. I can never repay him."

"You already have. Now, young man, how can I be of help?"

"First of all, sir, do you approve of the idea of liberating Florida?"

"I do indeed. It is a natural part of America. And, too, as you know, I have no love for the Spanish. First tell me about General MacGregor and his plan. Such ventures depend very much on leadership."

Briefly but succinctly Ames outlined MacGregor's five-point campaign and asked, "Did you ever meet him?"

"No, but as a member of Bolivar's staff he's undoubtedly capable. Bolivar expected the impossible from his generals and somehow he got it. I have great respect for Simon Bolivar."

"You know General Bolivar then?"

"Not really," answered Poinsett, "though I met him in Paris years ago." He stopped Ames's question with a wave of his cigar. "When I was sent to Buenos Aires I gave some slight assistance to José de San Martín. The dons offered a reward for my head and I fled to Chile. There I got involved with the independence movement of José Carerre and Bernardo

O'Higgins. These three generals, like your General MacGregor, served in the Spanish Army. Disgusted with the corruption of Spain, they returned home and plotted to free their countries and set up a United States of South America.

"They exchanged information with Bolivar and I read much of the correspondence. I found him the most sensible and practical of the revolutionaries." He puffed his cigar, frowned and spoke slowly. "They are strange men. Idealistic yes, but arrogant, conceited and with a monumental belief in themselves. I spent much of my time in Chile trying to get them to agree on political and military matters. Does Mac-Gregor fit the pattern?"

"In many ways," Ames reluctantly admitted.

Sensing Ames's chagrin, he said, "Don't be too upset, young man. At least he's raised some money. Did you know that José Carerre was in America last year trying to get funds for Chile. He went home empty-handed."

"No, I didn't," said Ames.

"MacGregor's campaign seems well thought out—formulated, I'm sure, under the direction of General Bolivar. When will he arrive in Charleston?"

"I expect him in the next two weeks." MacGregor was already two weeks behind schedule, but Ames decided not to mention his concern.

"Then we'll have him for supper. I'll invite Edward and we can get acquainted."

"That will be fine."

"One more question. What does MacGregor plan to do with all the escaped slaves in Florida?"

"He said he would offer them citizenship."

Poinsett almost dropped his cigar. "That won't win him any friends in the South."

"But, sir, Mr. Simms told me you disapproved of slavery?"

"That's true, but one must be practical. In time I believe slavery will die a natural death. It almost did a couple of decades ago. We realized that slavery was the most expensive form of labor. Abolitionist societies spread even more in the

South than in the North. Then Eli Whitney invented the cotton gin."

He paused, puffed his cigar and sang:

> "Who made the South rich?
> 'I did,' said Eli Whitney,
> 'With my little cotton gin.
> I made the South rich.'"

"I'm not sure that I understand," said Ames.

"It's simple arithmetic. Before the gin it took a slave all day to get the seed out of five pounds of cotton. A big cotton grower in those days produced two or three thousand pounds of cotton a year. Nobody ever expected cotton to be an important money crop.

"But it has. In 1796, the year the gin was invented, we grew two million pounds of cotton. Five years later it was forty million, and last year we produced over one hundred million pounds of cotton.

"Cotton growing is simple. It keeps the slaves busy most of the year and uses women and children. It's true that it's made us rich. Yet Charleston under its gaiety and good manners lives in constant fear. A feudal society that rules by the whip just can't last."

Poinsett was agitated. He rose to his feet and slowly paced the large room. "I understand that Mr. Jefferson would free his slaves if he could afford it. So would I. I'd manumit mine tomorrow if I knew how. But that's no solution. They'd only end in more terrible bondage. I say slavery must be terminated legally but the whole country should bear the burden. After all, a slave is worth about a thousand dollars and represents a lifetime investment for many planters. Free 'em and the South would be bankrupt—but we must find a way."

"Then why, sir, is it wrong for MacGregor to offer them citizenship in a new state?"

"I don't say it's wrong, it just isn't sensible now. Have you any idea how many Southerners feel about slavery?"

"No, sir."

Poinsett jumped to his feet and picked up a newspaper

from his desk. It was an Augusta, Georgia, *Chronicle*. "Read this," he said.

"Once and for all," the letter in the newspaper said, "we hold slavery to be a wisely devised institution of heaven, for the benefit, improvement and safety, both morally and physically of a barbarous and inferior race who would otherwise perish by filth, the sword, disease, waste and destinies forever gnawing, consuming and finally destroying.

"We hold the African under moral and just titles founded upon his characteristics, nature, his necessities and our own and our accountability is to the God of both races. We alone are in no way troubled in our relation to our rights to hold the negro in bondage." It was signed by a Henry A. Lawrence.

Silently folding the newspaper, Ames said, "He can't be serious."

"Oh yes, he is. This man believes it's God's will. It frees the white man from drudgery so he can pursue higher things. How do you think he—and there are thousands like him in South Carolina and Georgia—would react to MacGregor's scheme?"

"I'm beginning to understand," said Ames.

"Then make MacGregor understand. He's got enough problems without stirring up the hornet's nest of slavery. Give the problem to his Florida provisional government and get on with his trade—fighting."

"I'm sure he would listen to you."

"We'll talk when I meet the general—but enough of this serious, sober prattle. . . . How do you like Charleston?"

"Very much. It's so different from Litchfield—gay, pleasant and everyone is so courteous and friendly."

"That's because you are Mr. Simms's guest. Charleston can be cruel to a stranger. And one word of advice. Don't take Miss Thalia Cummings seriously."

"But, sir, I just met her!"

"And you are captivated?"

Ames grinned shyly. "I found her interesting."

"That's her trade. She is the most accomplished flirt in South Carolina. She collects men like a bounty hunter does scalps. Keep your hair and your sanity, young man, and don't get dazzled by her." He watched Ames for a moment. "So it's too late for that, eh? Well, remember this. She's a superb actress and you are her audience. Every word, every gesture, every smile, every glance is carefully planned. And never, and I repeat never, believe a word she says."

Jonathan thanked Poinsett for his hospitality and departed —unable to think of a sensible reply to his advice.

§ CHAPTER 5 §

Refreshed by his afternoon nap, Edward Simms sat in his favorite chair and meditated. Why had Jonathan Ames resigned from the Army and joined MacGregor? It was none of his business, yet he was curious. He had found Ames a quiet, rather shy young man, thoughtful and deliberate in his actions. He was glad Bill Crawford had written him about Ames. His presence in the big, lonely house had been a joy. The young Puritan had mellowed considerably the past few weeks and Simms knew he liked Charleston. Perhaps I should try to persuade him to remain and read law in my office. I'll miss him damnably.

The crunch of footsteps on the gravel walk interrupted his musing. He beckoned Ames to join him. "Did you have an interesting talk with Joel?"

"Yes indeed. He's a most remarkable man." He briefly summarized their conversation.

"I think it's a fine idea to have your general for supper with him. Joel has much experience with such men and I'd value his opinion. I'd hate to see you get misled by some fancy freebooter." He chuckled softly and added, "That was sound advice on Miss Thalia Cummings. You were kinda taken with her, weren't you?"

"Yes, sir, I was. I've never met anyone like her. It's really difficult to believe Mr. Poinsett."

"Difficult or not, it's true. She's a dazzler all right, and brimful 'er mischief. Probably a throwback to her old grandpa, who made his money selling rum and muskets to the Indians. He bought land on the Edisto, got rich on cotton and married his daughter to Thomas Cummings. Tom comes from an old family, had lots of education, went to Cambridge for two years but has no sense. He just sits at home, reads, writes a little and his wife runs things. She's trying to get ahead in Charleston society and claims she can trace her ancestors back to Charlemagne." He snorted in disgust. "Wouldn't be surprised if she had a little Cherokee blood. It would account for some of Thalia's wildness."

Ames laughed, repeated her remarks about the waltz and the lesson.

"And you accepted?"

"Well, no, sir. I wanted to talk with you first."

"Why me?"

"Mr. Simms, I'm confused. You heard Mrs. Cummings' denunciation of the waltz, yet her daughter offers me instructions. What would you do?"

Simms said promptly, "I'd decline." He smiled at Ames's expressions. "But then, I'm an old man. If I were a young fellow like you, I'd accept. But you better watch your step."

"Mr. Simms, if this will embarrass you in any way . . . ?"

"It's not me, it's you I'm concerned about. That brother of hers, Aristotle, is damned hotheaded. If he caught his sister in your arms he'd call you out. And he's a crack shot."

"You mean he'd shoot me for dancing with his sister?"

"Oh, he wouldn't just gun you in cold blood. He'd challenge you to a duel."

"But I thought duels were fought only when someone was insulted."

"Be sensible, Jonathan. The end result of this new-fangled dance, the waltz, is to get a girl in your arms, ain't it?"

"So I'm told."

"Then Aristotle would claim that you had sullied Thalia's reputation—you had soiled her beyond redemption."

Exasperated, Ames said, "What nonsense!"

"Maybe to you, but these young men have chivalrous notions. They have a great respect for ladies—almost a reverence. Her purity of mind, soul and body is her most precious possession. Any form of coarseness will soil it. Aristotle called out a young man from Savannah last spring. He had misjudged his capacity for juleps and cussed at the Jockey Club. The young lady escorted by Aristotle heard him."

"Wouldn't an apology have been sufficient?"

"No. It seems the only way to remove the stain is by the blood of the offender. If Aristotle killed a man for cussing, imagine what he'd do if he found Thalia in your arms. When is this lesson?"

"Wednesday at four."

"Then you got time to do a little serious thinking. Would you like to go to a cockfight on Monday?"

Last week the *Courier* had appealed to all "gentlemen who are lovers of this Royal Diversion" to bring their cocks to be matched against the Gentleman from Port Royal. Though Ames considered it a barbarous pastime, he accepted.

At sundown Monday, Ames walked to the lawyer's office on Broad Street. His host, at their midday meal, told him the fights would be held on a bluff overlooking the Ashley River because of the "mighty fine weather. My other guests will be your French friend, Laurent, for he has never seen a main either, and Captain Stratford. I've wanted you to meet Captain Billy. He's the man who'll bring me your letters for Mr. Crawford. My carriage will pick us up here."

Strolling along the wide, shady street, Ames sensed Charleston's excitement. People discussed the gamecocks, analyzed their strengths and weaknesses and placed bets. He knew Simms owned a breed of glossy brown gamecock that had the reputation of being the best fighters in South Carolina. He entered them only in important mains and devoted much time to preparing the birds. The past few days he'd fed Rusty Red, entered in today's principal main, a special mixture of corn meal, gunpowder and rum. Its proportions were secret, as he believed this gave his cock courage and endurance.

Ames entered the law office, greeted Charles Laurent and

shook hands with Captain William Stratford of the schooner *John W. Callahan, Jr.* A small wiry Irishman with fading red hair and hundreds of freckles, Stratford spoke with such a slow Georgia drawl that Ames at first had trouble in understanding. "Colonel Ames, sah, I'se mighty proud to make yer acquaintance, and honored, sah, to be of any service to my lifelong dear friend Mr. Simms." He bowed from the waist and Ames scowled at being called "Colonel."

"He's absolutely trustworthy, Jonathan," said Simms, "but explanations were necessary. I couldn't in good faith ask Captain Billy to sail his fine ship into Fernandina without mentioning the risk."

"Don't you worry none, Colonel. The *John W. Callahan, Jr.* is a trim ship, mounted with eight guns. Them Spaniards shore a mangy lot and don't scare me. Anyhow, I'm all fer gittin' 'em out 'er Florida."

Ames smiled his approval and asked, "Have you been in Fernandina recently?"

"Now, sah. I'se just returned from St. Augustine. Lots of trade there and mostly in American bottoms. I stays away from Fernandina, don't mess around with stolen goods brought there by them privateers. Ain't nothing but a bunch 'er damned pirates."

"What about Fort San Carlos?" asked Simms. "We understand it's in shambles."

"I expect you are right. Rode out a blow in the harbor 'bout six months ago. Them old tabby walls of the fort was a-crumbling and them guns guarding Amelia River was mighty rusty. Bet they'd blow up with a proper charge."

"That's good news," said Ames. "Captain Stratford, just what is tabby?"

"It's just sand, lime, oyster shell and water all stirred together. You just pour it into forms, let it git hard and it's mighty tough. Ain't you ever been to a tabby festival? More fun even than a cockfight."

The three men shook their heads.

"Next time they have one on St. Simon's Island I'll take you. It's like this," he explained. "You gotta have lime fer tabby.

Best way to git it is burning the Indian shell mounds—'kitchen middens,' they's called, though they's nothing but the trash piles of them shell-eatin' Indians.

"Anyhow, you pile layers of wood and oyster shells into kilns one on top of the other and set her afire. Folks gather, eat, drink, sing with the musicians, dance and keep them fires burning hot. Next day the powdered shell is lime."

"Well, I'm damned," said Simms. "Seen hundreds of tabby houses but never knew how they made 'em."

"And St. Augustine, is it in bad shape also?" asked Ames hopefully.

"No. Governor Coppinger runs a tight ship and the fort—it's called Castillo de San Marcos—ain't gonna be easy. It's undermanned, though, and a sudden attack from the land side might succeed."

"I understand," said Ames, "there are a few large plantations in Florida, mostly owned by Americans and perhaps a few British. How would they react to liberation?"

"They'd welcome anybody who'd restore law. Dons can't with a few soldiers on east and west coasts. I know some of 'em planters and like me they's interested in making money. They gotta arm their workers, their homes is barricaded at night, they is always on the watch fer Injuns and thieving whites. This costs 'em money—plenty money. They'll support yer general if his rule will increase profits."

A rap on the door and Simms said, "There's the carriage. Gentlemen, let's be away to the mains."

The fights had begun when they arrived. Someone said two pairs of stags, green birds, never before pitted, had been matched and fought. The four mains between Charleston and Port Royal were under way. A cheerful crowd, betting heavily, yelled excitedly as these matches ended in a tie.

First night sank over the Ashley River as time came for the principal main between Rusty Red and a rangy white Dominique owned by Dr. Armitage.

There was a slight delay as the pine-board pit was freshly sanded. Tall staffs of pitch pine were lit, throwing a flickering light over the crowded arena. Gentlemen in ruffled shirts and broadcloth mingled with homespun-clad farmers and fishermen. Tiny feathers drifted, settling on men's coats and in their hair, their faces cruel as they watched the death struggle of the proud cocks. Despite a gentle breeze from the river, the air was heavy with perspiration and tobacco smoke.

A stout gentleman in a blue gingham coat shouted, "This here is a fight to the finish between the birds of Dr. Armitage and Mr. Simms. Stand back, gents, stand back. These here birds can't fight if you don't give 'em room."

"Excuse me," said Simms to his guests, "but I always fight my own birds." He went to his corner of the twelve-foot-wide pit, stripped to his ruffled shirt and received Rusty Red from a Negro trainer.

The judges weighed in each bird at slightly over four pounds. Their spurs were carefully examined, as no steel gaffs were allowed. Constant honing with broken glass made them razor sharp. The cocks seemed evenly matched, judging from the betting.

The blue gingham coat shouted, "Gentlemen, bill your cocks." The two birds were held at arm's length but close enough for them to peck each other.

"On the line," ordered the referee. "One, two"—a long pause —"and a big three."

The birds were released and sprang at each other. They leaped high, wings thrashing, attempting to drive their spurs forward. Feathers flew, the cocks pecked and slashed but did little damage. The spectators shouted encouragement to their favorite and continued to bet as the odds shifted after each flurry. Simms had accepted all bets against Rusty Red and had over $1,500 on the fight.

Another flurry and the cocks circled and glared. The white rooster charged and jumped high, hoping to land on his opponent's back. Rusty Red ducked and attacked from the rear. He pounced on the Dominique, pecking and slashing. He worked his legs and drove a spur into the white's neck. Blood stained his feathers and he toppled sideways. The main was over. The cock crowed lustily and strutted to Simms, who washed and sponged his cuts with rum and water.

He was elated. He had won nearly $2,000 and again proven the potency of his secret elixir.

A faint lemon-colored sunlight bathed Charleston. There was a cutting edge to the wind off the harbor. In a fever of anticipation Jonathan Ames had arrived early at the Cummings house. Chilled, he walked briskly along King Street, circled the Battery and returned. The chimes of St. Michael's pealed the hour as he timidly lifted the heavy silver knocker. He rapped gently once, twice and then once again. There was no answer. He knocked again but no reply. She's changed her mind, he thought, and turned to go.

Suddenly the door swung open. Mrs. Cummings came out on the portico and glared balefully. She did not speak.

Hesitantly he said, "Good afternoon, Mrs. Cummings. Is Miss Thalia at home?"

"Not to you, sir." She literally spat the words.

He mumbled, "She suggested that I call."

"That, sir, was before she knew about you."

"I don't quite understand."

"My daughter does not receive servants." She started to close the door.

Angrily Ames said, "I think you had better explain. After all, I called at your daughter's suggestion."

"That, sir," she replied, "was before she discovered you had been a bound servant."

Ames flushed. "That was a long time ago. I've been a freeman for years."

"But not a gentleman. You, sir, are not welcome in this house. Mr. Simms and Mr. Poinsett should be ashamed to introduce you in polite society. I shall severely reprimand them." She re-entered her house, slamming the door.

Perplexed, he walked to Simms's office on Broad Street. The old lawyer bade him welcome. "You in trouble, Jonathan? You didn't have a run-in with Aristotle?"

"No, sir." He then repeated his conversation with Mrs. Cummings. Simms walked over and gave the disconsolate young man a kindly pat. Slowly he said, "I guess I'm to blame."

"You, Mr. Simms?"

"Yes. At the club last night I bragged about you. Praised you highly for overcoming the handicap of being bound out. I said some of our lazy young men might well profit by your example. I'm sorry, Jonathan. Damned sorry." His voice cracked and he managed a melancholy smile.

"It's all right, Mr. Simms," comforted Ames. "I'm not ashamed of being bound out."

"That stupid snob, Martha Cummings," ranted Simms. "Come, let's go home and dulcify ourselves with a mint julep."

The two men walked down Broad Street in intimate silence, each deeply engrossed in his own thoughts.

That evening after Simms had selected his cigar and was puffing happily he said, "I believe this will interest you." He chuckled and continued, "The house servants' grapevine is sure, swift and mostly accurate. Some say the doomsday rabbit brings them news." The lawyer rambled on, "Others claim it's the wind from the briar patch or the conjure bag. I don't suppose we'll ever understand the secret places in the back of their minds." He saw Ames's impatient frown. "My apologies, Jonathan. I'm just a garrulous old man. Jeff, the butler, just told me that Mrs. Cummings bundled Thalia off to Beaufort on the morning stage. When old Martha babbled you'd been a 'bound boy' and forbade Thalia to see you, she balked. She said this only increased her respect for you. Her ma exploded and sent Thalia to visit her Beaufort cousins."

Shrugging his shoulders, Ames said, "I'm glad she feels that way. Perhaps it's just as well. I'm too clumsy to waltz properly."

A servant entered and gave Mr. Simms a letter. "It's for you, Jonathan."

Ames scanned the note and sighed with relief. "It's from Mr. Blair. General MacGregor's ship has been sighted. He'll land tomorrow afternoon."

Jonathan slept little that night. Had General MacGregor changed his plans? It was now the middle of May and the general had promised to be in Charleston a month ago. Why the delay? Was it lack of money? Had the President intervened?

(84)

Had Spain ceded Florida to the United States? He had had one cordial letter from Mr. Crawford, but it did not mention Florida. Had something gone wrong?

Though concerned, he admitted the delay was pleasurable. He had found Charleston a city of contradictions. It glittered like a morning star full of charm, gaiety and splendor. Though his Puritan conscience winced, he enjoyed the theater, the Jockey Club races, the balls, the many clubs and the elegant leisurely life. He disapproved of the way planter aristocracy displayed and spent their wealth from rice, indigo and cotton plantations. He agreed with Joel Poinsett, who said a civilization built on slavery could not last.

Yet, he hated to see it go. The city had a grace and refinement of which he approved. He realized the ladies set its tone and regulated its behavior. The nod of a flowered bonnet, the wave of a dainty white glove could ostracize the sinner. Beneath their autocratic rule was a butterfly charm that fascinated Ames. He enjoyed their exaggerated compliments, their gay teasing, but he was never at ease. They were so different from the few Connecticut ladies he had known. And none more so than Thalia Cummings. She was a complete enigma —so lovely yet so unpredictable. He was bewitched by her dazzling beauty yet confused by her willful manner. He groaned as he recalled his conversation with her mother. Did Thalia have objections to his once having been bound out, or was she just annoyed with her mother for spoiling her afternoon date? He did not know, but he would like to find out.

Toward morning he sank into a troubled sleep. He dreamed he was at the St. Cecilia Ball waltzing with Thalia. She was so irresistible that he forgot the four-inch separation rule and pulled her closer. She snuggled into his arms and smiled provocatively. He was about to kiss her when a voice roared, "You damned Yankee rascal." It was her brother, Aristotle, pistol ready. He fired and Ames awoke, his body drenched in sweat.

It was almost sunset when General MacGregor, his wife and staff disembarked. He was superbly uniformed in cherry-colored trousers, half boots and a royal blue jacket edged

(85)

with gold, and a short coat, worn like a cape, glittered with braid and gold lace. His brown hair curled over his ears, his blue eyes flashed and wide shoulders tapering to a narrow waist made it easy to understand why his wife thought of him as "MacGregor the Beautiful." Señora Josefa MacGregor wore a long-tailed blue skirt and a form-fitting pink coatee with brass buttons. Her blue-black hair flowed freely in the light shore breeze. They were a handsome couple.

As Ames and Blair walked down the dock to greet the general the little Scotsman muttered, "Look like a couple 'er parakeets to me." Ames smothered a grin as he introduced Blair. The general said he was delighted to see Mr. Blair and his young American friend, Colonel Ames. He presented his staff: Colonel Jared Irwin, "a former congressman and a brave fighter in the Revolutionary War," and colonels John Carrol and Thomas Johnson of Baltimore. The three colonels bowed and shook hands with Blair and Ames, who was glad that Mr. Crawford had insisted on a colonel's commission.

Irwin was a wiry, taciturn man of fifty, with thin lips and a foxlike expression. He represented the financial group supporting the expedition. The impeccably dressed young men from Baltimore had no military experience but were friends of MacGregor's backers. They were cheerful, pleasant and excited.

Mr. Simms had sent his carriage with his matching blacks to the pier. The general admired them extravagantly as they rode to the Planters' Hotel.

The next fortnight General MacGregor proved a competent administrator. He knew what supplies he needed, bargained astutely and kept his staff on the run. He told Blair to purchase victuals for four hundred men. He growled, "Beastly pothouse politicians kept the British Army half starved. Want my army well fed. Daily ration will be one pound of beef, three quarters a pound of pork, eighteen ounces of bread, bacon, corn bread, plenty of beans, peas, coffee and one gill of rum. Need extra supply of whiskey or rum to dole out just before going into battle."

"Man alive," exclaimed Blair, "you'll have 'em too fat to fight."

"Mr. Blair," admonished the general, "my orders are to be obeyed, not questioned." The Scotsman smiled wryly and did not answer. "And have you found me a ship?"

"Yes, General, and a rare bargain too. She's a sloop, deep-beamed and fast and will accommodate couple 'er hundred men." Blair, who loved ships, spoke with great enthusiasm. "She's a hundred feet over-all, has a flying jib boom and a ninety-foot mast. She's rigged for afore and aft mainsail, a big square top sail and a small top gallant.

"Eight four-pound cannon are mounted on the gun deck, four more on the quarter deck and a swivel gun in her prow. The captain's and officers' cabins are ample and your soldiers can sleep in hammocks on the berth and gun decks. She's a lovely lass, General, and a rare bargain at three thousand and one hundred and sixty-five dollars."

"Buy her," ordered MacGregor.

"Don't you want to see her?"

"Mr. Blair, you know ships, I don't. I accept your estimate. If she is unsatisfactory I shall hold you responsible. When can I board her?"

"General, you will be more comfortable here in the hotel."

"Sir, if a soldier seeks comfort he is in the wrong profession. When will she be available, Mr. Blair?"

"I can buy her today. But she needs cleaning and painting. Her sailing master says her hold needs fumigating and scrubbing with vinegar and hot water. Another day or so I reckon."

"Move ahead, Mr. Blair, and paint Bolivar in gold letters on her bow. A fitting name for my flagship."

"Yes, General MacGregor," he said and left.

"Colonel Ames?"

"Yes, sir."

"Have enlistment notices printed and post them in the taverns and along the waterfront. Place a small advertisement in the *Courier*."

"Yes, sir. . . . General, Mr. Willington, the editor of the *Courier* is anxious to see you."

"Gad, no. Can't afford to waste time with ink-stained scribblers. We need four hundred men within the week. Set up a recruiting office on the gun deck of the *Bolivar*."

"At once, General, but . . . sir . . . the *Courier* printed a favorable article about the expedition several weeks ago."

"Did they now? Have you a copy?"

"I'll be glad to get you one."

"Do that, Colonel Ames. Meantime, do you remember what the *Courier* said?"

"Yes, sir. It was most flattering. It described in some detail your career in Spain and South America, your friendship with one of England's royal dukes, your knighthood, and remarked that you were 'not only a gentleman by birth, education and manners, but a man of considerable literary attainments.'" He paused and added, "If I might be so bold, sir, I'm glad to be on your staff."

The general beamed and said, "Thank you, Colonel Ames. On reflection, perhaps we should speak with Mr. Willington. Will you make the arrangements?"

"Certainly, sir."

"God's eyeballs," muttered the general, "but it's hot today." He wiped his brow with a linen handkerchief. "It's almost June and we are still in Charleston. We should be in St. Augustine."

"Might I ask," said Ames, "what delayed things? I was worried when you failed to arrive on schedule."

The general's good humor faded. "Penny-pinching, tight-fisted Yankees. Wouldn't put up the money unless that rascal Jared Irwin had the power to approve all expenses. By gad, sir, I refused. We wasted two weeks in Baltimore arguing. They finally accepted my terms but reduced their contributions and sent Irwin along as a watchdog. A pox on their skinflint souls. Why, Colonel Ames," he shouted indignantly, "that Irwin objected to my hiring a piper. I've never gone into battle without bagpipes playing!"

Jonathan turned aside to hide a smile and said perhaps they could recruit a piper in Charleston.

"Gad, sir, I'd be grateful." He scowled for a moment and

continued, "If only I could have seen President Monroe I'm sure I could have persuaded him to help. He knows and understands the importance of Florida to your country."

Ames changed the subject by asking if the general would like to set a date to dine with Mr. Simms and Mr. Poinsett.

"My apologies to your friends," said MacGregor. "I'm a wretched fellow not to have responded to their gracious invitation. I've been so harassed with monkey-nonsense."

"I've explained, sir."

"Deucedly thoughtful of you, but I'm sure these two gentlemen realize my first duty is to my command. I'd be delighted to meet them, especially Mr. Poinsett. I've heard of his exploits in Chile and I'm sure we have much to discuss."

Nodding, Ames asked if the general had any preference as to time.

"It's Tuesday, so shall we say Friday? By then my affairs will be tidy."

"I'm sure Friday will be suitable. I'll make all the arrangements."

"Thank you, Colonel Ames. You are a splendid young officer and should go far in our profession."

Pleased with the compliment, Ames saluted and went about his duties.

Though the food and wine were superb, the Friday night supper turned into a fiasco. President Monroe had summoned Joel Poinsett to Washington City. He had sailed the previous day and MacGregor was irked. He implied that Poinsett could have postponed his departure as "I was most anxious to meet Mr. Poinsett."

Joel could hardly have been aware of that, commented Simms. "After all we sent you a supper invitation the day you arrived and did not receive the courtesy of a reply for over two weeks."

Bristling, MacGregor said a soldier's first obligation is to his army. "But God's garter, sir, speaking of courtesy, I do not understand why none of the Charleston ladies have called on Señora MacGregor."

Simms blandly replied that Joel had hoped to have the general and his wife to one of his Sunday dinners and to introduce them to Charleston society. "It was regrettable the general has been so busy, but unfortunately in Charleston we consider it improper to pay calls unless introduced."

And so the evening went. MacGregor refused to discuss his campaign, fumed about the heat and mosquitoes and complained that the chimes of St. Michael's disturbed his sleep.

"It's too bad," said Simms. "The British regiment that stole the bells during the Revolution didn't melt them down. Instead they were offered for sale in London. They were bought by a Charleston gentleman and returned to their rightful place on St. Michael's steeple.

"And, sir, we'd prefer the sun not rise to silencing the lovely chimes of St. Michael's."

The supper ended on this acerbic note, and the chimes were not mentioned again by the general, Mr. Simms and especially not by Jonathan Ames.

As ordered, Ames had established a recruiting office on the *Bolivar*. General MacGregor insisted on talking with each volunteer. He would swagger on deck, his chest heavy with medals, and deliver a ringing oration on valor and courage. "The Spaniards are evil, vicious men, without honor and never to be trusted. But brave men in Venezuela, though outnumbered, won eternal glory by defeating and routing them. You, too, will earn a place in history by liberating Florida from the tyrannical yoke of Spain and adding another star to the American flag." Standing at attention, he would salute the startled recruits and return to his cabin.

The pay seemed to impress the men more than the general's visions of glory—$10 for swearing on the Bible "eternal obedience and fealty" to the Army of Liberation plus $15 a month was a generous wage and attracted dozens of volunteers.

Several young Charleston gentlemen, their blood stirred by the general's rhetoric, enlisted as cadet officers. The others were a motley crew of waterfront idlers, jobless sailors and soldiers, gamblers, farmers, fishermen and a few French émigrés. Many of the French flatly refused to serve under a former British officer. Others quarreled over rank. Charles Laurent accepted a captaincy. Jonathan was pleased, as he had become friendly with the scowling French officer who looked far older than the forty years he admitted.

Working diligently, George Blair accumulated the supplies requisitioned by MacGregor. In addition he had collected enough rifles, shotguns, pistols, sabers and even tomahawks to arm four hundred men. A merchantman, converted to a privateer in 1812, was bought. She was slow and poorly armed compared to the *Bolivar* but of greater tonnage.

General MacGregor was fretful and anxious to leave Charleston. His imperious manner had not endeared him or his wife to the South Carolinians. To them he was just another adventurer who wore gaudy uniforms and had bad manners. He had not been accepted or entertained. The hot humid weather had slowed recruitment. His Florida Army of Liberation now numbered 127 men. Enlistments had dwindled to one or two a day. Jared Irwin constantly prodded the general. Several times they exchanged fast and angry words. Finally, MacGregor announced that his army would sail on the morning tide for Savannah.

Jonathan Ames wrote a long letter to Crawford in Washington City. After deliberation he decided to confine himself to facts. He described the two ships, the size of the army, its supplies and equipment. He avoided speculation about the future and also comment on General MacGregor.

He delivered the letter to Edward Simms and enjoyed a last meal with his friend. Ames had been happy here and hated to leave. He had never imagined such gracious living, excellent food, fine service—and those wonderful mint juleps. Someday I'd like to live like this, he thought, possibly in Charleston, and almost laughed aloud at the absurdity of the idea.

His host promised to send all letters express to Crawford. He presented Ames with a silver flask of rare cognac and a long sword. "This is a tempered Toledo blade. Get that French fellow Butler to teach you a few tricks. Swords don't misfire like pistols, nor do they have to be reloaded. Finest of all weapons. This brandy is for a most special occasion—disaster."

"What?" exclaimed Ames.

Simms smiled fondly. This naïve young man with his rather priggish outlook had given him many pleasant hours. I'll miss him damnably, he thought. "Yes, Colonel Ames, this brandy is not for a victory celebration, not even for weddings or for christenings. It's for that dark hour when all seems hopeless. It will give you solace and courage. God knows, I hope you return to Charleston with a full flask. But it's there if you need it. Now bless you, Jonathan Ames, and good-bye."

§ CHAPTER 6 §

The *Bolivar* cleared the harbor on the morning tide. Under a full spread of canvas the trim schooner veered south at fourteen knots.

"She's a sweet-sailing ship, just as Mr. Blair claimed," said General MacGregor.

"That she is, sir," replied Ames.

Jim Smith, the sailing master, drawled, "If wind holds we'll be in Savannah by morning."

"Splendid. Colonel Ames, call a staff meeting at five. We need to plan our Savannah recruiting. I must have at least two hundred more men."

"Yes, General." He saluted as MacGregor went to his cabin on the aft deck. Ames walked to the starboard and watched the ever-changing shoreline.

"That's Port Royal Sound," said Smith. "And beyond you can glimpse Beaufort."

Beaufort reminded Ames of Thalia Cummings. She had not returned to Charleston. He was flattered when Mr. Simms told him "her ma won't let her come back till you leave." Had she introduced the waltz in Beaufort? He smiled and wondered if he'd ever see Thalia again. He doubted it and was sad.

The *Bolivar* dropped anchor at the Bull Street wharf. Ames

and Laurent went ashore to post their recruiting notices and call on the editor of the *Savannah Gazette and Columbian Museum.*

Savannah, thought Ames, was a lovely and spacious town. Its wide streets were lined with moss-draped live oaks and its many squares were luxuriant with palmetto, oleander and azaleas. The dry sand crunched under their boots, disturbing scores of buzzards that flapped to the tall pine trees surrounding the city. They paused to admire two highly polished brass cannon in front of a brick building that housed the Chatham Artillery Regiment. George Washington had presented them to the regiment for valiant service during the Revolution.

Unfortunately the editor was out of town. After an excellent meal at Tonti's Tavern, the two officers returned to the *Bolivar.* Then another two weeks of delays and frustration. Only seventy-eight men enlisted, though MacGregor would gladly have accepted anyone, even toothless old men and scraggly boys.

He spent much of his time in his cabin studying maps, charts and designing a uniform for his Army of Liberation. It was to have a bright green jacket faced with scarlet, white shoulder belts and a green-plumed helmet. When a Savannah tailor came aboard with a basted-up uniform, Jared Irwin sneered, "Battles ain't won with fancy feathers. By God, General, if you humbug my friends in Baltimore I'll have your hide. We've already overspent in Charleston and are short of cash."

MacGregor, after angry words with Irwin, agreed to borrow $30,000 in Savannah. John Turner, the spokesman for the syndicate, scoffed at the idea of liberating Florida and setting up another state.

He said bluntly, "Our only interest is making money. We want a percentage of all sales of smuggled goods and the right to buy thirty thousand acres of choice land at a dollar an acre. Also, you must open the slave trade. Big profits there since Lafitte banned it at Barataria."

"God's blood," spluttered MacGregor. "I'll never accept such exhorbitant demands."

"That's your privilege," replied Turner, "but those are our terms. Take it or leave it."

"If you don't pay your men soon, you won't have enough soldiers to liberate a pigsty," warned Irwin.

After three hours of futile argument over selling slaves, General MacGregor reluctantly approved the loan. He still insisted his army was too small and improperly trained. An adamant Jared Irwin and a worried staff persuaded him to sail fifty miles south to Darien, where he could drill and train his army. Such facilities had been denied him in both Charleston and Savannah. He was assured of a warm welcome in Darien, which had been settled in 1736 by a group of Scotch Highlanders.

Jim Smith skillfully tacked the *Bolivar* up the Altamaha River and anchored her alongside the long wooden wharf. A dozen men in kilts and war bonnets shouted greetings and two bagpipers squealed a welcome. A huge man waved a two-edged sword, which MacGregor said was a claymore.

Excited, General MacGregor waved and bowed. "By God, sir," he said to Ames, "it's like a gathering of the clans. There's a MacPherson, a McIntosh, a McKay, a McLaughlin and a McLeod."

"How can you tell, sir?"

"Easy, my boy. The MacPherson kilt has light gray crossbands with blue and orange lines. McKay is the one with a dark green background interspersed with blue and orange lines and the tartan of bright red with stripes of green and burgundy is a McIntosh. Over there is a McDowell in a—"

The thunder of two brass cannon interrupted further explanations. General MacGregor jumped to the dock. His fellow Scots surrounded him, yelling congratulations, good wishes and shaking his hand.

Ames had never seen General MacGregor so happy. His handsome face beamed, he revelled in this adulation. He had deeply resented the lack of attention he had received in Charleston and Savannah. Here among his fellow countrymen he was exuberant, laughing and joking.

A swarthy man in the McIntosh tartan signaled the pipers. They shrilled three short blasts. The tumult subsided.

"General Gregor MacGregor"—he bowed deeply—"I am John McIntosh. I've been asked by my fellow Scots in Darien to bid you welcome. It's an honor indeed to have the illustrious grandson of the great Laird of Inverardine as our guest. Most of us have had fathers or grandfathers killed by the wicked Spaniards. We know, sir, you will avenge our loss. There can be no peace in south Georgia until these evil papists are defeated and driven back across the sea. General MacGregor, we believe in and approve your mission. How can we help? We are yours to command, sir."

In a very husky voice and brushing away a tear, MacGregor said, "I only wish the old Laird MacGregor could be with us today. He'd be most gratified at the welcome you've extended his grandson. Your companionability, congeniality, your bonhomie would have delighted him, as it has me." He paused and wiped his eyes with a linen handkerchief. "Oh fellow Highlanders of the New World, what can I say . . . ?"

His abashment touched McIntosh, who whispered in broad Scottish, "What say, General, to a wee drappie of whuskey?" His companions cheered, waved their cloaks and scarves of tartan and some hailed him in Gaelic. They escorted MacGregor and his staff to the Eagle Hotel for a celebration. During the enormous meal of roast lamb, venison, duck, turkey and even haggis, consumed to the music of the bagpipes, General MacGregor outlined his requirements.

McIntosh said he could drill his army on the bluff north of Darien overlooking the river. "We'll help with victuals and see that you get them at a fair price. But powder, no. We are in short supply."

Expressing his appreciation, the General asked if he might enlist the pipers. "I'd rather have 'em than a brace of cannon."

Laughing, McIntosh said they were "freemen and can join up if they like. Sir," he continued, "I understand you are reopening the slave trade in Fernandina?"

MacGregor nodded and explained the necessity, adding

that he regretted having to do so. "But you own slaves in Georgia?" he questioned.

"We do," admitted McIntosh, "but many of us think it evil and rue the day that Georgia, swayed by the planters, permitted it."

"I don't quite understand."

"When General Oglethorpe founded this colony he forbade both liquor and slavery." He chuckled. "While no true Scot would agree that a wee drappie of malt spirits was bad, we na liked slavery. Rich planters from the Carolinas and Virginia bought land in Georgia and claimed they couldn't profitably raise rice or indigo without slaves. The argument went on for years, but finally in 1749 the Crown relented. In our petition against it we said, 'We cannot help but believe that one day it will be a scourge and a curse on our children and children's children.'"

"Let's hope you are wrong, Mr. McIntosh. But as I see it I have no choice." He sipped his madeira reflectively. "The name Darien, somehow it's familiar."

"It should be to most Scots," replied McIntosh. "A group of Highlanders established a colony in Panama and called it Darien. It thrived, to Spain's annoyance. The dons wiped it out, slaughtering men, women and children. Some eighty years ago General Oglethorpe recruited one hundred and thirty Scots for his Georgia colony. Some, like my grandfather, were involved in the Jacobite Rebellion. Others came seeking a new life. We established a fort here as protection for the southern colonies against Spanish raids. We named it New Inverness. There was constant fighting with the dons and almost in defiance of Spain the name was changed to Darien. Now you see why we ardently support your expedition."

Thanking his hosts for an unforgettable evening, MacGregor and his officers returned to the *Bolivar*.

Ames and Laurent went ashore to make arrangements for their camp. They found Darien a pleasant village of shady streets and comfortable houses enclosed by picket fences. Flowers bloomed in profusion and Ames was enthralled by the many orange trees. He picked and ate his first ripe orange, which was delectable.

With the aid of fifty slaves ground was cleared and a camp built a mile north of town. The army sweated in the blazing Georgia sun and complained of the stinging flies and mosquitoes. They spent each day in close order drill, bayonet and musket practice and parading up and down the sandy bluff.

They loafed, slept or swam at sundown, waiting impatiently for the sea breeze to freshen the long twilight hours. Ames and Wash often went fishing. The former slave rigged lines on cane poles, netted river shrimp for bait and always seemed to know the best spot for sheepshead, red snapper and an occasional pompano. The sweet flesh of these fish, previously unknown to Ames, was a welcome change from the regular diet of bacon or pickled beef.

The black man, Wash, was a joy. He made existence pleasant for Ames with apparently little effort. He cut wood, cooked, washed clothes, cleaned their quarters and laughed off Ames's protests.

"Sah, you is a colonel. If you don't let me wait on you it'll bring shame on my poor head. Colonels, sah, just don't work."

Ames enjoyed being spoiled and sensed that Wash was proud to serve an officer. He was equally proud to be a regular soldier. Ames had insisted that he take the oath of allegiance and be paid and treated like all recruits.

In their brief time together Ames had grown to respect the Negro. He bore himself with dignity, never complained and had an amazing knowledge of birds, animals and perhaps most important of all had an earthy sense of humor. His stories amused the tired, bored men. Their favorite was:

"On a cold winter morning a little ol' rabbit was a shiverin' and a jumpin' down the road when he met up wid a big ol' dog. Ol' dog asked little rabbit if he wasn't a freezin'. Rabbit allowed he mighty cold, especially his foots. They walks and talks together fer a spell den de rabbit asks dog whar he git such fine shoes from. He just smiles and admires them shoes until dog took pity on him and tole him to try 'em on—mebbe he could git some too, next time he go to the store. Little rabbit puts shoes on front paws, said they mighty comfortable but he slightly off balance—too high in de front. Old dog let him have two hind shoes. Rabbit smile and then he just high tail it down the big road. De dog barkin' and howlin', chased him. And ever since dogs been runnin' rabbits or tryin' to get their shoes back."

Wash's big face would break into an even bigger smile as the men guffawed. One young recruit said, "We'se been tricked like that pore ol' dog, but don't know exactly which way to run." That summed up the attitude of the men and why they liked the story.

Slapping ineffectually at the buzzing mosquitoes, Jonathan Ames got up, stretched and peered from his tent. It was that pale hour before dawn that was called "mornglown," the time when ghosts and "hants" run. A chill wind came from the water. He dressed and decided to go for a walk. It was Sunday, their one day of respite from MacGregor's stern discipline.

A mile north of Darien was the beginning of the Altamaha Swamp. The soldiers told many tales of its mysteries and horrors. He decided to see for himself. As he neared the swamp the black muck shivered beneath his feet. The gum and cypress trees were gloomy with clinging vines. A few flowers bloomed palely.

He came to a pond filled with decaying logs. A mist rose, white and curling. It seemed cold and menacing, filled with lurking horrors. Bullbats swept past him with their shivering notes and moths struck his face.

The water swirled and boiled. He saw a flash of silver and a dark shape in pursuit. The ripples widened and tiny waves lapped the tree roots. A sleek head appeared, two eyes looked around and a mink climbed out dragging a small bass. Its long slender body was covered with brown fur, which glistened in the pale light.

He jumped when a great bull alligator thundered and the swamp resounded with the ugly clamor of its bellowing. His hair rose in bristles, "I've had enough," he said to himself. He loped toward the river and soon reached an open field. He saw a few clouds tinged with yellow in a pale green sky. A rim of gold sneaked above the horizon and the rising sun was tinted orange, then a deep red.

A blue heron, standing on one leg, fished in the shallows of a salt-water creek. The chuckling calls of a white egret blended with the loud trumpet notes of a giant crane. There were woodpeckers with black and white wings, redbirds, bluebirds, wrens, doves and even a brilliant turkey gobbler. A mocking bird sang lustily from the shade of a scuppernong vine.

He heard the frightened squeal of a field mouse. Turning, he saw an olive green snake, ornamented with brownish black diamonds. The seven-foot rattlesnake moved swiftly after the mouse. A twig snapped sharply under Ames's foot. Instantly the snake coiled, his rattles trilled a staccato whir. For a moment he was mesmerized by its wicked eyes. The snake swayed and struck. He jumped and toppled into the low palmettos. He watched horrified as the rattler coiled. Before it could strike again a slim black body, almost like a rope playing out, darted at the rattler. Rattles whirring, the diamondback sank its fangs into the long thin snake. He struck again and again as the black snake whipped its slender coils around the heavy olive green body. The desperate rattler struck at the small oval head and missed. They rolled over in a tangled writhing mass and the black snake wound itself tighter and tighter. The rattler gasped, gave one final lunge and became limp.

Aghast, Ames staggered to his feet. He heard someone calling his name and saw Wash running across the savannah.

"Is you all right, sah?"

The stunned young man did not speak but pointed to the snakes. The black one slowly unwound itself, noticed the two men and glided away in the tall grass.

"Them kingsnakes is shore mean to rattlers," said Wash.

"But it was bitten half a dozen times. Why didn't it die from the poison?"

"Old kingsnake don't pay no never-mind, he just hug him clean out 'er breath. But you, sah, mighty lucky that ole kingsnake happened along."

Ames agreed and asked Wash how he "happened along."

"Sah, Captain Stratford docked this morning. He is a-lookin' fer you."

"Then we must hurry back to Darien."

"Ain't no hurry, sah. Captain Stratford can't sail until ebb tide." Wash pushed the dead snake on a rock and with one swipe of his curved machete severed its broad triangular head. Cutting wild grape vines, he tied the viper to a long pole and swung it over his shoulder.

Ames asked why.

"Tote him back to camp and bile him."

"You mean to eat him?"

Laughing at Ames's horrified expression, Wash said, "Nah, sah. Though many folks do. They claims a roasted snake better than chicken, but not me. I gnawed on one once and it riled me up fer days. But, sah, snake grease is finest medicine there is for aches and pains." He picked wild grape leaves and carefully wrapped the rattler's ugly head.

"Now what's that for?" asked Ames.

"Snake juice just fine for my blowgun darts. Look here, sah." Slowly he opened the rattler's mouth and pointed to a short brown needle projecting from the upper jaw. He pressed gently on the poison sac back of the eyes and a drop of venom came out. "Smear one drop on honey locust thorns and it'll kill birds and rabbits. Three or four drops will kill a man."

"And you use that in a blowgun?" questioned Ames.

"Yes, sah, I found some big wild cane by the river. I'se hollowed out a ten-foot piece. Put in a dart, give one mighty puff and out she comes at other end. Better 'n a gun—don't make no noise. Old Indian taught me all 'bout blowguns, sah."

"I see," muttered Ames. "Now we better get back to Darien."

"Yas, sah." As they walked back to the village Wash picked a dozen wild oranges, which he said boiled down was mighty good for fever. "We'se been lucky so far, only two or three soldiers been sick."

Ames went to the Eagle Hotel, where he found Captain Stratford sipping a rum punch. He hailed the young officer, ordered him a drink and said, "Fisherman in Savannah told me you folks was here. Thought I'd stop by and see how you all doing."

Ames said he was glad to see him and described their rigid training.

"All that marching mighty fine, but when is you gonna hit the dons? They shore as hell know 'bout yer army."

Admitting that he was concerned about the delay, he asked the captain if he would take a letter to Mr. Simms.

"That's one of the reasons I came," he said. Ames excused himself and hurriedly wrote to Mr. Crawford. Once again he confined his report to facts, size of the army, training and MacGregor's plans as he knew them. Though tempted, he did not speculate. He was aware of his mixed feelings about General MacGregor. It would be difficult if not impossible to put them in writing.

Ignoring his staff, General MacGregor continued his imperious way. He refused to see Jared Irwin and threatened court-martial. Slight annoyance was his reaction to Captain Stratford's report that the Spaniards were aware of his army. Drilling, marching, more drilling was the order of each day. Mutiny was in the air and desertions increased. Yet the general remained unperturbed. Each evening he met his Scotch admirers in Darien to drink madeira and reminisce about the Highlands.

Remembering Simms's suggestion, Ames asked Laurent to give him fencing lessons. The lithe Frenchman said it would be a pleasure as he'd "greatly admired that tempered Toledo blade."

He was strong, cunning and a splendid swordsman. "You attack and I'll defend," he ordered. "No fight was ever won by the defense."

Keeping his arm straight and firm, as Laurent instructed, Ames moved to the attack. Sweating and swearing, he never penetrated Laurent's flashing blade. Laurent kept bombarding him with orders. "Thrust, attack, thrust, move forward faster, faster, arm stiff, point straight. Thrust—don't lunge—thrust, attack, attack." He was a splendid teacher and showered Ames with orders and occasional insults. Each lesson improved

Ames's skill, though he knew Laurent could kill him in a fight.

Another week passed and both officers and men were near anarchy. Suddenly the general called a staff meeting. He announced that his Army of Liberation was ready and he graciously thanked his staff for their "efforts and forebearance. . . . We move against Amelia Island in three days. That's June 29, 1817. That will be a day to be remembered in the history of Florida, a day that will be celebrated like America's Fourth of July."

He spread a large map of Amelia Island on the sand and carefully outlined his battle plans. They were strategically sound and Ames understood how MacGregor, despite his bombast, had defeated the Spaniards many times in South America. His staff was impressed and even Jared Irwin approved.

"I spent a week on Amelia Island last year," said Mac-Gregor. "God's blood, what an uncomfortable, dismal place." Then, pointing with his gleaming sword to the map, he said, "As you can see, Amelia is a long narrow island. St. Marys River empties into the Atlantic at the north, the Nassau River at the south and the Amelia River connects the two, forming the island.

"On a high bluff facing the Amelia River is Fort San Carlos. It is old and its tabby walls are crumbling. The fort has four long Spanish sixteen-pounders, five four-pounders and one long carronade. They are rusty and might explode if fired.

"The garrison has about a hundred men. Most of them are old, worn out in the service of Spain in the New World. Their uniforms are faded, shabby and morale is low. Their commanding officer, Morales, is a dirty fat pig." The general wrinkled his nose in disgust. "He dined with me in a soiled shirt and he smelled of sweat."

Using his sword as a pointer, he continued, "The town of Fernandina is here, on high rolling ground. It's really a shabby village of forty or fifty frame houses with the exception of several imposing dwellings on the Estrada. The resident population of Fernandina numbers a few hundred, mostly slave traders, smugglers, undesirable Americans and assorted rascals. They detest Morales and I'm sure none will aid him.

"Troops from our merchantman will drop anchor here." He indicated a spot where Egan's Creek flowed into the Amelia River. "It's swampy and the Spaniards will not expect a land attack from there. Colonel Ames, you will lead these troops and assault the fort once the *Bolivar* has fired five broadsides. This will create a diversion for your troops and even our small cannon should crumble those walls."

"Pears to me it's easy pickings," observed Irwin. "Why did we delay for so long?"

MacGregor glared at the American. In haughty tones he said, "For two sound tactical reasons, Colonel Irwin. I had to be sure Fort San Carlos had not been reinforced by troops from Cuba. My latest intelligence says it has not. Secondly, a competent general values human life, never spills the blood of his army unnecessarily. Subtlety is more effective than a slashing frontal attack. I have persuaded several traders to spread rumors that my Army of Liberation is a thousand strong. Morales is a bloated poltroon and frightens easily. Such stories will not strengthen his resistance." He paused as if waiting for his staff to applaud. The officers chuckled and showed their approval of his strategy.

Sailing into St. Marys River on the morning tide the *Bolivar* slowly maneuvered within easy range of Fort San Carlos. The troopship dropped anchor near Egan's Creek and the two long-boats rowed Ames and his men ashore.

He was welcomed by Wash and Laurent, who had landed at sunrise to scout. Wash said the long marsh grass stood in "a couple 'er feet of water" and could be waded.

"It's a dirty, slimy mess," added the Frenchman.

"Can't be helped," said Ames. "What about snakes or alligators?"

"It's salt water," said Wash. "Mebbe a few crabs or sand fleas, but nuttin' much else."

Ames ordered his men to check their loading and priming and watched the *Bolivar* tack before the fort. The flag of Spain, imperial lion on a golden field, floated over the ramparts. Its gunports were closed and the fort seemed almost deserted. Four sentries walked the ramparts, pausing to look curiously at the trim schooner. Beyond, Ames could see the town, its houses tight-shuttered. He supposed they had fled to safety in the back country. Had Morales deserted and abandoned Fort San Carlos?

The *Bolivar's* guns roared and through the heavy black smoke Ames saw the round shot smash into the fort. Bits of tabby and a crushed palmetto flew into the sky. Several balls missed and buried themselves in the sand. MacGregor's guns did little damage and determined men could withstand a long siege.

Gunports opened and the ancient cannon returned the *Bolivar's* fire. Only two, maybe three at the most, were effective. Ames saw the round shot plump harmlessly into the harbor, far short of the *Bolivar*. The nimble ship swung quickly and fired her second broadside. This volley was more accurate and there were shouts and cries from the fort. A thin trail of smoke rose from a sentry shack on the parade ground.

Three more broadsides and we attack, thought Ames. He looked at his tattered army, each wearing a green fern in his hat instead of the splendid white and green uniform promised by MacGregor.

Once again the *Bolivar* put about, but before she could fire the imperial flag of Spain dipped. A soldier on the rampart frantically waved a ragged sheet on a bayonet point.

Fort San Carlos had surrendered. The battle was over.

"*Mon Dieu*," said Laurent with a shrug of his shoulders. "It's a comic opera—and a bad one at that."

§ CHAPTER 7 §

Wash found quarters for Colonel Ames at the tip of Garden Street overlooking Amelia River. It was a rambling frame house, comfortably furnished and shaded by bride of India trees. Scarlet hibiscus and elderberry bushes heavy with purple fruit dotted the small garden. The owner, a Spanish trader, had fled to St. Augustine.

Ames removed his sweat-stained jacket and kicked off his muddy boots. He sighed contentedly as he sipped a rum toddy, tangy with fresh lime. Wash, practicing his own form of magic, had located ice and a half box of Havana cigars. Ames lit one, drank more rum and meditated. Rum and tobacco—handmaidens of the devil. They'd dance one's soul down the daisy path to hell, where you'd burn and writhe in eternal perdition. So said the Holy Writ as expounded in the Puritan sermons he'd heard so many times in Litchfield. Perhaps I'm beyond redemption. He was reasonably confident that anything this enjoyable is not sinful. He turned his thoughts to the report he would send Mr. Crawford.

It had been a day to remember. After a brief parley, Fort San Carlos had capitulated. The terms were generous:

Surrender all arms and munitions of war belonging to the King of Spain.

All officers and troops will be sent to St. Augustine with their private baggage, which shall be respected.

The lives and property of all private persons in Fernandina shall be sacred and inviolate.

By high noon the Army of Liberation was ready to march through the town gate and occupy Fort San Carlos. Then came the delay. General MacGregor insisted on leading his troops on horseback, preferably a white stallion. He fretted, his wilted soldiers slapped mosquitoes and grumbled. Finally he accepted a bony mare.

In his sky blue coat, belted with a flowing red sash, General MacGregor was an impressive figure. He swung gracefully into the saddle, flourished a long sword and bellowed, "Forward march!" To the sound of fife and drum the tattered army straggled into Fort San Carlos.

A bugle sounded. The flag of Liberated Florida went up. It was white, bisected with one vertical and one horizontal green stripe forming a St. George's cross.

Astride his small mare, arms folded in Napoleonic fashion, General MacGregor graciously refused the sword of Captain Morales. He released the Spanish dragoons on "their word of honor" to remain in the fort until transportation could be arranged for St. Augustine.

Ames was forced to admit that he looked the part of an empire builder as he turned and saluted his men. He waved his long sword and shouted, "Glorious Army of Liberation, the twenty-ninth of June will be forever memorable in the annals of Florida. On that day a body of brave men, animated by a noble zeal for the happiness of mankind, advanced within musket shot of the guns of Fernandina and awed the enemy into immediate capitulation, not withstanding his favorable position. This will be everlasting proof of what the sons of freedom can achieve when fighting in the great and glorious cause against a government which has trampled on all the natural and essential rights which descend from God to man. Impelled by these noble principles you will soon be able to free the whole of Florida from the hand of Spanish despotism. The children of this noble country will re-echo your names in song, your heroic deeds will be handed down to succeeding generations and you will cover yourselves and your posterity with a never-fading wreath of glory.

"To perpetuate the memory of your valor I have decreed a shield of honor to be worn on the left arm of every soldier here today. It will be round, four inches in diameter, and of red cloth, with the device 'Vencedors de Amelia, twenty-ninth of June, 1817' surrounded by a wreath of laurel and oak leaves."

Sheathing his glittering sword, the general rode slowly across the *prado*.

"*Mon Dieu*," whispered Laurent. "He's the only man I ever saw who could strut sitting on a horse."

Ames smiled as he recalled the sardonic remark and asked for another drink. Sipping the tangy rum, he considered the report he had to prepare on today's events. It was not easy for him to put his thoughts on paper. But it must be done at once, as he knew the importance of Mr. Crawford having the latest intelligence. Beyond an accurate description of the capture of Fort San Carlos, he mused, it's now time I spoke of my hopes and fear for the future. General MacGregor has many admirable qualities and I feel a loyalty to him as my commanding officer. Yet I have a greater obligation to Mr. Crawford and must give him a candid appraisal of Mac-Gregor's strengths and weaknesses.

Wearily, he asked Wash if he could find pen, ink and paper. Wash said he would try. "Colonel, a soldier here a while back said special meetin' at general's headquarters toward sun-down." Ames groaned and glanced at the long shadows over the garden. "I'll have to go now," he muttered. "Come along, Wash."

"Yas, sah, Colonel."

Walking past the square Ames noticed that Fort San Carlos was deserted. No sentries on its ramparts, no guards at the portal. He quickly understood why. Fernandina's sandy streets were jammed with drunken soldiers, sailors and the town riff-raff. From the taverns along the waterfront came the sound of laughter, jeers, guitars and singing. The chorus of one song—"The good is doubtful/the bad is sure and certain"—seemed prophetic. The two men came to a short narrow street named Pasco de los Damas. They saw long lines of men standing in front of the cribs. Business was very good for the town's fancy ladies.

Beyond was Fernando Street, where General MacGregor had established his headquarters. Most of the houses, well screened by trees, were shuttered. The town's people had fled. A dim light shone in a rear window of an imposing two-storied house. Ames paused and said, "What was that noise?"

"Sounds like a cryin' baby," replied Wash.

They both listened intently. Again came the soft low wail. "It's a-sufferin'," murmured Wash. Ames nodded and walked swiftly toward the light. He peered into the window and said in a horrified voice, "God Almighty, Wash, look!"

A single candle guttering in a rum bottle gave enough light to show them a half-naked young woman stretched on a bed. Her long hair covered her face, her hands were roped tightly. Between sobs she was praying.

Two men sat at a low wooden table. Heaped before them was a collection of silver plate, goblets, bracelets, rings and perhaps half a hundred gold pesos. They swigged rum from a bottle and divided their loot. After carefully counting the money, the man with gold rings in his ears, a blue handkerchief knotted about his hair, said, "Now the doxie."

His companion, a gross mulatto said, "We'll share."

"Not with you, dog dung." He made a move for a knife at his waist.

"Softly amigo," said the dark man, swiftly drawing a dirk. "The dice will decide."

Ames tapped Wash on the shoulder and pointed to a side door. He moved forward and gently turned the knob. It was locked. Wash motioned him aside, crouched low and charged. His broad left shoulder tore the rotten wood from its hinges. The door fell forward, overturning the table, scattering baubles and knocking the two thieves to the floor.

Wash seized the mulatto by his ankles, swung him against the door jamb. His head split like an over-ripe melon. The second robber fumbled for his knife. Ames stomped his fingers and deliberately swung a heavy boot just below a dangling earring. He screamed, rolled on his back and vomited.

"Tie 'em up, Wash."

"Yas, sah." Wash grinned. He poked his opponent with his foot. "He's dead," he said calmly, "and yourn won't cause no more trouble tonight."

For a second Jonathan regretted kicking the man. No, the scoundrel got what he deserved. The woman had fainted during the brief but bloody fight. Cutting her bonds, he rubbed her chafed wrists and asked for the rum bottle.

Cradling her in his arms, he wiped her face and lips with the rum-soaked handkerchief. Except for a bruise on her left cheek she was not hurt. He pushed back her wavy black hair and saw that she was beautiful. Her fully rounded breasts were exposed. Her tiny pink nipples fascinated him. He had an overpowering urge to stroke them. He spoke to Wash, who ripped an old blanket into squares. Ames gently pulled it around her shoulders and squeezed more rum into her red mouth. The girl blinked and opened her eyes. She gave the two men a startled look. Screaming, she raked Ames's cheek with her fingernails and jumped to her feet. She grabbed the knife and slashed at Ames, who nimbly dodged. She backed into a corner, frantically waving the shining blade. The blanket fell, leaving her naked again above the waist. Between hysterical sobs she spoke rapidly in Spanish. The two men did not understand.

Protecting himself with a chair, Wash edged toward the frantic girl. Softly, as though speaking to a baby, he said, "Don't you cry little missy, you'se safe. This here is Colonel Ames. He wouldn't even hurt a little ole fly."

His voice seemed to soothe the weeping girl. Slowly she lowered the knife and glanced down. She blushed and tried to cover her breasts with her long curly hair. Wash picked up the blanket and gave it to her. As she adjusted it around her shoulders he moved quickly and plucked the wicked blade from her trembling fingers.

Fear filled her expressive dark gray eyes. She apprehensively watched the two men but did not speak.

Holding his bloody handkerchief to his cheek, Ames bowed. "Señorita, don't be frightened. Please." He smiled and waited.

She relaxed a bit and some of the dread left her face. In slow but perfect English she announced, "I am Señora Gonzalez, wife of Don José Gonzalez."

"Colonel Jonathan Ames of the Army of Liberation."

Anger flared in her voice. "Didn't your general promise to respect our lives and property?"

"He did indeed, señora."

"But within the hour I am attacked and robbed." Her eyes blazed indignantly. She said scornfully, "Army of Liberation—bah! Army of heretics—evil, vile men. Thieves, bandits and liars."

"Sah, these men ain't ours," said Wash. "This one"—he pointed to the dead man—"from Santo Domingo and him a sailor."

She stared haughtily at Wash. "Are you his slave?"

"No," said Ames sharply. "He's a soldier and my friend."

"A nigger friend?" She grimaced. "What a vulgar, dissolute country."

"Madame," flared Ames. "He saved you."

"From what?" she asked. Speaking directly to Ames she said, "I saw you kick that man in the head. It was vicious."

Ames disliked this arrogant, unreasonable woman. To his disgust he found himself explaining. "He had a knife, señora. It was no time for niceties."

"Niceties?" she repeated maliciously. "Does an American understand the word?" She pointed to the gold pesos, "Take that and go!"

His lips curled scornfully. He had never met such ingratitude. Controlling his voice with difficulty, he spoke to Wash. "Perhaps you better stay here for a while and help . . . er . . . er the lady," and strode out of the house.

Startled, Señora Luiza Gonzalez moved after Ames. She was confused and mortified. Yet she knew she was at fault. The afternoon had been a horror from the moment the two men entered her house. She had fought like a tigress. They had laughed, slapped her about, ripped off her silk blouse and collected their spoils. Their lewd comments left no doubt of their intentions. She must see this young American again, apologize and make him understand.

Perplexed, she turned to Wash. "My husband will reward you for this."

The big Negro shook his head. "I help 'cause he ask me. He a good man, little missy, and you not very nice to him."

"No, I wasn't. I'll send him a note of apology." She eyed Wash curiously. "I've never met a free Negro before."

"He free me," said Wash and told her about the slave auction in Charleston.

Señora Gonzalez nodded understandingly and asked Wash if he would help her straighten the house and guard her against intruders. While she collected her valuables he dragged the two men from the house. He nailed the broken door and escorted the señora to an upstairs room. He advised her to bolt the door and not show a light.

"I got 'er run a errand fer the colonel but I'll be back soon. Things be fine by sunup. General MacGregor mighty strict man. Won't stand fer this drinking and shouting. You'll see."

She replied that she hoped so and asked Wash to wait while she wrote a note to Colonel Ames. He asked if he could "borrow a little paper and pen," explaining that's what he was "supposed to git fer the colonel." She was glad to help and he left promising to return "in a little while."

Ames strode down the crushed-shell walk to headquarters, the largest house on Fernando Street. He entered and saw General MacGregor seated at a long table writing vigorously with a quill pen. Jared Irwin, Laurent and several other officers were in a far corner of the room. He went over, said "Good evening" and asked if anything was wrong.

Irwin said acidly, "The general is upset. His printing press is lost."

Astounded, Ames said, "What?"

Irwin spoke in rapid angry words. "That's right. The printing press he bought in Savannah is gone. He can't fight without one." He glanced at his commanding officer and spat in disgust. "He's busy writing proclamations when he should be planning to move on St. Augustine."

"Reminds me of a Mameluke," said Laurent.

"What in hell is that?" growled Irwin.

"I fought against them in Egypt and Napoleon slaughtered them outside of Cairo."

"Egypt, Cairo, Napoleon," snorted Irwin. "What's that got to do with us?"

The Frenchman smiled. "Perhaps nothing, Colonel Irwin."

"Doesn't the word 'Mameluke' mean slave?" asked Ames.

"That's right, my friend. They were purchased as children from poor peasant families in the Caucasian section of Russia, imported into Egypt and trained as mercenaries. Our general's love of braid and uniforms reminds me of them. The Mameluke warrior wore a coat of chain mail beneath a long green coat bounded at the waist by an embroidered shawl, a green cap wrapped in a yellow turban, red pantaloons and red pointed slippers, a brace of pistols, a long curving sword and carried an English musket with an engraved silver stock. Brave, bloodthirsty butchers but no understanding of tactics. The Emperor smashed them in every battle." He paused and added caustically, "Just a band of lawless adventurers like us."

"Mebbe," said Irwin, "but for God's sake don't mention 'em to the general. He'll want something similar. Red pointed slippers? My God!"

The men laughed, and Laurent, noticing Ames's cheek, said with a smirk, "A little bird scratch you?"

"A Spanish virago. Two men had robbed her house and were throwing dice for her. Wash took care of them."

"A gallant knight rescues the fair lady." Laurent grinned. "Did you bed her?"

"No," said Ames, blushing slightly as he remembered her full breasts. "She had fainted. I was sponging her face when she clawed me and went for us with a knife."

"She's marked you for her own," the Frenchman said, smirking. "Is she pretty?"

"I suppose so, but she's an ill-tempered wench."

"Probably just disappointed. Forget your Puritan ways, Jonathan. Go bed her and all will be well."

Such ribald comment disturbed Ames. His fellow officers laughed at his obvious discomfort. Irwin came to his rescue. "You damned Frenchies. Don't you ever think of anything but women?"

"Ah, Colonel, can you think of a more pleasant pastime?"

General MacGregor got to his feet and said, "Gentlemen, your attention please." The officers stood quietly and waited.

In his deep baritone the general said, "I shall read to you the proclamation of the Army of Liberation:

> "General Gregor MacGregor, Brigadier General of the Armies of the United Provinces of New Grenada and Venezuela and General in Chief of the Armies for the New Floridas, commissioned by the Supreme Director of Mexico and South America to the inhabitants of Amelia Island.
>
> "Your brethren of Mexico, Buenos Aires, New Grenada and Venezuela who are so gloriously engaged in fighting for that inestimable gift which nature has bestowed upon her children, and which all civilized nations have endeavored to secure by social compact; desirous that all the sons of Columbia should participate in that imprescriptible right, have confided to me the commandant of the land and naval forces.
>
> "Peaceful inhabitants of Amelia. Do not entertain any danger of oppression from the troops which are now in possession of your island, neither for your persons, property or religion, however various the climes in which you may have received your birth; they are never the less your brethren and friends."

Ames wondered how Señora Gonzalez would react to such a promise. His thoughts kept turning to her as MacGregor declared his eternal belief in human liberty and justice, outlined his plan to establish just laws in Amelia and then to deliver the rest of Florida from the cruel tyranny of Spain.

Could the Frenchman be right? Would he dare make love to such a lovely woman? Would she welcome him?

MacGregor paused and drank wine from a silver goblet. The silence brought Ames back to reality as the general concluded, "Friends or enemies of our present system of emancipation, whoever you may be, what I say unto you is the language of truth; it's the only language becoming a man of honor and, as such, I swear to adhere religiously to the tenor of this proclamation."

"Should we applaud?" whispered Laurent. The officers suppressed grins. Jared Irwin said laconically, "Right pretty, General."

The handsome general glowered. "This proclamation would be distributed to every inhabitant of Amelia if some fool hadn't lost my printing press. My secretary promises a dozen copies by morning. Colonel Irwin, see that they are posted in Fort San Carlos, the churches and the taverns."

"Yes, General. But what about St. Augustine—what are your orders?"

"It's been a long day, Colonel, and I'm weary. We will discuss tactics in the morning. Good night, gentlemen."

"Pompous ass," muttered Irwin as the general left.

That night he sweated over a long report to Mr. Crawford that described the capture of Fort San Carlos, the surrender terms and included a copy of MacGregor's proclamation. He wrote:

> In previous letters I've confined myself to facts. Now I think, to the best of my ability, I should venture an opinion about the future and give you my impressions of General MacGregor.
>
> At the memorable evening in President Madison's home, which I'll never forget, Mr. Jefferson asked the question "Can he organize and lead an army and then establish a stable government?"
>
> Sir, he has recruited, trained an army and captured Fort San Carlos. He has proved himself a competent

general, and even the staff officers who dislike him think his planning and strategy sound. As you know, the general is a handsome man always immaculately groomed and looks every inch the soldier. When he desires he can be witty, ingratiating and an excellent raconteur. He can also be overbearing and is given to black moods and atrocious temper. Perhaps his most grievous fault is a tendency to procrastinate. Amelia Island could have been easily captured two months ago and all Florida liberated. Even now if he moves swiftly against St. Augustine I believe victory possible. If he allows his restless army to drink and loot, as they are doing tonight, the Spaniards can strengthen their defenses and even bring in reinforcements from Cuba.

In fairness to the general I'm sure he has been deceived by his Baltimore company. He has not received the additional funds, ammunition or supplies promised.

Unfortunately a pompous young man from Charleston, Farquor Bethune, has been named mayor of Fernandina. I doubt his ability to establish a government that can control this lawless island.

I believe, sir, that the next few weeks will determine Florida's fate.

> Yours with esteem and respect,
> Jonathan Ames

He sealed the letter and gave it to Wash. "Captain Stratford promised to put in to Fernandina on his return voyage. Keep a sharp lookout for his ship and deliver this."

Wearily he wiped his brow and said he would be most grateful for a cold drink.

Wash said there was plenty of rum and limes but "ice mighty hard to come by. See what I can do, sah." He returned shortly with a frosted pitcher of rum toddy.

"You are a wizard," said Ames as he swigged the heady drink. "Where'd you find the ice?"

"Spanish missy down on Fernando Street. Asks you to call some afternoon so she can say she sorry she clawed you."

Rubbing the welts on his cheek, Ames remembered the softness of her full breasts. He flushed as he recalled Laurent's ribald suggestion. One winter he had tumbled a barmaid a few times in the hayloft. It had not been a very satisfactory experience. He had been steeped in remorse for weeks. Such thoughts are ridiculous and he damned the Frenchman. "I'll write her a thank-you note for the ice," he told Wash, "and you can deliver it in the morning."

Wash was not pleased with the decision but made no comment. He just did not understand white folks. Instead he said, "That shore must be hard work."

"What?"

"Er, writin'. You sweat more than a man pickin' cotton."

Laughing, Ames said, "It's not easy, at least not for me."

"Spose I could learn?"

Surprised, Ames said, "You mean to write?"

"Yas, sah, and to read them bugs you put on paper." His wistful tone touched Ames.

"Why sure, Wash," he replied enthusiastically. "I'll be glad to help you." The big Negro had a quick mind, a retentive memory and Ames was pleased with his request. "Did you ever go to school?"

"Nah, sah. No niggers do in South Carolina. I can count a little, up to 'bout twenty. And I knows my ABCs but don't know just what they means."

Puzzled, Ames said, "You can recite the alphabet?"

"Well, sah, I can sing it." In a big bass voice he did:

> "An A and a B and a big C,
> An a D E F G,
> An a H and 'er I and a J
> And a K L M N O.
> A P and a Q and a R
> And a S T U V,
> And a W X Y and a big ole Z.

(117)

For a moment Ames was tempted to applaud. "Who taught you?" he asked.

"Old preacher in Charleston come to Colonel Stovall's place ever month to hold services. My, but he was a stem winder, talk all de time. He gonna teach us young 'uns to read, but Colonel Stovall found out and run him off de place. Bout all I learnt was that little song."

"Why did Colonel Stovall object? It seems to me an education would increase the value of his slaves."

"He say it just make us niggers biggerty, but, sah, he was a kind man. Never whup us and we got plenty clothes and vittles."

"I guess I just don't understand."

"Well, sah, Colonel Stovall think of us 'bout like he does his horses and huntin' dogs. Treat us good, but he can't quite accept us as folks."

"What?"

"Sah, my name is George Washington Lewis. When I first started huntin' with Colonel Stovall, cleaning his guns, pickin' de birds, holdin' his horses—things like that, he called me George. One day after a few juleps he say, 'Goddamnit, George ain't no fit name fer a good nigger like you.'

"I say I got other names and tell him. He mighty surprised and allowed he never knowed before that niggers had last names. He say Washington all wrong fer a nigger, he shortened it to Wash and I'se been called that ever since."

Ames noticed his hand shaking as he gulped his rum. Now, more than ever, he was determined to teach Wash.

"I'll find some books and we'll start at once. You can do it, Wash, but it'll take time and lots of work."

"I'se willin'," said Wash.

Despite the withering heat, the general moved with vigor the next week. He established a post office and a Court of Admiralty, which levied a tax of 16 per cent on gross sales. Pirates and privateers were invited to make Fernandina their home port for refitting and "victualing." Jared Irwin was named treasurer of "free Amelia" and instructed to issue notes negotiable on the faith of the new government.

Another printing press was ordered from Savannah and the general made plans for a newspaper. He named it the Amelia *Liberator* and said it would faithfully report all actions of the new government. Troops were ordered to forage for horses and food. Settlers indignantly refused payment in "Amelia notes" and the soldiers blandly took what they wanted. Thirty-one Negro slaves were "liberated," then sold for the benefit of the government.

This enraged the influential owners of the large slave-run plantations. Many of the small farmers, cattlemen, hunters and fishermen had welcomed MacGregor. Any new government, they thought, would be an improvement. They soon became disillusioned.

General MacGregor issued ringing proclamations urging the "freedom-loving citizens" of Florida to enlist in his army. They laughed and ignored his appeals.

Tension mounted as the sultry August days crept by. An angry Jared Irwin demanded an immediate march on St. Augustine. MacGregor protested that he needed more time to plan his attack, more intelligence about the size of the garrison and the strength of the fort.

"With such shilly-shallying," bluntly replied Irwin, "you are making a rod with which you will be scourged yourself."

"Sir, you forget that I am your commanding officer. I demand your respect."

The old Revolutionary soldier scratched his head thoughtfully and said calmly, "My God, you are a fool and will soon regret your folly."

The general's handsome face flamed scarlet. His eyes bulged. "Sir, you are insolent. Colonel Irwin, I demand—"

Irwin interrupted, "I've had a bellyful," and stalked out, leaving MacGregor gasping like a landed fish.

Ames and Laurent found Irwin late that afternoon in a tavern on Long Wharf. He waved them to a seat at his table and considered the two officers with bloodshot eyes. He pushed a bottle of Jamaican rum toward them and shouted for more glasses. Gulping more of the potent spirit, he wiped his thin lips and shouted, "Rum shall set you free."

"And make you drunk, too," laughed Ames. "Easy on, Colonel."

Irwin scrutinized the young officer for a long time. "Why?" he blurted. "Why, Jonathan Ames. Why?"

Ames fumbled with his answer, though he understood perfectly. "What are you talking about?"

Winking slyly at Laurent, Irwin said, "The Frenchie here and me are a couple of rascals. We'll never die in bed. For God's sake what brings you to this hellhole? You're too smart to be taken in with all this talk about freedom, liberation and justice, ain't you, Jonathan Ames?"

Without waiting for an answer he rambled on, "I'm here 'cause I'm well paid. Folks up Baltimore way sent me along to keep an eye on the mighty General Gregor MacGregor. They are only interested in a profit on their investment, don't give a damn 'bout evil dons, tyranny or another star in the flag. Reckon I oughta be satisfied as long as we have Fernandina, that's where the money is. But damn me, I hate to see that popinjay piss away such a chance. If he'd moved against St. Augustine all Florida would be ours by now." He belched and drank more rum.

In an amused voice Laurent said, "As one rascal to another, do I detect a note of patriotism?"

"What's wrong with that?" bellowed Irwin. "I fought the lobsterbacks for four years. Saw 'em surrender at Yorktown." He blinked and hummed softly. "By God, that's it. Things are as upside down here as they were for Cornwallis. Remember?"

The puzzled men shook their heads. The old soldier staggered to his feet, waved a rum bottle and sang in a cracked voice:

"If ponies rode men and grass ate cows,
    And cats should be chased into holes by the mouse.
    If summer were spring and the other way round,
    Then all the world would be upside down."

"That's the song a British band played at Yorktown." He lifted high the bottle, spilled more than he drank, smiled foolishly and crumpled to the floor.

As Wash predicted, General MacGregor restored order on Amelia Island. A number of residents returned and opened their houses. They apparently had no feeling against the Army of Liberation. "Been invaded so many times, they're used to it," said Jared Irwin.

The officers were invited to suppers and small dances. Ames refused all invitations. It did not seem right to accept the hospitality of a conquered people. Laurent told him he was wise. "The music is stiff and tuneless, the cotillion about as exciting as high mass and the bumbo just frightful. Ah, what I'd give for a good bottle of claret."

"Ask Wash," suggested Ames. "He's a wizard at finding things."

"I will. And, Jonathan, I met your Señora Gonzalez. She's lovely and dances with the graceful flutter of a song sparrow. I wish I were twenty years younger and bore her mark."

Ames rubbed the welts on his cheek. "Ungrateful woman," he muttered.

"How do you know?" Laurent leered. "Seek her out. You Puritans just don't understand women."

Perhaps I am acting foolishly, thought Ames. She had written a charming note of apology, asking him to call so that she could explain her "inexcusable behavior that terrible evening." He wanted to accept but was scared. Suppose, just suppose, Laurent was right. What would he say? How would he behave? A sweat of fear dampened his forehead and he sent a refusal by Wash.

She had given Wash additional paper, a new quill pen and a second gracious invitation. He returned the next day saying, "Colonel Ames sorry, missy, but he mighty busy and can't come."

Señora Gonzalez' black eyes flashed. This young American interested her. She was accustomed to having her way with men. When she didn't get it she flew into a rage.

She was a pampered only child. Her father was Bruce Halloran, a Jamaican planter, her mother the lovely Maria Herrez of Havana. When she was ten her father was drowned in a September hurricane. Her mother returned to Cuba and Luiza was reared a strict Catholic. At eighteen she had married Don José Gonzalez, a rich widower who had often aided her impecunious family. He was a swarthy but dapper man in his late fifties who desperately wanted an heir. Years of tropical sun and too much madeira had impaired his vigor. Luiza had dutifully tried to stimulate him. At first it was a game that appealed to the Irish sense of humor that lurked just below her strict training. She wore clinging gowns, used exotic perfumes, spiced his wine with "love charms" and even performed provocative dances in the nude. It finally became a bore as Don José failed to respond. She became irritated and frustrated. And Don José blamed Luiza for his disappointment. He now treated her like a wayward daughter, avoiding the humiliation of her bed. Yet, he was still jealous and insisted that she travel with him. He found an attractive wife useful in his business and Luiza was amusing. They lived in Havana but owned a house in Fernandina. As East Florida representative of the English firm of Forbes & Company he bought and sold merchandise, horses and slaves in St. Augustine and Fernandina.

He had been in the St. Johns River country when Fort San Carlos was captured. A cautious, sensible Spaniard, he waited a few days before returning to Fernandina. He was sure Luiza was in no danger.

Luiza had given little thought to her husband's absence. It had happened before. The accumulation of gold was his chief satisfaction. She was more concerned with the young American who had spurned her invitations. He piqued her curiosity. She had never met an American she liked. The ones doing business with her husband were mostly bearded sea captains or gimlet-eyed traders. They were, to her, scruffy uncouth men. Was Colonel Jonathan Ames different? She was determined to find out. Suddenly she smiled to herself. The solution was simple. She would call on him and apologize.

She dressed carefully in a simple white gown with puffed

short sleeves that left her slender arms bare. A tiny trellis of green and gold embroidered the hemline, which she adjusted to three inches above her shapely ankles. This was most improper but she didn't care. For reasons she did not understand, a well-turned ankle, the calf of a leg, interested men. She wanted to excite this indifferent American. Her hair flowed freely beneath a bonnet of soft green silk. She swirled before a tall mirror and was satisfied.

Just at twilight she walked slowly to Ames's quarters on Garden Street. The house seemed deserted. She knocked, hesitated, knocked again and then turned to leave. She heard the low splash of water. Someone was there. Had Ames seen her and refused to answer the door? This was too much! Her temper flared, she entered the house and tripped down the long hall. She came to a closed door and rapped angrily.

A pleasant voice called out, "Come in, Wash."

She entered the room and gasped. Ames sat in a long tin tub, half filled with steaming water. His back was toward the door, his head against the back rest. He seemed half asleep. He said, "A bit more hot water, please, Wash."

Luiza giggled and poured water from an oaken bucket into the tub. Ames washed the soap from his neck, face and arms. "Now the towel, please."

She tossed it beside the tub. Annoyed, he turned his head. His mouth dropped open. He snatched the towel and tried to cover himself. He sat in embarrassed silence.

Impishly the girl walked slowly around the tub. Her dancing eyes roved over his lithe body. She liked what she saw. She took a step forward, peering closer, and in a mocking voice said, "Good evening, Colonel Ames. Can I scrub your back?"

This was too much for the humiliated man. He roared, "Get out!"

"*Por Dios*, such manners. And such a handsome man, too. Broad shoulders, lovely muscular thighs and soft black hair." Her expressive face lit up with amusement.

"Get out you damned Spanish Jezebel," shouted Ames. "Get out—go!"

He wadded the soggy towel and threw it. She dodged nimbly and poured a bucket of cold water over him. He swore and lunged forward, overturning the tub. She lost her footing in the soapy water and fell. Her hair cascaded over his glistening chest. His wet arms went around her, pulling her over him. She did not resist. Her fingers brushed his cheek and her eyes flickered sensuously. He crushed her soft lips and felt her breasts harden under the thin muslin dress.

The next few minutes were always hazy—a wonderful blur to Jonathan Ames. He ripped off her dripping clothes and somehow they were in bed. Her body became vibrantly alive as he wildly kissed her mouth, her eyes, her pointed breasts. Without a word he took her, brutally, completely. She responded passionately.

Exhausted, he tried to speak. She held him tight and her warm lips silenced him. "No regrets, no apologies. I wanted you to love me." She smiled happily.

Supremely unconscious of her nakedness, she sat up in bed and looked at her sodden dress. Laughing, she said, "You will have to send Wash for dry clothes, but"—she turned and snuggled against him—"in the morning, please, señor."

§ CHAPTER 8 §

In Washington City, William H. Crawford smoked his morning cigar as he pondered Ames's report. The prediction
that the fate of Florida would be settled in the next few weeks
disturbed him. His friend Edward Simms had included a letter
saying the "patriot army is being criticized for not moving
against St. Augustine. Several of our young men who enlisted
have returned to Charleston disgusted with General Mac-
Gregor."

Crawford brooded and decided that prompt action, which
only President Monroe could instigate, was necessary. As Secretary of the Treasury this was hardly his concern, but as temporary Secretary of War it was. Swearing softly, he wished
Monroe would fill the post. The President had been in office
six months and had not found a Secretary of War. Henry Clay
had bluntly refused, Andrew Jackson was not interested and
it was rumored that John C. Calhoun of South Carolina would
resign from Congress and enter the Cabinet. Crawford hoped
this was true, for the country's deplorable financial condition
required his full attention.

Meantime there was the vexing problem of Amelia Island.
Additionally, Crawford felt an obligation to Jonathan Ames
and was proud of him. Here was an opportunity to bring his
service to the attention of the President. Tossing aside his

cigar, he went to his office and made an appointment to see Monroe that afternoon.

Entering the President's office, Crawford was irritated to find the Secretary of State, John Quincy Adams, there. "I invited Mr. Adams," said the tall wrinkled President, "as any action we take might affect his negotiations to buy Florida."

Nodding glumly, Crawford sat down and glared at the short, stout, baldheaded New Englander. He knew Adams had once described him as a "worthless and desperate man, a worm preying on the vitals of the administration." He thought Adams a gloomy misanthrope with his grim, peevish mouth and rheumy eyes, which leaked tears down his cheeks.

"I understand, Mr. President. This morning I received the latest intelligence from Amelia Island. I think it deserves your immediate attention. Jonathan Ames reports that—"

"Who is Jonathan Ames?" interrupted Adams.

Crawford tersely explained that Jonathan Ames was a West Point graduate who, at the request of President Madison, had resigned from the Army and joined MacGregor to keep the United States informed of his Florida campaign.

Snarled Adams, "Why wasn't I told?"

The President said placatingly, "That was my fault, Mr. Adams. I had so many other concerns that I suppose it just slipped my mind." His face became stern. "However, I knew and approved Mr. Madison's plan."

"I understand, Mr. President. This Ames," he questioned Crawford, "is he reliable?"

"Yes. He's a fine young man, completely trustworthy." Crawford ghosted a smile and added, "He's from your part of the country, Mr. Adams. He's from Litchfield, Connecticut."

Adams reached for the report. "Let me see it," he demanded.

The President intervened. "Summarize it for us, Mr. Crawford. It will save time."

Chuckling at Adams' irritation, he said, "Ames is worried at the failure of General MacGregor to mount an attack on St. Augustine. Morale is low, desertions are frequent and the army is more interested in loot than in liberating Florida. This delay will permit General Coppinger at St. Augustine to bring troops from Cuba and counterattack Amelia Island. Ames believes the fate of Florida will be determined in the next few weeks."

"Why does it concern us?" asked Adams. "Let MacGregor stew in his own juice."

"That's all very well, Mr. Adams," said Monroe, "but anything that happens in Florida is of vital interest to the United States. I'd hoped MacGregor would be successful and Florida would be invited to join the Union. We aren't getting anywhere in Madrid. Two years of talk and no agreement in sight. Perhaps this expedition will increase the pressure on Spain to sell or cede us Florida. If we can help in any way, I think we should."

Adams blurted, "You don't mean we should send troops to this, this . . . er . . . adventurer?"

"No, Mr. Adams. Mr. Crawford, at President Madison's instructions, made it very clear to General MacGregor that he could expect no aid from the United States." He paused and glanced at Crawford.

"That's true, Mr. President, but Mr. Madison gave the expedition his unofficial blessing. He believed that the acquisition of Florida is essential to our future security. He felt that any scheme that might accomplish this should be encouraged."

"Those are my feelings, too, Mr. Crawford, as long as we avoid a war with Spain. Have you any suggestions? Or have you, Mr. Adams?"

Both men were silent. Finally Crawford spoke. "If Coppinger retakes Amelia Island there'll be chaos in north Florida. Spain lacks both the force and the will to police the land. Disorders will increase. Even now the Seminoles are constantly raiding south Georgia and Alabama. Homes burned, cattle stolen, crops ravaged and many settlers killed. I'm told the escaped slaves—there must be several thousand in Florida— are rebuilding old Fort Negro on the Apalachicola River."

"Is that the fort that General Gaines destroyed two years ago?" asked Monroe.

"Yes, Mr. President. A lucky shot dropped a hot cannon ball in the fort's powder magazine."

"But where are the Negroes getting supplies, in particular, guns and powder?"

"From the English traders."

Adams said, "That's difficult to believe, Mr. Crawford."

"Not if you understand the English. They have a trade monopoly in Florida and intend to keep it. If we get Florida, Forbes & Company, Arbuthnot and the other English traders will have competition. It will cost 'em plenty, and this always upsets the English. They'll arm the Indians, the slaves, the Spaniards—do most anything to prevent it."

"I see your point," said the President. "I've had many complaints on the lack of law and order in the area. Georgia is your state, Mr. Crawford, what do you recommend?"

Crawford frowned and thought for a minute before speaking. "Mr. President, you have the right and the obligation to protect our settlers. Order General Gaines to patrol the border and smash the raiders. Follow them into their Florida if necessary, burn their villages and camps and rout out and destroy them."

"But that means war with Spain, perhaps England," said Adams.

"I doubt that, Mr. Adams," growled Crawford. "Instruct General Gaines that if they take refuge in a Spanish fort, leave 'em be. The Spanish won't object."

"Why not?" asked the President.

"Spain is far too busy in South America. The revolutionaries are beating her armies in Chile, Peru and Venezuela. Spain is bankrupt after the years of French occupation, not a spare peso in her cupboard. And King Ferdinand, or Ferdinand the witless, as he's known in Europe, is hardly an inspiring leader. He spends most of his time knitting."

"Come now, Mr. Crawford," laughed Monroe.

"Oh yes"—the robust Georgian grinned—"the King is very proud of his skill. He especially likes to knit petticoats."

Monroe chortled and even Adams' thin lips puckered into a wry smile. "Perhaps a king," said the President, "wielding knitting needles isn't too dangerous." He stood up and thanked the cabinet members for their advice and comments and said he would "sleep on it before making a decision."

"Mr. Crawford, if you get any new intelligence from Amelia Island please inform me at once."

"Yes, Mr. President. And, sir, I think young Jonathan Ames should be highly commended."

"Yes indeed. Please express my appreciation to him."

"Perhaps a letter from you . . . ?"

"No, Mr. President," Adams said. "Posts sometimes get lost with most embarrassing results."

"I expect you are right." To Crawford he said, "Do let Ames know we are grateful for his service to his country. When he returns to Washington City, bring him to see me. I'd like to personally thank him."

Crawford said Ames would be pleased.

Georgia's sultry August brought increasing days of confusion to General MacGregor and his Army of Liberation. The soldiers refused to accept "Amelia notes" in payment and so desertions increased. The hesitation and indecision at headquarters seeped down to the men. They were disgruntled and befuddled.

The torrid heat covered Amelia Island like a soggy blanket. Daily thunderstorms with jagged lightning and ear-splitting thunderclaps brought no relief. The men guzzled rum, gossiped and complained. Fistfights were common and two men were killed in a row at dice.

Trading, however, prospered in Fernandina. The harbor was filled with ships. Some were privateers sailing under the Mexican flag; others boastfully acknowledged that they were pirates. Plunder piled high on the long wharf and in the tabby huts facing the Amelia River. Merchants from Savannah, Charleston and even Baltimore and New York bought and asked no questions.

Slave auctions increased. The pirate Jean Lafitte, after aiding Andrew Jackson in his defeat of the British at New

Orleans, became an American citizen. The United States prohibited the importation of slaves. Lafitte decided to obey the law and the thriving slave trade at Barataria moved to Fernandina. Many Negroes were brought direct from Africa. Slaves from Georgia and the Carolinas who had escaped into Florida were captured and sold.

His patience long exhausted, Jared Irwin scornfully abused General MacGregor for not attacking St. Augustine. A visit by the Savannah backers increased the turmoil. Unable to exercise their option to buy land at one dollar an acre, they demanded repayment of their loan. The general fretted, fumed and insisted he needed more ammunition and supplies.

The daily bickering at headquarters disgusted Ames, but the nights were a delight. The young lovers joyously taught each other in the ancient ritual. The frustrations that had been locked in Luiza for the past two years vanished. Young Ames's Puritanism was forgotten with Luiza in his arms. He possessed her with a violence he would not have believed possible. She responded with equal abandon. There was a fury in their love that shook them deeply.

When Ames attempted to talk about the future Luiza would curl her beautiful body against him, her hair cascading over his chest and close his lips with her long slender fingers.

Her husband was in St. Augustine. One day he would return and she would go with him to Havana. As a good Catholic she had no choice. I'll probably roast in hell for my sins, she thought; as a loyal Spaniard, taught to despise Americans, I'll suffer triple torture, but come what may I'll never forget or regret. She sighed and murmured, "Jonathan, don't be remorseful. We slake our thirst at the same fountain."

At times her straightforwardness embarrassed him. His Puritan scruples continued to harass and torment, but he found this sensuous, ingenious girl fascinating. He knew he was living in a fool's paradise. The thought made him despondent. As though she sensed his confusion, Luiza said, "Love comes unbidden and without permission." She turned in his arms, dug her fingers into his back and whispered fiercely, "Love me!"

General Gregor MacGregor summoned his officers to a special staff meeting. Eyes flashing, his handsome face distorted with rage, he waved a Charleston *Courier* at the assembled men. In a furious voice he read:

> "We have received several letters from St. Marys and Amelia Island which confirm the verbal accounts received here a few days since, that the prospects of the patriots were by no means so flattering as at first represented. Had MacGregor pushed for St. Augustine immediately on his landing, while the Spaniards were panic stricken and flying before him, he might have gained possession of the fortress, but he has lost that opportunity by his delay. His followers have become dissatisfied while inhabitants of Florida are taking alarm from the misconduct of his outposts. The planters are petitioning the American government on that frontier to take their negroes into our territory for safe-keeping."

He crumpled the *Courier* and tossed it to the floor. Glaring at his officers, he roared, "God's blood, gentlemen, we have traitors in our ranks. Beastly wretches sending dispatches to a newspaper. By God, sirs, heads will tumble. I demand a full investigation. The guilty will be shot."

The words tumbled forth in a senseless flow as his fury mounted. "Now, General," interjected Irwin, "no point in getting your dander up. That paper spoke the truth. Just what we've been telling you the past few weeks."

"Gad, sir, I am a professional soldier. A trained British officer. I'll not be dictated to by newspaper scribblers. I refuse to risk my army without proper intelligence."

Irwin grunted and in his nasal tone said, "Soon you'll have no army to risk."

"We will march on St. Augustine as soon as possible."

Irwin spat, "When is that?"

"When the troops are ready."

"They've been ready for weeks, but it's nigh on to a hundred miles of wild rough country between here and St. Augustine—what about victuals, ammunition and such?"

MacGregor gave him a withering smile and unfolded a map of Florida. In the measured voice of the trained soldier he said, "We'll divide our forces and attack from two sides. Colonel Irwin, lead your regiments down the St. Johns River to Fort Picolta, then march overland toward St. Augustine. I will march due south on the old King's Road. We rendezvous here at Fort Moosa." He indicated a spot on the map very near St. Augustine. "It's only two miles from the city's walls. A determined two-pronged assault will deceive General Coppinger as to our strength."

Once again Ames was impressed with MacGregor's planning. His officers' approval showed on their faces. They were ready, eager for action.

"But first, gentlemen, I must have the latest intelligence from St. Augustine. Colonel Ames, you are a trained observer. That blackamoor of yours knows the country. Scout the fort, its strength and weakness and especially the size of its garrison."

"Yes, sir," said Ames.

"Then we sit here at Amelia for another week?" scornfully asked Irwin.

"No. We march at dawn. Colonel Ames, report to me at the King's Road crossing of the St. Johns River. Your best estimate of the time required to get this information is . . . ?"

"If we take a fishing vessel, land a few miles north of St. Augustine, it shouldn't take more than three days, maybe four at the most." Ames paused for a moment. "That's provided we don't get caught by the Spaniards."

"Then don't. That's an order," said MacGregor. He walked over to Ames and extended his hand. "God be with you."

"Thank you, sir," replied Ames.

Ames found Wash and described their mission. The big Negro nodded, said he would find a boat and be ready to sail within the hour. Ames went to Luiza's house but she was not there. Probably riding, he guessed, and left a brief note. Explanations were unnecessary as Luiza would soon learn of the decision to attack St. Augustine.

He walked rapidly to the docks at Egan's Creek. Wash had discovered a small, light sloop that two men could handle. He had stocked her with food and water and told Ames he was ready to "up anchor." With Ames at the tiller Wash raised the jib, then the mainsail on their single-masted vessel. A spanking breeze moved them southward at better than ten knots.

After studying a rough map of Florida's coastline, which he had obtained from the *Bolivar*'s sailing master, Ames said, "If this wind holds we should be near St. Augustine by daybreak."

Squinting at a low bank of clouds about twenty miles off the port bow, Wash said, "I don't care fer the looks o' the sky. Might be in fer a blow."

"Oh, I don't think so," said Ames.

Wash scratched his head and laughed. "Hope you's right. Anyhow, too early fer a big hurricane. They come in September."

"That's good. Now here are my plans. We'll sail up the St. Marks River, which is only a couple of miles north of St. Augustine, and hide the boat. Then we'll scout the approaches to the fort and try to sneak into the town late at night."

"Naw, sah. I'll go into St. Augustine. You stay hid."

"But, Wash, I have my orders."

"I knows, but you get caught and them Spaniards cepo you."

"Cepo? What's that?"

"Captain Laurent say dons is wicked folks. Throw a line over a limb and hang you up dare by your balls. He say hanging by the neck is less painful."

Laughing, Ames commented, "I don't want to be hung at all."

"I'll go alone. Don't think anyone mess wid me." He flexed his huge arms. "Dey better not."

"Wash, no fighting now."

"Yas, sah."

"Have you your freedom papers?"

He pulled a leather pouch from beneath his cotton shirt. "Keep 'em wid me all de time."

"That's good. There are lots of free blacks in St. Augustine. If anyone questions you just show 'em your papers and say you are looking for a job."

"Yas, sah. Now what you wanna know about St. Augustine?"

"If the garrison has been reinforced by troops from Havana. The strength of the fort—the thickness and height of the walls, the condition of their cannon, how many entrances and can they be breached? Also how the people feel toward the Spaniards. Are the Seminoles friendly? Any English ships in the harbor? Get all the information you can."

"Yas, sah." A sudden freshening of the wind sent a whitecap over the sloop's bow.

"Better shorten sail," said Ames.

Wash looked at the angry sky, a dull gray streaked with yellow and orange. Pointing to the shore, he said, "Make fer that little salt-water creek." His voice was shrill above the rising wind and his placid black face showed signs of terror. Ames spoke soothingly. "Just a little wind, Wash. Nothing to worry about."

Wash managed a grim smile. "I don't swim so well and I'se scared of being drowned. Hates the idea of all them little fishes 'er nibblin' on me."

Ames swung the tiller hard and headed directly for the creek, which he could now see just beyond a grove of mango trees. "We'll feed no fishes today, Wash. Soon as we get into the creek, drop anchor."

"Can't do that, she'll drag and pound to bits on the shore. There's a little beach just beyond the cove. Head for it and I'll pull her ashore."

Ames steered the sloop into the breakers. Wash leaped into the raging surf, stumbled and recovered his footing in the waist-deep water. He jerked the anchor from the bow and tossed it ashore. Grabbing the anchor chain with both hands, Wash dragged the sloop up the beach. Ames dropped the tiller and pushed frantically with a ten-foot pole. He jumped into the water and heaved. Somehow they managed to get their little craft onto the sand. They careened it. Wash jerked the jib from the mast and spread it over them. It was just in time.

The rain gushed from a rolling, heaving mass of black clouds. Marble-sized drops beat a steady tattoo on the sloop's bottom. It was midnight dark though only late afternoon. Flashes of lightning followed each roaring thunderbolt. The high wind swept the shallow water over the low-lying land. Ames and Wash clung desperately to their sloop, digging their feet into the soft sand. For a minute Ames thought they would feed the fishes. But suddenly the wind abated, the rain stopped and within half an hour blue sky appeared again.

"We'd better camp here tonight and push ahead at first dawn," said Wash. Ames agreed and asked if they could risk a fire. He was cold, hungry and wanted to dry his clothes.

"Ain't too much danger. I'll git some dry wood." Suddenly the twilight was shaken by a hideous bellow. "Just ole bull alligator," said Wash and scrambled up the beach. "We'se landed on a small island. Big swamp just over de ridge. You safe here, just stay close to de boat. I'll go find some wood."

"All right," said Ames. "I'll get the kettle ready for coffee." He watched the big Negro walk down the shoreline and felt a sense of terror. New noises blended with the din of the bellowing alligator—a chorus of bullfrogs, the squawk of wild birds, a panther screaming and the howl of wolves a long distance away. Ames carefully loaded his two pistols, his rifle and waited.

Wash found plenty of driftwood but no dry grass or fronds that would catch fire from sparks of flint and steel. Several hundred yards down the beach he saw a four-hundred-pound turtle scooping sand from beneath her body. In less than twenty minutes she would lay dozens of soft-skinned eggs, the size of wizened apples. The heat of the sun would hatch the eggs and the young ones would scratch their way out of the sand and return to the sea. Wash disliked turtle eggs, for the whites would never firm, remaining a soft mass, regardless of how long they were cooked. Turtle meat would be a delight after their diet of salt meat and fish. He knew a turtle could not bite beyond the reach of the forelegs and was helpless when flipped on its back.

The sloop's long push pole was just what he needed to overturn the great turtle. Approaching their camp site, he heard Ames shout "sooey pig—sooey." He ran forward and saw him flapping his wet shirt at a gray, bristling, humpbacked pig. The big porker grunted, squealed and its reddish eyes glittered behind its bloodstained, razor-sharp tusks. It was a wild boar, descendant of the swine brought into Florida centuries ago by the Spaniards. Far more vicious than the bear, wildcat or even an alligator, the four-tusked boar had been known to attack men on horseback, killing both the rider and his steed.

Ames continued to wave his shirt, urging the beast to go away. He was unaware of his danger, thinking of the pigs he had fed slop in Connecticut. The big boar pawed the mucky ground and charged. Ames dodged behind the sloop's hull. Grabbing the ten-foot push pole, Wash slapped at the boar's stumpy legs. The ferocious beast turned on Wash, who nimbly skipped aside and smacked its ugly snout.

Fumbling with the pistols at his belt, Ames drew one and pulled back the hammer.

"Don't shoot," called Wash. "Them little old shots only rile him up. Won't kill him." He smashed the boar with the heavy pole and jumped high over its charge. He circled, swung his club in a great arc and mauled the boar's forelegs. It screamed and rushed at Wash, who scrambled up the sand dune.

Ames dropped his pistol, got his rifle and waited, not daring a shot for fear of hitting Wash.

Slowed by the heavy sand, the raging beast charged. The enormous black man, gripping his club like a quarterstaff, cracked one of the boar's forelegs. It squealed and limped toward its tormentor.

Ames triggered his rifle but Wash came into his sight as he backed down the sand dune holding his cudgel ready. The boar snorted and followed. Suddenly Wash leaped over the beast, clouted its rump with a sledge-hammer blow, knocking it into the black swamp water. The shrieking pig thrashed toward shore. A great bull alligator lashed the wounded animal with its giant tail. A second gator crushed the porker's rear leg in its powerful jaws. The boar screamed once, rolled over and the alligators tore and ripped his carcass. A wide smear of blood stained the dark swamp water.

"My God," said Ames, as he wiped his sweaty face, "what a country!"

"Ole gators," laughed Wash. "Think a nice fat pig the best supper there is. Don't reckon you ever saw such a ornery critter."

"No," admitted Ames. "In Connecticut pigs were fat, lazy and harmless."

"Bout the same in Charleston, but them ole wild hogs git powerful mean. Hunted 'em with my old massa on Hiltonhead Island. One boar kilt five dogs and a horse 'afore we got him."

Shuddering at the thought of those bloody tusks, Ames thanked Wash. Embarrassed, Wash said, "Come along and help me kill big sea turtle. Mighty fine eatin' and we have a good supper, too."

At dawn Ames crawled from under the sloop, yawned and pulled on his wet boots. Waving his big index finger over his lips, Wash whispered, "Just heard a hoot owl call couple 'er times."

Noticing Ames's frown, he explained, "It wont no owl but an injun. Seminole probably."

"How do you know?"

"I just knows. Injuns mighty good at bird calls. I knowed one could call a covey 'er quail out of the broom sedge. But they just don't git owl so good. Last hoot kinda out 'er tune."

Ames nodded and suggested breakfast.

"Yas, sah, but no fire. Can't tell if 'em injuns friendly."

The two men silently munched cold turtle and watched a red sun rise over the swaying marsh grasses. It would be another hot and hazy day. Once again came the ominous sound of a hoot owl.

"Colonel, sah," said Wash, getting to his feet, "let's git." Ames nodded and helped push the sloop into the salt-water creek. Standing erect in the stern, Wash poled their light craft downstream into the ocean. He raised the mainsail, adjusted the jib and Ames steered their boat southward. A brisk wind howled them along at ten knots or more. Wash pointed off the starboard bow. "Must be St. Johns River."

Ames saw a broad tidal stream flowing into the Atlantic and knew from its size that it was the St. Johns. He snapped open a small silver watch. It was seven o'clock. He said, "If the breeze holds we'll be close to St. Augustine in the early afternoon."

"I reckon," said Wash. He pulled a coiled fishing line from a locker, baited the hook and tossed it over the stern. He let out two hundred feet and tied it securely to a davit. Watching, Ames asked why.

"Sah, when I gits to St. Augustine I'd like to have a nice string 'er fish to sell. I'll just walk around cryin' 'nice fresh fish' and no one pay me any mind. Most harmless thing there is, is a fish peddler."

"Maybe, Wash, but I've been thinking. I can't let you go into St. Augustine. It's my job."

Looking stubborn, Wash replied, "No sah . . ."

"But, Wash, I'm sure I can—"

"No sah," interrupted the Negro. "Them Spaniards shore will kill you."

"They won't catch me. I'll sneak over the wall at midnight and—"

Wash shook his head and interrupted again. "Colonel," he said with a persuasive smile, "you is being downright foolish. Besides, I promised that nice Spanish lady I'd look after you. What good you be to her without your balls?" His laughter was contagious and Ames found himself chuckling.

Wash shouted, "I gotta fish!" He pulled in the hand line and a five-pound red snapper flopped on the deck. "'Bout six more like him and I'se ready fer business." He baited his hook and threw it into the sea. "When we lands I wanna pay a little visit to Fort Moosa. Lots 'er black folks live there. Might even find a cousin or two."

"All right, Wash," replied Jonathan, remembering Mr. Simms had once told him in Charleston—"Never argue with a nigger, for you always lose." Anyhow he felt better for the effort. The idea of scouting St. Augustine frightened him and the thought of "cepo" was terrifying.

The breeze slackened and it was midafternoon before they tacked up the St. Marks. Wash lowered the mainsail and poled their sloop under a clump of overhanging muscadine vines. He whacked palmetto and white oak branches and covered their small boat.

"You safe here, sah, but stay in de boat." He jumped ashore, scaled and gutted his fish, three large snappers and a dozen or more sheepheads and croakers. Wrapping them carefully in a twined basket of wild grape leaves, he grinned. "White folks lazy, hate to clean fish. Git a better price fer 'em this way anyhow." He declined the offer of a pistol, saying, "Poor fisherman never have fancy gun like dat." Picking up his machete, he walked toward Fort Moosa.

As long as he could remember he had heard stories about Fort Moosa, or the black fort, as it was called in Charleston. In their quarters at night the slaves talked endlessly about the freedom land of Negrito. Here, under their own king, escaped slaves from Georgia and the Carolinas lived happily under Spanish protection.

Wash wondered how much of this was really true. He had learned much about white men and their ways in the past few months. Despite General MacGregor's promises of freedom, the Negroes liberated in Florida were auctioned to American slave traders.

Wash was the only Negro in the Army and he was considered a curiosity—"That Yankee colonel's pet nigger." He was liked by the men, as he was cheerful, polite and always willing to do a favor, but he was not accepted. Were the Spanish different? Would they treat the Negroes at Fort Moosa as equals? His former master, Colonel Stovall, claimed they were "far worse off than slaves." The Spaniards had no responsibility for feeding or clothing them and when labor was needed they were dragooned into service. Well, he would soon find out.

As he walked through the knee-high palmettos, now brown and scorched by the long summer, the angry whirring of a rattlesnake interrupted his thought. The ugly reptile coiled to strike but a quick swipe of the machete severed its head.

Suddenly he heard children crying and dogs barking. He must be near Fort Moosa. He quickened his pace and through the scrub pine loomed high tabby walls. He creeped to the main gate but saw no one. Inside there was the sound of laughter, the crack of leather striking flesh and hoarse cries of anguish. He peeked around the corner. A Spanish officer in a sweat-stained red and yellow tunic counted as two swarthy soldiers flogged a young mulatto. He screamed each time the leather thongs crossed his bloody back. Horrified and without thinking, Wash stepped into the courtyard.

The Spanish captain turned and saw a magnificent Negro barefooted and in mud-stained trousers. Drawing his gleaming sword, he asked, "Who are you?"

"Just a poor fisherman, General, sah." He knew the officer's rank but had found flattery effective in dealing with whites. Aware now of his danger, Wash spoke in the patois of the street vendor. "Nice fresh fish, sah. Cleaned, gutted and scaled. Cheap, sah, real cheap. Look." Kneeling, he removed the grape leaves, revealing his catch.

Ignoring the fish, the Spaniard pointed his sword. "Where do you live?"

"Up St. Marks River, sah."

"Why haven't you reported to Castle of Santa Maria?"

"Sah, I'se just poor fisherman."

The Spaniard snorted. "Governor Coppinger needs porters for his troops. All able-bodied men in the district were told to report to the castle. This scum"—he pointed to the crumpled mulatto—"refused. You look strong as a mule. Carry him to the castle," he ordered Wash. "He'll hang for this," he added.

"General, sah," protested Wash, "I'se just er—"

"That's an order," snapped the officer to one of the soldiers. "Give him a taste of the cat—that'll quicken his understanding."

The soldier snapped the rawhide, ripping and searing Wash's chest. A second blow nicked his cheek and he became an enraged animal. He kicked aside his fish and picked up his hidden machete. The ten-foot coil snapped around his wrist.

The machete clattered to the crushed stone. A blow from the second whip split his forehead, narrowly missing his eye. Half blinded with blood, he charged. Before the man could strike again Wash grabbed him by his broad leather belt. He lifted him high and flung him at the captain, who had rushed forward with a cocked pistol. The gun exploded harmlessly as the two men fell.

Wash turned on the other soldier. One glance at the snarling, bleeding Negro sent him racing in the direction of St. Augustine. The officer scrambled to his feet and picked up his sword. Wash dodged a wicked thrust, circled, grabbed his wrist, twisted and the bone snapped. He gave a short agonized scream and fainted. Still groggy, the soldier staggered to his feet. A clubbed right to his jaw sent him reeling, unconscious.

Picking up the young mulatto, Wash muttered, "I'd best get out of here quick." He had gone less than one hundred yards from Fort Moosa when he was surrounded by a group of young women and children. They jabbered excitedly in a tongue Wash did not understand, and motioned to the man in his arms. He nodded and gently placed him on the ground. One woman gave him water from a leather bag, another briskly rubbed his open wounds with a thick black grease.

A boy spoke in halting English. "We saw. We humbly and graciously thank you. That my brother Pedro." His admiring eyes swept over Wash's huge frame. "Big, big, mighty big man. Beat soldier good." Grinning, he bowed low and extended his hand.

Wash enclosed it in one great fist and patted the twelve-year-old on the shoulder. He heard a low cry, turned and saw Pedro sitting up and sipping rum. He smiled and offered Wash a drink, who refused. Two women pushed him to Pedro's side and began to wash and clean his wounds. They rubbed in the greasy salve. It staunched the flow of blood and he felt better. "Thank you," he said, and asked Pedro what happened.

The handsome brown-skinned man sipped more rum, his eyes brightened and in a husky voice he said, "You just in time. A few more licks 'n' those soldiers would have killed me. Can't thank you enough. Who are you? Where you come from?"

Wash ignored the question. "Why they beat you?"

"I didn't want to serve the Army and go with 'em to fight the American slavers at Fernandina." He took another swig of rum and explained. "I lives in St. Augustine, looks after Mr. Sullivan's horses. I'se in Fort Moosa seeing my family. All the men run 'n' hide in the swamps when the soldiers come. They only find me, and when I tells them where I work and can't go with the Army they gives me the cat. That Captain Lopez mean, vicious fellow. Did you kill him?"

"No, just busted his wrist. Ain't Fort Moosa under Spanish protection?"

"They don't bother us much in peacetime, but now things is different. Governor Coppinger mighty worried when the Americans captured Fernandina. Most folks thought they'd come right down to St. Augustine, but now it's too late."

"Why?"

"Five hundred of the Royal Cuban Guards landed on Monday. Governor Coppinger say he gonna run all 'em rascals out 'er Florida. Expect he will send his army north in next day or so."

"How big is it?"

"Besides them Cubans, a couple of hundred Florida militia rode into St. Augustine the past week. I hears they don't like Americans at Fernandina, as they takes cattle, crops and things and pays fer it with no-account paper money. That gives him 'bout seven hundred men."

"St. Augustine strong place, ain't it?"

"Oh yes. It got twelve-foot-thick walls made 'er tabby. A creek, or moat, as them Spaniards calls it, surround the fort and there's two doorways with drawbridges. Insides there's plenty of fresh water from three drinking wells. My boss man say St. Augustine safe from any land attack. Gunboats coming up the Mantazar River into harbor the only way to take St. Augustine."

Noticing Pedro's voice weakening, Wash thanked him for the information, refused offers of food and drink, said goodbye and loped toward the river.

When he reached the sloop Ames noticed his slash marks and asked what had happened.

"Just a little fuss," replied Wash. "Now let's go—and fast."

The two men slid their small boat into the St. Marks River and Wash poled it swiftly downstream. He raised the mainsail, adjusted the jib and, with Ames at the tiller, set the sloop on its northbound course.

Wash told of his "little fuss" with the soldiers and described in some detail the strength of the fort in St. Augustine. "Now that Governor Coppinger has been reinforced with the Royal Cuban Guards, he's gonna march north, retake Fort San Carlos and chase General MacGregor's men back to Georgia," he added.

This was bad news indeed, thought Ames. How would General MacGregor react? Would he attack Coppinger's larger force or retreat? Perhaps he would ambush the Spaniards as they marched north?

Scores of ideas went through his mind as they sailed toward their rendezvous with MacGregor. If this wind holds we'll reach the St. Johns River by noon tomorrow. Then I'll report the facts and the general can decide.

§ CHAPTER 9 §

Their small sloop, her last bit of canvas belling, sailed up the broad tidal river at sunset. Consulting his watch, Ames reckoned they had logged the thirty miles from St. Augustine to the St. Johns River in record time. He motioned to Wash to shorten sail and straighten his tiller while he watched for the Army of Liberation. A gull cried in the blue stillness of the afternoon, a raccoon eyed them curiously and disappeared in the pine barrens and two graceful white herons stalked fish in the muddy shallows. There was no sign of General MacGregor's army.

Ames shaded his eyes and saw a small hill jutting above the green sweep of palmettos. He swung his tiller starboard and held his course until the sloop's bowsprit crashed into the dense marsh grass that fringed the bank. Wash deftly dropped the mainsail and picked up the heavy push pole. In a puzzled voice he asked, "What we do now?"

"I thought I saw a tent near the top of that mound," said Ames.

"You did," answered a laughing voice from the shore. It was Captain Laurent. "I wanted to be sure it was you before I spoke."

"What in hell?" said the astonished officer. "Where is the army?"

"In Fernandina, I expect."

"But why?"

"It's a long story. Come along and I'll explain over a glass of wine." In some mysterious way the Frenchman always managed to have a bottle of wine. For him it was the panacea for all problems and Ames knew from past experience that explanations would come at Laurent's pleasure. The two men followed him up a sudden path to the dry ground of the crumbling hillock.

"Was this an old fort?"

"Yes, Jonathan. It's the site of Jean Ribault's Fort Caroline. He tried to establish a Huguenot colony here some two hundred years ago."

Ames inspected the ruins, realized the ramparts were hand dug where wooden barricades had long ago crumbled into dust. "What happened?"

"The Spanish objected. The New World belonged to them by papal decree. The French were considered both pirates and heretics and were righteously put to the sword. Several hundred men, women and children were massacred. A few escaped and went home. It ended the attempt of France to colonize Florida and the Carolinas." He glanced at the serene river and murmured, *"Le Fleuve de Mai*—the River of May is what Jean Ribault named it. Suits it better than St. Johns, don't you think?"

"Perhaps." Impatiently he asked again, "What happened to General MacGregor?"

Laurent deliberately opened a bottle of claret, sniffed and said, "Drinkable but not delectable." He ordered the two soldiers with him to build a fire and fix supper. He gave Ames a pewter mug and sloshed in a large dollop of the ruby liquid.

"Your good health, my young American friend. Wine should only be served in crystal glass. No bouquet or flavor in these."

"Tastes fine to me," said Ames. "But for God's sake, Charles, get on with it!"

The Frenchman spread a large blanket near the trunk of a

white oak tree. "Come sit, relax, for we can't return to Fernandina tonight."

"Return?" said Ames. "Don't we move on St. Augustine?"

"I don't know. I was told to come here, find you and bring you back to Fernandina. I might add that there's much talk and confusion at headquarters." Sipping the wine, he added, "Ah, this is delicious for a young wine."

"Damnit, man," raged Jonathan, "facts, Charles, facts. No more fancy words."

"Patience, my young Puritan. Patience. The morning after you left the former high sheriff of New York City, Ruggles Hubbard, arrived in the brig *Moriana*. He's a big blustery Yankee, blows his nose like a foghorn, talks constantly but says little. MacGregor expected him to bring money, additional supplies and ammunition. He didn't. The woolgathering Scotsman howled he had been deserted and double-crossed and refused to order the army to march. Said he would return to South America, where Simon Bolivar appreciated his genius." He grinned sardonically and drank his wine.

Ames frowned and spoke in an anguished voice. "I wonder what the general will do when he gets my report on St. Augustine." Charles listened carefully as he gave a brief summary of the Spanish forces.

"You are saying that the dons outnumber us about five to one?"

"I expect so."

"Then MacGregor won't fight. He's always wanted the odds in his favor. Expect he'll work out a trade with the Spaniards or go back to Bolivar." He thought for a second and added, "But Irwin will fight."

"Do you think so?"

"Yes, he has no choice. He must hold East Florida for his backers or go home a beggar. And America does not welcome beggars." He scowled and said bitterly, "I know."

The two men were quiet for a time, drinking wine and pondering. Finally, Laurent asked, "When will Coppinger move?"

"Soon. Next day or two I expect."

"By sea?"

"Yes. He has the troopships from Havana. This way he can get his army to Amelia Island in three or four days. By land it would take weeks."

Charles drained his mug. "No more wine. Let's have supper, such as it is. We'll sail with the morning tide. I'll go with you. My boat leaks."

Ames agreed.

Chuckling, Charles added, "Can't wait to see the strutter's face when you tell him about that Cuban regiment."

As they swept into Amelia harbor, Jonathan counted five ships anchored near the *Bolivar*, which he noted was stripped for action. Perhaps MacGregor means to fight after all. The other privateers, their colors as varied as their flags, swung peacefully at their berths.

Landing at Long Wharf, the two officers climbed the bluff to the town above. Most of the houses along the *prado* were shuttered. Fernandina, wise in the ways of filibusters, had fled to the mainland. Perhaps they knew of Coppinger's plan. A mysterious grapevine seemed to bring them news faster than the military got intelligence. Certainly they knew the Army of Liberation, weakened by desertion, had little brawn.

They entered the wooden portcullis of Fort San Carlos and marched across the sandy courtyard. The green crossed flag of new Florida whipped in the breeze. There were no sentries and only a few ragged men lolling on the sand. One said "Howdy" and told them the general was in the watchtower. They climbed the ancient wooden steps to the ramparts and entered a small room. A man in faded blue, his face to the sea, peered through a tarnished telescope. He turned on his spindly booted legs and barked a welcome.

Surprised, Ames asked, "Where is General MacGregor?"

"The general, his staff and that plump pretty wife of his vanished during the night. I'm in charge."

"Ah, General Irwin is it?" Charles grinned.

He fixed Laurent with his pale fish eyes. "That's right, Captain, and I'll have no nonsense from you."

Ames said, "My congratulations, sir."

"Don't be sarcastic, Colonel Ames."

"Sorry, General, but may I ask what happened to Mac-Gregor?"

"He's gone. He expected money and ammunition from Sheriff Hubbard. He didn't get 'em and was in a tantrum. Late last night he told me he was shipping out for Nassau, felt he could recruit British soldiers there and maybe raise some money. General said his army just wasn't strong enough to assault St. Augustine. He was one disappointed man. I kinda felt sorry for him."

"Do you think he will return?" asked Laurent.

"If he can round up support he'll be back. He did leave the *Bolivar* and headed for Nassau on a fishing schooner. Damned shame." He paused and in a compassionate voice added, "Poor fellow with his dreams of glory. He was so sure Florida would rally to his cause of liberty. If he'd only attacked instead of writing all them fancy proclamations." He chuckled softly. "Guess you might say he was kinda weighted down with his own rhetoric. . . . Now what's the news from St. Augustine, Jonathan?"

"Bad," he answered and gave a brief summary.

"I ain't surprised," said Irwin. "Coppinger fought with Wellington on the Peninsula. He's no milksop like Morales. I reckon we have four, maybe five, days to prepare a welcome for the dons." He glanced at Ames, who nodded in confirmation.

"Then we fight?" asked Laurent.

"We do," he answered scornfully. "I ain't impressed with them Cuban Guards and their fancy uniforms. Won't stop a bullet any better than homespun."

A tattered soldier poked his head in the door and said, "There's a Spaniard here with a message from Governor Coppinger."

"Ah," said Irwin. "Send him in."

A thin man, immaculate in black broadcloth and silver-buckled shoes, entered. He stroked his graying beard and

(148)

looked distastefully at the three men. Ames and Laurent were mud spattered and filthy from their night on the St. Johns.

The Spaniard bowed stiffly. "Don José Gonzalez, official emissary of His Excellency Governor Coppinger." He paused and when no one spoke he said, "Which of you is General Irwin?"

"I am," replied Jared Irwin.

"I assume you are in command since MacGregor fled?"

"Sir," bristled Irwin, "state your business."

"I bring you peace terms from Governor Coppinger." He sniffed at Ames and Laurent. "I prefer to discuss this alone."

"Colonel Ames and Captain Laurent are on my staff. I have no secrets from them."

"As you wish." He paused and squinted at Ames. His lean face was ugly. "Are you the young American who befriended my wife?"

"Yes, I am."

"I'm indebted, sir," he said coldly.

"It was my pleasure," replied Ames. Laurent smirked and a slight flush crept over the Spaniard's narrow face.

"If I personally can be of service, do not hesitate to call on me. But I prefer you not to see Doña Luiza again."

Before Ames could reply Irwin snapped, "Time's a-wastin'—what's Coppinger's offer?"

He tapped his buckled shoes, which had been built up to give him added height. "Governor Coppinger requires your immediate surrender."

"Does he now!" said Irwin.

"But on most generous terms . . ."

"Yeah?"

"You will be allowed to sail on the *Bolivar* with all your men and their personal possessions. I'm sure the *Bolivar* will hold what's left of your army of liberation," he added sarcastically.

"Ain't interested!"

"Additionally," added Gonzalez, "I'm instructed by several St. Augustine merchants to offer you ten thousand pesos to be paid when the Spanish flag flies over Fort San Carlos again."

"Ten thousand pesos . . ." mused Irwin. "What's that in real money—dollars?"

"About the same. We'll give you dollars if you prefer."

"I do," he chuckled. "That's a mighty reasonable bribe."

"Let's say it is just compensation for any embarrassment you might suffer from a quick departure."

Irwin laughed and scratched his head. Ames realized he was teasing the Spaniard and for the first time he was impressed with Jared Irwin. He might resemble a clerk, but Ames liked his dogged courage and his broad humor.

"As I said, that's a reasonable offer but I can't accept."

"What?" said Gonzalez. "You can't be serious."

"You heard me. . . . No."

His small birdlike eyes glittered. "Governor Coppinger warns he will be merciless if you refuse. He'll put you and your filibusters to the gallows."

"Mebbe Coppinger is counting his chickens before they are hatched. He ain't in Fernandina yet."

Gonzalez controlled his anger and spoke like a courtroom lawyer. "General Irwin, I know you have less than a hundred men. How can you expect to oppose our superior forces? Five hundred Royal Cuban Guards and a crack militia company. It's absurd sir . . . idiotic!"

"Mebbe, but it's my choice. . . . Captain Laurent?"

"Yes, sir."

"Chuck this arrogant dandy in one of them dungeons. Can't have him wandering around Fernandina. He might get into mischief."

"I protest, sir. I'm here as the legal representative of the governor of Florida. I demand the normal courtesies of war."

"You Spaniards shore take the cake. One minute you call us filibusters, the next you is talking about courtesies."

"You must allow me, sir, to report your rejection of the governor's terms."

"Coppinger will know soon enough. Jonathan, you and Laurent spread the word we ain't quittin' but gonna fight. News gits back to St. Augustine mighty quick."

His ugly face contorted with rage, Gonzalez shouted, "I'll have you on the rack."

"Ain't gonna hurt you, little man," said Irwin. "If Coppinger wins you got no worries. If we beat him I'll send you and your wife to St. Augustine."

"General Irwin, I appeal to you as a gentleman, Fernandina under siege won't be safe for a lady."

"We don't make war on women. Besides," he chuckled, "I'll order Colonel Ames to keep an eye on her." His voice was hard again. "And you, you insolent bastard, can cool your heels in a dungeon. Take him away, Captain Laurent."

"It's a pleasure, sir," replied the Frenchman as he none too gently pushed the Spaniard down the rampart steps.

Turning to Jonathan, the general said, "Go home, young man. This ruckus no longer concerns you."

"But, sir," said the surprised officer, "that would be desertion."

"By God, Jonathan, be sensible. This ain't no army of liberation. That Spaniard was right about us being filibusters—pirates if you like. Go back to Washington and rejoin the Army. They need trained officers and your experience here should be useful. Never understood how a nice young fellow like you got mixed up with MacGregor."

This was sound advice and Jonathan knew it. His mission was complete. Yet he hesitated. Would Irwin, despite the odds, defeat the Spaniards? He had a strange confidence in the old Revolutionary soldier. And there was Luiza. He walked to the ramparts and tried to sort out his thoughts about her. Was this a touch of midsummer madness? Was he just being silly? I can't leave her in this hellhole. I must get her to safety.

Irwin walked up to him, patted his shoulder and said gently, "It ain't that Spanish hussy, is it?"

"Sir, I resent that."

"Sorry, boy. I'm just fond of you. I'll admit she's mighty pretty and I suppose she's your first, eh?"

Flushed, Jonathan stuttered, "Sir, I don't—"

"Easy, Jonathan," interrupted Irwin. "I'll get you into

Georgia in a few hours." He squared his shoulders and in a hard voice said, "Colonel Ames, do you go or do you stay?"

"I'll stay, sir. And I'll fight."

Smiling sadly, Irwin said, "I shore need all the help I can git."

Captain Laurent returned to the ramparts. "I don't understand Spanish very well but that don said some hard things about us. Just for that I put him into one of the lower cells. It gets about a foot of water in high tides."

Irwin grunted. "Better than he deserves. If Coppinger catches us we'll end up in Cuba in the dungeons of Fort Morro. Expect they'll put me in the cave of the lowering knife."

"What's that?" asked Laurent.

"The dons are experts in torture. Knew a sea captain out 'er Baltimore that often traded in Havana. He claims in this cave a man is chained to the floor, a heavy iron blade suspended over him. It's lowered by the tides. Takes about four tides to kill a man, but most of 'em go crazy fore the knife strikes."

"*Mon Dieu*," spluttered the Frenchman. "Even more cruel than cepo."

"Well, gentlemen, if we expect to keep our balls there is much work to be done. . . . Captain Laurent?"

"Yes, General Irwin." Ames thought he detected a new respect in his voice.

"Can't have this lovesick ninny on my hands. Better get rid of the trouble."

"Ah, remove the *femme fatale?*" said Laurent as Ames blushed.

"Exactly." He scribbled a brief note. "Find that big black, Wash, and have him escort Señora Gonzalez to St. Marys. Use force if necessary, but git her out 'er Fernandina. This is a letter to Georgia friends of mine. They'll take care of her."

Laurent saluted and trotted down the rampart steps.

"Even all the fancy ladies on Pasco de Damas have gone to Georgia. Don't want your gal to get hurt, do you?"

"No, sir." He was irked that he would not see Luiza but was

glad she would be safe. Irwin's sharp voice cut across his musings. "Colonel Ames?"

"Yes, sir."

"Go aboard the *Bolivar*, get the ship's carpenter, any additional help you need, and fix me about fifty Congreve rockets."

Ames looked puzzled and Irwin said, "Don't they teach you nothing practical at West Point? Never heard of the Congreve rocket?"

"No, sir."

"We damned near lost Baltimore to the British on account of those rockets. Don't do much damage but they scared hell out 'er the militia. I was in Fort McHenry and watched 'em half the night. Ever hear that song 'bout 'watching fer the flag through the rockets' red glare'?"

"Oh yes, we sang it sometimes in barracks. 'Oh say, can you see, by the dawn's early light . . .'"

"Yup, that's it. But we got no time fer singing. Them rockets, invented by a British artillery officer by the name of William Congreve, is easy to make. Just get some metal tubes, fill 'em with powder and cap 'em with a warhead. Then tell the carpenter to build half a dozen bombarding frames. Rockets are mighty unpredictable. Sometimes they go up in the air, sometimes on the ground. If you ain't ever seen one they're terrifying as they whiz by."

"Then you have a battle plan?"

"Yes. Come to my quarters tonight and we'll talk it over. You can get on them rockets, make 'em about ten-pounders. I gotta talk with the men. Get 'em in a fighting mood. They ain't done nothing the last month but drink rum and complain."

"You think they'll fight?"

"Yep. They think I'm a greedy Yankee only interested in money. They joked about MacGregor and all his talk about liberty and freedom. They don't give a damn about Florida— they only want money. And they'll get a fair share if we win. If Coppinger retakes Fernandina we'll cut and run."

"Cut and run?" questioned Ames.

"Yep. Coppinger is a sensible man, won't try to force the harbor. He knows I've repaired the guns of Fort San Carlos. He'll land on the lower tip of Amelia. As they outnumber us, a determined sally with cutlass and bayonet might beat us. But then we'll get aboard the *Bolivar,* hoist sail and run." He chuckled. "That Gonzalez was sure right about the *Bolivar* holding all my men. Now, fix those rockets and come to see me at sundown."

"Yes, General Irwin."

When Ames got to headquarters he noticed that the general had shaved, cleaned and polished his boots and was puffing a long cigar. He said 'Good evening' to his staff as they reported for duty. The officers seated themselves on benches or stools and waited. There was no conversation. They were curious to hear their new commander.

Irwin got to his feet and stood in front of one of MacGregor's huge maps. He seemed to strut but Ames was quickly reassured by his low-voiced confidence. Irwin pointed to the tip of Amelia Island. "Dons will land here. We ain't got strength to prevent it. But once they get ashore we'll give 'em a warm welcome."

"Sir," questioned Laurent, always thinking of Napoleon's motto of "Attack, attack and then attack," "if they mount a determined assault won't they overpower us by sheer numbers?"

"They might if Governor Coppinger was in command, but he'll be in St. Augustine. Just got word from a privateer captain. As Florida's governor he's forbidden to lead the army in the field. Damned lucky for us, as I'm told that Irishman is a fighting fool. Cubans and militia will be commanded by Colonel Cervantes, just out from Madrid. I'm betting he's one of those European-trained dandies that only thinks of siege. They'll take McClure's Hill, mount cannon and bombard us. Set fire to a few houses, do some damage, but won't hurt no one under cover. And you see to that—keep your men in the fort or behind the barricades. . . . Colonel Ames?"

"Yes, sir."

"Go here." He pointed to a section of the Atlantic coast two miles below the island. "Take three soldiers and have them collect fronds, dried grass, sticks, driftwood—a big mound of stuff that'll make a roaring fire. Tell 'em when they see Spanish sails on the horizon to start her and hurry back here."

"Yes, General Irwin."

"And Captain Laurent?" Somehow the Frenchman had obtained a clean uniform. Very dapper, he stood and saluted.

"Yes, *mon Général.*"

"Speak English, you goddamned frog eater." The men laughed and Laurent in a broad accent said, "Yas, sah, Mr. General, sah."

Irwin joined the amused titter. "All right, no more foolishness. You're mighty good with the sword. Select twenty-five or thirty men. Arm 'em with cutlasses, bayonets, swords if you can find any. Have 'em razor sharp and give 'em a few lessons in their use."

"Yes, sir, and then what?"

"I'll give orders later. Jim"—he turned to a lanky Georgian chewing tobacco—"I've seen you bark a squirrel at a hundred yards. Ever miss?"

Jim chewed for a minute. "Seldom," he answered and spat juice in a corner. "Why?"

"That sheriff from New York had two dozen Lancaster rifles on his brig. I kinda persuaded him to part with 'em. You form a rifle company, select men who know how to shoot but teach 'em fast loading. How many shots can you fire in a minute?"

"Mebbe three, four if I hurry."

"We'll see to it that you hurry," ordered Irwin. He resumed his seat and found a tinder box and relit his cigar. The officers no longer doubted his purpose and tenacity. "Ain't much else we can do 'cept wait for that bonfire. Set a twenty-four hour watch on the ramparts, Colonel Ames. Get a bugle and tell 'em to blow like hell when they sees it. Good night, gentlemen."

An officer in the rear of the room said, "No proclamations, General?"

Even Irwin laughed as the men dispersed.

Three, four, five days, but no Spaniards. Rumors were as plentiful as the September mosquitoes that plagued the bored men. Irwin had accepted a bribe and there would be no fight. President Monroe had decided to seize East Florida. Spain had sold Florida to Great Britain, to the United States and even to France. General MacGregor was returning with crack regiments of Simon Bolivar's Venezuelan Army. The notorious pirate Luis Aury, once an associate of Jean Lafitte, but now privateering under the Mexican flag, was sailing to their rescue. The Seminole Indians, under Chief Billy Bowlegs, had joined the Spanish forces.

The jaded men were roused from their doldrums by a story in a recent issue of the *Savannah Gazette and Columbian Museum* brought to Amelia by a fisherman. General Irwin nailed it to the flagpole so all his soldiers could read it. It said:

> Early this AM, the Patriots under the command of General MacGregor, General Aury and Colonel Irwin and many more gallant generals and officers were mustered at Amelia and marched direct to St. Augustine. This important movement was conducted with all the prudence and correctness which always takes place when great generals and brave soldiers are united. When they arrived at St. Augustine the wary Spaniards were on the lookout and opened fire. But the brave MacGregor, not in the least disturbed, calmly ordered his two wings to open fire and his artillery returned fire.
>
> Fortune favors the brave and the armies of the gallant General MacGregor prevailed. The Fortress was carried and the haughty standard of Spain was drowned in blood. The Patriots were triumphant and the whole of Florida free.

The men were incredulous, then the ironic humor of the article struck them. Their grins and snickers erupted into gales and shrieks of laughter. They shouted, howled, roared and guffawed. A beaming General Irwin told the hysterical men he planned to send the newspaper to the Spaniards. "Mebbe if they discovered we've already beat them and taken St. Augustine, they'll surrender."

With a broad smirk, Captain Laurent said he expected any time to hear that Napoleon had escaped from St. Helena and was marching to their aid.

"If we get back to Savannah alive I'm shore gonna decorate that editor. Finest laugh I've had in many a day." In a serious tone Irwin added, "With the dons it's always mañana, but they'll come."

And they did on the ninth day. The signal fire blazed, bugles sounded and the soldiers went to their assigned posts. The rifle brigade manned the gunports and loopholes at the town gate. Laurent's group, armed with sabers, cutlasses, pikes, three swords, two axes and a pitchfork waited orders behind a barricade of palmetto logs. The big cannon of Fort San Carlos were trained on the harbor entrance. The *Bolivar* raised anchor and readied for action.

Colonel Ames led his rocket brigade to the ramparts, where they had built five bombarding frames that were nothing more than a tube and tripod. He had tested several rockets and found them wildly inaccurate but terrifying as they streaked across the sky.

General Irwin mounted the ramparts and adjusted his telescope. As he had predicted, the Spaniards landed in small boats on the southern tip of Amelia Island. First were the Florida militia, Coppinger's best troops. They were mostly Americans and British who had settled in Florida. These were the men MacGregor had expected to rally to his flag of liberation but who had turned against his marauding army. Adjusting his glass, Irwin saw the Royal Cuban Regiment—five hundred strong, their black faces glistening and their red tunics brilliant in the hot sun. To the steady beat of drums they marched in parade-ground formation through the sand dunes into the scrub oak behind McClure's Hill.

Last came five mortars, roped to wooden rafts that the Spaniards somehow landed. Cursing and sweating, half a hundred men got them to the top of McClure's Hill. Their ugly snouts pointed toward Fort San Carlos. Gunners made ready, the guns thudded and heavy black smoke twisted skyward. The battle for Fernandina had begun.

Round shot banged against the fort's tabby walls and bounced off the palmetto barricade at the town's gates. A second salvo and the iron balls ricocheted into the deep sand. Another blast from the mortars and a rooftop on the *prado* splintered and blazed. The *Bolivar* swung to the starboard and fired a broadside at McClure's Hill. They overshot and the balls tumbled down the hillside. Irwin gave his first order. "Signal the *Bolivar* to use grapeshot and aim at the militia. Them mortars ain't gonna hurt us."

For the next hour the mortars whanged away, wasting powder and shot. Irwin ordered his men to hold their fire, and then he waited. "Guess those Spaniards think all that cannon fire will make us strike our colors." He spat, rubbed his sunburned face and said, "Damned sure those Cubans won't move until the wall is breached. But where's the militia?"

He scanned the oak and pine barrens and saw the Floridians crawling through the thigh-high palmettos. "Where in hell is our lookout?"

The answer came quickly. A long rifle spat and a man in a faded green uniform screamed, spun to his feet and crumpled. Brandishing guns, knives and machetes, the militia charged. Rifles cracked, one or two at a time, but there was no volley. The enemy slowed as men dropped, but then, encouraged by their officers, regrouped and moved ahead.

"Damned fools," muttered Irwin. "They must be drunk. Thought all grog shops in Fernandina had been closed the past week." He was right. Someone had sneaked a gallon of rum into the barricade. Many of the men were smoking, talking and dozing when the attack came.

"Colonel Ames," shouted Irwin. "Fire your rockets."

Before Ames could give the order, Captain Laurent's men hit the right flank of the militia. They fired their muskets, pistols, shotguns and charged with gleaming cutlasses, swords and bayonets.

A man howled as a pitchfork ripped his belly. Another spouted blood from a saber cut. The surprised Floridians braced against the onslaught and lashed out with knives and machetes. Ames saw Laurent cut off a wrist with his shining sword, dodge and expertly slash a man's cheek.

The stunned rifle brigade was unable to fire for fear of hitting its own men. Furious and half drunk, they poured over the barricade, clubbed their rifles and smashed into the militia.

Tripping over corpses, stumbling in the shifting sand, the men howled, screamed and cursed. Smoke and dust threw a curtain over the fight. Irwin twisted his telescope and swore. He could only hear roars, grunts, terrible animal noises and occasional gunshots and a high voice screaming, "Oh Christ, oh Christ!"

Irwin now swung his glass and pointed excitedly. Ames turned. The Royal Cubans, as if on parade, marched forward. Formed in columns, company after company swung into his sight. Led by officers in scarlet tunics and white gaiters, the men, arms shouldered, kept step to the beating drums. The high note of a bugle sounded. The Cubans broke into a slow trot. It was an awesome exhibition of Spanish power.

"Like them buzzards," said Irwin, glancing at dozens of black vultures soaring overhead, "coming for the feast when the fighting is over. Can you reach 'em with your rockets?"

"I think so."

"Let 'er rip then."

Ames aimed the rockets, lit the fuses from a tinder box and watched as they streaked toward the Royal Cubans. They whined on take-off, whistled past the startled Negro troops and burst with a tremendous roar when their warheads struck the hillside. A second salvo burst high over the advancing men, but the third rocket blast was right on target. Five more rockets whizzed toward the advancing troops, now hidden by great pillars of smoke. Faintly, Ames could hear hysterical cries and a wailing sound like small children crying. He reloaded the tripods and aimed another salvo of rockets.

"Wait," ordered Irwin.

Ames paused, looked and wondered if his eyesight had failed him. A shore breeze had lifted the smoke curtain and the Royal Cuban Regiment had disappeared. They didn't fall back in any kind of order, they just dissolved. In the distance Ames could see the terrified Cubans jumping into boats and paddling to the troopship. Others dropped their guns and swam.

The rocket crew watched in shocked silence. It was a complete rout, accomplished in less than five minutes. Irwin shouted words of praise and said, "Colonel Ames, get down to the gates quick. Order our men back behind the barricades. Fight's over. Florida militia alone can't hurt us none. Git word to them they can take their dead and wounded back to their ships. Don't take no prisoners. Hardly got enough food fer our own men."

Ames saluted and dashed down the rampart steps.

§ CHAPTER 10 §

Tumult reigned on Amelia Island. The waterfront taverns swarmed with dirty, tired but happy men. Laughing, singing, swigging tankards of rum, they cursed the "damned Spaniards of the Main" and shouted "On to St. Augustine." Toasts were drunk to the Congreve rocket, which had routed the Cuban regiment and made an easy victory possible.

An exhausted Jonathan Ames, knowing there would be no sleep in Fernandina tonight, wandered beyond the town and climbed McClure's Hill. With Wash's help he'd spent the twilight hours bringing the wounded into Fort San Carlos. Twenty-two men were killed in the fight with the Florida militia, and over thirty wounded. Most of these, he knew, would die from lack of medical attention.

The silent Spanish mortars and the dead among the palmettos were a grim reminder of the brief but bloody battle. There had been no time to organize a burial detail—this unpleasant task would have to be faced in the morning.

He dropped in the warm sand, removed his boots and rubbed his aching feet. A copper-red moon shone over Fernandina. The last of the fires set by the dons' cannon were doused. A few hardy folk lurked behind closed shutters, glad the fighting was over and indifferent to the winner.

Tomorrow the refugees from the mainland would return and it would be business as usual. The whispering wind that swept Amelia Island at night soothed him. Reclining in the warm sand, he drifted into a reverie, speculating about the future and puzzling over the past.

Two years ago he had graduated from West Point determined to do his duty to God and country. I'm glad, he mused, that I volunteered to join MacGregor and I hope that Mr. Madison and Mr. Crawford have found my reports useful. His disappointment in the dashing, handsome Scotsman troubled him. I was fooled by his stirring proclamations, the strange fire in his dashing eyes, yet I'm sure he was a dedicated revolutionary, passionately believing in his mission to liberate Florida. If only he'd been more decisive, less inclined to dawdle, all Florida would be ours. I have no resentment, only pity for this sad, disillusioned man. Will he return from Nassau with reinforcements and attack St. Augustine? I doubt it. If he does will I support him?

No. I've no faith in MacGregor's leadership. Florida is ripe for the taking and we should have it. Besides its strategic importance it's a fertile, beautiful land. A company of Regulars could smash the Spaniards in a few weeks. That's what I'll tell Mr. Crawford. I'll talk to Wash in the morning and somehow will get to Savannah. There I can secure passage to Washington City.

Suddenly he sat up, wide awake. Luiza would soon return from St. Marys. The thought of leaving her was unendurable. Could he take her with him? Would she go? What about her husband—would General Irwin send him back to St. Augustine? Probably, as his chief concern was profit and Gonzalez represented Forbes & Company. A trade agreement with them would certainly please Irwin's Baltimore backers.

Would Luiza go with her husband? He almost retched at the idea of that sinister old man touching his lovely Luiza. He recalled their delight in making love. Must he give up this beautiful, sensual woman? Smiling, he remembered how Luiza would kneel by their bed and silently pray for a few minutes. She told him she was asking God's forgiveness for finding so much happiness in each other. While he didn't understand, he realized her religion was important. Would a devout Catholic consider a divorce or marrying a Protestant? Did he want to marry Luiza? He just didn't know. His Puritan conscience stirred. Did God deliberately create sin to tempt man? He thought of the long sermons of Ebenezer Camp in the Litchfield meeting house. Camp preached the true faith, garnished with Greek and Latin quotations, and damned toleration as the liberty to blaspheme and seduce men from the living God.

Ames groaned as he recalled old Ebenezer's favorite sermon on the redemption of sin. "Every natural man," he had said, "is born full of sin—as full as the toad is of poison, as full as ever his skin can hold, mind, will, eyes, mouth—every limb of his body and every piece of his soul is full of sin. The heart is a foul sink of all atheism, sodomy, blasphemy, murder, whoredom, adultery, witchcraft, buggery. So if thou hast any good in thee, it is but a drop of rose water in a bowl of poison."

Reared in this stern Puritan creed, Ames felt he should be concerned with his own eternal welfare. Instead he could think only of Luiza's rounded breasts, her full mouth and the joy they shared. He scrambled to his feet and loped down McClure's Hill. He was frustrated, angry and confused. He went to his house and searched out the flask of old cognac that Edward Simms had presented him for a special occasion —disaster. This was it, he decided. He kicked off his boots and gulped the fine old brandy. Once again he attempted to think, to sort out his problems. It was no use. Fully clothed, he fell on his bed. Sleep came quickly, with wild and troubled dreams.

The bright autumn sun roused him. Blinking, he saw Wash standing beside his bed with a cup of steaming black coffee. Moaning, he sat up. Inside his head a huge bell seemed to be ringing.

With trembling hands he grabbed the coffee. It burned his lips but drove the cobwebs from his brain.

Wash said, "Sah, General Irwin wants you soon as you can git there."

Ames got up, dashed cold water in his face, and drank more

coffee. "I want to go to Savannah or Charleston. Where's the sloop we sailed to St. Augustine?"

"It's down at Long Wharf, but don't expect we can git outa the harbor. Look."

Ames went to the window and saw a strange ship blocking the harbor entrance. Its red sails were furled and a gaudy flag flapped in the wind. Its twelve long eighteen-pounders were manned and ready. Squinting, he saw *Mexican Congress* painted on her bow. "What the devil . . ."

"Ain't old Satan, sah, but mought as well be. That's Luis Aury, the pirate you folks been talking 'bout. He come in on morning tide while soldiers were still rum-fuzzled. He say Amelia now belongs to Mexico. He take Fort San Carlos and is now talking with General Irwin. You'd better git down there, sah."

Without shaving, Ames hurried to the fort. A dejected Irwin stood in a far corner of the large room. A swarthy man in a brilliant green and white uniform sat talking with Señor Gonzalez. So this was Luis Aury, but why was he so friendly with the Spaniard? The two men ignored him and continued their conversation. Occasionally Aury would laugh and nod to Gonzalez. Ames decided he had never seen such an evil man. His black hair was neatly curled above a long nose. His chin was narrow, his forehead high and small slitted eyes peered from beneath bushy black eyebrows. A gold ring dangled from his right ear and he constantly fingered his wax mustachio.

Noticing Jonathan, Irwin walked over and softly said, "Ain't this a hell of a note," and pointed to a proclamation on the wall. Another MacGregor, thought Ames to himself as he quickly read, "The inhabitants of Amelia Island are informed that tomorrow the Mexican flag will be located on the fort with the usual formalities. They are invited to return as soon as possible to their homes, or send persons in their confidence to take possession of their property, which is held sacred, existing in their houses. All persons desirous of recovering their property are invited to send written orders, without which nothing will be allowed to be embarked." It was signed "Aury, Commander in Chief." It was businesslike and to the point compared with MacGregor's bombastic prose.

(164)

In a sibilant voice Aury said, "General Irwin, this young man, is he one of your officers?"

"Yes, he's my aide. Colonel Ames, this is Captain Luis Aury."

Aury's black eyes gleamed wickedly. "*Mon Dieu,* stupid Americans! In the future you'll address me as Commodore Aury or taste the cat."

Aury turned to Ames. "You are a disgrace—unshaven, dirty boots and rumpled uniform."

"We had a little tussle with the dons yesterday," said Irwin. "Or ain't you heard?"

Ignoring Irwin, the pirate continued, "I insist that officers be well groomed. Never appear before me in such a deplorable condition."

Controlling his temper, Ames blandly replied, "That's no problem. I'm leaving Amelia today."

"With whose permission?"

"I take orders from General Irwin. He has approved."

In an angry voice Aury said, "I command here, not Irwin. No one leaves without my consent."

"I'm sailing on the evening tide."

Furious, Aury said, "That remains to be seen. Why, you may not be alive by sunset," and he chuckled maliciously. "My friend Señor Gonzalez tells me you are a spy."

"A spy!" exclaimed Ames. "For whom?"

"It matters not," purred Aury. "I don't like spies. Yes, I'll have you shot, or do you prefer the rope?"

Irwin rasped, "Gonzalez is just a jealous old fool."

"Jealous, eh?" His small black eyes flickered with interest. "Explain, sir."

"It's an old story," said Irwin. "A dried-up old goat"—he glanced at Gonzalez—"with a young wife—"

"Ah," interrupted Aury. "And a lusty young man. I understand."

"I thought you would," dryly observed Irwin.

"So you trompered this gentleman?" questioned Aury.

"What?"

"Cuckolded, bedded his wife?"

Ames flushed. "I resent your . . ."

A cynical laugh stopped his protest. "Don't deny it. You reek of guilt."

Jumping to his feet, Gonzalez, in Spanish, cursed fluently. "Give me a sword. I'll gut the *bastardo*."

"Gently, my friend, gently," admonished Aury. "No woman is worthy of such an outburst. Sit down, Señor Gonzalez, there'll be no fighting here. This young stallion is my problem. But he'll bother you no more, I promise."

Gonzalez seemed satisfied, even slightly relieved. He resumed his seat next to Aury. Eyes flashing, Ames moved forward.

"No, Jonathan, no," said Irwin. "He's only baiting you. Look." A silver-mounted pistol had magically appeared in Aury's hand.

"Control this hotspur," he ordered Irwin. To the Spaniard he said, "When does Señora Gonzalez return?"

"Late this afternoon, I believe."

"She will be escorted to your house. Keep her there, locked in her room if necessary."

Gonzalez nodded and the pirate lowered the hammer of his pistol. He lit a slender cigar and puffed. "This *enchanteur* piques my curiosity. With your permission, señor, I'll do myself the honor of calling this evening. Now go with God, señor."

"We shall be honored, Commodore," replied Gonzalez and departed.

Aury blew smoke toward the ceiling and turned his malevolent eyes on the two officers. "The great country of Mexico and Señor Gonzalez representing Forbes & Company are partners. No one will hinder this developing trade. General Irwin, control that rabble that you call the Patriot Army. No heroics!"

Stifling an oath, Irwin said, "There'll be no fighting. We are outnumbered, outgunned."

"A wise decision, though my black dogs will be unhappy. They like blood." To Ames he snarled, "If you try to see or speak to Señora Gonzalez, I'll have your balls on a cutlass."

"Come, Jonathan, let's consider our problem over a rum toddy. Mebbe it'll sharpen our wits," said Irwin.

"I take leave to doubt that," said Aury. "Ames, make no attempt to flee this island or you'll be shot. I'll consider the spy charges against you in the morning."

A reply would be futile, thought Ames and walked toward the door with Irwin. Aury called spitefully, "I'll give your regards to Señora Gonzalez. If she be so *magnifique* I might even relieve you of your problem. After your puppy scrambling I'm sure she'd welcome my charming expertise."

Turning, Ames thundered, "Touch Luiza and I'll kill you."

Irwin pushed him through the door with Aury's satanic laughter ringing in their ears.

"That goddamned son of a bitch," muttered Irwin. He spoke swiftly and sternly to Ames. "I must talk with my men, quiet 'em down, keep 'em from acting foolishly. Killing comes as easy to Aury as breathing. Go to your house and stay off the street. Tell Wash to find Laurent. We'll meet at the Long Wharf Tavern at sundown. That's an order, Colonel Ames."

A discouraged Ames returned to his quarters. If he attempted to escape and was caught, Aury would kill him. Luiza's return was an additional complication. Could Gonzalez protect her? Aury's taunting jest haunted him. I'll talk with Irwin this evening. Perhaps he can suggest a way to get her to St. Marys or St. Augustine. His thoughts turned to Jared Irwin. Would he stay in Fernandina or return to Baltimore? What would happen to remnants of MacGregor's Army of Liberation? All hope of freeing Florida was dead.

This made him think of Mr. Crawford. So much had happened so fast that he had not sent a report in weeks. He must do so at once. He found a sharpened goose quill and wrote that General MacGregor had feared his army too weak to attack St. Augustine and had sailed to Nassau to find reinforcements.

It's doubtful if MacGregor will return and Jared Irwin was left in command of the patriots. This week he defeated a much larger Spanish army that attacked Amelia Island. Disorganized, confused and

(167)

with great losses in both men and material, the Spaniards have fled to St. Augustine.

Immediately after Irwin's victory, Luis Aury, a pirate, landed here. Outnumbered and weakened by their battle with the Spaniards, Irwin offered no resistance. On September 20, 1817, Aury annexed Amelia Island to Mexico and raised the Mexican flag over Fort San Carlos. He issued a proclamation to the local inhabitants urging them to return home and promised business as usual.

Sir, without being presumptuous, may I suggest that the President invoke the Congressional Act of 1811, which gives the United States the right to occupy Florida if seized by a foreign power? Mr. Madison discussed this with you and Mr. Jefferson that evening at Montpelier. Aury is a devil and border disorders will increase. Spanish Florida is in chaos. With one bold stroke the United States could easily acquire this territory.

I had planned to make this report in person but Aury claims I'm a spy and won't allow me to leave Amelia Island.

I am enclosing a clipping from a recent Charleston *Courier* which I believe you will find interesting.

In possession of Amelia Island, General MacGregor was surprised and embarrassed by the avidity of plunder which activated so many of his soldiers. In South America the patriots required no pay, not so with the followers of the Green Cross. Arguments about pay and rations increased and no reinforcements arrived. The Baltimore bankers backing MacGregor were perfectly happy for him to stay in Amelia. With a rendezvous for their privateers and a court of admiralty for their prizes the fate of South America gave them little concern—theirs was the glory of piracy and the trophies of the purse.

Views so dissimilar to those of MacGregor could not last. I am sorry he has been deceived because of his zeal, enterprise and valor. He has left Amelia Island in possession of Colonel Jared Irwin (late member of Congress from Pennsylvania) and I presume under the flag of the northern company for South American Emancipation.

(Signed) Verisimilis

Sealing the hastily written letter, he found Wash, explained its importance and said he must find a way to get it to Washington City. Wash allowed as how he'd try and told Ames he had seen Captain Laurent and he and General Irwin was expecting him, come nightfall, at the tavern. "And, sah, you better sneak thar by the beach."

Ames looked puzzled and Wash continued, "Mighty mean folk out tonight. Most evilist people I'se ever seen."

"Aury's cutthroats, eh?" replied Ames. "Any idea how many?"

"Guess 'bout three hundred, half of 'em niggers."

Recalling Aury's remark about his black dogs, Ames said, "The blacks, who are they?"

"Most of 'em from Santo Domingo. Strapping big mens, even bigger than me. Got machetes, long knives, cutlasses— whack you up fer noggin' 'er rum. Many of 'em fought in Haiti. Calls theyselves Aury's bloodthirsty dogs."

"I see," said Ames, thinking of the stories he had heard in Charleston about the Haitian massacre, men, women and even children slaughtered, their homes burned. "I'll be careful, Wash."

"Mebbe I'd better tag along. You might need me."

"No. Find a ship going to Charleston and post this to Mr. Simms. He'll speed it to Washington City."

"Yas, sah," muttered Wash, obviously displeased.

Jonathan found his two friends seated at a small table in the rear of the tavern. Irwin ordered rum toddies, "with an extra fresh lime." They sat quietly drinking, each man deep in his own thoughts.

A dozen or more Negroes pushed their way to the tavern

bar. Several wore dirty uniforms, the others, bare-chested, barefooted, were clad only in colored pants, brilliant reds, greens and yellows. Well armed with knives or machetes, they noisily swigged rum and glanced at the three white men with obvious contempt.

Pointing to them, Ames whispered, "Aury's black dogs," and told them of his talk with Wash.

"He's right," said Laurent. "They are vicious hounds from hell and Aury is the devil incarnate."

"Just who is Aury? Know anything about him?" asked Ames.

"He's a Paris-born purse snatcher—a damned filthy *cochon*— a miserable . . ."

"*Cochon?*" questioned Irwin.

"Pig, swine," answered Laurent. "I vomit to think he's French."

"I reckon you don't like him," said Irwin. "But where'd he come from?"

"I drank wine this afternoon with several French refugees who came with Aury. They now fear and hate him, can't wait to desert. He was a lieutenant under Jean Lafitte but they never got along. Lafitte, I understand, is a gentleman, and Aury, as I've said, a swine. He's crafty, vicious, and his crew, even those blacks, cringe when he speaks. His weakness is women. He's had 'em by the score. Keeps 'em a few weeks and then tosses them to those niggers."

Irwin noticed Ames whiten under his tan. With assurance he said, "I believe he'll behave on Amelia. Fernandina will become a depot where pirates and privateers can sell their plunder, where blackbirders can land their slaves. For trade to flourish he must have law and order." Drinking more rum, he added, "Why he even offered me a post in the Mexican Republic of Amelia, and a share of profits, if I'd police Fernandina."

"What did you say?" asked a surprised Laurent.

"Well, I told him I was flattered and would like a few days to consider it." Sensing their dismay, he added, "Goddamnit, what else can I do? Can't fight him, he ain't gonna let us sail away on the *Bolivar*, but I do think time is on our side. Main thing right now is to keep alive. Don't rile this bloody bastard, just wait. Something is shore gonna happen."

"You think the Americans might chase him out?" asked Laurent.

"Don't know what those piss buggers in Washington City'll do. Florida is shore ripe fer the taking and they just talk."

Ames told them about his letter to Mr. Crawford.

"Might help," admitted Irwin. "Being from Georgia he'll understand. Crawford is a 'hard chewer,' but can he influence the President? Anyhow it'll be weeks before your letter gits to Washington City. Meantime, I say don't do nothing rash."

It was sensible advice and the officers nodded. A loud burst of ribald laughter came from the bar. The ragtag crew had doubled and the tavern was jammed.

"Trouble 'er comin'," said Irwin. "Let's go." He tossed four pesos on the table and pushed back his chair. Beside him stood a Spaniard resplendent in a green uniform trimmed in gold braid. He bowed and said, "Good evening, señors."

Irwin barked, "What do you want?"

The intruder balanced on his toes, his right hand fingering the hilt of his sword. Instantly Laurent recognized him as a skilled swordsman.

"You Señor Ames?"

"I am," said Jonathan.

"Ah," minced the Spaniard. "Yanque *pícaro, perro.* I spit on you."

"What's he saying?" growled Irwin.

"He's trying to start a fight," replied Laurent. He jumped to his feet, but the Spaniard dodged and spat in Jonathan's face. "Yanqui *bastardo,*" he shouted, drew his sword and ripped Ames's coat.

Irwin dashed his rum toddy in the swordsman's face. Blinded, he slashed wildly with his gleaming weapon. The old soldier, moving swiftly, clubbed him with a heavy pewter mug. He dropped his sword and tottered. Another blow from the mug, a heavy boot to the crotch and he crumpled to the floor.

"Goddamned murdering papists. I hate 'em," said Irwin as he hurried his astonished companions out of the tavern.

(171)

§ CHAPTER 11 §

A brisk wind from the sea whipped the palmettos. There was chill in the morning air. It's almost October and time for a change in the weather, thought Ames. It would be a pleasure after the long, hot, humid summer. There would be frost in Litchfield and the gnarled maples around the Green would be tinted red and gold.

He noticed that Wash had pressed his uniform and shined his boots. As he slowly dressed he pondered the tavern incident. He was sure Irwin's assault of the Spaniard had been reported to Aury. What would he do? Why had the Spaniard deliberately insulted him? There was no mistaking his intent. He had planned to kill me, but why? I'd never seen him before.

It was very puzzling and he was glad when Wash called, "Breakfast ready in the back yard." He ate, with enjoyment, a slice of melon, fried shrimp and hominy swimming in butter. He lit a cigar while having his second cup of coffee and asked Wash about his letter to Mr. Simms.

"I went to the docks at first light and found a schooner upin' her anchor fer Charleston."

"Weren't there any guards?"

"Yas, sah, but they mistakes me fer one them men from Santo Domingo," laughed Wash, who was barefooted and wore only green cotton trousers.

"You think my letter will reach Mr. Simms?" questioned Ames.

"Yas, sah. I give the captain a dollar and told him letter mighty important. Tole him if it don't git there I'd find him someday and stomp his insides. Now don't fret, Colonel, everything gonna be all right. Look what I brung you." He placed a foot-high cedar keg on the breakfast table. Inside, placed end on end, were more than a hundred Havana cigars. They were hand rolled and their aroma was delightful. A gold label said they were "*especial para el Rey de España.*"

"Special cigars for the King," he slowly translated. "Where'd you find them?"

"Last week 'em pirates took a Spanish ship off the Florida Keys. Lots of cigars, 'bout a thousand kegs."

Ames said, "And they gave you these?"

"Not exactly, sah. I kinda persuaded 'em." He flexed his right arm and jabbed lightly with his huge fist. He laughed and Ames joined him. He thanked Wash for the cigars, but warned him to keep out of trouble.

"Now," said Ames. "What about a lesson? We haven't had one in weeks."

"That's right. Hope I ain't forgot all I learned. I'll git the books."

Ames was delighted with the Negro's progress in such a short time. He knew the alphabet and could print block letters. He'd begun spelling with the aid of Noah Webster's book, which he had found in Fernandina. I must get a child's storybook and start him reading, thought Ames. The only available thing was a Bible and a few back copies of the Savannah and Charleston newspapers. These Wash found confusing, especially the Bible.

Wash returned with paper, a goose-quill pen and his speller. Smiling, he sat at the table and awaited instructions. At first he did not understand Jonathan Ames. It took him a long time to realize that Ames judged him as a man, not just a Negro. This was a new experience for Wash and at times difficult to believe. Yet, he knew it was true and he was grateful. He was proud of Ames's confidence in him and resolved to be worthy. He carefully printed words as Ames read them to him and explained their meaning.

At noon Laurent called and said Amelia Island was quiet, though full of rumors. He had heard nothing about the tavern fight and did not know if the Spaniard was living or dead, and didn't care. He refused to dine, saying he wanted to talk a bit more with the pirates and see what he could find out. He promised to have a drink with Ames around sundown and left.

That afternoon, just before sunset, a squad of Aury's "black dogs" surrounded Ames's house. A huge Negro, in a faded purple uniform, smartly saluted and told Ames he was to report to Commodore Aury at Fort San Carlos.

Ames returned the salute and said he would be there very soon.

"My orders," said the pirate, "are to fetch you now." As argument was useless, he buttoned his jacket, buckled on his sword and marched to the *prado* in front of the old fort. It was jammed with pirates, traders, remnants of the patriot army, citizens of the island and even several "ladies" from Pasco des Damas.

Commodore Aury, resplendent in a bright orange uniform, sat on a long mahogany bench. With him were Señor Gonzalez, his wife and an officer that Ames recognized as his tavern foe.

He was surprised but delighted to see Luiza, though he wondered why she was present. It was his first glimpse of her in weeks. She had never looked more lovely. Long black hair, loosely tied with a green ribbon, cascaded over a red linen coat. She glanced at Ames and gave no sign of recognition. He walked to her and bowed. Before he could speak one of the pirates spun him around to face Aury.

"The gallant American," sneered Aury. Turning, he said, "Captain Fuilla, is this the man?"

"*Si*, Commodore."

"This American with those two ruffians"—he pointed to Irwin and Laurent—"assaulted you last night?"

"*Si, si*," excitedly replied Fuilla. "I was drinking in the tavern, dreaming of Madrid when, without warning, these three men beat me."

"Why you lying scoundrel," shouted Irwin.

"Shut up," ordered Aury. "Do you dare question the probity of one of my officers?" With a sardonic smile he said, "Fifty lashes each. Next time the rope. Are you satisfied, Captain Fuilla?"

"Gracious Commodore Aury, may I ask a favor?"

"Yes."

"This man," and he looked at Ames, "insulted me, spat in my face. My honor can only be redeemed in his blood. He has a sword, let him use it."

"You challenge him?" asked Aury.

"With your gracious permission, Commodore."

"A duel—how delightful! Permission granted."

The Spaniard smiled wickedly, unsheathed his gleaming sword and saluted. Laurent moved near Aury and spoke rapidly in French. The pirate's pleased expression vanished, his eyes were hard. Ignoring his displeasure, Laurent continued in his persuasive voice and gestured with both hands.

Aury listened carefully, nodded twice and finally said, "I agree, Captain Laurent. Now let's get on with the duel."

Laurent went to Ames and whispered, "It'll be a fair fight and I'm your second."

"What did you tell him?" asked the puzzled young man.

"I titillated his conceit, the lousy pig," replied Laurent. "He thinks of himself as the Emperor of the New World. I told him that, like Napoleon, he must place honor above all else. He beamed at the comparison and when I slyly suggested that Captain Fuilla would certainly kill you, he consented to a proper duel."

"So you think he'll kill me?" asked Ames, ignoring Laurent's other remarks.

"He will if you don't follow my instructions. He is conceited, sure of himself, look at him gloat." They saw Captain Fuilla chatting with several pirates and casually whipping his sword. "He thinks you're a yokel, he'll make fancy passes, nick you a few times and then run you through. That is, if you let him. You are younger and stronger, Jonathan, so you must attack and attack. Force the fight. Don't give him a moment's respite and, above all, watch his blade. Never take your eyes from it, regardless of his remarks. Being a conceited Spaniard, he'll abuse and insult you, but that can't hurt. Move ahead, force him, press the attack."

Ames said he understood, drew his sword and waited. Captain Fuilla moved opposite his opponent.

"You will rigidly observe the code *duelo*," ordered Aury. His voice was husky and he gulped rum from a stone jug. "No dirty tricks, no blinding with sand, gouging or kneeing. Your swords alone will decide the issue." He paused for a minute and shouted, "On with the fight!"

Their swords rang together, feinting, seeking an opening. Ames attacked, forcing back his opponent, though he skillfully parried every stroke. He smiled at the crowd, almost disdainfully blocking Ames's blade. He gave the impression he could end the fight when he chose.

The spectators hooted, screamed and one or two gave Indian war whoops. The pirates tried to bet on Captain Fuilla. Aury waved his silver-chased pistol at Laurent and barked, "One hundred pesos on the don." Laurent shrugged and the pirate said, "Two hundred pesos to fifty if he kills the American."

"Done," replied Laurent, thinking, I've got only ten pesos to my name.

Captain Fuilla sped up the pace and went on the offensive. Ames refused to retreat and the men fought on even terms for ten minutes. Fuilla's face clouded. He had not expected this. He had counted on killing the American with ease. He scowled and concentrated on vital spots. Now he was out to kill quickly and Ames saw it in his face. With a flash of inspiration he noticed that Fuilla exposed his forearm with each thrust. A quick turn of his wrist would reach it. He sidestepped and flicked his blade. A red streak appeared below the Spaniard's elbow. The seconds shouted and halted the fight.

Though Ames had drawn first blood, Laurent knew the

wound had little significance. But the buccaneers screeched their approval and a few bets were made on Ames.

Fuilla refused a bandage, as it would hamper the movement of his right arm. His second washed the skin-deep scratch with rum.

"On guard," roared a slightly tipsy Aury. "Go."

Eyes flashing, Fuilla, dripping blood from his forearm, attacked. He was mad but remained cunning and resolute. He moved with lightning speed, slashing, lunging, thrusting. Dripping perspiration, Ames desperately parried the wicked blade. It was a bitter ordeal. Only Laurent's coaching those long afternoons on the Altamaha kept him alive. His throat contracted, dry as the sand under his feet. Doubts tormented him. Could he last? Only the surprised weariness in his opponent's eyes revived his hopes. For a second he thought Fuilla's arm had faltered and he attempted a straight thrust to the body. It was a mistake and left his side open. Fuilla countered with a deadly riposte. Blood gushed. He had no idea how badly he was wounded. He saw the exultant look on Fuilla's face, faintly heard the cries of the seconds.

Laurent swiftly bandaged the wound. "This will hurt like hell in a few minutes," he said.

"Sooner I get back, less I'll feel it," muttered Ames. Needles of pain stabbed his wound. He knew he would never last another long reprise. A quick analysis of the fight gave him an idea. It might work but he must act quickly. Laurent gave him a sip of watered rum and spoke confidently. "He's worried. Keep attacking, keep pressing, keep him off balance. If he gets you on the defense all is lost."

Ames nodded and gazed at the spectators. The pirates yammered and howled approval. The fight was far more exciting than they had believed possible. Many of them shouted encouragement to Ames, saying they were betting on him. All the clamor seemed to amuse Aury, who drank rum and offered to double his bet. Laurent refused.

Luiza's face was taut with apprehension. Her lips moved as if in prayer. She blinked away tears as she watched Laurent adjust the crimson bandage on Ames's left side. Her husband sneered, hate glittering in his small eyes. He whispered to Aury, who laughed and commanded, "Go."

Their clashing blades met. Ames wasted no time in testing his plan. He rushed Fuilla, feinting at the cut just below the elbow. The Spaniard parried almost too quickly, anxious to avoid the pain and humiliation of another nick. Ames's sword veered from the feint and its point went between the ribs to the spine. Fuilla staggered, dropped his weapon and fell. He was dead before he hit the sand.

There was a moment of stunned silence, then wild cheers. Aury roared above the bedlam, "I've been tricked—hood-winked!" He turned on Laurent. "You cunning bastard. So this is his first duel, and he's just killed the best swordsman in the Caribbean. This is murder—yes, murder, and you will hang. Both of you." Aury blubbered in his rage.

"No!" screamed Luiza. "No!" Eyes blazing, she faced Aury. "He deserved killing."

"Goddamnit, what are you screeching about?" thundered Aury.

"My husband paid him"—she pointed to the dead man—"one thousand pesos to kill Colonel Ames."

In a low soothing voice Gonzalez said, "Luiza, you are dis-traught—very upset. Come, I'll take you home." He moved toward his wife.

"No. You are responsible, not Jonathan. You and your paid assassin."

Bewildered at the sudden turn of events, Aury said, "Is this true, Señor Gonzalez?"

"It's none of your concern," retorted the Spaniard.

"Ah, there I beg to differ." He leered drunkenly and mocked, "Spanish pride just couldn't stand being cuckolded, eh?"

Spluttering oaths, Gonzalez went into a wild rage. His com-bustible temper boiled over and he hit the pirate sharply across the face.

Aury blinked in astonishment. As casually as if he were squashing a mosquito, he shot Gonzalez. Deliberately reload-ing his pistol, he said laconically, "Nothing like a jealous old fool with a young wife."

(178)

Appalled at Aury's brutality and weak from loss of blood, Ames collapsed. Luiza rushed to him, knelt and cradled his head in her arms. Wiping his grimy face, she kissed him tenderly.

"Why waste that on a man who's as good as dead?" said Aury. He spoke sharply to one of his "black dogs," who brushed Luiza aside and pushed Ames into Fort San Carlos. Two pirates seized Laurent and dragged him behind Ames.

"Come with me, señora," coaxed Aury. "I'll escort you home." He pulled Luiza to her feet, gripped her arm and tried to lead her from the *prado*. She resisted, freed her arm and walked swiftly away. Aury followed, caught Luiza and ripped her coat in a clumsy embrace. His men laughed and offered ribald suggestions. Luiza screamed, *"Estúpido!"* and slapped him. Grabbing her long hair, he flung her to the sand. Fuming, he yelled, "Bitch, filthy bitch," and swung his heavy boot. Luiza dodged, jumped to her feet and raked his cheek with her long fingernails. The pirate howled and attempted to draw his pistol. A raging Luiza snatched the weapon and smashed his nose. The gleeful men cheered the girl and laughed at their leader's plight. She flung the pistol at Aury, kicked off her shoes and ran swifter than a young doe toward the river.

Jonathan Ames spent a fitful and restless night in his damp cell. His wound throbbed though it no longer bled. He was cold, hungry and disheartened. Thoughts of Luiza flicked through his mind: bravely confronting Aury, denouncing Gonzalez and weeping softly as her tender lips brushed his cheek. What would happen to her now? Her husband murdered, though God knows he deserved it, by that inhuman savage Aury. Laurent, and he supposed Irwin, jailed. He had last seen her struggling with Aury as he was dragged away. There was hell in his soul as he vowed, somehow, he'd kill him.

The door to his cell clanked open. Half light from a barred window outlined a huge Negro, clad only in red cotton trousers. Another of Aury's "black dogs." What does he want?

A low voice said, "Colonel, sah?"

"Wash," he gasped. "Wash . . ."

The big man put a finger to his lips and pointed to the straw pallet. Ames sat while Wash cleaned and put a fresh bandage on his wound. "It's clean, ain't deep. You be all right soon," he whispered. From a sail cloth bag, he produced a bottle of wine, bread and three oranges. Ames ate hungrily, sighed and wished aloud for a cigar.

Wash grinned and shook his head. "Em guards smell a cigar and they know I ain't no pirate. You know, sah, I had trouble finding one with big-enough pants to fit me." He dissolved in soft laughter and added, "He won't need 'em no more."

He looks like one of Aury's "black dogs," admitted Ames to himself. Abruptly he asked, "Luiza? Have you seen her?"

"She's safe, well and sends love and says fer you not to worry."

"Where is she?"

"Maybe best you not know, sah."

"But why, Wash?"

"That Aury devil done gone crazy. He's maddest man I ever saw." He described Luiza's fight and how she smashed Aury's nose with his own pistol. "He say five thousand pesos fer finding her. He might ask you. If you don't know, you can't tell him."

"That's true," said Ames. "But you're sure she's safe?"

"Yas, sah, when she run towards the river, I followed and hid her."

"I'm most grateful, Wash. Can you smuggle her off Amelia —perhaps to St. Marys?"

"Mebbe later, not now. All them pirates searchin' fer her. That's heap 'er money fer a lady."

She's worth every penny, thought Ames, and then he asked about Laurent and Irwin.

"Captain Laurent in here. I'll try and git him some food. Don't know about General Irwin. In all the fuss, he just got hisself lost. He's foxy man, he'll take care of hisself." Wash got to his feet and said he'd return tomorrow.

"Bring writing materials so I can send Luiza a letter."

"No, sah, too dangerous. I'll take messages, but no scribble."

Reluctant to reveal his feelings to Wash, Ames said, "Tell her I'm glad she's well. She's very brave and I'm most grateful for what she did yesterday."

"Spanish missy mighty fine lady," said Wash and left.

Early each morning Wash sneaked into the cell with food and fresh water. One time he brought a blanket, for the nights were cold, another, a clean shirt and socks. He always had a message of love and encouragement from Luiza and the latest news of Amelia Island. Fernandina, he said, was "ole Satan's back yard, drunks 'er fighting and yelling and lots of folks done moved to the mainland or St. Marys. Old Aury is still a lookin' fer Miss Luiza and cussin'."

Slowly the days limped by. From marks he'd made on the tabby walls, Ames knew he'd been in jail for fifteen days. It seemed like months.

One dreary morning came a sharp rap on his cell door. It was Jared Irwin in a blue and white uniform. He grinned at Ames's puzzled expression, gave him a bottle of rum and asked, "How do you feel?"

"Pretty good," said Ames, "but what are you—"

Irwin interrupted. "I'm now the adjutant general of the Mexican Republic of Amelia Island."

"Then get me out of here."

"Can't do that yet, Jonathan. But give me time. That drunken lout Aury," he explained, "let things get out of hand and it hurt trade. Killing Gonzalez didn't help, either, for Forbes & Company won't do business here. Anyhow, Aury offered me this job and, being a realist, I accepted. Damned sight better than fifty lashes. Some of the old patriot army are helping and I've got Laurent freed. Mebbe you next. Just be patient. Aury has dropped the murder charge against you. He found all those pesos in Fuilla's luggage, which proved Señora Gonzalez's bribe story. Strange how she vanished, ain't it?"

"Wash told me she got away."

"Do you know where she is?"

"No. Do you?"

"No." He chuckled. "Neither does Aury. It's driving him crazy. Can't decide whether he wants to bed or beat her.

Mebbe both." Smiling, he added, "You should see his big nose. Mostly black and blue where she whammed him with the gun butt. Too bad she didn't shoot him."

"I'm glad she didn't. That's my job. If I ever get out of here, I'll kill him," raged Ames.

"Take it easy, Jonathan. Aury says you are a spy and insists you'll have to stand trial."

"What a farce."

"Don't think so," replied Irwin. "He's got enough troubles without hanging an American and he knows it. Folks in Georgia are complaining about his Negroes stealing and raiding. Mebbe your letter to Mr. Crawford might stir 'em up a little in Washington City."

"I doubt it," he gloomily replied.

"Don't be downhearted, Jonathan. Laurent and I'll git you outa here. I promise." He walked to the door. "But don't rile Aury if you see him. Won't help matters none." He waved good-bye.

§ CHAPTER 12 §

Wash's daily visit at daybreak is the only thing that keeps me sane, thought Ames. Besides food, fresh fruit and clean water, Wash brought news of Amelia. Luiza was still safe though Aury had increased the reward to 7,000 pesos. "Fernandina is jammed with pirates and rascals and the few decent folk have fled to the mainland. Last week two black-birders anchored in the harbor and over eight hundred Africans were sold at auction. Traders from Georgia and the Carolinas buy them and sneak them across the St. Marys River at night. While General Irwin is doing his best, brawls and street fighting continue," Wash told him. "Wish I could get Miss Luiza away, but only safe place for her would be St. Augustine. I'd be gone a week and you'd git mighty hongry on bread and water. Don't worry, sah, I'll git you out 'er here real soon. Miss Luiza, too."

Though Ames had confidence in Wash, he was deeply discouraged. He had been in this uncomfortable cell for sixty-one days. Without Wash he would have starved, for his daily ration was a jug of dirty water and a wedge of cornbread. His wound had healed and he had kept in shape by running. He reckoned five thousand paces were about a mile. Daily he would prance or skip up and down for five miles. This was his only diversion. It was too dark to read, even if Wash could have smuggled in books or old newspapers.

Late in the afternoon of his sixty-third day of imprisonment, four Santo Domingo Negroes kicked open his cell door. Without a word the pirates, clad only in yellow and blue cotton pants, escorted Ames to the inner court of Fort San Carlos. It was sunset and a cooling breeze came from the sea. He breathed deeply and blinked at the unaccustomed light. Before him stood a sardonically smiling Luis Aury, elegant in his green uniform, a gold ring in his ear. His long black hair was freshly curled. He certainly needs a haircut, observed Ames, and laughed silently at the absurd thought.

The buccaneer frowned as he walked around his prisoner. He had expected to see a dirty, half-starved man. Instead Ames was freshly shaved, robust and obviously well fed. Aury's thin lips curled upward. He was irritated. Hate glittered in his black eyes. He would enjoy killing this American, if for no other reason, that Luiza loved him. He expected to get from Ames a confession he could produce at a trial. Once Ames admitted being a spy he could be shot or hanged at Aury's pleasure.

"*Mon Dieu*," he rasped. "Prison life certainly agrees with you."

Remembering Irwin's instructions, he bowed and said, "Good evening, Commodore Aury."

In a sarcastic voice Aury said, "And it's even improved your manners. So, after weeks of bread and water I find you glowing, almost radiant." He roared, "Who's been feeding you?"

Ames shrugged and did not reply.

"Never mind." He smirked. "We have more important matters to consider. The truth, I find, flows more freely with gentle persuasion."

He spoke in French to the four black men. Moving swiftly, they strapped Ames to an iron post, leaving his arms free. Long slivers of bamboo, feathered with egret tails, were inserted under his fingernails. They held his hands high above his head. The breeze rustled the feathers and the sensitive flesh under his nails prickled. He squirmed but was helpless. A sudden gust of wind and the pain was excruciating. He writhed and tried to free his arms. The "black dogs" laughed and turned his hands to catch more of the wind.

"Lower his arms," ordered Aury. "I have a few questions for you. Answer truthfully and all is well. Lie to me and" —he jerked his thumb skyward—"understand?"

"Yes," groaned Ames.

"Yes, what?" spat Aury.

"Yes, sir."

"Perhaps this will teach you respect for your betters. What's your correct name?"

"Jonathan Ames."

"Your home?"

"Litchfield, Connecticut."

"A damned Yankee. Always sticking their noses in other people's business." He stuck a long cigar in his mouth but did not wait for a light. "You are a graduate of the United States Military Academy at West Point?"

Surprised, Ames was slow in answering.

"Don't lie, Ames. Several soldiers have so described you."

He nodded and flexed his fingers trying to loosen those prickly darts.

"Then you are a lieutenant in the regular army?"

"I was, sir."

"Was?" questioned Aury.

"I resigned last year and enlisted with General MacGregor."

"Why?"

"I approved of his plan to free Florida and bring it into the Union."

Aury gave a waspish chuckle. "That pompous peacock. If you were so devoted to him, why did you remain in Amelia?"

"I thought he'd return with reinforcements and we'd attack St. Augustine according to plan."

"Up his hands," ordered Aury. His men complied and Ames's fingers ached and throbbed. He writhed in agony. "Such exquisite pain," gloated Aury. "Now the truth!" He motioned and the pirates lowered Ames's aching hands. "You and the patriot army had lost faith in MacGregor, hadn't you?"

"Yes, sir," murmured Ames.

(185)

"But you stayed here and fought with Jared Irwin against the Spaniards?"

"Yes, sir."

"Why?"

"I respected General Irwin, sir, and hated all Spaniards. Besides it was my duty to the Army of Liberation."

"Very noble, I'm sure. You joined Irwin because you are still an American officer."

"I told you, sir, I resigned."

"Then you are a spy," accused Aury, "reporting to Washington City, urging your government to seize Florida."

"No, sir."

"Another lie," snarled Aury. "What has President Monroe decided? Is he sending American troops?"

"I've had no correspondence with the President."

"But you admit with someone. With whom then?"

"No one, sir."

"I warned you," said Aury and waved to his "black dogs." They jerked Ames's fingers high in the freshening wind. The feathers fluttered merrily, making his hands throb. The pain was unendurable. He gasped, closed his eyes and fainted.

When he regained consciousness he noticed Aury had lit his cigar. "Perhaps," he said, "I've been too lenient, too gentle. A more vigorous treatment seems indicated." He exhaled a blue cloud of smoke and ordered, *"Eau la torture."*

The four blacks bound his arms and retied him to the post. One held his nose, another, using a knife blade, pried open his mouth. The third pirate poured water in his open mouth. Some of it spilled over his face and chest. It was cold and refreshing. An angry shout from Aury and the pirate poked the jug's neck down his throat. The water gurgled and his stomach billowed out like a sail in the wind and cramps racked his body. He felt he would explode any minute. Suddenly his mouth was gagged by a huge black hand. The pressure on his nostrils eased and he breathed once. Two pirates beat a rapid tattoo on his belly. Each blow sent water spurting from his nose. His face turned crimson, he gasped from lack of air and thought he would suffocate. Aury, enjoying Ames's suffering, blew smoke in his face and shook his head.

"Don't think he's quite ready to tell the truth. Better wash a few more lies out 'er his system." One of the blacks went to refill the large jug.

Someone shouted from the ramparts. It was Jared Irwin, excited and gesturing to the harbor. The boom of a long carronade drowned his voice. Aury and his men raced up the steps and joined Irwin on the ramparts of Fort San Carlos.

Four ships, flying the American flag, sailed up the Amelia River. They shortened canvas and sailors manned their guns, ready to fire. A hundred or more marines, bayonets gleaming, crowded the deck of the larger ship, the corvette *John Adams*. It was flanked by the brigs *Enterprise* and *Prometheus* and in its wake came the schooner *Lynx*. The American warships swung broadside, ports open, ready to pound either Fort San Carlos or Aury's ship, the *Mexican Congress*. A brass cannon on the corvette's beak-head belched black smoke.

"It's a signal," said Irwin. "Better dip your flag."

"I'll see 'em in hell first," raged Aury and ordered the pirates to the guns of Fort San Carlos.

"You are daft," said Irwin. "Before you can get those guns ready they'll smash the *Congress* and the fort, and storm Amelia Island. Look, they want to parley."

A tender from the corvette, flying a white flag, headed toward Long Wharf. "Might as well see what they want," grumbled Aury and went to meet the Americans.

Irwin told the pirates to stay away from the cannon "unless you want to get us all killed," and followed Aury. They obeyed the order and left the fort.

Drenched and still spitting water, Ames was alone in the courtyard. He realized that for the first time since he was a child he had peed in his pants. Less painful than through my nose, he thought, and tried to free his hands.

Wash ran to the post, slashed him free and carried him to his cell below.

"Why back in this dismal place?" spluttered Ames.

"Two reasons," explained Wash. "I've got a key to this cell

and it's the last place they'll think of looking fer you. How you feel, sah?"

"Like a drowned rat."

Wash scratched his head. "Good time to git you out 'er here. I'll find a boat and return 'bout midnight when things quiet down."

Ames said that was fine but be sure and bring Luiza. "We can escape together."

"Yas, sah," he replied.

The tender pulled into Long Wharf. A marine captain in an immaculate blue uniform jumped ashore. A company of marines, muskets cocked, covered him as he strode to the waiting pirate.

"Is Luis Aury here?" he asked.

"I'm Commodore Luis Aury."

The officer gave a scornful glance at the dapper pirate with his long hair. His nostrils twitched distastefully. "I have a letter for Luis Aury from Captain J. D. Henley of the United States Navy. Will you accept it?"

Aury's face reddened at the marine's rudeness. For a moment Irwin thought he might refuse the letter. "Better see what Captain Henley wants," he whispered.

"When I want advice from you, I'll ask for it," snarled Aury, but he accepted the letter.

"Captain Henley told me to be explicit on this point. You have until noon tomorrow to answer," said the American.

"Who is Henley?" asked Aury.

"He is the commanding officer of this squadron. And I'd recommend, Mr. Aury, that you'd be wise to address him correctly."

Aury cursed softly in French. "What does he want?"

"I suggest you read the letter," said the marine and jumped aboard the tender.

"Impudent bastard," he said and ripped open the letter. As he read his small black eyes flashed furiously. He turned to his men, "This Henley says he's been ordered by President Monroe to seize Amelia Island and hold it in trust for Spain.

If we don't depart by noon, he'll use force." He fingered his gold earring and glanced at the guns of Fort San Carlos.

"What you gonna do?" asked a frightened voice.

"We is outgunned and outnumbered," said another.

"Likes to fight 'em Spaniards," muttered a black, "but don't want to mess with 'em Americans. They hates us niggers."

Aury crumpled the letter. "Irwin, round up my officers and meet me at headquarters in an hour. This island belongs to Mexico and I ain't about to give it to those goddamned Americans."

Jonathan Ames restlessly paced his cell. It was long after midnight and Wash had not returned.

He could see the faint rays of a new moon through his cell bars. Though he had no watch he reckoned it about two o'clock. What had gone wrong? He flung himself on the straw pallet, overcome with despair.

At last Wash appeared with dry clothes, bread and cheese and a small flask of rum. Eating hungrily, Ames said, "You are late. Anything wrong?"

"Yas, sah, plenty."

"Luiza? Where is she?"

"She's fine. But 'em pirates planning to blow up the American boats."

"What?" exclaimed Ames.

"Yas, sah. They's busy now 'er filling rum kegs with powder. They's making rafts from old boards, swim 'em out, tie 'em to the ships' sides and light a long fuse. Ships go boom, boom like this," and he clapped his hands.

"Where is General Irwin, and Captain Laurent?"

"They's been arrested 'cause they refused to fight the Americans."

My God, thought Ames, I must get word to them!

"When will this happen—tonight?"

"No, sah, ain't ready yet. But tomorrow night fer sure."

"I must warn the Americans."

"I figgered you'd want to tell 'em. That's reason I left Miss Luiza behind."

"I see," said Ames. "You got a boat?"

"An old pirogue down by the docks. I'll row you out to a ship."

Ames nodded and said, "Let's go." Wash opened the cell door and peered down the long dark passage. He signaled and Ames followed him out of the fort. The fresh air was more refreshing than old brandy and he breathed deeply. They sneaked to the river and Wash paddled the clumsy pirogue to the corvette.

"You go back and keep Luiza safe," ordered Ames as he caught the rope ladder and climbed to the ship's deck.

A sleepy sentry said, "Who goes there?"

"A friend," whispered Ames. "Take me to your captain."

The soldier flashed his lantern on a young man in cotton trousers and a torn shirt.

"Who the hell are you?"

"Never mind, I must see the captain at once."

"Captain Henley chew my ass out if I woke him. I'll take you to the duty officer." He poked Ames with his musket and guided him to a small cabin on the aft deck. "In there."

Ames entered and saw a young lieutenant asleep on his bunk. The sentry banged the floor with his musket butt. The officer opened his eyes and said, "What the hell?"

"Don't know, sir. This man came over the side and says he gotta see the captain. Might be one of 'em pirates."

Annoyed at being disturbed, the lieutenant said, "Who are you?"

"I am an American and I have a most important message for your captain."

"Is that so," sleepily replied the officer. "What is it?"

"Aury is planning to blow up your ships."

"Nonsense. That pirate wouldn't dare."

"You don't know Aury. He's a cunning devil and fearless."

The officer said scornfully, "And you want me to disturb the skipper with this wild tale?"

"I insist, sir. I must see the captain."

"Do you now," wearily said the lieutenant. "Put him below

decks," he told the sentry. "I'll speak to Captain Henley in the morning."

With his musket ready the guard ordered Ames to march. When they arrived at the ship's stern he said, "Open that hatch and git below." Ames complied and the guard banged the hatch and secured it with a heavy chain.

The sun over the yardarm indicated less than an hour to midday and no word from Luis Aury. An incensed Captain Henley paced up and down the quarter deck of the *John Adams*. His wintry blue eyes scanned Fort San Carlos, the wharfs and Fernandina's shaded streets. He saw no unusual activity, no evidence the pirates were planning to evacuate Amelia Island.

Several men lolled on the docks, talking and smoking their long-stemmed pipes. Two sentries strolled the fort's ramparts. The Mexican flag flapped in the mild breeze. The fort seemed deserted, its gunports closed.

Captain Henley focused his telescope on the *Mexican Congress*. Its sails were furled, its decks almost empty. One man fished from its port bow, another dozed in the warm December sun.

By God, thought Henley, that damned pirate is ignoring my ultimatum. He glanced at his dollar-size watch. It was eleven-thirty. His red face purpling with anger, he said in a ringing voice to his sailing master, "Mr. Johnson, clear the decks for action. Signal the other ships."

"Aye, aye, sir."

"Tell Major Burns to get his marines on deck. Full equipment, ready to land."

"Aye, Captain Henley."

The lookout shouted, "Boat to starboard."

Rowing slowly, two pirates eased the boat to the *John Adams*. "Permission to come aboard?" shouted one, dropping his oars.

"Granted," replied Captain Henley. The man scrambled up the boarding ladder, saluted and presented the captain with an elaborate scroll, sealed with gold wax and neatly tied with a green ribbon.

The captain ripped the document open and read swiftly. He cursed, removed his cap and rubbed his bald head. He looked again at the message and fumed. "That arrogant son of a bitch!"

"What'd he say?" asked the sailing master.

"That damned filibuster wants to know what authority the United States of America has to interfere in Mexican property. He says the inhabitants of Amelia Island are not subjects of the United States and he cannot understand why a great republic like the United States of America would act for that tyrant the King of Spain. He considers my demand to leave Amelia idiotic and he refuses to consider it until I answer his questions."

"Mebbe a few rounds of grapeshot would knock some sense into his head," said Johnson.

"Don't tempt me, Mr. Johnson. . . . Where is that pirate?"

"He's left," said Johnson and pointed to the boat headed for shore.

"Mr. Johnson, take a squad of marines and find Aury. Tell him my orders are to take Amelia Island and I've no time for political arguments. If he doesn't sail on the morning tide, I'll open fire."

"Aye, aye, Captain, but why not now? Teach 'em a lesson."

Henley said with a grimace, "I was instructed to avoid trouble with Mexico if possible. I'm giving Aury a last chance. If he doesn't take it, then by God I'll blast 'em to hell and hang every pirate I catch."

Inwardly raging at his restrictive orders, Captain Henley walked briskly up and down the corvette's deck. He paused at the ship's stern and decided a pipe might be comforting. He patted the side pocket of his worn blue serge uniform. The pipe wasn't there. Damnit, he remembered he had left it in the cabin. Grumpily he kicked the hatch. An answering thump came from below. Surprised, he banged the hatch again. A dull thud replied.

"Open this," he bellowed to a sailor. Out came a dirty, unshaven young man.

"Jesus Christ," swore Henley. "How long have you been down there?"

"Since last night," gasped Ames, inhaling gulps of fresh air.

"Who the hell are you?"

"I'm an American and I must see the captain."

"I'm Captain Henley. What do you want?"

"Sir, Aury has a plan to blow up your fleet tonight."

"How do you know?"

"I escaped last night from Fort San Carlos and came to warn you. Instead I was arrested and tossed down there."

A most unlikely yarn, thought Henley as he scrutinized the speaker, wondering if he were a pirate. He barked, "What's your name?"

"Jonathan Ames, sir."

The captain gave a startled look. "Jonathan Ames, did you say?"

"Yes, sir."

"Come with me," said Henley and walked to his cabin. They entered and the officer pointed to a chair. Ames sat down, thinking, How can I convince this stubborn man I am telling the truth?

"So you claim to be Jonathan Ames," accused the captain.

"That's my name," flared Jonathan. "But what difference does it make—"

Henley interrupted. "Do you know Mr. William Crawford?"

"Yes, I was his aide."

"What's he like?"

Both irritated and perplexed, Ames gave a quick picture of Crawford, his career, his size, his jovial manner and his fondness for wine and good cigars.

"What's the name of his friend in Charleston who posted your reports?"

"Why, Mr. Edward Simms," he replied.

A smile glimmered on Henley's thin lips and he extended his hand. A slightly bewildered Ames responded.

"Sorry about the examination, but I had to be sure you were

Jonathan Ames. With my orders from the President was a letter from Bill Crawford. He told me of your mission and the service you'd rendered our country. He said, 'Keep your eye peeled for young Ames and if you find him see that he gets safely back to Washington City.'"

Ames relaxed and said he was glad to get Mr. Crawford's thoughtful message. Noticing his gray, taut face, Captain Henley ordered food and hot coffee, saying, "Make you feel better. Now what about Aury blowing up my ships?"

As Ames tersely described the pirate's scheme, the navy captain angrily drummed the table with his fingers. "A question, Mr. Ames. Why didn't he attack last night?"

"He wasn't ready. Takes time to fix those kegs and make the rafts."

"That tricky bastard," exploded Henley. "That explains his letter."

"What, sir?"

"Aury sent me a long document this morning—full of arguments and questions. It was a ruse to gain time. By God, I'll fix him."

Someone knocked. A steward entered with a tray of bread, cheese, cold meat and a pot of coffee. Jonathan ate greedily and sipped the hot coffee. He felt better and thanked Captain Henley, wondering what he planned.

"Has Mr. Johnson gone ashore?" Henley asked the steward.

"Yes, sir."

"Tell the watch to have him report to me as soon as he returns."

"Yes, sir."

Henley told Ames why he had sent his sailing master ashore. "Soon as he gets back I'll attack, sink that rascal's ship and destroy the fort."

"You'll bomb Fernandina too?" asked Ames, thinking of Luiza.

"If the pirates take refuge there, I will."

"Sir, I think there's a better way."

A slightly startled Henley said, "Go ahead, Mr. Ames."

"The powder magazine is underneath the rear wall of the

fort. There is a tunnel to it. Give me a dozen men and at sunset we'll sneak in and blow it up. Without powder Aury will be helpless. Bombard and you'll kill lots of innocent people. A number of Spaniards and their families are still in Fernandina. Storm the beaches and you'll have heavy losses. Those pirates, expecting no mercy, will be desperate. They are skilled, vicious fighters and will kill many marines."

This argument made "plenty of sense" admitted Henley. He was supposed to be considerate of the Spaniards. Destroying their property and killing would not endear the Americans. "There is something in what you say," he reluctantly told Ames. "Though I'd like to get my hands on Aury."

So would I, thought Ames, wincing as he remembered his torture. He deserves killing and, given a chance, I will do it with pleasure. Speaking in a persuasive voice, Ames continued his argument. "The *Mexican Congress* is almost deserted and I'm sure a company of marines could easily board her. Then there's no escape for Aury and you can dictate terms."

"I'd hang Aury if I had my way," said Henley. "But he's flying the Mexican flag and the President wants no trouble with them. My orders are to evict him without incident. Perhaps your plan is best. We'll try it first. Exactly what do you require?"

"I want a dozen men armed with knives and pistols. No muskets. They are too clumsy and we'll need to get out of the fort in a hurry. Have 'em barefooted and their faces blacked with grease or burned cork. Most of all, three or four signal rockets."

Frowning, Henley asked why.

"There are two large, open bins of powder, plus a few additional barrels from the ship. That's where the kegs are being fused. Aury is a lubberly fellow and I'm sure there's loose powder around. Rockets will detonate the magazine and we'll run for our boat."

"It's dangerous but it might work. . . . What time?"

"December days are short—it should be dark by five. Can we be ready by six?"

"Yes," replied Henley. "I'll see to it. You rest for a couple of hours. Don't reckon you were too comfortable last night."

Ames grinned and stretched out on a small bunk. It was pitch dark when Henley roused him. "Have a good snooze?" he asked.

"Yes, Captain, and my thanks."

"Come on deck then. The men are waiting."

He followed the chunky naval officer topside. He introduced him to the marines. "Mr. Ames is a special emissary of the President of the United States. You are to obey his orders implicitly." He waited for a minute and said, "Any questions?"

The marines shuffled and stared at Ames, but no one spoke. A sperm-oil lamp cast a dim light on their blackened faces. Armed with pistols, knives and cutlasses, they were a tough crew. Ames was satisfied and outlined their mission. "Where are the rockets?" he asked. A marine pointed to a canvas bundle.

"Let's go," said Ames. "Be quiet—absolutely no talking." They nodded and got into the longboat.

"Mr. Ames," said Captain Henley.

"Yes, sir?"

"I'll give you two hours. If you are not back by then I'll order my ships to fire."

"Two hours should be ample, sir."

"Then, go with God."

Oars muffled, the marines paddled toward the marsh grass at the mouth of Amelia River. They beached their boat and walked single file behind Ames. He led them toward Fort San Carlos, half a mile away. The sound of their bare feet crunching the sand was barely audible. A breeze rustled the low palmettos, the new moon was a silver crescent on the horizon.

As they approached the fort a low voice said, "Colonel Ames, sah?"

"Wash," he whispered and signaled the men to halt. "I'm sure glad to see you, but how did you know?"

"I'se been watching the ship since first dark . . . figgered you'd come ashore and I might help."

"You surely can." He described their plan to blow up Aury's powder supply.

"It'll shore make a big noise." Wash grinned. "Bombs all finished but pirates won't raft 'em out until midnight. Don't think more than two or three guards, and this'll take care of them." He waved a ten-foot bamboo blowgun.

In five minutes they reached the tunnel. They crept down the long passage and tipped up the stone steps to the inner court. Two pirates leaned against the tabby walls, smoking and talking.

Wash slipped forward and raised the blowgun shoulder high. He filled his lungs and gave one big puff. There was a soft twang. One of the guards grunted, dropped his gun and crumpled to the ground. His startled companion knelt, shook him and spoke excitedly. Wash put another venom-smeared dart in the reed and puffed. The second pirate screamed and tried to pull the feathered missile from his cheek.

"Quick," said Ames. "This way." He ran for the powder magazine in the far corner of the fort. The marines raced behind. "The rockets! Toss 'em in that door." The men obeyed.

A surprised sentry on the rampart yelled, "Halt!" and aimed his musket. A pistol cracked and the pirate fell.

"Light the rockets and run like hell," commanded Ames. Pistol shots ignited the fuses and the raiders dashed for the tunnel. A musket whanged from the rampart. A marine shrieked and went down. Half a dozen pirates emerged from the guardhouse above and fired. A volley of pistol shots sent them scuttling for cover.

The din was terrific. Ames bellowed to the marines to get back to the boat. He doubted if they heard him. Above the noise and confusion came a great roaring gust, like the eye of a hurricane. Then a giant blast that tinted the sky a bright yellow. The rear wall collapsed and bits of tabby floated in the air. The ground trembled and Ames tripped. Jumping to his feet, he roared, "Hurry, hurry—make for the boat."

A jagged piece of tabby struck his shoulder. Blood gurgled in his throat, stifling his agonizing cry. He crumpled and fell unconscious.

§ CHAPTER 13 §

General Jared Irwin and Captain Charles Laurent strolled past the deserted wharfs along Amelia River. The noonday sun shone brightly in a deep blue sky, already haunted with spring. It was more like April than January. Fernandina was again a sleepy fishing village. The admiralty courts were closed. The long warehouses, once packed with loot, were vacant. The bargain-hunting merchants from Charleston and Baltimore had vanished. The shrill cry of the slave auctioneer had been silenced. Aury's crew and the privateers who had roved the Caribbean were gone forever.

The two men sought the shade of a green water oak. Parakeets on the high branches chattered and whistled. A scarlet tanager, only a few feet away, eyed the men and preened its brilliant feathers.

"A bit warm, ain't it?" said Irwin. "Hard to believe it's winter."

Laurent nodded and looked at Fernandina's wide sandy streets. The American flag fluttered over Fort San Carlos. Marine sentries slowly paced the broad ramparts. It was so peaceful that it was difficult to believe only a few weeks ago Amelia Island had been a roaring hellhole. "The Americans have certainly changed Amelia," observed Laurent.

"Shore have," agreed Irwin. "Captain Henley is a damned good man."

"Yes, he is," said Laurent. "He neatly foxed Aury."

"Wish he'd hung the scoundrel."

"Why didn't he?"

"Orders from those Washington milksops. Take Amelia but git into no fuss with Mexico. Hold her for Spain until she can send enough troops to restore order in East Florida." He spat in disgust and fumbled with his pipe.

"But that isn't possible."

"I know it, you know it. Everyone does except those fools in Washington City. Take four or five thousand men to police it, and the dons can't spare even a squad. Understand Bolivar and those rebels in South America are beating the beejesus out of the Spaniards."

"Then why return Amelia Island?"

Irwin scratched his head and thought for a minute. "I'd guess long before the dons can garrison the fort, Florida will belong to us."

"I hope so. It's a charming little village and should prosper under the Americans. I expect I'll miss it."

"Sure you want to go?"

"I've no choice. Fighting is my only trade."

"You'll get your bellyful with Andrew Jackson," said Irwin.

"You know him well?"

"Not exactly, though we were in Congress together some twenty years ago. Jackson was a skinny, red-headed, hot-tempered lawyer from Tennessee. Land speculator, too. Sold thirty thousand acres owned by the Indians to some folks in Philadelphia. When settlers moved in, the Indians complained and President Washington had 'em thrown out by the Army. Jackson fussed and fumed—he hates all Indians—and suggested George Washington be impeached." Irwin chuckled and lit his pipe and continued. "Since then, 'Old Long Knife,' as the Indians call him, has made quite a name for himself. He smashed the Creeks at Horseshoe Bend and went on to defeat the British at New Orleans."

"That where he beat the British regulars?"

"Yes, with the help of Jean Lafitte's pirates and a bunch of coon hunters from Tennessee. He just murdered 'em red coats."

Laurent was impressed and said so.

"You know," mused Irwin, "if he'd commanded our army, instead of MacGregor, we'd now not only have Florida but 'Old Hickory' would be fighting the dons in South America."

"Old Hickory?" questioned Laurent.

"That's what his soldiers call him. A good name, too, for he's mean, tough and can whip his weight in wildcats. He's fought several duels, been shot up a few times and hates all foreigners, especially the British."

"*C'est formidable*," commented Laurent. "But why do you think he'd welcome me, a Frenchman?"

"It's simple. He needs soldiers and you are a good one. I've written Jackson a long letter about you. I am sure he'll remember me. We often disagreed but settled things with a toddy or two. Besides, I'm sending twenty-two good men, the last of the patriot army. You'll command them."

"I'm most grateful for your kind consideration and generous assistance," said Laurent.

"What fancy language." Irwin smirked. "Anyhow, you sail on the morning tide for Mobile, Alabama. Old Hickory is someplace in the south Alabama Territory, if he ain't already licked them Seminoles."

"Let's hope not." Laurent smiled. "I am most anxious to see your great general in action. One of the soldiers called him a backwoods Napoleon."

"Wouldn't know," replied Irwin. "But you'll shore get plenty of action. Old Andy is riled up plenty. Last month the Indians ambushed an army supply boat on the Apalachicola River. Killed thirty-seven soldiers, seven wives and four children. He shore gonna fix 'em Seminoles—Spaniards, too, if they try to help."

"Never dreamed that one day I'd be in this wild country fighting red Indians," said Laurent. "Should be fascinating."

"Mebbe, but remember a war arrow kills just as quick as a musket ball."

"I'll remember. Do you suppose I might tell Jonathan Ames good-bye?"

"Don't think so. The doctor from Savannah says no visitors for another week."

"Please give him my fondest regards. He's a fine young man."

"He is that, and a damned lucky one, too. Hunk 'er tabby nearly busted his head and bits of oyster shell ripped open his back. That Spanish gal sewed him up and nursed him night and day for two weeks. He'd be dead if it weren't fer her and that big nigger of his."

"Wash is a splendid man," mildly reprimanded Laurent. "Did you know he's learning to read and write?"

"Don't hold much with such notions. But he's best nigger I ever knew. When 'em rockets exploded, and hell was bustin' out all over, Wash went back and toted Ames home. He and that Spanish piece fixed his wounds, washed and fed him. Somehow they kept him alive when he should 'er croaked."

"Señora Gonzalez is a lovely and brave lady. I'll never forget how she clawed that pirate. I do hope she and Ames will be happy together."

"A papist and a Puritan double-teamed? It would never work. Anyhow she's gone. Sailed for St. Augustine last week with the few Spaniards left on Amelia Island. General Coppinger requested their return and Henley agreed, even though she begged to stay until Ames was well. Seems her folks in Havana are pretty important and they're anxious to git her home."

The Frenchman shrugged and said he better pack. "And, General Irwin, if I may be so bold, what are your plans?"

"I gotta go back to Baltimore and see the folks who put up the money for MacGregor."

"They, I suppose, are annoyed?"

"I suppose so, but they got no real complaints. They received a percentage of admiralty sales and recovered their original investment. Their land options, if Florida joins the Union and Washington City honors them, will make them rich. But greedy folks just ain't ever satisfied."

"God's eyeballs, a pox on them," said Laurent with a heavy

British accent. They both laughed, shook hands and wished each other good luck.

When Captain Henley was told that Jonathan Ames could have visitors he called at once and asked if he could see Mr. Ames.

"Yas, sah, Captain. He up fer de first time today. Come along, he's a restin' in the back yard." He guided the naval officer to a small walled-in garden. Eyes shut, Ames relaxed in a canvas sling chair, soaking up the sun. His head and back were bandaged and he'd lost weight. He was pale, haggard and there was a sad expression on his face.

"Sah," said Wash, "Captain Henley to see you."

Blinking, Ames said in a weak voice, "Afternoon, sir, please sit down."

The officer pulled up a stool. "How do you feel?"

"Weak, tired and I get a little dizzy when I try to walk."

"A blow on the head does that. It'll soon pass."

"I hope so, anyhow that's what the doctor says. And sir, Wash tells me you got the Savannah doctor. My thanks."

"Least I could do," said Henley. "Doctor says his trip here was a waste of time. Señora Gonzalez had you in good shape by the time he arrived."

"You know, Captain, I don't remember anything after the explosion. Wash says I was unconscious for two weeks, but I dreamed constantly. The wildest sort of dreams—that Luiza was feeding me, washing my hands and face, dressing my wounds and even singing me to sleep. Now I find that it wasn't a dream. She was really here."

"That's right, Mr. Ames. Day and night, she never left your bedside. She, with Wash's help, gave you every attention."

"I'm most grateful, but I wish I could have seen her before she went home."

"I'm afraid that's my fault," admitted Henley. "She wanted to stay until you had fully recovered, but I sent her back to St. Augustine with the other Spaniards."

"Why?"

"Orders, Mr. Ames. Co-operate with the Spaniards, no incidents and no trouble. General Coppinger demanded the Spaniards on Amelia Island be sent to St. Augustine. He asked especially about Señora Gonzalez, saying her family wanted her in Havana. I'm sorry, Mr. Ames, but you, too, are a soldier."

Ames groaned and shut his eyes. Softly he replied, "I understand, Captain Henley. Did you see her, talk with her before she sailed?"

"Yes, we talked for several hours."

"Did she leave me a letter?" he asked eagerly.

"No letter. She had tried to write but was too upset. However, a message . . ."

"What did she say?"

"Señora Gonzalez is a most remarkable lady. She's not only beautiful but she's got a big dose of what I call horse sense."

"I know," said Ames. "But what did she say?"

Captain Henley was not to be hurried. "I had a long and most interesting conversation with Señora Gonzalez. She was annoyed at being sent to St. Augustine." He grinned. "Annoyed, hell, she was furious. She called me a heartless, inhuman old man and then lapsed into Spanish. I understood just enough to know it wasn't complimentary." He laughed, pulled out his pipe and tamped down the black tobacco.

For God's sake, get on with it, thought Jonathan. He squirmed impatiently.

"After a time she kinda ran out of breath and tears came to her eyes. She desperately needed to talk to someone. I asked a few questions and out it came like a spring freshet." He deliberately lit his pipe and puffed clouds of smoke.

"Señora Gonzalez is deeply concerned and worried. She loves you very much but fears she might be a burden. She is a Spanish Catholic, you are an American Puritan. This is a vexing problem. She wants time to think and then she'll write." He smiled benignly and added, "She's a mighty sensible and unselfish lady. That briefly is what she wanted me to tell you." He relit his pipe and waited.

Ames sat quietly for a long time. He remembered the passionate joy they had shared—her tender lips and her beautiful

(203)

body. He thought of her courage in facing Aury and the long tedious hours she had spent nursing him. Once or twice after they had first met, he had tried to discuss their future, but she had always shushed him. Her husband was alive then. Now she was free. Did he want to marry her? He had never considered it before. He only knew the thought of being separated from Luiza was unbearable. He asked Captain Henley, "When will I hear from her?"

"I don't know. I gave her Mr. Simms's address. She will write you in Charleston."

"Perhaps I'll go to Havana."

"No," said Henley. "Give her the time she requested. Women are much more sensible about such things than men. Besides, you have an obligation to your country. Go to Charleston and stay with Mr. Simms until you are fully recovered. Then to Washington City and give Mr. Crawford a full report. That's your duty, sir."

"I suppose so," ruefully admitted Ames.

"Cheer up, young man. I've written President Monroe how you saved our fleet. Your mission was successful—we lost only two men. Aury, without powder, raised the white flag and sailed the next morning. By God though," growled Henley, "if I'd known then how he'd tortured you, I'd have hung him, even if it meant a war with Mexico."

"He's a devil and deserves hanging."

"I'll get him yet. I'm stationed at St. Marys with orders to rid the Caribbean of pirates and privateers. If I see Aury's ship and I don't give a damn what flag he's flying, I'll sink it."

"I wish you luck, sir."

"Thank you, Mr. Ames. Now can I make arrangements for you to get to Charleston?"

"Sir, with your permission, I'd like to take the sloop Wash and I sailed to St. Augustine. He'll get me to Charleston safely."

"She is all yours," said Henley. He got up and patted Jonathan gently on the shoulder. "Mr. Ames, if I can ever be of service, command me." He saluted and left.

Ames asked Wash if he knew where the sloop was docked. He replied that it was hidden in the marsh grass by Egan's Creek.

"Is it shipshape?" asked Ames.

"Bottom is sound but some new canvas and rope would be handy."

"Find out what we need and I'll send the captain a note. I'm sure he'll help."

"Yas, sah, but you ain't well enough to go no place."

"By the time you fix the sloop," said Ames, "I'll be ready."

Captain Henley willingly provided canvas for the jib and the mainsail, and new cordage. He assigned two sailors to help Wash, and within a week they had careened the boat, scraped her free of barnacles and painted her hull a bright blue.

"Little boat is ready," reported Wash. "The Navy has give us a frying pan, coffeepot, ax, few knives and forks, enough food and even a jug of rum."

"They have been most generous," said Ames. "Did they supply weapons?"

"No, sah. Claims they is in short supply of guns, powder and shot."

"Should be an easy voyage. Don't suppose we'll need them anyway."

"Can't ever tell," said Wash, "this might help," and produced a short-barrel musket.

"Why it's an old Brown Bess!" exclaimed Ames. The gun was clean and free of rust but lacked a flint with which to ignite the powder in the firing pan. Wash said he'd get a new flint for "What'd you call it?"

Laughing, Ames explained. This type of musket had been standard equipment in the British Army for many years. "It's always been called Brown Bess, booms like a small cannon, but you can't hit the side of a barn with them at ten paces."

"I'll take along my blowgun," said Wash. "And your sword, which I picked up when them pirates dragged you into the fort."

Ames thanked Wash, saying he was delighted to have the sword. "Now all we need is a map."

"Got that, too. Gift from Captain Henley."

"Then we'll sail in the morning."

"You still weak as 'er kitten. Better wait a week."

"No," said Ames, who was restless and anxious to leave Amelia Island. "I'll just sit at the tiller, that won't take much effort."

Unfolding the map, he saw Captain Henley had charted their course and attached a long explanatory letter. He had drawn a heavy blue line between the chain of barrier islands off the Georgia coast and the mainland. "Georgia's Golden Islands—Cumberland, Jekyll, St. Simon, Sapelo, St. Catherines and Ossabaw—will protect you from the Atlantic ocean. You might also be interested to know that a Scottish nobleman, just a hundred years ago, planned a settlement on these islands which he described as an early paradise and named them the Golden Isles of Georgia. This failed, but they are inhabited today. I know from experience that the islands welcome visitors with lavish hospitality."

The map indicated it was about 150 miles to Savannah. He reckoned it would take a week and another five days to Charleston. Perhaps two weeks with good weather, which would land him there in March. It didn't seem possible that it was just a year ago that he came to South Carolina.

During the next few days, as they sailed north, Ames saw that the islands were well named. They were serene, beautiful and heavily wooded. Long-leaf pine, oak, magnolia, palm, cypress palmetto and cedar grew almost to the beach. Long streams of Spanish moss hung from the spreading water oaks and the tall cypress. Between the islands and the mainland were acres of sea marsh crisscrossed with salt-water creeks.

Though tempted to visit one of the islands, Ames decided against it. As they sailed past Cumberland Island, with acres of gardens and olive-bordered terraces, he saw the immense four-storied mansion of Dungeness. It had been built by General Nathaniel Greene, and his family still lived there. He would have visited Dungeness except that his shabby clothes were not suitable for such an elegant establishment.

At twilight Wash dropped anchor in an inlet. While the days

were pleasant and the winter sun surprisingly warm, the nights were cold. As soon as they got ashore Wash started a fire, cooked supper and made a pallet of pine straw or moss. Exhausted, Ames often fell asleep before finishing his meal. With the morning sun he felt better. His wounds had healed and the dizzy spells were less frequent.

To pass the long days at sea he resumed Wash's lessons, including arithmetic. The multiplication tables, once he understood their use, fascinated him. He mastered them in record time and grinned happily at Ames's praise.

"Ever thought what you'd like to do when we get to Charleston?" asked Ames one day.

"I likes working fer you."

"But, Wash, I can't pay you. I've no money."

"Tain't no matter."

Yes it is, Ames said to himself, though God knows I'll miss him. The smartest thing I ever did was buy Wash. He's been loyal, devoted and I'd probably be dead if it had not been for him. How can I make him understand that he is free and must earn a living. Speaking slowly, he said, "Wash, you have been the best friend a man ever had."

"I'se glad, sah."

"Damnit," exploded Ames, "stop that sah, sah, sah all the time."

Wash asked in a baffled tone, "Why?"

"You only say sir to your elders or an official like a governor or Captain Henley. You and I are the same age and, the Lord knows, I've got no title."

"You is Colonel Ames." He paused, grinned and added "sah."

Laughing in spite of himself, Ames replied, "Colonel of what? I'm just a man, with no job and no money."

"I'se got some money."

"You!" exclaimed Ames. "Where'd you get it?"

"Spanish missy give it to me fer hiding her from Aury." He reached in his canvas bag, found a small pouch, opened it and dumped gold pesos on the deck.

Ames counted the coins and said, "Why, Wash, you are rich. That's about five hundred dollars."

"Heap 'er money," agreed Wash. "You take some."

"No," replied Ames. "This will help you get started in Charleston."

"Don't care fer that place. I like the ocean much better."

"Then become a trader. You can have this sloop. Fill it with knives, fish hooks, pots, pans—all the things the island people need. Sell or exchange them for fresh fruit, cigars, rum, coconuts—anything folks in Savannah and Charleston will buy."

"Sounds mighty fine. I'd shore like that."

"I'll get Mr. Simms to help. He'll know how to make the necessary arrangements," said Ames enthusiastically.

Beaming, Wash said, "This boat ain't got no name. If you don't mind, I'd like to call her Miss Luiza."

"I'm sure it would please her very much." He thought for a minute. "Where did you hide Luiza?"

"In your little house back 'er the fort."

Ames was astounded. "Why there?"

"With you in jail, last place old Aury thought 'er looking. I kinda let my hair git bushy and wore yellow or blue pants. I reckon I looked like one of 'em pirates. No one bothered me. I got around, stole some food and kept Miss Luiza comfortable."

"I'm sure you did," said Ames gratefully and finished stacking the gold pesos.

The fair weather held. Her mainsail taut from the brisk wind, the sloop skimmed over the water like a soaring gull. As they sailed north past Sapelo, St. Catherines and Ossabaw islands, Ames passed the time by tutoring Wash in writing and arithmetic. He could write his name and simple sentences in block letters and had an aptitude for numbers. Wash, in turn, taught Ames the names of many of the birds that called the Golden Isles home. He liked to watch the gulls, terns, pelicans and ducks swooping over the waves, the sandpipers and willets running along the beaches, the cranes, the blue and white herons fishing and the lovely egrets in the shallows, the water turkeys and wood ibises soaring over the marshes. The forests, marshes, creeks, rivers and ponds of the islands attracted birds of every description—swimmers, divers, cooers, warblers and singers. He was fascinated and learned to identify them by their plumage, flight or song.

On the eighth day they passed the Savannah River, which divides Georgia and South Carolina. Their water and food was ample so it wasn't necessary to stop in Savannah. They plotted their course on the inland water route by Hiltonhead Island, then into Charleston harbor. They tied up at the Ashley Dock and Wash said he'd store the sails and bring their gear to Mr. Simms's home.

Stiff from days at the tiller, Ames walked slowly along the shaded streets. He was dirty, tired and hungry. He wondered if Mr. Simms would welcome him. After all, it had been a year. He had sent a letter from Fernandina, but posts were unreliable. He turned into the walk of the Georgian house and saw its owner dozing in a rocking chair. Treading softly down the side porch, he shook Simms gently and said, "Good evening, sir."

Simms blinked at the thin, rather shabby young man standing over him. Recognition came, he struggled to his feet and embraced Ames. "It's you—safe. My God, Jonathan, I'm glad to see you." He hugged Jonathan again and mumbled, "Let's celebrate with a drink."

Jonathan saw him brush away a tear. There was no doubt about the warmth of his welcome. It was good to be in Charleston again.

§ CHAPTER 14 §

Jonathan Ames felt like a goose being fattened for Christmas. For over a week he had eaten three enormous meals, nibbled cake, cookies, pralines between and drunk goblet after goblet of sweet milk. He had slept eight to ten hours every night and napped in the afternoon. His gaunt cheeks filled and his husky voice vanished. Each day he was stronger, and though his vertigo persisted, he was on the mend.

His host asked no questions, though he was bursting with curiosity. He encouraged Jonathan to eat and rest, regaling him with ludicrous and roguish stories about Charleston. The old lawyer enjoyed talking and kept his guest relaxed with his wry comments and his amusing anecdotes. To the best of his ability he answered Ames's questions about West Florida. Intelligence was slow and the *Courier*'s news limited.

Simms explained that John C. Calhoun of South Carolina had resigned from Congress in December and been appointed Secretary of War. One of his first acts was to order General Jackson to Georgia with orders to "adopt the necessary measures to terminate the conflict.

"That simple language means beat hell out of the Seminoles, who raid, steal and kill settlers in Georgia and in Alabama and run back and hide in Spanish Florida. Jackson is someplace on the border with eight hundred Regulars and nine hundred

Georgia militia under his command. He's an able and restless man who won't hesitate to follow the Seminoles into Florida and even fight the Spaniards, the British partisans, or anyone else that might interfere."

One evening Simms said, "I'm most interested in what happened to you on Amelia. I think it's about time for you to do some talking, instead of me."

Jonathan agreed and that night over coffee and brandy he described General MacGregor's expedition, his capture of Fort San Carlos and attributed his subsequent failures to indecision. He told how Jared Irwin had rallied the army and defeated the Spaniards, how Luis Aury had seized the island and turned it into a pirate hell. He lauded the bravery of Irwin, Charles Laurent and said that Wash had saved his life and his sanity.

Simms waved his cigar and said Wash was a "good Negro, smart, too. I've changed his pesos into dollars, got him credit for trade goods and he sails for Nassau and the Out Islands next week. He'll do fine," said Simms. "He can add faster than I can."

Ames said he was appreciative, as he could never fully repay his obligation to Wash.

"He's got more payment than he ever expected," shrewdly observed the lawyer. "Your respect and friendship. He certainly deserves it." He lit a fresh cigar and poured more brandy. Jonathan declined, saying he still had bouts of giddiness and spirits made it worse.

"You got quite a blow on the head when you blew up Aury's powder supply," said Simms.

"How did you know?" he asked in surprise.

"Captain Stratford was in my office this afternoon. He'd just arrived from Fernandina, where he'd dined with Captain Henley. He gives you full credit for saving his fleet and routing the pirates."

"Captain Henley is too generous. The marines he put at my command made it possible."

"Modesty is a fine trait," commented Simms. "But don't

overdo it. I've written Bill Crawford that you should be decorated and commissioned a major in the Regulars."

Frowning Ames said, "I don't want to rejoin the Army."

"Now, that's interesting. Why?"

He hesitated. It was difficult to put his feelings into words. "I still have nightmares when I remember all those dead Spaniards on McClure's Hill. I hate killing and the sight of blood makes me sick. I'll never be a good soldier."

"Seems to me you've already proven yourself wrong." Simms smiled. "I'll admit fighting is damned silly, seldom accomplishes anything useful. But what would you like to do?"

"I haven't given it much thought. I just know, as soon as I'm able, I must go to Washington City."

Simms nodded his approval. "Crawford is an honest man. He'll see that you get fair treatment."

"I only want to give Mr. Crawford a full report on Florida. I'm not asking anything."

"Never refuse anything you can get from your government. Just consider yourself lucky."

"All right, sir," laughed Ames.

Puffing smoke toward the ceiling, Simms bluntly asked, "Ever consider the law?"

"Why, no, sir."

"It's not a bad profession. Why, I even know one or two honest lawyers," he said in a mocking tone. "See Crawford, discuss it with him if you like, but come back to Charleston, read law in my office, pass your bar exams and I'll make you a partner."

Jonathan was overwhelmed by the offer. He knew Simms had one of the city's most lucrative practices. "It's most generous of you," he stammered.

"No. I'm selfish," replied Simms, thinking of his dead son who would be about Jonathan's age now. "I'm lonesome in this big house. I'd like you to live with me, Jonathan. Probably add ten years to my life." He chuckled and added, "Some folks might think that a bad idea. Anyhow, think it over and we'll discuss it again."

Ames promised he would.

March was a delightful month in Charleston. Fresh crisp mornings, hot but not oppressive during the day and refreshingly cool evenings. Jonathan had never seen so many beautiful flowers. The deep shade of the water oaks and magnolias accentuated the brilliance of pink and red azaleas, purple wisteria and hundreds of daffodils.

He received numerous invitations to teas, suppers, the races or to drink at one of the many gentlemen's clubs. He declined politely. He still had sudden attacks of dizziness. They came without warning and lasted only about ten minutes but were disconcerting. Simms had insisted he see a Charleston doctor. Again the same diagnosis that he had gotten on Amelia Island—not serious and with rest and proper diet they would go away.

Every morning after breakfast with Mr. Simms, Jonathan went to the library. He enjoyed reading the *Courier*, but its lack of news on Florida distressed him. He smiled at the thought of suave Charles Laurent fighting under Old Hickory. They were indeed an odd pair, but, as experienced soldiers, would respect each other. The French officer had talked with Wash before sailing from Amelia. He had sent Ames "good wishes for a speedy recovery" and promised to write. No letter from Laurent though, or Crawford or, more important to him, none from Luiza. He fretted at the inefficiency of the post.

Luiza had been in Havana at least a month. Though American relations with Spain were tense, trade continued. The *Courier* listed Havana sailings several times a week. There had been ample time for a letter. Why—what had happened? He would like to write Luiza but had no address. Why don't I go to Cuba? There is so much I want to tell her. The idea appealed to him. Then he recalled Captain Henley's advice to give her time and his own obligations to Mr. Crawford. This only deepened his black mood.

His glumness worried Simms. While accepting the doctor's prescription of "rest and quiet," he began inviting friends for a drink or coffee after supper. Jonathan was courteous but quiet. He smiled occasionally, seldom laughed and spoke only when questioned. At times Simms wondered if his head injury had permanently affected him.

The one exception was Simms's good friend Joel Poinsett. This handsome, elegantly groomed man stimulated Ames. He realized that beneath the quick wit and gracious smile was a vast fund of knowledge.

Poinsett was very curious about MacGregor's expedition. He asked questions by the score and deplored the failure to take St. Augustine. The scarcity of news from West Florida, he admitted, was disconcerting, but "I have great confidence in Andrew Jackson."

"Young Calhoun made a wise choice," said Simms, "in sending old Andy to clean up the Seminoles."

"Yes, he did. John is shrewd, cunning and very ambitious. He wants to be President."

"He's only thirty-five," said Simms. "Monroe will get a second term and in 1824 Bill Crawford will be elected."

"If the election were held this week your friend Mr. Crawford would win. But lots of things can happen in six years. He'll probably have plenty of competition. Jackson, Henry Clay and John Quincy Adams among others."

"That sniveling, baldheaded Yankee? He hasn't a chance."

"Now, Edward," laughed Poinsett, "don't let your prejudice show. Adams is well educated, lived in Europe for many years, which gives him an understanding of foreign relations, and would probably make a good President."

"Maybe, but I'll lay you two to one on Crawford. With Jefferson, Madison and Monroe supporting him he can't lose."

"Wouldn't be too sure about the President. He's a slippery fellow. What about Jackson?"

"I like the old devil but he doesn't want it. His wife hates Washington." He grinned. "Can you imagine fat old Rachel, with her pipe, as first lady?"

Both men smiled and Poinsett told Simms he talked like a Charleston snob. "Seriously, Edward," he continued, "I think it's true that Jackson doesn't want to run for President, but he's the great hero of the West and his ardent supporters will force him to stand. Then don't forget he hates Crawford for

(214)

giving the Cherokees back some of their land that he took at the Fort Jackson treaty."

"That was a swindle and you know it, Joel."

"Certainly. But stealing Indian lands never lost a politician any votes. To the contrary. And what of Mr. Crawford's views on relations with the Indians? As I remember, he said in a speech, 'Let intermarriage be encouraged by the government. It will preserve the Indians, give them civil liberties and social happiness.' What will your Charleston friends think?"

"They won't like it," admitted Simms.

"I'm sorry," Poinsett said to Ames, "but when Edward and I begin to argue, we forget our manners."

"It's most interesting," said Jonathan. "Go ahead. Please don't mind me."

"A most courteous retort, sir," said Poinsett. "Did you by any chance know John C. Calhoun when he attended law school in Litchfield?"

"No, though I remember him. He was very tall, with long black hair. Also he scandalized Litchfield by going on long Sunday walks instead of to church."

Poinsett laughed. "Don't ever tell anyone. It's a mortal sin in Charleston to miss Sunday services."

"Yes, let's keep his secret," agreed Simms. "Perhaps fifteen or twenty years from now he might get to be President. Be rather pleasant to have a President from South Carolina."

"But not John C. Calhoun," Poinsett said sternly.

"With his cabinet service and perhaps a term as Vice President, he'd be mature enough."

"No, Edward. He'll destroy our country with his nullification doctrine." Noticing Ames's puzzled look, he explained. "Calhoun thinks the states should have the authority to say what federal statutes they'll obey. This would lead to anarchy, disunion and even civil war."

"I think you go too far, Joel," admonished Simms. "The tariff bill of 1816 protects Yankee industry and makes things cost more for us."

"I agree the tariff isn't fair, but our recourse is to Congress or the federal courts. Chief Justice John Marshall said, 'If the legislatures of the several states nullify the tariff law, we produce direct collision between the authority of the state and the authority of the Union. We trap the innocent citizen between duty to his state and duty to his country. A man cannot obey two masters.'"

Jonathan listened with rapt attention. Poinsett's arguments were convincing. He waited for Simms's reply. The old man took a linen handkerchief from his pocket and mopped his face. It was obvious he was impressed by Poinsett's sincerity. "I'm the lawyer, not you, Joel," he said lightly, "though I admit you'd make a good one. I still insist this high tariff will ruin the South."

"You must not blame the tariff for the North's prosperity or our poverty. Northerners are industrious and frugal, while we, unfortunately, are idle and extravagant. Has the tariff really reduced property values in South Carolina, or is it the cheap land in Alabama and Mississippi that has lowered cotton prices and caused our headaches?

"But enough of this gloomy discussion. Jonathan, I am having a supper the night before the Jockey Club races. That's April tenth and I insist you must come."

"I'd be delighted, if I'm able."

"Nonsense. Sweet music, wine and charming ladies. That's the best cure for all ailments. I'll expect both of you."

The mysterious grapevine among the Negroes, which Jonathan did not understand but found accurate, brought the news that Wash's sloop would dock in the morning. Hoping that his trip to the Bahamas had been successful, he decided to meet him and find out. As he walked slowly to the waterfront he sought the shade under the old trees. The early morning sun was hot. Charleston had a muted mellow beauty. Heat, damp and rain had faded the crumbling walls and old houses into delicate hues of pink and blue. Fires, wars and hurricanes gave the city a time-worn look.

The bustling harbor fascinated him. The fishing boats were in and moored to the tangle of small wharfs. The boatmen haggled over prices with the peddlers while their carts lined the quay waiting to be filled and trundled through the streets. Their cries and chants of fresh fish, all kinds, prices and sizes, Ames found musical but unintelligible.

He was impressed with the harbor activity. Ships of British, American, Dutch, French and Spanish registry were loading cargoes of rice, lumber, resin, sugar, molasses and cotton. Everywhere he looked he saw mountains of cotton and the adjacent warehouses were filled with cotton bales. Was Poinsett right when he predicted that cotton would eventually strangle Charleston?

In the waterfront taverns he heard the accents of New England, Georgia, Virginia and a bewildering number of foreign languages. Ships of all sizes and rigs dotted the harbor. Just beyond a brigantine, with a fore and aft sail, he spotted the blue hull of the *Miss Luiza*. Wash lashed the sloop to a wharf and he jumped aboard.

The big Negro was pleased at Ames's welcome and spoke enthusiastically of his voyage. With one assistant, he had sailed the *Miss Luiza* to Nassau, to several of the inhabited Bahamas and as far south as the Turk Islands. There was a ready market for his trade goods and he had returned with a cargo of grapefruit, oranges, limes, lemons and sponges. He also had a strange greenish-pink fruit, apple-sized, which he said was a papaya. "Taste it," he urged and cut thin slices, dousing them with lime juice.

Their tangy sweetness was a new flavor to Ames. It was delicious. "Where did you find them?"

"They grows wild on most of 'em little cays. Bahamians eat 'em for breakfast with grilled fresh fish. Mighty tasty," added Wash. He packed a basket of papayas and pineapples and asked Jonathan to give them to Mr. Simms.

"I'm sure he'll like papayas and tell his friends about them," replied Ames. He advised Wash to load up with papayas on his next trip as "I think there's a ready market for them in Charleston."

"I'll do that," agreed Wash and asked Ames if he thought it was safe for him to go to Cuba.

"Why?"

"Mr. Blair said he'd like five thousand Havanas but they cost more in Nassau than in Charleston. A thing called duty makes 'em so high."

Everyone seems to be complaining about tariffs, thought Jonathan. I suppose the English are trying to protect the markets for their Jamaican cigars, which do not have the delicate flavor of Havanas. Pointing to several Spanish ships in the harbor, he said, "I expect you'll find plenty of American bottoms in Havana. They won't mind, especially as you'll go to buy."

"If Mr. Blair will double his order, think I'll go."

"If you do, would you try to find Señora Gonzalez?"

"You ain't heard from little Spanish missy?"

"No. And I'm worried."

"I'll do my best. If I finds her, what you want me to say?"

"Tell her I hope she's safe and well. That I can't understand why she has not written and that I miss her."

"Quit yo' worryin', Mr. Ames. If she in Cuba I'll search her out."

The afternoon of Poinsett's party Simms received a letter from William Crawford. He wished Jonathan a quick recovery, said there was no hurry about coming to the capital and under no circumstances should he make the long trip until he was well. He added there was no late news from Florida—just rumors. "Though you can be sure Jackson is active. I'm told that the President has to fortify himself with two brandies before opening Jackson's dispatch box."

Ames told Simms, "If the doctor approves I think I will go to Washington City next month. I feel better every day and I've had no vertigo recently."

"We'll see," replied Simms. "Now I think we had better dress for Joel's supper."

An unexpected visit from one of Simms's clients made them late. Poinsett waved aside their apologies and ushered them into the long dining room. He said to his seated guests, "This gentleman is Mr. Simms's good friend Jonathan Ames. And mine, too, I add proudly. He begs forgiveness for his late arrival but he was delayed while Edward accumulated a few extra dollars by advising some rascal how to thwart justice."

The assembled company laughed and teased the lawyer. Ames was seated between two young girls who said they were thrilled to meet Mr. Ames for they had heard so many complimentary things about him.

Their flattery gave him a pleasant glow. He nodded to several people he remembered from Poinsett's last party. At the far end of the table he saw Thalia Cummings. Her red hair, flowing loosely over her shoulders, shimmered in the soft candlelight. For a moment he was dazzled by her beauty. She caught his stare and smiled. Her mischievous green eyes seemed to mock him. Blushing slightly, he turned to the young lady on his left, who was lamenting that cotton had dropped two cents a pound and they probably could not afford Newport this summer.

While the delectable meal of roast wild duck and baked oysters was served, Thalia Cummings carefully studied Jonathan Ames. This was not the bashful young man she had met a year ago. She had been told of his gallantry at Amelia Island, his torture by the pirates and his almost miraculous escape from death. His experiences had aged him. There was a sadness in his face that gave him a distinguished look. He was not handsome, she decided, but interesting. She approved of his dark unpowdered hair, neatly clubbed with a black ribbon, but his black broadcloth coat wrinkled at the shoulders. I'll remind him to speak sternly to his tailor, and she giggled at this possessive thought.

Ladies' gossip reported that Mr. Simms had offered Jonathan a partnership in his law firm and that he would name him his heir. If this were true he would be one of Charleston's richest bachelors. Thalia had few doubts, for she knew Mr. Simms had great affection and respect for him. At a Christmas party, mellow with rum punch, he had confided that he missed Jonathan and hoped to persuade him to stay in Charleston. He had bragged of Ames's friendship with Mr. Crawford and how he had dined with President Madison and Mr. Jefferson at Montpelier.

For the first time Thalia was seriously considering marriage. She was nineteen and by Charleston standards an old maid. Then, too, her mother's complaints were shriller. Why had she refused so many eligible young gentlemen? Heaven knows she'd had plenty of proposals, but she had never met a man she wanted to share her bed.

She glanced again at Jonathan's face and thought he had suffered and that that should make him kind. Anyhow, she was positive she could manage him, or any man for that matter. She approved of his Washington City friends and said to herself, I'll get him elected to Congress, perhaps even to the Senate. She liked the idea of living part of the year in the capital, meeting the President and those foreign diplomats. Maybe I'd better brush up on my French. By the time coffee was served Thalia had decided to marry Jonathan Ames.

At an early age this willful girl knew what she wanted and how to get it. The servants and even her parents were terrified of her tantrums. She would kick and scream until she got her way. The only person she feared was her tough old grandpa, who once said she was like a female spider, deadly but irresistible.

Joel Poinsett moved among his guests and announced that there would be dancing. Jonathan heard the scraping of fiddles, then the stately music of the minuet. He walked toward the orchestra and somehow was not surprised to find Thalia Cummings at his side. He said, "Good evening, Miss Cummings."

"What a pleasure, Mr. Ames. I'm delighted to see you again and looking so handsome after your tribulations in Florida."

The sound of the music made Thalia think of their last meeting. Smiling, she asked, "Did you ever learn to waltz?"

"No, Miss Cummings."

"My invitation still holds."

"What about your mother?"

"Ma sent me packing to Beaufort 'cause she thought I showed too much interest in a young Yankee."

"I'm flattered."

"Then you'll come for your first lesson. Say, on Wednesday at five? The waltz is really quite respectable now."

He couldn't resist asking, "Do you observe the four-inch separation?"

"That depends on your partner," she answered gaily. "The minuet is quite safe though. Shall we?"

"I beg to be excused."

This was a new experience for Thalia. She was not accustomed to men refusing her. Angry flecks showed in her eyes, her smile was like the silver plate on a coffin. She waved to a gentleman and without another word left Ames.

As he watched Thalia dance, a faint disturbing dizziness touched him, almost an instinctive fear. That night as he slowly undressed Jonathan recalled Thalia's bold look when he bowed good night. He did not understand this beautiful girl. The smoldering light in her green eyes and the sweet curve of her pink lips intrigued him. She was that mysterious thing, a clever woman who was lovely and feminine. The combination made him uneasy.

"I'll avoid her in the future," he said to himself. "And first thing in the morning I'll send a note saying I'm too ill to accept her invitation." As he got into bed he was shocked at his conceit. Thalia had many beaux and was invited to every party. Why should she be interested in me, a Yankee and a nobody in Charleston? he asked himself. Perhaps it's my imagination, but wasn't there a predatory look in her lovely eyes? He wished somehow that he could explore her mind, find out what she was thinking.

He would have been surprised if he could have seen Thalia at that moment. She had returned from Poinsett's in a melancholy mood, perplexed by Jonathan's rebuff. She had flirted enough to know he was interested. What had she done to . . . to, well, frighten him. Yes, that was the word—frighten. She had seen it in his eyes. She pirouetted before a full-length mirror, pleased with her rounded breasts and long graceful legs. She had been told many times that she was beautiful, lovely and exquisite. She believed it. Besides, she knew the mirror did not lie.

Why did I fail to captivate him? The thought made her furious. I will never speak to that priggish young man again and I will refuse to receive him when he calls. But, what if he doesn't come?

She recalled her decision at supper to marry Jonathan. Now she was even more determined. She brushed her long hair and considered. As she got into bed she was planning and scheming—dozens of ideas flashed through her mind.

Neither Thalia nor Jonathan slept very well that night.

At Mr. Simms's urging Jonathan began to accept a few of his many invitations. "Charleston in the spring is paradise," said the lawyer. "Its inhabitants' chief concern is the pursuit of pleasure. Enjoy it, my boy, while you are young."

Ames did. He visited dozens of men's clubs where whist was played half the night for high stakes. These were convivial gatherings. Gentlemen discussed politics and the price of cotton, told bawdy stories and drank indifferent wines. Race days were gala occasions, for the entire town turned out. Ladies, in the latest finery, sat in a special gallery. Captains complained that they could not get their ships loaded—all their men were at the races.

There was the theater, concerts, lectures, the stylish St. Cecilia Ball and wining and dining nightly at some mansion.

A foolhardy gentleman was indiscreet enough to write in the paper that the ladies should spend more time at the distaff and spinning wheel.

He got a scorching reply, saying it proved little for her sisters to card and spin while the men continued to spend both time and substance in what they call parties of pleasure. There is not one night in the week in which they are not engaged with some club or tavern, where they injure their fortunes by gaming in various ways and impair their health by the intemperate use of spiritous liquors and keeping late hours. The writer damned horse races, heavy betting and said, "Some gentlemen will even risk large sums on the chance stroke of a cock's heel, so addicted are they to extravagant dissipations which they falsely call pleasure."

In the long South Carolina spring Jonathan often saw Thalia. Depending on her mood, she was haughty and cruel or gay and tender—almost affectionate. Other times she simply ignored him. This was disturbing, for he admired this lovely girl. Her wit was odd and entertaining. She dismissed one admirer with the remark that his "fatiguing loquacity was tedious." The first time she saw Jonathan, after he had declined her waltz lesson, she said with a bewitching smile, "I'm sorry, sir, that your indisposition was not more serious," and left him gasping.

At parties he often found himself watching Thalia, usually surrounded by a group of men. Her acerbic comments and shrewd remarks impressed and amused them. And always she seemed to be bursting with happiness. Though she made no effort to speak to Jonathan, she adroitly maneuvered near him. Occasionally she would give him a provocative smile, a quick flicker of her soft green eyes. She was so desirable, so tempting that he often wanted to crush her in his arms. Instead, at night, lusty and rapacious dreams tantalized him.

The perceptive old lawyer watched them with tolerant amusement. He had once congratulated Thalia on perfecting the art of flirting. She scornfully replied it was not an art, just hard work and understanding the male ego. The most effective method she said was indifference. Every man thinks he is irresistible. That you believe otherwise is a staggering blow to his conceit. He will do anything to convince you the errors of your ways. Be charming, gracious but pretend to ignore him. He will be on your doorstep and you can have him, if you want him.

For reasons which he did not understand, he sensed Thalia wanted Jonathan. Her technique was working perfectly. God help him, for he's unaware of his danger. She'll have him at the altar before he knows it.

Simms decided he would have a talk with Jonathan. One evening he said, "You find Thalia attractive?"

"Yes, sir."

"Have you ever thought of marrying her?" he inquired bluntly.

A startled Jonathan blurted, "Why, no, Mr. Simms. She dislikes me."

"I doubt that."

"But, sir, she avoids me."

That shrewd, cunning little bitch, thought Simms. Preening, smiling, doing anything to catch his eye and then pretending disdain. And, it was effective.

"Jonathan," he said in a fatherly voice, "I know Thalia. She's set her cap for you."

"You can't be serious, sir."

"Very much so, unless you love her. Then, you have no problem."

Jonathan was astounded. Was Simms teasing? No, there was a worried note in his voice. "I like Miss Cummings. She's beautiful but, sir, at times she terrifies me."

"Then run before it's too late."

"What, sir?"

"Run. Escape—get away for a time."

Ames could hardly believe his ears. This was absurd. The idea of running away from a slip of a girl. He didn't know what to say and so was silent.

The lawyer finally spoke in pre-emptory tones. "The schooner *Santee* sails for Washington City in the morning. Be aboard her. Stay here and your goose is cooked."

Jonathan thought for a time, smiled and said, "All right, I will."

§ CHAPTER 15 §

Eleven days out of Charleston the *Santee* dropped anchor in the Potomac River. As Jonathan Ames came ashore he was pleased to see William H. Crawford. The tall Georgian swept him into a bear hug. "My God, Johnny, I'm glad to see you." He carefully scrutinized him. "You look well, young man."

"I'm fine and I greatly appreciate you being here to meet me. It was most kind of you, sir."

"Nonsense, Johnny. I send you on a wild-goose chase to Florida with that pompous MacGregor. You get jailed, tortured and damned near killed. Least I can do is show my big face and say I'm mighty sorry."

"Don't feel that way, sir. You didn't send me. I volunteered."

"Now, Johnny," laughed Crawford. "You hurt my feelings. You mean my persuasive hints didn't influence you?"

"Well yes, sir." Ames smiled. "If you put it that way."

"I always say there is nothing like an honest man. Come, here is my carriage."

As they rode down dusty Pennsylvania Avenue, Jonathan noticed many changes in Washington City. The buildings damaged by the British invasion had been repaired and painted. A dozen or more new houses graced the wide tree-lined street.

The President's palace, a gray black ruin a year ago, glistened a pristine white in the brilliant June sun. "Took four coats of paint to cover all the smoke stain," said Crawford. "Everyone now calls it the White House. Much better than the 'palace,' don't you think?"

"Yes, I do."

"Sorry the President isn't in residence. He's in New England shaking hands and making speeches. He's anxious to meet you. Wants to thank you for those excellent reports on Florida."

Ames said that he would be honored.

A jovial and skilled raconteur, Crawford amused his companion with his stories of capital society. "The ladies, bless 'em, just love to gossip. Dolley Madison liked giving parties and her charm and social adroitness made them fun. In contrast, Mrs. Monroe is cold, a bit haughty and her drawing rooms are . . ."

"What, sir?"

"Drawing rooms. That's what they call a party at the White House. They are stiff, tiring and mighty squeezing. Just too many people. Bands play, and wine, tea and ices are served. There are no cards or dancing, the town's favorite amusement. Also the President gets poorer every day. He receives only twenty-five thousand a year and no expense money. It's a damned disgrace. Like Mr. Jefferson and Madison, he'll be deeply in debt when he leaves office."

Jonathan agreed it was most unfair.

"It is that. If the taxpayers want the White House to be almost a public tavern, they ought to be willing to pay for it. And the diplomats criticize the President for occasionally serving scuppernong wine instead of madeira to save a little money."

Crawford said he had built a new house on the corner of Massachusetts Avenue and Fourteenth Street, which friends call my "country home." "It's a bit far from the Capitol, but the town will grow that way. Mrs. Crawford is delighted to have you as a guest. She's heard me speak of you so often."

That evening, over brandy and cigars, Jonathan underwent a grueling examination on Florida. It was easy to understand why Crawford had been a successful lawyer. At midnight

Ames concluded by saying that he was sorry MacGregor's expedition had failed.

"He failed but you didn't. We'll soon have Florida. Your report on Aury's seizure of Amelia Island gave us the opportunity we needed."

"I don't quite understand, sir."

"Your intelligence was both comprehensive and timely. The reference to the Congressional Act of 1811, which gives the President the power to seize Florida if occupied by a foreign nation, was masterful, and Aury did annex Amelia to Mexico." He paused and smiled. "You have the makings of a good diplomat, Johnny. Anyhow, when the President read it he smacked the table and said, 'The young man is right' and ordered the Navy to expell the pirates."

"Luis Aury was the devil incarnate. His 'black dogs' were raiding south Georgia, stealing and killing. It seems to me the President could have just booted them out, without worrying about any congressional act."

"No, Johnny, that would have violated the Constitution. Don't you remember our conversation at Montpelier? If any President ever commits an act without congressional approval that might involve us in a war with another nation, he should be impeached. Not that Monroe would for he's a strict constitutionalist, sired as it were by Mr. Jefferson and Madison."

Jonathan was awed by Crawford's solemn voice. "I understand, sir."

Crawford nodded approvingly. "Now one final matter. The Secretary of War is with the President. We've talked about you several times and Mr. Calhoun wonders if you would like to rejoin the Army and teach at West Point."

"Me, at West Point? Why I don't think so, sir."

"Sleep on it before you refuse. An officer with your experience would be a great asset to the academy. It's being revitalized and brought up to date. A Major Sylvanus Thayer has been appointed superintendent."

"So they finally got rid of Old Pewter?"

"Who?"

"When I was at the Point, Captain Alden Patridge was in

charge. We called him 'Old Pewter' because he wanted every-thing gray—uniforms, barracks, cannon and even gray-backed test books."

Laughing, Crawford said, "An apt name. Am I correct in assuming you don't have a very high opinion of . . . er . . . Old Pewter?"

"Well, sir, he liked to hire his relatives. The mess was ter-rible and there was much drinking and gambling. I am sure Major Thayer will be an improvement."

"I hope so. You look tired. Go to bed, Johnny, get some rest and we'll talk of this again."

Everyone in Washington City seemed to be determined to make Jonathan's sojourn pleasant. He was deluged with in-vitations to teas, dinners and suppers, or to cockfights, racing or cards. While he enjoyed being feted he didn't really under-stand.

"Simple," drawled Crawford. "I've mentioned your Florida adventures to a few people and news spreads fast. Why, Johnny, in this town, devoted wholly to politics and society, some ladies even scan the hotel registers looking for people to entertain."

The hospitality, while pleasant, was both exhausting and expensive. He had been amused when Crawford had told him that Portuguese Minister De Serra had described the capital as "a city of magnificent distances." Houses were widely sep-arated, and daily he was spending six or seven of his dwin-dling dollars on coaches. Nor did he like their pitching and plunging over ruts, through dusty lanes and across vacant lots. Crawford had invited him to a three o'clock dinner at the In-dian Queen. It was time he decided to return to Charleston and he would tell him today. As he stood under the lurid paint-ing of Pocahontas over the entrance to the hotel he thought he saw a familiar figure.

Had the hot June sun tricked him? It just couldn't be, but it was. A sardonic voice he knew so well said, "Jonathan, to use an overused cliché, it's a small world."

"Charles, Charles—what a pleasant surprise!" They shook hands, smiling at each other.

"Sorry I'm late, Johnny," boomed the deep voice of Crawford.

"Mr. Crawford, this is Captain Charles Laurent. You will remember . . ."

"Indeed I do. You mentioned his courage several times in dispatches. This is indeed a pleasure, Captain Laurent," he said, shaking hands. "Come and dine with us?"

Laurent said he would be most happy.

They walked to the spacious dining room where Jesse Brown, the landlord, in a large white apron, said, "Senator Crawford, a welcome to you and your friends."

"Thank you, Jesse. Could we have a corner table?"

"Certainly, sir." Brown seated them, waved to a waiter who brought decanters of whiskey and brandy. "A bottle of my special madeira for the senator," he ordered.

"You know my weakness, Jesse," laughed Crawford. To Laurent he said, "What brings you to the capital, Captain?"

"A special dispatch from General Jackson."

His eyes glistening with excitement, Crawford said, "When did you leave Florida?"

"I sailed from Pensacola on the first of June."

"Pensacola? You mean Jackson has captured it?"

"Yes, Mr. Crawford, and the rest of Florida also."

"My God," he blurted and poured the madeira. "Do tell us what happened."

The Frenchman rolled the wine in his stemmed glass and drank deeply. Noticing his haggard look, Jonathan said, "Charles, you must be hungry."

"I'm half starved," he replied and finished his drink.

"My apologies, Captain Laurent," said Crawford and replenished his madeira. "Not a word until you've had dinner. The Indian Queen isn't elegant by Paris standards, but the food is good. Simple, well cooked and there's plenty."

"After months of parched corn and salt pork with such occasional delicacies as fried alligator tail or roasted raccoon, this is sheer heaven."

(229)

The two men waited impatiently as Laurent ate. They watched in awe as the wiry man devoured huge slices of roast beef, lamb, duck and turkey, generous portions of corn, beans, squash and potatoes. He gave Crawford a grateful smile when the waiter uncorked a bottle of claret. For a half hour Laurent said not a word but concentrated on his dinner. Finally, sipping wine, he said, "*Magnifique!* Mr. Crawford, your obedient servant, sir."

"It's a real pleasure to see a man enjoy his victuals," observed Crawford. "Now tell us what Jackson has done in Florida."

Ames spoke up. "Start at the beginning, Charles. I believe you left Amelia just after Christmas?"

"About the middle of January. When we got the news of General Jackson's appointment, Jared Irwin, who'd served in your assembly with him, wrote a letter recommending my services. Twenty-two Georgians, who'd enlisted with Mac-Gregor in Savannah, sailed with me to join Jackson." He looked at Jonathan and continued, "I was sorry I couldn't say 'good-bye' to you but your doctor forbade visitors."

"Wash gave me your message. I thank you. Why didn't you write as you promised?"

"With what in those miserable swamps?"

"I understand." He saw Crawford squirming restlessly. "Get along with your story."

"When we got to Mobile we were told that Jackson was at old Fort Negro on the Apalachicola River. We got some ponies, 'tackies' I believe you call them, and started. The streams were bank-high and the trail a quagmire." He rubbed his bottom gently and sipped more claret. "Those bony little horses were uncomfortable but we reached the fort on March fifteenth and I reported to the general at once." He paused, wrinkled his brow and reflected for what seemed like minutes. "Have you ever met General Jackson?"

"No," answered Ames, but Crawford said, "I know him quite well."

"Then you can imagine my surprise. He is a tall, gaunt man, red hair tinged with gray, and he wore a faded uniform, dirty high boots and a greasy little leather cap. He bade me welcome in a shrill voice and read Irwin's letter. In a much more friendly tone he said he was glad to have the services of a professional soldier and assigned me to the Georgia militia. He questioned me sharply about Amelia and said, 'By the Eternal, Captain Henley should 'er hung that scoundrel Aury. I'm told some of his pirates have joined the Indians around Pensacola.'"

"Did you see any of Aury's men in Florida?"

"No, Mr. Crawford." He drank more wine and continued. "Next day we got word the Seminoles had taken refuge in the Spanish fort of St. Marks. Jackson marched at once but when we arrived the Indians had fled. His only prisoner was a kindly old Scotsman, Alexander Arbuthnot."

"The British trader?"

"Yes, Mr. Crawford. He was arrested and held for trial. Then Jackson plunged into the jungle for the Suwannee River, one hundred miles east.

"His army was wet, tired and hungry—been on half rations for weeks. The militia wanted to go home. Jackson damned them to the 'deepest pits of hell.' Called them 'fireside patriots' and said he would shoot the first man to falter. They knew he meant it. We marched there in eight days. The Indians in the village of Chief Bowlegs had scattered like quail into the swamps. Our only prisoner was a Lieutenant Robert Ambrister of the Royal Colonial Marines who stumbled into our camp by mistake."

"A British officer?" exclaimed Crawford. "What was he doing there?"

"He planned to help Chief Bowlegs train his men. Jackson marched his army back to St. Marks—this time in five days. No wonder the militia call him 'Old Mad Jackson.' He convened a court-martial and tried Ambrister and Arbuthnot. The white-haired old man was convicted of inciting the Indians to war, spying and giving aid to the enemy. Seems to me his principal villainy was treating the Indians decently. Anyhow, Jackson hung him the next morning."

Crawford groaned at this treatment of a British subject. "What about the lieutenant?"

"They convicted him of assuming command of the Indians in a war with the United States." He paused and had more wine. "Makes one thirsty, all this talking. I felt for Ambrister as a fellow soldier. He'd been wounded at Waterloo and been one of Napoleon's guards on St. Helena. I was sorry to learn that the Emperor is in bad health and not expected to live much longer." Noticing Crawford's frown, he said, "Sorry, Mr. Crawford, for digressing. Ambrister was an attractive man, well liked by the American officers who petitioned Jackson to show him mercy. Several members of the court reconsidered their verdict and reduced his sentence to fifty lashes and a year in jail. Jackson ignored them and had him shot at sunrise."

Crawford and Ames sat in shocked silence. They realized the enormity of Jackson's act and its implications.

In a very quiet voice Laurent said, "There was a girl in London waiting to marry the lieutenant. I posted his last letter to her this morning."

"My God," exploded Crawford. "A respectable merchant hung and a young officer shot. Some of us were worried about trouble with Spain and now it's England, too. They'll not take this lightly."

"The British lion will roar," agreed Laurent, "but Mr. Crawford, strictly from a military standpoint, they were guilty as charged."

"I hope so. What next? How many Spaniards did he kill?" he asked anxiously.

"None, so far as I know. They wouldn't fight. Jackson invaded West Florida, had a couple of minor skirmishes with the Seminoles, attacked Pensacola on May twenty-fifth. Three days later it surrendered and the dons were shipped to Havana. He appointed one of his colonels as military and civil governor, seized the royal archives and declared in force the laws of the United States. He wrote a long dispatch, which he ordered me to bring here, and went back to Tennessee, saying his wife was sick."

It's incredible, almost unbelievable, thought Crawford. How

(232)

dare Jackson seize Pensacola and St. Marks? He had no such orders from the President or the Secretary of War. In addition, he had summarily executed two Englishmen. This exercise of power by Old Hickory would have the capital in an uproar. He turned to Laurent. "Did you deliver the Florida dispatches to the War Department?"

"Yes, sir."

"When?"

"About an hour ago."

Crawford knew the President and the Secretary of War were expected back in Washington City tomorrow. The President will certainly call an emergency cabinet meeting. I had better get that dispatch and have copies made. "I have problems, gentlemen," he said with a wry smile. "Please excuse me." He jumped up and hurriedly left.

"He's a fine gentleman," said Laurent. "But seems a bit disturbed."

"And why not?" asked Ames. "I'm sure it never occurred to him or anyone that General Jackson could be so rash."

Laurent shrugged and sipped the last of his claret.

"What are your plans?"

"I'm going to Georgia, to a town called Elberton."

He couldn't have been more surprised if the Frenchman had said he was leaving for the moon. "What will you do in this place?"

"For one thing I'll get three meals a day. As usual, Jonathan, I'm short of funds."

"Have you a job?"

"Not exactly. While in Florida I got to be friendly with a Lieutenant John Banks of the Georgia militia. He is an engaging young fellow, with a quick mind and boundless curiosity. You see, he had never been away from home before. Told me this was the first time he'd eaten in a tavern or paid for a meal. Banks peppered me with questions about Europe, my years with the Emperor, how people lived in cities like Paris and Rome. He invited me for a visit and I accepted. He said I might get a job teaching French at Franklin College, which is in Athens, a nearby town. Perhaps I might open a fencing school."

"Franklin College, Athens, Elberton? I never heard of any of them."

"Nor I, until I met Banks. I looked on a map, though, and found them." He smiled cynically and asked, "What about you? Had enough soldiering?"

"Yes," replied Jonathan, explaining that Mr. Calhoun had offered him a teaching post at West Point, but he was going back to Charleston and read law.

"Too bad. You were a good officer and someday you might get to be a general."

"Heaven forbid," laughed Jonathan.

"And Señora Gonzalez?"

"In Havana, I think. She told Captain Henley she wanted time to think about us, then she would write. I've had no letter," he added in a despondent voice.

That damned Spanish doxie, Laurent said to himself. She fooled me, for I thought she loved the lad. I suppose she just wanted a vigorous lover after all those dreary years with an old husband. Now that she's in Cuba with her family and friends she has no further interest in an impecunious young American. This was Jonathan's first love and he was obviously disconsolate. He said, "Perhaps it's just as well. Ladies are rather like wine. Each bottle you open, while pleasant, is just a bit different. And there are plenty of bottles around." He abruptly changed the subject and asked, "When are you returning to Charleston? Maybe we can sail together."

Ames said he thought that was a good idea and suggested they meet at the Indian Queen in three days.

"That's fine. I'll find out about ships and it gives me time to collect some expense money from the War Department."

The news of General Jackson spread angry confusion through the capital. The *National Intelligencer* and the Washington *Gazette* denounced his actions and the President for not controlling Old Mad Jackson. Many eastern congressmen agreed. The western representatives and newspapers praised

Jackson, comparing this venture to his great victory over the British at New Orleans. The Cabinet met daily at noon, dispersing at six, exhausted by the heat and acrimonious arguments.

The arrogant Spanish Minister Don Luis de Onís routed the Secretary of State at midnight. "In the name of the King, my master," he told John Quincy Adams, "I demand a prompt restitution of St. Marks, Pensacola and other places wrested by General Jackson from the Crown of Spain. I demand indemnity for all injuries and losses and the punishment of the general." The friendly British minister, Sir Charles Bagot, was more circumspect. He said, "His Majesty's Government deplores the treatment of our subjects by General Jackson and requests an official explanation from the American Government."

The Cabinet was in a turmoil. An irate Calhoun said Jackson had disobeyed orders and should be reprimanded. The President and Crawford concurred. Adams contended that Jackson's proceedings were justified by necessity. The Cabinet agreed unanimously that Pensacola and St. Marks should be returned once Spain provided a garrison adequate to control the Indians. To retain the forts, said the President, would be tantamount to a declaration of war against Spain, a power exclusively vested in the Congress.

Finally the Cabinet sent a note to De Onís saying that General Jackson had acted on his own responsibility and would not be censured but the forts would be given up.

The controversy was far from settled. Rumors flooded the Capitol. The House of Representatives would consider legislation condemning Jackson. Old Hickory was en route to Washington City to "horsewhip Calhoun and Crawford" and break with Monroe. Spain and England would declare war on America. The London newspapers denounced Jackson as a "ruffian" who had murdered "two peaceful British traders." Public opinion demanded instant apology and reparation or war.

The Secretary of the Treasury remained in his office long after the Cabinet adjourned. He was deeply troubled, especially about British relations, though he scoffed at the stories of Jackson coming to the Capitol.

Jonathan seldom saw his host during those turbulent days. He met Laurent, who said there was little shipping to Charleston in midsummer. The first available passage was the last week in July.

"That's fine," replied Ames. He was relieved, for he did not want to leave the capital now—there was too much happening. "Can you manage?" he asked Laurent.

"I think so. The Indian Queen is—why it's *incroyable!* For slightly over a dollar a day I get a clean room, three enormous meals and all the wine I can drink. If I had the money I think I'd board with Jesse Brown the rest of my days."

One morning Crawford said, "Mr. Madison is in Washington City. He's coming here for supper. Would you like to join us?"

It was impossible for Jonathan to conceal his joy. "That's most thoughtful and I'm grateful." Perhaps he thought he would get answers to some of the many puzzling questions, and besides it would be a pleasure to see the former President again.

At twilight, to everyone's surprise, Madison arrived on horseback. Spry as a cricket, he dismounted and exchanged greetings with Crawford and Ames. The wizened sixty-seven-year-old Virginian explained, "Horses are much more comfortable than carriages and a damned sight cheaper. Those livery owners must be making a fortune. Their prices are outrageous. Bill, can you stable this old mare?"

Laughing, Crawford said "Sure" and escorted his guest to the dining room. At the former President's request they had a simple meal of poached eggs, grilled ham and fresh fruit. After supper, comfortable in large leather chairs, the three men talked over coffee, cigars and brandy.

Madison said he was pleased to see Ames so well and fully recovered from his injuries. "Mr. Crawford sent me copies of your Florida dispatches. They were excellent. Only an hour ago the President told me your timely report on Aury gave him the information he needed to justify the seizure of Amelia Island."

An embarrassed Jonathan stammered his thanks. Once again, under Madison's shrewd examination, he described the success and the failure of the patriot army.

"Was it really a failure?" mused Madison. "I wonder. It's tragic that MacGregor didn't liberate Florida when, with one decisive move, he could have captured St. Augustine. But we now control Amelia and St. Augustine. This gives us a wonderful opportunity to force Spain to cede Florida and to accept a satisfactory boundary for the Louisiana Territory. Don't you think so, Bill?"

"Yes, Jemmy. I believe Madrid is at last convinced it's better to sell Florida before we just take it. Both MacGregor and Jackson proved how easy that is."

"Then, Mr. President," asked Ames, "you think this time we'll really get Florida?"

"Indeed I do, Jonathan. Spain is now a second-rate power. Despite her imperious bad manners, she can't hide this fact from the rest of the world. We should thank our lucky stars for King Ferdinand. That imbecile, when he regained the throne three years ago, tried to restore the old colonial system in South America. Their leaders rebelled, just as we did against the British. He dispatched troops and they, like the British, didn't understand fighting revolutionary forces in their own country. It's only a matter of time before they are wiped out."

"I think Spain is already finished," said Crawford. "Last year when José de San Martin led his troops over the high Andes and slaughtered the Royalists at Chocobuco was the beginning of the end. Chile is now a republic under O'Higgins and Bolivar is pushing the Spaniards out of the Orinoco valley."

"My good friend, Joel Poinsett, must be pleased," said Madison. "Do you know him, Jonathan?"

"Yes, sir. I've had the pleasure of dining with him several times."

"And I'm sure you had a wonderful meal, perfectly served."

"Why yes, I did."

"Did you know that beneath his impeccable grooming and charming manners Poinsett is a tough, ruthless revolutionary?"

"Really, Jemmy," said Crawford. "I thought Poinsett was just another rich young Charlestonian."

"He's probably rich all right, but he truly believes in a democratic form of government. When I sent him on a trade mission in 1814 to South America he spent most of his time encouraging and counseling the revolutionary armies. The British termed him 'scourge of the American continent' and once sent a warship to Chile to capture him. Somehow he escaped, crossed the Andes on a mule to Buenos Aires and took a fishing smack to Charleston." His eyes brightened as he tasted his brandy. "A most interesting man," he continued. "Jonathan, get him to tell you sometime of stealing a latticed cart full of girls destined for a Turkish harem, or why the Czar of Russia offered him a colonel's commission in the Imperial Guards. Sorry, gentlemen, I didn't mean to bore you. Jonathan, do give him my regards when you next see him."

"It will be a pleasure."

"Also, you might tell him," added Crawford, "that Peru, Chile and the Argentine are now requesting recognition by the United States. I favor it."

"So do I," agreed Madison, "but not until we get Florida. De Onís, as we both know, is a tricky knave and would probably demand nonrecognition as a condition of sale."

"Spain can't dictate terms to anyone today," said Crawford in an angry voice.

"Exactly, Bill, but they are experts in evasion and procrastination. I discussed this with the President and he plans to present De Onís with a virtual ultimatum—immediate cession of Florida and extending our western boundary to Mexico and in the north to the Pacific Ocean, subject of course to cabinet approval."

"He'll get it," said Crawford. "But will Madrid accept?"

"They have no choice," replied Madison. "But if they dawdle the President will ask Congress to approve taking Florida."

Crawford nodded. "Congress will back President Monroe to-day just as they should have supported you five years ago when you wanted to aid Georgia's invasion of Florida."

"Perhaps, Bill, but we were at war then and Congress feared Spain might side with the British. There's no excuse now and certainly Spain is about as dangerous as one of Dolley's kittens."

"What about England?" asked Jonathan. "The newspapers say they are indignant over Arbuthnot and Ambrister. Might they support Spain?"

"I doubt it," said Madison. "England is war-weary and deeply in debt from her long struggle against Napoleon. She wants peace, trade and profits."

"Wars, Johnny," commented Crawford, "never improve your bank balance. Besides, the British minister told the President that the two men had no official sanction, and while the incident was regrettable, His Majesty's Government would make no formal complaint."

"My God," said Madison, popping to his feet and holding high his goblet, "a toast to a new state. We've been trying to get Florida for fifteen years and at last we've succeeded. I know Mr. Jefferson will be pleased." Crawford and Ames drank. "Now," said Madison, "Bill and I should drink to you, Jonathan Ames. We are in your debt."

Crawford smiled approvingly and raised his glass.

"Young man," continued Madison, "what are your plans? I'm told this old fox"—and he glanced at Crawford—"has gotten you reinstated in the Regulars and a teaching post at West Point."

"That's true, Mr. President, and I'm most grateful, but I've decided against it. I've had enough fighting." He turned to Crawford and said, "My apologies, sir, for not telling you sooner, but I've had no opportunity since all this . . . this . . ."

"This bedlam and confusion," injected Crawford. "Forget it, Johnny, but what will you do? Can we be of help?"

"No, sir. I'm going back to Charleston. Mr. Simms wants me to read law in his office. He's offered to take me in his firm when I'm qualified."

Both men agreed that this was an excellent opportunity and offered their congratulations and good wishes.

Glancing at the wall clock, Crawford said, "With your permission, Mr. President, I'm off to bed. It's been a long day." He bowed solemnly.

"Permission granted, Mr. Secretary," chuckled Madison. To Ames he said, "Dolley sends her kindest regards. She's never forgotten you and instructed me to invite you to Montpelier."

Jonathan was pleased but said he did not want to be an imposition.

The small man gave a hearty laugh. "You, one man, an imposition? Why Dolley had ninety people for dinner on the Fourth of July. Do come, Jonathan, but I warn you Dolley is a great matchmaker. Probably wants to marry you to one of our Virginia girls. Some of them are mighty pretty," he added.

"I have passage to Charleston next week. The sooner I begin my law studies the better. Perhaps, sir, at a later date?"

"You will always be welcome." His gray eyes twinkled as he swigged the last of his brandy. "Surely the law can't be that interesting. You must have a girl waiting for you."

"Oh no, sir." Thinking of his experience with Luiza and Thalia he said, "I just don't understand women. I don't believe I'll ever marry."

"I wonder," replied Madison in a kindly voice, "how many thousands of young men have said the same thing. What's wrong, Jonathan? One of those soft-talking Carolina ladies jilt you?"

"It's not that, sir. It's all very . . . confusing . . ." he stuttered.

The amiable old gentleman said sympathetically, "Want to tell me about it? Sometimes just talking is helpful."

Suddenly Jonathan knew he wanted to confide in this good-hearted man. Words tumbled over each other as he talked about Luiza and Amelia Island.

Madison listened quietly. It was a strange and fascinating story and he sensed Jonathan's inner conflict. This was obviously his first experience with a charming, sensual lady. Did the young Puritan love her or was he simply bewitched? He asked bluntly, "Ever thought of marrying her, now that she's a widow?"

Jonathan hesitated before replying, "Well, yes I have but—"

Madison interrupted. "I can highly recommend widows. They make excellent wives. I know, for I married one." His soft laughter brought a half smile to Ames's face. Madison's compassionate voice became stern. "Go to Cuba and find Señora Gonzalez. You'll never be satisfied until you see her again."

He slowly got to his feet. "Good luck, Jonathan, and good night."

§ CHAPTER 16 §

Low clouds scudded past on the rising wind as the schooner tacked into Charleston harbor. The white spire of St. Michaels gleamed through the mist and its bells chimed six o'clock as the ship tied up at the Ashley River dock. Jonathan saw Mr. Simms's carriage waiting on the wharf and it gave him a feeling of well-being.

At supper Simms and his friend Joel Poinsett questioned him for hours. They wanted detailed information on General Jackson, Florida, Congress, possible war with England and what President Monroe planned. His report on the Madison–Crawford conversation they found both interesting and reassuring. Poinsett was obviously pleased with Madison's message and said, "I'll write him tonight."

Simms said, "I'm happy you decided to return to Charleston. I've missed you, Jonathan. We'll plan your law studies tomorrow." Then in a whimsical voice the lawyer added, "Thalia Cummings is on the 'grand tour' with her mother. Will be away six months."

Jonathan gave an audible sigh and the two men smiled. "Relax, young man," said Simms. "With all those Europeans to charm she's probably forgotten you. Though I'll admit you were a new experience for Thalia. First time a man didn't come running when she crooked her little finger."

There is an old Charleston saying that there is plenty of time to do everything. Jonathan found it was not true. Though a gracious host, Simms proved to be a stern taskmaster when it came to the law. He insisted a good lawyer needed more than knowledge of codes and statutes. He must know the history of common law over the centuries, going back to the Magna Carta and tracing the slow development of the court and jury system and why every man is presumed innocent until convicted in a fair trial. Only then will come an understanding and appreciation of our system of justice.

He set a schedule that gave Jonathan little opportunity for pleasure. He spent his mornings reading in Simms's office. In the afternoons he studied in Charles C. Pinckney's extensive library. Here among the hundreds of books, bound in soft Italian leather and edged in gold leaf, he found the answers to many historical questions posed by Simms. Jonathan enjoyed his studies. He was satisfied that he had made a wise selection, though he knew it would require two years of "diligent effort" before he would be ready for his examinations.

Every day Simms and Ames scanned the *Courier* for Washington City news. The negotiations for Florida were slow. It required weeks to get letters from Madrid and De Onís lacked the authority to make decisions. Finally word came from the Spanish Minister of Foreign Affairs that restoration of the forts was not enough. General Jackson's actions must be disavowed and he must be suitably punished or talks would end.

The American reply was a withering blast. It said the President would neither inflict punishment nor pass censure on Jackson as the vindication of his actions was written in every page of the law of nations—self-defense. The President, in turn, demanded suitable punishment of the commandant of St. Marks and the governor of Pensacola for their defiance and violations of the engagements of Spain with the United States. Spain must properly defend Florida or cede to the United States a province of which she retains nothing but nominal possession. The twenty-page document reviewed Florida's history: Amelia Island and MacGregor, Luis Aury, a haven for escaped slaves, arming the Indians, Arbuthnot and Ambrister

(243)

and the British partisans. It was labeled a "narration of dark and complicated depravity, a creeping and insidious war, a mockery of patriotism" and warned, "If it becomes again necessary to take the forts and places in Florida, they will not be returned."

"Thank God," said Simms solemnly. "The President at last is showing a little courage. I'll bet it caused old King Ferdinand to drop a couple of stitches."

Jonathan laughed, glad that the President had been tough with Spain, as Mr. Madison had advised.

Each time Wash returned from the Caribbean he came to see Jonathan. He always brought a gift—cigars, a keg of rum, baskets of fresh fruit and once half a dozen giant sponges. Trading was profitable and with the help of Mr. Blair he was saving money. Soon he hoped to buy a larger boat.

"I'se been to Havana three times this fall," said Wash, "and ain't seen hide nor hair of Miss Luiza, but if she's there I'll find her. I'se got friends and they's nosing around like a pack of hound dogs, 'cause whoever finds her gits five gallons 'er rum."

"I can't thank you enough," said Jonathan.

"Wait till I finds her"—Wash grinned—"then mebbe you be sad, mebbe glad."

That, thought Ames, is a good description of my feelings. But Mr. Madison was right—I'll never be content until I see Luiza again. He asked Wash to "keep trying" and the big Negro said, "Don't fret, we find her sooner or later."

Autumn in Charleston was neither bitter nor swift. It lazed along, one warm day after another, and suddenly it was Christmas. The city was never gayer. Dinners, parties, dances or the theater every night. At Simms's suggestion Jonathan put aside his books for a week and enjoyed the festivities.

Early in January of 1819, Simms got a long letter from Crawford saying the aggressive dispatch had brought Spain to her senses. Adams and De Onís are parleying and he thought an agreement would be reached in the next few weeks. He was right. On February 22, Spain ceded all her lands east of the Mississippi, together with her claims to the Oregon Territory, in return for $5 million. In addition, the boundary between the United States and Mexico was determined.

When the news reached Charleston, Simms sent for Poinsett and Ames and served champagne. Poinsett called for a toast to "Florida, our new territory and may she soon become another star on our flag." Equally interesting was the report that President Monroe would visit Charleston in April.

Not since George Washington came to Charleston in 1791 had the city been so excited. To the annoyance of numerous hostesses, the President was to be quartered in the new St. Andrew's Hall on Broad Street. He would be in Charleston for a week and already enough entertainment had been suggested to keep him busy around the clock. "The poor man has got to have time to sleep," Poinsett told the welcoming committee. After days of bickering it was decided the President's program would include dinner with the Society of Cincinnati, a visit to the harbor forts, fireworks that night, breakfast with Poinsett and a special St. Cecilia Ball and concert.

The April day that the President, accompanied by John C. Calhoun, his Charleston-born wife and Major General Thomas Pinckney, arrived, the city was in a festive mood. By carriage, horseback, wagons and even on foot came thousands of people from the surrounding countryside. It was a cheerful crowd and a holiday spirit prevailed. Jonathan saw soldiers in uniform, planters in broadcloth and wide-brimmed hats and hundreds of Negroes. The variety of costumes was marvelous. Muslins and velvets, laces and homespuns, ladies with dainty parasols and even one or two old men in knee britches and silver-buckled shoes.

Cannon boomed a twenty-one-gun salute, bands played and the people waved flags and cheered as the Washington Light Infantry escorted the President to St. Andrew's Hall.

Jonathan had received invitations to Poinsett's breakfast and the St. Cecilia Ball honoring the President. He was glad that he had not attended the Cincinnati dinner when Mr. Simms described it at breakfast.

"The hall was hot and crowded and you never saw so many

different colored uniforms. Most of 'em were a bit snug and reeking of camphor. The society, as you probably know, is limited to Revolutionary officers and their direct descendants. I'll wager some of my friends hadn't worn their uniforms in forty years, forgetting how their middle and bottoms had spread." He laughed and continued, "By the time we'd drunk twenty or more toasts the food was cold and hardly edible."

"Twenty toasts?" exclaimed Ames.

"At least that many. I lost count after the first eight or nine, though I quit drinking wine, just raised my glass and puffed out my cheeks."

"How did they find so many subjects to toast?" asked Jonathan.

"No trouble at all. Started with one praising the Constitution of the United States and next came Washington." In the unctuous voice of the skilled toastmaster Simms said, "To George Washington, a name associated with every ennobling quality of man, his fame is identified with our history and its luster will be reflected upon ages yet to come. All the guests stood up, drank bad wine and said, 'Hear, hear.'" He was a good mimic and Jonathan was amused.

"Then came the President, the state of South Carolina, the gracious city of Charleston, Mr. Calhoun, General Jackson, and lord knows how many more. We'd been there all night if Mr. Monroe hadn't complained. Won him more friends than anything he's done in a long time."

The lawyer frowned, gulped black coffee and said, "I'm exhausted, think I'll go back to bed."

Poinsett's breakfast for "gentlemen only" was at ten o'clock the following morning. Jonathan came early, stood at the rear of the long hall and watched the tall, stoop-shouldered President acknowledge introductions and speak cordially to each guest. Jonathan was too shy to push through the crowd and meet Mr. Monroe.

An enormous meal was arranged on the mahogany sideboard. Ham, bacon, sausage, fried shrimp, grilled trout, eggs scrambled, poached or baked, hominy swimming in butter, hot biscuits, rolls, muffins and waffles. Jonathan had never seen so much food. It would feed a Connecticut family for a week. Joel Poinsett whispered, "The President was asking about you. He wants to see you after breakfast."

Too surprised to speak, he just nodded. Toying with his food, he waited. At a wave from Poinsett he followed him into the library. The President arrived in a few minutes. A friendly smile appeared on his wrinkled face as he shook hands.

"This is a pleasure, Mr. Ames. For a long time I have wanted an opportunity to thank you for your Florida dispatches. They not only kept me informed but helped me to convince the Cabinet that our Spanish policy was correct. I am grateful, sir, and so is your country."

An embarrassed Ames mumbled that he was glad his reports were useful.

"They were indeed," replied the President. "So much so that Mr. Madison, who approved your enlistment with MacGregor, thinks you deserve a reward. I heartily agree. We think it appropriate that the government grant you one thousand acres in Florida."

"One thousand acres!" gasped Jonathan, hardly believing his ears. "It's too much, Mr. President. I just don't deserve—"

"Let us be the judge," interrupted Mr. Monroe. "We think it a most suitable award and it has ample precedent. The state of Georgia gave General Nathaniel Greene a large plantation near Savannah in recognition of his service in the Revolutionary War. Other states have made similar grants."

Still dumfounded, Ames murmured, "It's far too generous, Mr. President. I just don't know what to say."

"Why don't you just say 'Thank you very much, Mr. President,'" suggested Poinsett with a smile.

This was good advice, thought Ames. "Mr. President, I thank you very much and, as we say in Connecticut, I'm most beholden to you, sir."

The two men laughed and the President said, "I assume you'd like your grant on or near Amelia Island."

"If I have a choice, sir, I'd like it on the St. Johns River."

"Where is that?" asked the President.

"It's about fifty miles south of Amelia. I camped there after scouting St. Augustine. It's a beautiful place, has a fine harbor and someday there'll be a city there. Besides, sir, I'd just as soon forget Amelia."

The President said he understood and would make the necessary arrangements.

The St. Cecilia Ball was the climax of the President's visit. As Jonathan waited in the receiving line he heard the sweet music of the violins. In the ballroom he could see the ladies in brilliant silks, their escorts in black broadcloth. They bowed and smiled as they moved through the intricate steps of the minuet.

A low voice said, "Good evening, Mr. Ames." It was Thalia Cummings, in a forest-green satin dress with matching slippers. Her soft red hair, braided, was swept up into a coronet. A single strand of pearls was her only ornament. She was extraordinarily beautiful.

Startled, Jonathan said, "Evening, Miss Cummings. When did you return?"

"Last night. You didn't think I'd miss the only St. Cecilia Ball in history honoring a President, did you?"

"I suppose not."

She clasped his arm, her green eyes twinkling. "I have heard so many wonderful things about you, Jonathan Ames. Honored by the President and awarded a big Florida plantation. All Charleston is singing your praises and I'm so proud of you." She gave a little tinkling laugh, squeezed his arm and said, "Introduce me to your friend the President."

The astonished young man, by now standing before Mr. Monroe, said, "Mr. President, may I present Miss Thalia Cummings?"

She curtsied gracefully and spoke in a coquettish voice. "I'm so thrilled. It's like a dream come true, meeting the President of the United States. And Charleston, sir, is indeed honored to have you as our guest."

The tall man bowed, thinking what a lovely girl. "Charleston is a most delightful city, Miss Cummings, and certainly the many stories I've heard about its charming and beautiful ladies are not exaggerated."

Pleased with the compliment, she drawled softly, "Mr. Ames has told me how kind and wonderful you've been to him."

"Not me, Miss Cummings, but a grateful country."

Jonathan felt a sudden tension. He knew Thalia was acting. What was in this capricious girl's mind? He attempted to move her past the President. Instead she snuggled closer and gushed, "We are so happy and we can't thank you enough for everything." She paused, blushed and added, "I mean, sir, Jonathan can't thank you enough for all the things you've done for him."

The President gave a perceptive smile. "Am I right in assuming, Miss Cummings, that felicitations are in order?"

In a shocked voice she said, "Oh no, Mr. President. It's supposed to be a secret."

"If I'd won such a lovely girl I'd want the world to know. My heartiest congratulations, Mr. Ames."

This is an incredible nightmare, thought Jonathan. Still dazed, he found himself shaking hands with Mr. Monroe and accepting good wishes from dozens of people. Someone called for champagne and the President said, "May I be the first one to kiss the bride-to-be?" Thalia moved quickly into his arms and kissed him warmly.

It was generally agreed that this was St. Cecilia's most exciting ball.

At breakfast Mr. Simms gave Jonathan a quizzical look. "I understand from the servants that congratulations are in order. May I say I am surprised?"

"*I* am absolutely dumfounded."

"You mean Thalia tricked you?"

"Yes, sir," said Jonathan and explained.

"My God, what a woman! And compromising the President, too. That conniving little devil has been like that since she was six." He shouted for more coffee, "strong and black," and lit a cigar. "The question is—what are you going to do?"

"I don't know," glumly replied Jonathan.

"If you don't marry her there'll be one hell of a scandal."

"Maybe Mr. Cummings won't consent."

"He'll do what his wife says and I'm reliably informed she is delighted."

"Why? Once she disliked me."

"That was a long time ago, before you got so friendly with Presidents." Noticing Ames's dejected expression, he apologized. "Sorry, Jonathan, I didn't mean to tease." He puffed his cigar and reflected. "My boy, you are in a mess. The ladies run Charleston and never forget it. Walk out on Thalia and they'll make your life miserable. Perhaps you'd better consider carefully. She is a damned lovely woman."

"She's fascinating and clever but, Mr. Simms, I won't marry her."

The old lawyer thought for a long time before speaking. "Jonathan, I've never asked, for it was none of my business. Captain Stratford said you were, shall we say, involved with a Spanish lady on Amelia. Does she have anything to do with your feelings about Thalia?"

Jonathan blushed. "No, sir. I haven't heard from Señora Gonzalez since I left Amelia. I guess," he said bitterly, "now that she's in Cuba with her family she's forgotten me."

"Perhaps it's just as well," said Simms, who didn't approve of foreign women. "I suggest you stay at home today, don't see anyone and we'll have a strategy meeting at six."

"Thalia ordered me to report this morning so that we can make plans."

"Are you going?"

"No, sir. If I did I'd be tempted to either whip or rape her."

"Why not send her a note saying you are overcome with happiness and that you'll see her in a few days?"

Ames said he would and, with a half-sorrowful smile, went to the library. The butler rapped, opened the door and said that Wash was on the back porch and would like to see him.

"Show him in."

"In here, Mr. Ames?"

"Yes."

"You mean, sir—"

"Damnit," said Jonathan, "bring Wash to the library."

Wash walked into the room laughing. "That the most upset nigger in Charleston, having to show me, a field hand, into Mr. Simms's house."

"I'm glad to see you. Sit down."

"I'll stand, sir. I'se dirty. Come here straight from the docks. Mr. Ames, I'se found little missy."

Ames jumped to his feet. "Where? When? What did she say? Did she send me a message?"

"I didn't speak to her."

"Why not, Wash?"

"I was too shook up."

Exasperated, Ames said, "What?"

"She was walking along with an old lady and a little bitty boy. Fer a second I thought some conjure woman done shrunk you up. He's yer spittin' image, even walks like you."

Jonathan blinked in astonishment—too surprised to speak. Wash continued softly, "No doubt about it. You've got a son."

"A son?" repeated Ames. "I've got a son." He collapsed in a chair and rubbed his forehead. This startling news might be the answer to the questions that had tormented him the past year. Was this why she hadn't written? Was she ashamed of having a child? Did she regret their passionate love when they first met on Amelia Island? But what about his son? Was he considered Gonzalez' child and would he be reared as a Spaniard? "No, no," he said aloud and jumped to his feet. Do you, he asked himself, want Luiza as your wife?

There was only one way to find out. Go to Havana. See Luiza and his son. Then he would know what to do.

Turning to Wash, he asked, "When are you returning to Havana?"

"On the morning tide. Sloop being loaded and provisioned right now. I figgered you'd be in a hurry."

Ames scratched a hasty note to Mr. Simms. "I am," he said to Wash. "Let's go!"

POSTSCRIPT

Although the Adams–Onís treaty ceding Florida to the United States was signed in 1819, Spain delayed ratification for two years. She hoped for British intervention that would forestall giving up Florida and even offered the territory to Britain for $6 million. Britain refused and when the United States, annoyed at Madrid's procrastination, threatened to seize Florida, the Spanish capitulated. Florida was organized as a territory in 1822 with General Andrew Jackson as its first governor. On March 3, 1845, Florida entered the Union as our twenty-seventh state.

The fate of the lesser-known characters in this story might be of interest. William H. Crawford was generally considered the leading presidential candidate in 1824. Then tragedy intervened. In September of 1823 he left Washington for a visit to Virginia friends. The jovial fifty-one-year-old Secretary of the Treasury seemed in the best of health. But a week later he was paralyzed, speechless and nearly blind. Most historians believe the stroke was induced by an overdose of lobelia, which had been prescribed by a country doctor in treating an attack of erysipelas.

Crawford, his mind clear, refused to withdraw from the race. The opposition, especially the press, exaggerated his condition and many of his supporters wondered, if elected, could he serve.

None of the candidates—Andrew Jackson, Henry Clay, John Quincy Adams or Crawford—received a majority in the electoral college and the contest went to the House of Representatives. Clay, promised the post of Secretary of State, threw his support to Adams and elected him.

The next day a letter from the new President arrived urging Crawford to remain in the Cabinet. Broken in health, he declined, returned to Georgia and served as a local judge until his death in 1834. Perhaps his most cherished possession was a letter from Thomas Jefferson expressing his "frank regrets" over the presidential election.

The flamboyant General Gregor MacGregor never returned to Amelia Island. He captured Puerto Bello, lost it in much the same way he failed in Florida and finally settled among the Poyais Indians in Central America. Here he adopted the title of "Grand Cacique," planned a republic, obtained a bank loan in London (which he never repaid) and encouraged Scottish emigration. This failed and in 1839, desperate and broke, MacGregor appealed to the Venezuelan Government for naturalization in the republic and restoration to his former military rank. The Venezuelan Government granted his request and decided that in view of the eminent services rendered by him during the wars of liberation he be restored to his rank of General of a Division with his former seniority and that a sum of money be granted him. MacGregor moved back to Caracas and died a few years later.

Joel Poinsett was elected to Congress in 1821 where he urged the recognition of the South American republics. In 1825 he was appointed the first American Minister to the Republic of Mexico. He got involved in the turbulent politics of the young republic and finally was recalled in 1830 at the request of the Mexican Government. He returned to South Carolina and became the leader of the Unionist party and supported President Andrew Jackson in his bitter fight against John C. Calhoun and nullification. In 1833, at the age of fifty-four, he married Mrs. Mary Izzard Pringle, the widow of his deceased friend John J. Pringle, and retired to his plantation. President Martin Van Buren called him from retirement in

1837 to become Secretary of War. Long a student of military affairs, he was an energetic and excellent administrator. He improved the status of the regular army, organized a general staff and broadened the course of study at West Point. Again he retired to South Carolina and, though no longer active in politics, bitterly opposed the secession movement.

Despite his long and devoted service to his country, he is, ironically, best known for the poinsettia flower, a traditional Christmas decoration. He brought a cutting from Mexico, rooted it and gave plants to his friends, who named it after him.

The notorious pirate Luis Aury and the taciturn Jared Irwin, after leaving Amelia Island, seem to have faded into the mists of history.

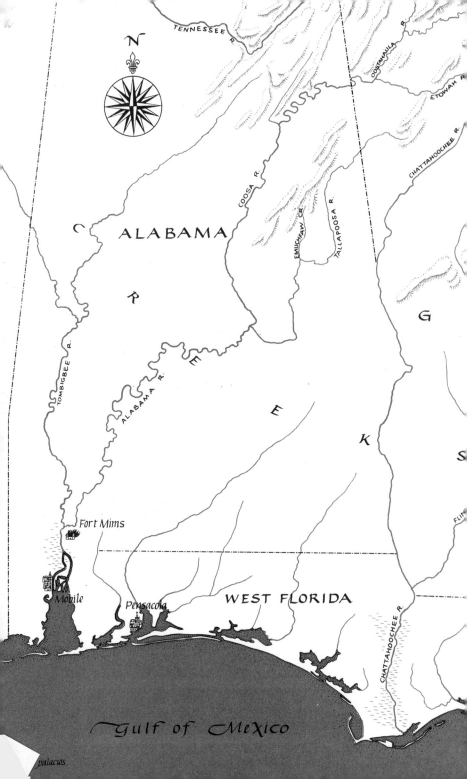